Fools Playing Fools
A Hugo Miller Mystery

Joseph Allen

Published by Rogue Phoenix Press, LLP
Copyright © 2020

ISBN: 978-1-62420-518-7

Credits
Cover Artist: Designs by Ms G
Editor: Kitty Carlisle

Dedication

For Rudy, Angus, Kitty, Arlo and Christine

Chapter One

When I heard the commotion in the hallway outside my door, I opened the door a crack and looked out. Cops, white-coated CSI workers. They were talking to each other, but it was so muffled that I couldn't understand what they were saying. I guessed someone had died.

We were in the middle of a thunderstorm, an almost every-afternoon phenomenon anywhere near the Hudson River or New York harbor in the sweltering summer humidity. Zeus was slinging thunderbolts right, left and center, and the giants were bowling in the sky, creating rolling peals of ear-splitting, bomb-like explosions. It was the kind of storm that throws boats onto dry land and smashes sailing vessels against rocks and piers. Fortunately, these summer storms usually come and go fairly quickly, and then the sun comes out to dry the streets and sidewalks.

The apartment the CSIs were filing into was occupied by a young man whom I had not met, mostly because he had just moved in. Because it was still summer, I was trying to keep windows open when it wasn't raining and frequently propped the front door to the apartment open with a small but heavy fake-marble lion statue I bought at the Metropolitan Museum some years back. A cross-draft is a blessing in a New York heat wave. So, I had seen the young man going back and forth when he moved in. Never said hello.

He was boyishly handsome with almost shocking rock-star hair of a chestnut-auburn color, a fashionably scruffy almost-beard, enormous dark eyes and the regulation Levis and black t-shirt but with black leather lace-up shoes. He had a problem with his right side, holding his right hand in a cupped position that was at odds with the angle of his arm, and he almost dragged his right leg when he walked but didn't use a cane and walked in a straight line. Looked like a long-term problem, not the consequence of a recent fall off a motorcycle.

He wore a headset and was clearly listening to music or a radio show, was smiling and occasionally laughing quietly. Not talking on the phone. He looked happy. I paid attention because for some reason I was surprised that someone who looked to be crippled was in such a good mood on moving day, which I surmised must have been difficult at best for him. I considered introducing myself, but he seemed to be busy, so I thought I'd wait.

Well, it turned out I missed my chance to say hello because when the CSIs arrived a couple of days later, he was dead. Couldn't possibly have been over thirty, maybe as young as twenty-five.

My name is Hugo Miller, and I'm mostly retired from a business I started that specializes in public relations for sports teams and players. But I am also a civilian criminalist with the NYPD—mostly an honorary designation that lets me work on cases assisting a detective I know in the Midtown North precinct of Manhattan, Mike di Saronno. I kinda fell into this because of a homicide case in Manhattan where I was potentially a witness of something relevant. That was several years back, and since then I've worked with Mike on four or five cases.

That's all well and good, but I live in an area of Queens called Long Island City that's on the East River directly across from the east end of 42nd Street and the United Nations. My Manhattan credentials don't carry much weight with the local cops. To be fair, I used to live in the theater district on 48th Street—until I got priced out of Manhattan by skyrocketing rents. And although I continue to work with Mike when he calls me, I hadn't introduced myself to anyone at the 108th precinct that was a couple of long blocks up my street.

I called Mike, who poked around and told me what he found out. The victim was Ned Savage, twenty-seven, an Equity actor who had worked on Broadway and in smaller theaters in the area. Went to acting school in Los Angeles where he grew up but had lived in the theater district for several years. He rented the studio apartment on my floor and told the leasing agent he would be living there alone. Apparently, someone had conked him over the head with a brass candlestick.

"Must have happened quickly," I said. "My apartment is directly next door, and I think we share a wall in my guest bedroom. I never heard anything, so there must not have been much of a scuffle."

He said he thought the detectives would be knocking on my door to ask me some questions since my apartment shares a wall with Mr. Savage's place. As it happens, though, my apartment is a large two-bedroom, and I sleep on the opposite side of my floorplan from the hall or that apartment.

"Still, I think if there had been people throwing things or yelling, I would have heard some noise," I told the detective who was now asking me questions. "And since it's been hot, I've been keeping the sliding glass door open to the balcony to catch some breeze." I showed him and his partner the living room, with the sliding door open, a screen door keeping bugs out, and balcony directly upstairs forming a ceiling that kept it mostly dry during rainstorms. "If the balcony in that apartment was open like mine, I would for sure have known what was going on."

They were there to get information, not to give it to me, so I didn't bother to ask them anything, because I knew they'd clam up if I did. Figured Mike could find out and let me know.

I don't trust coincidences, but Mike told me Ned had moved into the apartment next to me from a high-rise across the street from where I used to live on 48th Street. I'd been living in Long Island City for almost five years and when I heard that, I tried to remember if that building was even ready for occupancy when I moved away. Anyway, he had to be well-off to live in a new luxury building in that area, because rents were sky-high; through-the-roof ridiculous. When I moved out of the theater district my rent was almost five times what it had been when I moved in ten years earlier.

"For sure I don't remember seeing him when I lived on 48th Street," I said. "I would have remembered. Very striking fellow. Combination of rock-star and person with disabilities. Like somebody who had fallen off a trapeze with no net, or been thrown from a horse jumping over a hedge."

Mike suggested it might be good if he and I could get together. It was almost mid-day so I suggested we meet for a quick lunch at Ariana, a hole-in-the-wall Afghan restaurant on 9th Avenue at about 49th Street that combined good food and cheap prices. He agreed.

To get from my place to Times Square is easy. Take the 7 train from my subway station, three stops—maybe eight minutes—and you're at Times Square, exiting onto 43rd Street. It was a warm day, no rain, so I could walk to Ariana in ten minutes. I took a quick shower, decided I didn't need to shave, and was on my way, tapping on my cellphone to retrieve text messages from relatives in California.

These days there is free WiFi on the subway platforms, so I stood and texted until the train pulled up, about three minutes after I got there. I was at Ariana before Mike, who only had to walk five blocks from his office. Go figure.

I'm fond of Mike, though we are not friends in a social sense. He lives right near where I used to live and before I met him professionally, I would see him in this and that restaurant or bar from time to time and never knew he was a cop. But I have a good memory for faces and after a couple of sightings, I recognized him, but we never were introduced or shook hands. So, when I did meet him, it was a shock that he was a police detective. Very normal-looking, Italian features, slightly bronze, even in the winter, good symmetrical features, hazel eyes, taller than normal but not as tall as me.

I grabbed the table in the front bay window so I could watch for Mike and stare at people who walked by. I am a born voyeur; there's nothing more fascinating than watching people, even if they're just walking by. It's a little like watching a fire in a fireplace, very calming and I can't take my eyes off the parade of people meandering or scurrying by.

Mike was all apologies for being late.

"You're not late. I was early. No prob."

He told me before he looked at the menu that he was going to be working on the Savage case. The guy had been directing a production of *Twelfth Night* at an off-Broadway theater just off 8th Avenue in the 40s. Talk was that he was a *wunderkind*, a young prodigy. The kind of charismatic genius that everybody loves, especially in show biz.

"He looked really young, almost like a kid."

"Maybe you're getting old, Hugo. I never met him, but his photos don't look like a kid to me." He told me some of the things the CSIs had found. First of all, Savage didn't seem to have any immediate family, or at least there were no entries on his computer or in an old address book. They packaged up a drawerful of manila envelopes with papers in them and took them to the lab to make copies. At that point there was no next of kin to notify.

Second, the apartment had not been ransacked. Savage's body was found on the floor between the coffee table and the front door. The cushions on the couch that was also a pullout bed were rumpled, so it appeared that he might have been sitting there before whatever transpired that left him on the floor. The candlestick that appeared to be the cause of his death was on the floor but closer to the door than the body. It had blood and bits of hair on the base, indicating it had been grabbed by the top. The wound was on the right side of Savage's head, indicating that if the person holding the candlestick was facing Savage, he or she was left-handed. If he or she was behind Savage, then the indication would be right-handed. The M.E. would have to make the determination as to where the assailant was standing or sitting.

Mike went on to say it seemed logical that I help him on this case if I had time. Since I had an official tie to the department, there would a modest paycheck attached to the assignment. Enough to cover expenses and maybe go out to eat—once.

"Got nothing but time, Mike," I said. "Okay if I talk to Ruth and Gabriele?"

He smiled a friendly grin and nodded vigorously.

I texted Ruth and Gabriele on my way to the subway to see if we could meet up that evening for a drink. "The game is afoot," is how I ended the texts. It's a quote from Sherlock Holmes, and it actually comes from what the Brits call "shooting." The "game" are the birds—grouse, whatever—the shooters are after. And they can be heard running around in the brush, so "the game is afoot." I always thought it had something to do with a game, like a game you play. Nope. Brits are different from Americans.

Yes and yes. We agreed to meet at Dominie's Hoek, a watering-hole on Vernon Boulevard about a block and a half from the subway station on the 7 line. It's an old Dutch name for the area from before the Brits took over in 1664. Kind of a silly operetta of a take-over. The Brits arrived in the harbor and signaled to the Dutch that they were going to lay siege to the city, which was then just a cluster around what we call Battery Park. The Dutch figured they were joking, said no, go away. Then the Brits signaled that if the Dutch resisted they would "sack" the city--in other words, burn it, steal everything they could find, and rape the women. Seemed like an over-reaction, so the citizens of New Amsterdam refused to defend the city from the English ships. They gave up, much to the chagrin of Peter Stuyvesant, who had been the director-general and autocrat of the colony of New Netherlands for eighteen years. He was known to history as Peg Leg Pete, because he lost a leg in a naval battle somewhere in the Caribbean. Even though he was no longer in charge, he hung around on his big estate on the East River and died in Manhattan in 1672, so it couldn't have been a terribly hostile time between the two Protestant powers. He was buried in St Mark's in the Bowery, which was built on the site of the Stuyvesant family chapel.

Anyway, Dominie's Hoek is a place where you can get a good drink and sit outside in warm weather in a garden-ish patio in the back. They make burgers and such. Mostly it's a noisy neighborhood bar where you can wave at people you recognize, even if you don't know their names. Just about everybody is in a good mood.

Gabriele was early and arrived downstairs at my building at about six. The concierge called up, and yes, of course, send him up. He rang the bell, and when I answered, he was gesturing at the yellow crime-scene tape that was all over the end of the hallway just feet from my door. I nodded and he came in.

"Kid just moved in a day or two ago. Young guy, apparently in the theater business, directing a Shakespeare play near Times Square."

"What happen?"

"Well, I guess that's what we'll be trying to find out. Mike is heading the investigation because the kid was working near Mike's precinct and used to live in that zombie Irish building on 8th Avenue, the tall, super-skinny one. You remember it?"

He nodded and hugged me. He's a hugger. He's from Capri, with a lot of relatives in Naples; not sure, it seems different from time to time. He and his cousin, Dante, have a popular white-tablecloth restaurant in downtown Manhattan called Ora di Pranzo ("dinnertime"). Heavenly food.

Gabriele is one of those confident Italian guys who attracts every eye in every room he walks into. I always look at his hair, since I am thinning/balding myself, but remember how nice it was to have hair when mine was still brown. I met him because he was a person of interest in a fairly sordid homicide several years back. He didn't do it, and we found out who did do it. Gabriele and I have been fast friends ever since. He says he's in love with me, which I try to smile through, but secretly it pleases me. Myself, I'm a two-time loser, two ex-wives with assorted kids, all on the West Coast. Limited contact. Not interested in hooking up again, but if I were, I would be aiming at Ruth, not Gabriele.

I live on the tenth floor; nice view of the Chrysler Building and the UN. Also that crazy tall Trump building that's across from the UN. Since he was early, we had a very short snort of whisky at my apartment to get loosened up and then walked over to the bar to meet Ruth.

Ruth is a fashion plate for the modish set who are into "classic" looks. In Ruth's case, that means older Chanel clothing, nubby fabrics that approach Turkish toweling at times, kinda Joan Crawford shoulders sometimes, usually worn over fairly tight tailored jeans that made it clear she had Betty Grable legs. Ruth is comfortably well-off, a widow with some family issues--her husband's ex-wife and her own brothers. Her father was a rabbi, and Ruth was observant, at least at the important times of the year. "Acerbic" would describe her personality, but smiley and sweet on top of the film-noir attitudes. She was a picture in Chanel pink that evening, with pink and white Vans. Gotta love a woman in comfortable shoes. I read somewhere that an average woman in spiked heels exerted the same amount of pressure on the floor under the spike as a full-grown hippopotamus. Impressive.

She does good entrances and paused in the doorway at Dominie's Hoek to be silhouetted by the sun.

"You did that on purpose, didn't you?" I asked as I bussed her on both cheeks like a European.

"Did what?"

"Stood in the doorway with the sun behind you."

"Pish-tush," she said, pulled out a chair at one of the tables and sat down. She made me smile every time I saw her. I re-appreciated that she didn't carry three handbags, which is what a lot of New York women do. Men use pockets more, and women use pocketbooks, purses, or backpacks, sometimes all three.

So I briefed them on what Mike had told me about Ned Savage. "I guess there was no real evidence of any kind of tussle, so the assumption is that either he was surprised or he knew whoever it was that hit him and didn't feel in danger. Nothing yet on next of kin, or whether he had any close relatives."

"Did you say he was an actor?" Ruth asked.

"What I was told was that he was directing a production of a Shakespeare play," I said. "I think it was *Twelfth Night,* in some off-Broadway theater."

"WSR," she said. "West Side Rep. I'm on their mailing list. I've met him. He was Bottom in their *Midsummer Night's Dream* a year or so ago. Good looking, has a limp." She pulled out her cellphone and tapped on it. "Here," she said, flashing a picture of Savage. "Brings out the mother instinct in me," she smiled.

"Yeah, that's him," I said. "Small world?"

Gabriele grabbed the phone from Ruth and looked at it. "He come Ora di Pranzo maybe two times, *con amici. Parl' Italiano, ma bruto. È una brava persona.*" (*He brought his friends and spoke Italian, but not well. Good man.*)

I wouldn't say that's why I love both of them, because it's not. I've loved them for years on their own merits. But the fact that Ruth is involved in what seems like every arts charity in Manhattan and Gabriele owns a restaurant that you have to reserve a month in advance to hope to get in--it don't hoit, as they say. There I was, living next door to an apartment where a man was murdered a couple of days before, and both of my best friends knew him. Go figure. What? Eight million people living in the five boroughs? I live in Queens. Ruth lives in Manhattan. Gabriele lives in Brooklyn. All three of us turn out to know this one guy, and I had only seen him, never met him even though he lived next door.

I made a mental note to look up West Side Rep and see what I could find out. A waiter took our orders. Glass of red for me, glass of white for Ruth, dirty vodka for Gabriele. It felt good to be sitting with them on a warm summer day and to be working together on a puzzle. When I was a kid, my favorite thing was to work on jigsaw puzzles--big ones, lots of little pieces, lots of areas of color that look the same on the boxtop. You find all the edges you can find, and work your way in toward the middle. There's a lot more in the way of blind alleys and dead ends when you're dealing with a homicide—don't get me wrong—and it's a good deal more somber than trying to fit the pieces together in a picture of bright seas and sailboats.

Gabriele said that Savage had been to Ora di Pranzo at least twice, both times with a group of young people, probably actors or people he was working with. I asked if they were well-behaved. He said something noncommittal, like he didn't remember.

Chapter Two

Later when I was back home, I was throwing darts with Google Chrome trying to find out what I could about Ned Savage. It turned out he was indeed a member of Equity, the actors' guild in the United States, and had done several stints on nighttime television dramas, although always as a guest actor, no repeating roles. I was surprised as I read the names of the shows he had appeared in, because several were shows I had seen many times. But I didn't recall seeing him. Maybe the *comprimario* roles just go in one side and out the other, or whatever the right saying is. They're not memorable.

He had appeared and been favorably reviewed in several plays I knew when they were produced in the West End in London, including the Jean Anouilh masterpiece, "Becket," which was made into a high-profile movie with Peter O'Toole and Richard Burton in the 1960s. He was in demand enough that he had several gigs going at once, it seemed from his Internet Movie Database (IMDb) profile. He did a stint on a soap opera in New York while he was playing Sir Henry Percy, called 'Hotspur' in *Henry IV, Part 1* at a full-on Broadway theater that was newly renovated with money from Disney, at 42nd Street near Times Square.

I called to ask some basic questions of Mike di Saronno and to tell him that both my cohorts had actually met Savage.

"The CSIs collected a lot of fingerprints. We'll try to run them all, but there was nothing on the candlestick that killed him."

"Wiped clean?" I asked.

"Maybe, or maybe just held with a cloth or a paper napkin."

"And no sign of a fight?"

"Nothing out of place, some dust that showed things hadn't been moved or cleaned. They vacuumed up some fibers from the rug, but you can bet if there's any hair or whatnot, it's from the previous residents or the property managers or the movers, since he'd only been there for a couple of days at most. Even if there is a hair from the killer, we'd have no way of knowing."

"Useless then?"

"We'll hold onto everything. Could be helpful in placing someone in the apartment if we come up with a suspect."

I told him about the IMDb biography I had found. He had printed it out and read through it already. "Early bird gets the worm," he said. "But in this case, it wasn't me, it was one of the guys doing background checks."

"I'm sure I must have seen him, maybe on television, or more likely on stage. I'm a big Shakespeare fan, like he seems to have been. But honestly if I have seen him, I don't remember it."

"People look a lot different in a hallway than they do on stage with makeup and a costume."

"But he had a really obvious handicap of some kind. He wasn't like a cripple, but he walked oddly. I would've thought I'd recall that. Ruth saw him in *Midsummer Night's Dream*, and she remembered that he had a pronounced limp."

"Eyewitnesses miss things like that all the time. For one thing, most of us are used to ignoring people with disabilities, or at least not looking at them. It's like that old movie where the postman is the killer. Nobody remembered he was there because they ignored him; part of the backdrop."

"And maybe he was able to hide it on stage too. Right?"

"The Medical Examiner said it was pretty obvious, especially his arm and hand. Like Hotspur likes to wave his sword around. Would have to figure out other ways to make him seem super-macho, or he would have to have a really good fencing master teach him how to look like Errol Flynn."

"Really? You remember Errol Flynn?"

"Late movies when I was a kid. I remember *The Crimson Pirate*."

"You're thinking of *Captain Blood* probably. Burt Lancaster was in *The Crimson Pirate*."

"Whatever."

"Don't fool a fooler," I said. "I was a night clerk in a motel when I was in college, and I bet I saw every movie made before 1960 at least twice. I could be on a quiz show about black-and-white movies."

"Yeah," he said. "We all have these secret troves of stuff we know. I used to watch soap operas when I was in school, helped me keep on schedule at lunchtime because they were an hour long. Addicted to *All My Children in* the seventies. Had lunch with Phillip Brent and Tara Martin every day for a while there."

"People in the soap opera?"

He chuckled and I imagined him nodding. It's nice working with friends. You develop shorthand for some things after a while.

"It turns out he does have next of kin. A brother and two sisters, all of them in the Los Angeles area."

"My old stomping ground. Whereabouts? Do you know?"

"The brother, yes, the sisters not yet. Does Hollywood Riviera mean anything to you?"

Of course it does, I thought. "Nowhere near Hollywood, to start off with. Part of the city of Torrance where I went to high school. Right on the sand near the south end of Santa Monica Bay. Next to Redondo Beach. And someone got in touch with him?"

"Yeah, he answered his phone. His name is Edgar Savage. Our man was born Edward Savage, became Ned Savage along the way as an actor. If it'd been me, I would've preferred Ned to Eddie. Parents divorced years back, father moved away, no contact. Mother died from some kind of cancer. There are some other relatives, but the family doesn't seem to be very close."

I told him that he probably had an agent that wanted him to have a new name, so the past won't jump up and bite them when they're in the public eye, or so anything in the past won't get in the way of the future. I didn't mention it, but I had written some magazine articles under assumed names when I was younger. One of the articles was signed with an obviously made-up woman's name, just to see if anyone would figure out that it was fake or that I was a guy. It was Ariadne van Kalkin, I think. Nobody said anything, but that could be because not many people even read it.

"Well, if you need somebody to go out and talk to Edgar in Hollywood Riviera, I'll toss my hat in the ring."

"Might take you up on it," Mike said. "But first we gotta talk to the folks at West Side Rep. See if he had any girlfriends or boyfriends or ex-wives or whatnot. See if they might know anything that would help us."

"Let me know if I can help."

"Actually, maybe you and Ruth both could help. Make it less threatening. No idea what they are doing about their play. No cancellation notice yet, no ticket refunds."

"It's probably a showcase production. If it is, the actors are basically footing the bill so they can invite agents and casting directors to see them perform. Common thing to do, audiences get a bargain too. Tickets are almost always cheap, and the guilds and unions look the other way because they're typically in non-union theaters."

He said this production was set for St Benedict in Hell's Kitchen, an Episcopal congregation that moved downstairs to the basement and deconsecrated the main church so it could be rented out.

Since I used to live in the neighborhood, I know the church. Pretty old Gothic-style with soaring ceilings, pointed arches. Better at night because the stained glass in the windows is mediocre at best, washed-out and cheap-looking. I wouldn't be surprised if they sold the original windows. I believe I recalled that the liturgy was moved to the basement, which became the main church for the parishioners. Probably, I figured, the congregation had shrunk to the place where they were having a hard time keeping the main church in good repair. Not uncommon for churches to be used for concerts and plays—they have good acoustics lots of times. And yes, non-union.

The Episcopal Church in general is well-heeled in New York, because King George III (yes, that one) gave a lot of land to Trinity Church down at the end of Wall Street, and that packet of real estate stood the whole diocese in good stead for well over two hundred years.

Nothing lasts forever, though, and the cathedral of St John the Divine, on Amsterdam Avenue at 113th Street recently caused a public outcry when it sold off a slim parcel of land on its north side. In so doing, they gave up on the uber-traditional 1888 cruciform floor plan in order to make room for luxury condominiums that basically paid for finishing construction on the cathedral, which was begun in 1892 and has been under construction ever since. Some claim it is the largest Gothic cathedral in the world. Hard to believe if you've been to Milan or even to York (the one in England). But it's a noble building and a civilizing sight in a city that is increasingly crowded with character-less glass boxes that look like they will blow over or send glass swords down toward the street in a really stiff wind.

Ruth and I hiked over to St Benedict's after slipping in for a quick snort at Joe Allen on 46th Street, one of our favorite watering-holes. St Benedict's still looks like a church, at least until you read the glass-covered bulletin board at the top of the few stairs leading up to the front door. It now reads "Theater at St Benedict's." There was a poster for *Twelfth Night*, still planning to open for a three-week run. There was also a poster for a dance company that was planning a week's "residency" shortly after the Shakespeare play closed.

The front door was locked, so we couldn't get in. I had my tablet with me, so I jotted down the email address and telephone number for tickets. Ruth took several shots of the poster with her phone, so we would have the names of the cast. There were no indications of which person would play which role, but we had something to launch a browser on anyway.

We decided to go over to Ruth's apartment on Park Avenue and 60th Street to do some research together. I had my tablet, and Ruth's apartment is all high-grade WiFi, so we were set. She took on looking up the names listed for the cast. I decided to look up the history of St Benedict's as a theater and whatever the congregation of the former St Benedict's Church called themselves. Who knows? They could feel anger at being shut out of their own church—even though it was, we were told, their own doing.

First of all, I was happy to read, the congregation of St Benedict's was intact. As it turned out, they still have Sunday Mass in "the theatre," which is how the old church is referred to on their website. They are proud of their activist history of including gay and lesbian people, their service to the poor, their sponsorship of the ministry of women, and what they refer to as their "creative liturgy," which I took to refer to the Sunday Mass in the "theatre."

There is already an Episcopal Church designated as "The Actors Church," and, oddly enough, it's nowhere near the theater district. It is the Church of the Transfiguration, more commonly called "The Little Church around the Corner," on 29th Street between 5th Avenue and Madison. But I was tempted to bring it to the attention of the Presiding Bishop that St Benedict's might be a better venue for actors. St Benedict's claims to be one of the oldest off-Broadway theatres, with a good fifty years of productions. I had been to a memorable production of "The Witch of Edmonton" there maybe ten years back. It was a period-accurate, bloody, gory production of a seldom-done Jacobean revenge drama from the 1620s. You didn't know whether to laugh or throw up at some of the theatrical effects, but in the end, it was a hair-raising, but rollicking, good time.

Ruth had found that three of the cast members were, in fact, sisters, in spite of their having three different last names. They were called Liesel Blackburn, Annette Hicks, and Melinda Tesserla. But according to Ruth's computer, they were born Faith, Hope and Laura Tate, from a little town in Texas.

"Reminds me of *The Mikado*," she said.

"Sorry, I don't follow."

She chirped in a squeaky soprano while wagging her head like a dog's tail: "Three little maids from school are we/ Pert as a schoolgirl well can be/ Filled to the brim with girlish glee/ Three little maids from school." She sounded like she was running out of breath there at the end.

"There aren't three female roles in that play," I offered.

"Well, there are so. There's Olivia, Viola, and Maria at least."

"Hardly three little maids from school. One's the countess or whatever she is, one's disguised as a boy for virtually the whole play, and the third is a wisenheimer that's in love with an old drunk."

"Whatever," she said, rolling her eyes. "Tough crowd tonight."

"Any names I might recognize?"

"Not many that I recognize, although I think I have seen one or the other of them someplace in a small role. I don't have a photographic memory for playbills."

"How about the lighting, sets, costumes?"

She said the poster hadn't listed the off-stage or back-stage people. "That's not uncommon in these showcase productions," she said. "The production people are frequently paid for their work, although probably not union wages, so their names never get printed. The actors don't get squat, except free tickets they can give to their agents or people they owe money to."

"But somebody killed the director."

"Maybe it had nothing to do with the play?" She said it like a question.

"You never know. Somebody got into his apartment and killed him. That's all we know right now. We know he has a brother who lives in the wilds of La-La-Land somewhere near the Beach Boys. We don't know if he had a girlfriend, whether he had bad habits like gambling or drugs. The medical examiner will decide what killed him and check to see if he had any alcohol or drugs in his blood, but even the M.E. isn't going to be able to tell us who did it."

"On TV, the CSIs or the forensic somebodies can tell you how tall the killer was, where he was standing, stuff like that. They can tell from the angle that the weapon hit them. But that's TV, I guess."

"Or her."

"What?"

"Killer could have been a woman, right? Hit somebody over the head with a candlestick, you don't have to be an Olympic athlete to kill him."

"I thought it was usually a guy when there's a murder," she said.

I didn't know how to respond to that. "Umm, well, they say women almost never use guns. I've heard that, don't know how true it is though. I remember hearing a knife is a woman's weapon. Or poison. But I doubt there's a consensus on which sex is more likely with murder by candlestick. In the parlor. By Colonel Mustard."

"Okay, I agree. Him or her, whichever."

"See if you can find out if there were any sponsors, like people who gave money to help the production," Ruth said.

"Ladies of B'nai B'rith?"

"Or men of the Elks Club?" she countered. "More likely Disney or some corporation that's Netflix-y or owns huge cable empires."

Tit for tat.

I looked at the WSR website for donors. There was a button to click if you wanted to make a donation. "Here's how you can support West Side Rep" was the headline. No list of patrons that I could find.

"See if there are cast lists or programs of productions they've done in the past."

I looked and there was a button to click for Past Productions. I clicked that and scrolled down through the cast and WSR Staff to a button called Program, and clicked on that. After I scrolled through a number of bios of actors and staff, there was a section on institutional supporters and then a list of various levels of gifts, no indication of how much, but with names like Dukes and Duchesses, Earls and Countesses, Barons and Baronesses, Lords and Ladies. Like, "Be an aristocrat and give us money." I showed it to Ruth.

She scanned down the lists. "These are people who support all kind of things," she said. "No help. And these are probably all the people who gave money that season too, not just for this production."

We kept on for a while longer, and then Ruth stood up. "I gotta get something to eat."

I checked my tablet for how much battery it had left. Plenty. I powered it down. "Whatcha got in mind?"

"I dunno. Chinese?"

"Not."

"Ok, what?"

"Any place near here that might have a turkey burger?"

We decided to go to a place called The Smith, a nice but casual grill with tablecloths and a good bar. It's not really a chain, but there are three or four of them in Manhattan, so it might as well have been a chain in New York parlance.

Chapter Three

I'm a fan of *Twelfth Night*, one of those plays that never seems to lose its freshness or its punch. Other than *Macbeth*, I think it is the Shakespeare play I have seen most often. It has such wonderful slapstick comedy scenes, and I marvel at the ways a good director can make the audience laugh on cue, in spite of the fact that the language is obviously over four hundred years old.

As I looked at the material online about the WSR production, I was taken aback at one casting choice. Malvolio, arguably the antagonist in this dark comedy, was to be played by a woman. That would have all the opportunities a director could need for silly laughs, because Malvolio's failing is that he falls in love with his employer, Viola, when he finds what he thinks is a love note addressed to him from Viola.

"You know," Ruth said, "I know the actress who's playing Malvolio. Brilliant idea."

"Who dat?"

"Her name is Lily Rasmussen; she's made a career out of playing old maids and schoolteachers. Tall, gangly and awkward, with electrified hair that stands out from her head. You feel like laughing immediately when you see her." She showed me a photo online.

"She looks vaguely familiar. Looks like a descendent of Margaret Hamilton when she was the Wicked Witch of the West. Like a hayseed Mrs. Malaprop."

"Never thought about it that way, but I take your point."

"But you know her?"

"What I meant was that I know her work. She was a hoot in a production of that Noel Coward play about old actresses, *Waiting in the*

Wings, a few years back. Stole the show, hilarious laughter. I would love to see a Malvolio who steals the show instead of just being the butt of all the laughs."

"She looks to be fifty-ish."

"Probably, yeah. Maybe more. She's looked the same for quite a while, I think."

"I kinda doubt she would have been alone in Ned Savage's apartment with an opportunity to kill him."

"Did we establish that there was no one else there but Ned and the killer?'

"Funny you should say that. As I said that about her being alone, I realized I was making all kinds of unwarranted assumptions. Nothing to say a middle-aged actress wouldn't be there alone, especially if she was in the cast. Nothing to say there was nobody else there, could have been. And most of all, nothing to say it wasn't a woman who did this."

"Maybe we should talk to Lily Rasmussen then."

"No idea how we would go about that."

"Well, as it happens, she is a member of the Opera League, so she should be in the directory."

"So, you do know her, not just her work."

"Not really. I've just seen her there on Monday nights for a long time. Don't recall ever speaking with her." She took my tablet and launched a browser. A minute or two later she had a phone number and email address.

"You are a miracle worker at times, ma'am."

The actress responded right away to Ruth's text, so we headed over to talk to her. Lily was a good deal less a caricature at home than she might be on stage. She was near my height (6'4"), not skinny but not inclined to be heavy, sixty-ish. Slump-shouldered as tall women were apt to be when society expected them to be shorter than their husbands, even when wearing high heels. Her hair was curly, cut fairly close to the head and clearly bottle-brown with some lighter streaks—I thought when I first saw her that she was wearing a wig. A wide mouth jammed full of teeth and a smile that would read well in the second balcony. Hard to describe her voice, sort of a gurgling alto, on the edge of laughter much of the time. Dimples. Still the look of a Valkyrie; a hint of majesty as you would expect from the daughter of a god.

Lily remembered Ruth from the opera ("Of course I do"). Firm handshake when I introduced myself, and strong eye contact. I felt comfortable with her immediately. Ruth clearly felt a little stand-offish but smiled a lot.

"Are you Scandinavian?" I couldn't resist asking.

She nodded. "*Ho jo to ho* and all that," she said, quoting Brunnhilde's war cry from the Wagner opera. "You wanted to talk about Ned. Nasty business, that, so young and talented." She cleared her throat.

I explained that Mr. Savage's apartment was next door to mine in Long Island City, and that I had seen him but not met him when he moved in.

"Startlingly handsome, didn't you think?" Lily looked directly into my eyes.

"Yes, I noticed he was good looking, although only I saw him in the hallway with the movers. The impression I had of him was emphasized by the limp and the problem with one of his arms."

She cocked her head and half-smiled. "You're very observant."

"I find that one advantage of getting older is that no one notices when I stare at them. Even on the subway." I tried to put on a different, more serious face. "Was Mr. Savage well liked at West Side Rep and at St Benedict's?"

"All directors are irritating," she said. "But Ned balanced his direction. I don't recall a time when he didn't have a smile and attentive eye contact. Yes, I would say he was popular with the cast and crew. Very helpful in little ways. Big thing for me, he told me to keep my hands within the envelope of my body, that it would increase the impact I made on the audience when I reached out. He was right. I've always had a tendency to wave my hands around, like Zasu Pitts."

"Do you have any idea why someone would have wanted to kill him?"

She made a motion of shaking something off or shivering in a cold wind and shook her head negatively.

"Is there any time in *Twelfth Night* when someone picks up a candlestick and waves it around?" Ruth asked.

"Interesting. No, and even though this production was to have been an innovative approach to the play, nothing super-different that I saw in any of the rehearsals." She pursed her lips a bit and said, "You're wondering if there was a rehearsal in process. No, I don't think so."

"How about a sword or a bottle? Something that a candlestick could be for rehearsal purposes?"

She looked up and dragged her right hand from her chin down her neck while she thought. "Well, Sir Toby is a drunk," she said, referring to one of the characters in the play. "He could be waving a bottle around, I suppose, but I don't recall anything like that."

Ruth nodded. "Did he rehearse any of the actors separately from the rest of the cast?"

"Possibly, I suppose. I don't know."

"Did he work with you one-on-one?"

"No."

I jumped in. "I keep wondering why he wanted to cast Malvolio as a woman."

"He didn't. Malvolio is a man; has to be to be enough of a fool to make a pass at his boss, Viola. He wanted a woman—me—to play a man, which is different from pretending Malvolio is a woman. I suppose because that's already a theme in the play with Olivia falling in love with Viola dressed up as a boy, and it can get a lot of laughs. You know Hamlet is sometimes played by a woman?"

"How did you get involved?" Ruth asked.

"Been part of West Side Rep for years, but I didn't audition for Malvolio. He approached me."

"Is that unusual?"

"Not with Ned. I think he cast almost everyone that way. Like he kept a rolodex of people he wanted to work with or something like that." She paused then added, "We had worked together before, you know."

"No, I didn't know that. Also Shakespeare?"

She harrumphed a bit and shook her head. "Tennessee Williams. Play called *Sweet Bird of Youth*. I was Alexandra del Lago, a movie star kinda like Gloria Swanson in 'Sunset Boulevard'; alcoholic and drug addict running from a recent movie that flopped. Ned was a bartender in the hotel I was staying in."

"You mean the hotel you were staying in while you were in the play?" I asked.

"No, the bartender in the play. The character was named Stuff, which originally meant it was intended to be a Black man since it was set in the South when it was still completely segregated. Ned had a way of attracting attention even in a small role, and that was probably the first role he got in New York. He moved here from LA, you know. The bartender is a snitch for the bad guy in the play, fellow named Tom Finley Junior."

She paused, smiling, remembering. "Probably six years ago or so. I liked playing Alexandra del Lago. I wasn't paired with anyone, just a character that made the plot go forward. Not all that different from Malvolio I guess, in some ways. She called herself Princess Kosmonopolis because she wanted to be incognito. We ran for six weeks."

"Also West Side Rep?"

"No. Independent production where we got paid scale. Not much money but good exercise."

"I saw you in *Waiting in the Wings*," Ruth said.

Lily beamed. "You should talk to Gianfranco Mirabella. He's in the production, but he was Perry in 'Waiting in the Wings.' So you saw him when you saw me. Amazing that when Noel Coward wrote that play, the first producer dropped it because it was too old-fashioned. It's really hilarious, lots of loud laughing in the audience." She pulled a notepad out of what I had presumed was a knitting bag and jotted something down and handed it to me. "Tell Frangooch I sent you."

It was mid-afternoon when we left Lily's apartment, and I was hungry. I texted Mike di Saronno to see if he was around. He said to come over. I asked if the Halal truck was there; I could see him smiling when he said yes. Both Ruth and I love falafel, a faux meatball made in the Middle East from garbanzo beans and deep-fried. Stuffed into pita bread with tomatoes, pickles, yogurt/mayonnaise sauce and fiery hot sauce.

We walked into Mike's office carrying paper bags with falafel sandwiches. "Here," I said, "brought one for you too."

He took us into one of the interrogation rooms. We sat down and ate, drank ginger ales from the Halal truck. Heaven.

Ruth told him about meeting Lily Rasmussen.

"I don't know about Ruth, but I didn't hear anything from her that would tell me there was anything hostile going on in the production he was directing."

"I didn't either," she said. "But she's an actor. She wouldn't go into something she didn't want to talk about. She did say she worked with Ned once before, in a Tennessee Williams play about an actress."

"He told us to get in touch with Gianfranco Mirabella who's playing a drunk in *Twelfth Night*."

Mike said the CSIs thought there might have been several people in the apartment. "But it's impossible to tell, because he had just moved in, so it could have been from the days before he was killed—movers, friends helping out, whatever. There was some residue of marijuana on the coffee table."

Ruth shrugged. "That would be true in my apartment too."

"I didn't mean it proves anything, just telling you what they told me."

"Anything more you found out?" I asked.

Mike shook his head. "Oh, wait. Ned had a car, and it's still in the garage. The CSIs went over it too. Not much help. And there was a letter in his files from a Turkish writer, with the stub of a check for $50,000. The stub said it was for Ned's 'project'."

I took out my cell and called the number for Mr. Mirabella. It went straight to voicemail, which probably meant his phone was turned off. It probably also meant the number was a cellphone. So I sent a text message telling him that Lily had told us to give him a call.

Ruth and I left with the intention of going over to the park to walk off some of the falafel, which is delicious, but very filling. Instead, my phone made a clunking sound that indicated a text message had arrived.

How can I help you? It was Gianfranco Mirabella.

Working with NYPD about Ned Savage. You have time to see us?

He responded with an address in the West Village. We walked over to the subway at 50th Street, jumped on a number 1 train and got off at Christopher Street, West Village.

I was feeling very full after the falafel, felt like I needed to wash out my digestive track, like maybe drink a bottle of water in one long gulp. Not a good idea.

He was the opposite of what you would expect of Sir Toby Belch, who is usually a bear of a drunk, clumsy and inclined to bump into things. "Frank," as he told us to call him, was shorter than normal, maybe 5'7", wiry and black-haired, not the least bit English-looking. And slightly prissy.

"Ned Savage was setting role types on their ears, wasn't he?" Ruth asked as we shook hands.

"You don't think I'm intimidating?" he said sweetly, like a boy trying to please a teacher.

She smiled.

Then he growled like a dog and suddenly screamed like a banshee, loud enough to hurt my eardrums. Ruth was startled.

"Point made," I said.

"The thing is, if you change one part, you end up changing several to balance things," Frank said. "You make Lily into Malvolio, you create a balancing surprise by shrinking Toby to me. But you keep the characters what they were. Malvolio is a bumbling fool, and all the funnier for being a tall, awkward woman who's all elbows. Lily is a genius at that. With me, Toby is like a tipsy troll peeking out from under a bridge instead of the drunken grizzly bear he usually is. Together we put the audience off-balance every time one of us walks onto the stage. And in this production, Maria is played by a kid who looks like an NFL tackle, so the supposed servant girl towers over Toby. Great wig for Maria too. Nice not to be typecast as a postal clerk for once. Don't forget that Viola is pretending to be a boy for ninety percent of the play."

He sat us down in his cozy living room and scurried off to the kitchen where a teakettle was whistling, returning with a plate of cookies and a pot of tea. There were teacups in the bookshelf next to the sofa. "Lemon? Sugar? Milk? Shall I be mother?"

"You're British, aren't you?"

He smiled. "Not hardly. I grew up in New Mexico, and my name isn't Mirabella, which is fake Italian, it's Martinez. My first language is

Spanish, but I got into Yale on scholarship and learned how to speak English several different ways, so I can be an Aussie, mate, a pahk-the-cah mick from Boston, or give me a fat suit and I can be Falstaff and sound like I was born in Bow Bells."

"So, nothing is what it seems to be. Like Willy Wonka's chocolate factory," Ruth observed.

"Or on the wrong side of the looking-glass," Frank said with a sly look that made me wonder for a second if he was going to pounce at us. He didn't.

I asked how it was working with Ned Savage.

"He had a knack for making it seem like I was directing myself." He cocked his head. "Does that make sense?"

"Can you give me an example?"

He looked up and then down and said, "Since Toby is constantly drinking, I was starting off staggering and slurring. Ned asked me if that's what I would do if I had been drinking. I said no, I would try to act sober, try to walk a straight line.

"He didn't respond, but when we did the scene again, I tried it that way, and it worked so much better. I know that is what he wanted, but he didn't try to tell me to do it that way. Got it?"

I was getting a basic education in acting. I had taken some acting classes when I first moved to New York, but it was different. The "method" then was all the thing. If your character was a druggie, then hang out with druggies and learn what to do by being with them. Actually, that only works if you are doing slice-of-life plays. You can't learn how to be Captain Hook by living with pirates in flying ships. And it seldom works for comedy.

Ruth shifted positions on the couch and looked at Frank. "Who would have had a problem with Ned?"

"Anybody could have, but it didn't seem to me like anyone did."

"Somebody killed him though."

"Yes, I know. I don't have a script for that. Sorry, I just don't know what to say. I liked him. I thought everybody liked him." He picked up the teapot and gestured, to see if we wanted a refill.

I stood up and said, "I'm afraid we ought to push on, Frank. I forgot to tell you that Lily said to say hi to Frangooch for her."

He smiled. "Lily-belle is always looking for laughs."

As we left, Ruth said to me, "I'm beginning to wonder if we're going to find out anything helpful at West Side Rep."

I observed that some situations are like onions, in layers, each layer obscuring the one underneath it.

"Antonin Artaud you ain't, honey."

"Well at least you could tell what I was aiming at." Artaud was a famous writer on the theater, and I was assigned to read one of his books when I was at UCLA. Trivia.

Chapter Four

Whether West Side Rep was an onion that needed peeling or not, we decided to try to learn more about other parts of Ned's short life. I texted Gabriele and asked him if he would like to join us for dinner. He answered yes, but only if it was at his restaurant, because they were expecting a crowd. I don't have to be asked twice about having dinner at Ora di Pranzo. The food is heavenly, because Gabriele's cousin, Dante, is a genius in the kitchen. I had a picture of a bowl of *zuppa di pesce,* which, contrary to what it sounds like, isn't soup at all, but a stew made from all kinds of seafood.

He had reserved a table for four in the front of the restaurant, meaning he would sit with us, but would have to get up to greet people who were arriving. The small tabletop was already covered with *contorni*, roasted veggies, cheese, olives and salami, even though he knows I don't eat meat. He told me once it just looks wrong without the salami or at least some *prosciutto* (Italian ham).

He was in the process of seating a table of ten or twelve toward the back of the restaurant, up a half-flight of stairs on a semi-balcony area. A waiter pointed out our table, so we sat down. Before we could order a drink, a waiter brought us dirty vodkas straight up with olives. Perfect. And a glass of red for Gabriele, who would doubtless also eat the salami that Ruth and I wouldn't want.

My phone burped to indicate a text message. I looked. It was Mike: *Call me.*

Gabriele was wearing a tuxedo, slim pants with a satin stripe on each leg, patent leather shoes and an intricately embroidered vest that seemed to have gold thread in it. Kiss-kiss, hug-hug, and he sat down with us, picked up the wine and drank half the glass in one gulp, and followed that by swallowing half a glass of water. I put down my phone, deciding to call Mike back in a few minutes. I wanted to ask Gabriele about Lily and Gianfranco, though I doubted he would know them. They didn't seem to be the type to frequent popular, fully-booked eateries in SoHo.

But as fate would have it, the phone rang. Mike. I clicked to answer the call, but the ambient noise around the table made it difficult to hear. I excused myself from the table and stepped outside onto the sidewalk, where it was measurably quieter, but still difficult to hear.

As it turned out, the Medical Examiner had found some surprises in the autopsy. First of all, although Ned probably died from being hit with the candlestick, he was almost dead before he was hit. Probably on the floor, which accounted for the hit from the back, if he was on his stomach. He was in anaphylactic shock, and had apparently stuck himself with an epinephrine pen to try to keep from passing out. Could have been a food allergy, Mike said. Ned's face was swollen from exposure to an allergen, which the M.E. said might have been a common one, like peanuts or chocolate, or an insect bite. And the odd part was that the exposure could have been some time earlier, even an hour. His throat was swollen, so he was probably having difficulty breathing.

"Could it have anything to do with whatever affected his arm and leg?"

Mike had no idea, but he would ask.

"Why didn't the epinephrine work?" I asked.

"I wondered the same thing," Mike said. "M.E. said it might have worked, but somebody smashed in his head and killed him before it could have helped much."

"Was there anything in his wallet about an allergy? Or was he wearing an ID bracelet with a warning on it?"

Neither. But he obviously had a syringe with epinephrine in it, so the anaphylaxis was something he was aware of.

I explained to him that I was at Ora di Pranzo with Ruth and Gabriele and told him I would talk to them and get back to him, possibly in the morning if that was okay. He agreed.

When I told Ruth and Gabriele, Ruth was shocked, but Gabriele wasn't.

"He say he allergic with something when he eat here. I ask in kitchen, maybe they know, make book for allergies so we not forget. I not remember what he say is allergic." Gabriele shook his head like he was trying to dislodge a memory. "Maybe he say he not eat *funghi.*"

"Mushrooms? Really? I am too," I said, as though he didn't already know that. I have an ID bracelet that says I am allergic to mushrooms, but I never wear it.

I asked Gabriele what Ned was like when he was there.

"He with many people, big table. *Amichevole, ride con gusto.*" (*friendly, laughed a lot*)

"Did you talk to him?"

No. "He very nice for eyes."

It takes one to know one. People stare at you all the time, signor. Glad to know you stare back sometimes.

"Maybe a party on opening night of a new play?"

He shrugged and put his palms up to say he didn't know.

Gabriele had ordered *branzino* (sea bass) for all three of us, with mashed potatoes and rapini. A bottle of Cannonau, a hearty red wine from Sardinia. He fileted the three fish himself, making it look easy. The only time I ever tried to do that, the fish ended up in small pieces like it had been flaked. And some on the floor.

"How do you do that?" Ruth asked.

"Do many time and then is easy."

She rolled her eyes and scrunched up her mouth. "Some day you show me. Do it slow so I can remember what you're doing."

He nodded and put on a fake smile. *When pigs fly.*

The fish was delicious. Nobody knows how to make a simple dish like the Italians. A plate-sized fish, whole, roasted in olive oil and herbs. Nothing more simple than that, and at the same time nothing more difficult to get right. There are ten or twelve ways to make it wrong and only one way to make it the way it's supposed to be. Italians don't make mashed potatoes in Italy, but in New York it's different, and the platter sauce from the fish is pure ambrosia on lumpy mashed potatoes. Rapini is good any time of any day, sautéed with oil and thin-sliced garlic, but still only partially cooked so it is firm.

When we finished, Gabriele sprang up, made a signal to one of the runners, and moved toward the front reception area, kissing the women he passed by and patting the men on the back. I wondered if he knew who they were but admired the way he made everyone feel welcome. Natural-born. The front-desk talent is what makes a restaurant successful. The kitchen talent is important too, but the kitchen seldom has direct contact with the patrons. People go to Ora di Pranzo because Gabriele treats them like royalty.

The waiters whisked all the china and cutlery off our table in seconds, poured more wine into our glasses and removed the empty bottle, putting three after-dinner flutes on the table. After a couple of minutes, Gabriele re-appeared, smiling.

"*Si*," he said. "*Funghi*."

A plate of cannoli appeared unbidden, looking as fresh and light as manna from heaven. No chocolate chips, just lemony ricotta cream with tiny chips of peppermint candy whipped in. Gabriele walked over to the bar and brought back an unlabeled bottle of yellowish liquid which he poured into the three after-dinner glasses.

"*Fatt' in casa*," he said, dropping a vowel along the way like a Neapolitan. It meant the bottle contained something that was "home made."

"*Caprese*?" I asked if the lemons were from Capri.

"*Si, la mia nonna,*" he said, the lemons were sent to him by his grandmother. I didn't ask how he got them through customs.

Limoncello is the perfect end to an Italian seafood feast. As sour as a lemon drop with a mouth-heating bite of alcohol. A few sips and it's over, like throwing back a tequila slammer after you bang it on the table top.

We had been at Ora di Pranzo for nearly three hours from start to finish. What I had learned was that Gabriele only remembered Ned because of his looks and his demeanor. He didn't have a chance to get to know him. That in itself was interesting, because it meant that Ned was not as outgoing as I had guessed he would be as an actor.

Ruth and I shared a cab; she dropped me off at Grand Central so that I could take a subway to Long Island City. When I got to my apartment, there was a text message on my phone that Gabriele was on his way over.

He brandished the bottle of limoncello as he walked in. I had put on some coffee because I suspected he wanted to talk, or talk and drink. I grabbed two small sherry glasses and he poured about a half-inch of limoncello into each one. We threw them back.

He was looking sheepish. I could have guessed what he was worried about, as it turned out. He knew Ned from several years back.

"He must have been very young," I said.

"He more older than he look."

"So, you knew him. Are you worried that might mean you shouldn't be working with me on this?"

He nodded.

"That's not something I would worry about."

He stared at me and said nothing.

"You mean you had sex with him?"

He nodded again and looked down at his hands.

"He gave you money?"

No.

"But did you stay in touch with him after that?"

No.

"I'll talk to Mike, but I don't think it will make any difference to him. Ned was killed. Do you still have feelings about him?"

He stood up and walked to the kitchen. I could see him through the pass-through as he took down a martini glass from the cabinet and opened the freezer. He poured three fingers of vodka into the glass, took a slurp and walked back into the living room carrying it with his fingers around the rim, the stem below his hand.

"I forget about him for long time, but I very sad now I know."

"So, what you told me about him being at Ora di Pranzo, that was not true?"

"Was true. He not remember me. He not know me. Maybe I look much different at Ora di Pranzo. I not talk to him, go in kitchen and talk Dante then go home."

"You were sad that he didn't know you?"

He shook his head. "I dress different, have different name. He change. He look different. He with friends, not notice me. Not sad, just want be away from Ora di Pranzo when he there."

He was dejected. I couldn't ignore that. I put my hand on his shoulder. He looked up at me and I hugged him. I felt like saying something comforting but nothing came out. Half my age, he's like a son for that reason, but less like a son because he is out front about being attracted to me in a not-fatherly way. I can't get used to that part; it's just odd, the May-December part. But also I'm just not capable of entering into that kind of relationship with a man--or probably not even with a woman, for that matter. No balls, two strikes, two outs in the bottom of the ninth in the matrimonial game. One more strike and it's over.

I have been friends with Gabriele for several years, and in all that time I never heard him talk about anyone the way he talked about Ned. Sadly, Ned may not ever have known that Gabriele was apparently carrying a torch for him.

I thought about Ruth. There was a time when I thought I was falling in love with her, and that maybe she was feeling the same way about me. But then she met Murray and they were clearly a love match for the decade they were married before he passed. I never thought she would take off that big emerald-cut diamond he bought her, but after he died, I never saw it again. She kept wearing the plain platinum band though. The more I have gotten to know her, the fonder I am of her—but also relieved that we never took a step too far with each other.

I feel something for Gabriele, but also he is close to the same age as my son, whom I haven't spoken to in ages—a result of the corrosive divorce that his mother and I inflicted on each other. I have for the most part not had any libido since then. My fault, although I have told lots of people it was her fault. Occasionally of course, nature arouses the dirty old man in me, but so far nothing that I have pursued.

If I could adopt Gabriele, I would. All that parenting that I gave up earlier in life has built up like the pond behind a beaver dam in a stream, and there is pressure building that may make a torrent of fathering inevitable one day. I guess I should get a dog and see if that helps. Dogs are huggable too.

Too much information.

I asked Gabriele if he would pour me some vodka like his. Of course he did and plopped a big green olive in it, too, with a slight tipple of olive juice from the jar. What they call "dirty" in a bar. I turned on ESPN and sat back on the couch to watch three retired baseball players talk about the day's games. I'm a Yankee fan, I guess, though I still have a soft spot for the Angels, who were my home team for a long time. And my son went to baseball summer camp that was run by the Dodgers. Gabriele had refilled his glass and seemed relieved when I put the television on. I doubt he understands much about the super-arcane rules of baseball, but like a lot of guys, he can watch almost any sport.

After a while, I felt like I was nodding off so I wandered into my bedroom and got a towel and washcloth for him and pointed him down the hall to the "guest" bedroom. It was a balmy night, but not super-sticky, so I had most of the windows open and the ceiling fans rotating. I think I was asleep in record time.

Chapter Five

I woke up hearing Gabriele cracking eggs in the kitchen, which is just outside my bedroom. The smell of coffee was strong when I opened the door. He was smiling his usual good-humored smile, wearing boxer briefs and nothing else. I sleep in a t-shirt and pajama bottoms, keeps from getting sweat stains on the sheets.

"How 'bout them Yanks?" he tossed at me. It was a comic line from a play.

"You okay?"

He poured some whisked eggs and cheese into a skillet for an omelet, something I have never been able to master. I can't flip them over, partly for the same reason I can't putt a golf ball—I'm shy about just doing it. My dad said putting is a young man's game, because they don't worry about it so much. But also because I have tried flipping an omelet, and it has gone wrong one-hundred percent of the time. He flipped it high above the pan with a quick glance at me to make sure I was watching.

"How do you do that?"

"Same like take bone out of fish. Easy after do wrong many time."

"You mean you have dropped an omelet on the floor like I do?"

"Throw many omelet on floor and on stove." He was smiling like the sun in splendor. "More hard clean up on stove." The moroseness of the evening before was gone.

I booted up my cellphone and it rapidly made several beeping noises, indicating new messages or emails. "My public is calling me," I said, thinking of a classic movie. *All right, Mister DeMille. I'm ready for my close-up.* Gabriele was doing a corner-of-the-eye look at me, trying to see me without looking at me; he clearly wasn't picking up on my old-movie reference.

I put some plates and flatware on the table on a couple of placemats and some paper napkins, something that would have been *verboten* when I was a child. But of course when I was a child, each cloth napkin was hand-ironed by the maid. Cloth napkins don't add to the trash going into landfills, so I still use them fairly often, but I just wash them and fold them; they don't get ironed. I have no maid. And I keep a backup supply of paper napkins too (sometimes folded paper towels from the kitchen roll).

Gabriele is a smiler-meeter-greeter at his restaurant, the guy in the fancy handmade suit who tells someone which table is yours and makes you feel as though you have just come home. He also debones your whole fish if you are smart enough to order one. Dante is the chef, definitely a cook to write home about. But the unsuspected truth is that Gabriele is no slouch in the kitchen either.

There have been times when they both have collaborated to cater meals for me. There are a few times when I feel like a jet-setter or a millionaire (which I'm certainly not), but when Gabriele and Dante take over the kitchen for dinner, it's like being king for a day. And when Gabriele makes a princely breakfast, and does it in his skivvies, the same monarchical transformation comes about. Hey, I may not be gay, but I'm not blind either.

He slid the omelet onto a platter and then disappeared down the hall, returning in jeans and a Yankees t-shirt, barefoot. He had made coffee that was strong enough that a spoon could have stood straight up in it but countered that with a fresh *bellini*, a drink that mixes mushed-up blended peaches with something alcoholic—properly Prosecco (the Italian answer to champagne), but in my case, vodka, because I react badly to carbonated cocktails—no rum and Coke, no champagne, no scotch and soda. At any rate, the coffee and the bellini balanced each other, especially since I had already downed a quick blast of vodka.

He is such a sunny person in the mornings that it emphasizes his youth particularly well. I find that I am slower in the mornings than I used to be. I tend to sit on the side of the bed and stare at the wall before I stand up and head into the bathroom for morning ablutions. It's not that I'm afraid I would be light-headed if I stood up more quickly, it's that I just am not ready to start the day until I am more fully awake, a process that seems to take more time with the passing years.

My new dining table is glass-topped, and the chairs are matte black metal with tall, thin, stiff leather backs. The glass is easy to clean, but more importantly, it doesn't take up visual room like the old wooden table did. I don't have a dining room, just a dining-place between the kitchen pass-through and the sliding doors to the balcony. I tend to use placemats instead of throwing a tablecloth over it, because I love the Turkish carpet under the table and like staring at it. Gabriele is so observant that I think he knows all these details of my peculiarities, and I find that comforting.

He brought out the omelet with a flourish and put a stack of perfect English toast in the middle of the table, with a properly softened stick of butter and some orange marmalade (my favorite jam). What's not to love?

"What we do today about find Ned killer?" He was a study in nonchalance.

I told him that we needed to learn more about the people involved in the play Ned was directing at St Benedict's and briefed him about our talks with Lily Rasmussen and Gianfranco Mirabella. "Mr. Mirabella is cast as Sir Toby in the play, a drunk and very funny if it's done right. I got the impression from Lily that he might be carrying a bottle around with him onstage, although bottles might not be period-accurate, now that I think of it. I've heard it is very difficult to do a good drunk scene without the audience seeing right through it." I told him I found myself wondering whether there was a rehearsal of sorts going on in Ned's apartment when he was killed. "Like maybe he was waving the candlestick around like it was a bottle of booze or something."

"But he hit Ned with *candeliere* and kill him. You think *per errore*?"

"No way to tell if it was an accident, but the coroner said Ned was dying already when the candlestick hit him."

Gabriele stood up suddenly. "Why he dying already?"

I explained the best I could that he probably had an allergy attack that put him into anaphylactic shock, which is *shock anafilattico* in Italian. "He had stuck a syringe needle in his leg to try to stop the reaction, but it may have been too late. So he knew what was happening with the allergy and had what they call an EpiPpen with the medicine in it."

"So *candeliere* not kill him?"

"Oh, it killed him for sure, or at least that was what I understood from Mike. But his head was bashed in before the medicine could act, so the two things must have happened almost at the same time. Look, I'm not a doctor, so I don't know exactly what must have happened, but from what Mike told me, he would have been okay if the candlestick hadn't hit him over the head. The cause of death was blunt force trauma caused by the candlestick, which had blood and hair stuck on it."

"And no *scazzottata*?" He was asking if the two people had been fighting.

I told him there was no way I could know the answer to that. "But Mike told me there was no obvious mess. No broken glasses or things that had been thrown around the room."

"Maybe we talk more people from play?" He sat down at my computer and tapped away on the keys, finding the website where tickets could be bought for *Twelfth Night.*

"If music be the food of love, play on," I said.

He looked puzzled.

"It's the first line of the play, and maybe one of the most famous lines in all of Shakespeare's plays. It's a silly play in lots of ways; very funny, makes the audience laugh, even more than four hundred years later. Almost everyone in the play is in love with the wrong person. The Duke, who says that first line, is in love with a woman who herself is in love with another woman, who happens to be pretending to be a man."

He wasn't interested, or wasn't following what I was saying, or both. "We go to theatre and talk to people?"

I said I needed a shower and would be quick. He smiled.

About twenty minutes later I was ready to go. It was sunny and hot-looking outside. Accuweather said it would be ninety-two by late afternoon, so I was wearing a short-sleeved linen shirt and khaki chinos with a pair of fisherman sandals. Gabriele had put on shoes and, annoyingly, looked like he just stepped out of a high-end menswear catalog, where I frequently look more like a walking garage sale.

I texted Ruth to let her know what we were up to. She texted back that she might join us if we were going to be there for a while.

We took the number 7 subway to Times Square and walked to St Benedict's, only about four or five blocks away. So much for being actually "Off-Broadway." The front doors were unlocked and we let ourselves in but were intercepted at the door by two young men who said the rehearsal was closed to the public. I flashed my NYPD identification as a civilian criminalist and told them we would like to observe and possibly talk to some of the cast or backstage folks when there was a break.

They scurried off and returned a few minutes later with an okay but a request that we sit in the back of the auditorium and turn off our cellphones.

The actors were carrying scripts and clearly trying to come up with blocking—deciding where they should be on stage for each part of the scene, and how they were to go from place to place without distracting the audience from the progression of the storyline. It was a scene that started off with a silly bit between Olivia's maid, Maria, and Olivia's jester who ends the opening with a tossed-off verbal jewel: "Better a witty fool than a foolish wit."

I was interested to see that Lily was taking over the director's duties, although her character, Malvolio, was also involved in the scene, initially showing jealousy concerning the jester. In some ways the plot revolves around Lily's character who is a high-level servant in Olivia's home, a major-domo, more or less. In a big home today he would be the Head Butler. She had altered her way of walking to thrust her pelvis forward in a way that was intended to burlesque a conceited man but had slumped her shoulders down and forward, possibly to conceal her breasts, since she was playing a man.

Gabriele was watching intently. It occurred to me that he was watching the scene the way a child would. He probably had little ability to understand the Tudor English, especially since it was spoken so fast as the actors spat it out. Children are used to not being able to understand what is being said, so they take their cues from what's happening, rather than what's being said. That's why they prefer comedy to drama, because comedy is frequently more visual than verbal.

He looked at me and said, "Is very good, *e divertenti, no?*"

"You know the play?" He had said it was funny, by which I gathered he meant the words, since they were not doing much acting.

He nodded. "Even in *Capri e Napoli,* we study Shakespeare," which he pronounced "Shock-ay-spay-AH-ray", hitting all the vowels the way you would in Italian. "Is very *comico.*" There was more than a touch of sarcasm in what he said.

So much for watching it like a child. I whispered to him that Ruth and I had spoken with Lily, the tall woman who was playing a man. He nodded to me.

Then Gianfranco Mirabella entered, wobblingly drunk, and I told Gabriele we had spoken with him too. He squinted as he looked at Gianfranco, one of a pair of bookend fools in the play with alcohol as an identifying characteristic. Shakespeare was a genius in many ways, but for sure one of his most outstanding talents was in creating very funny characters who had a world of possible improvisation built into them. No wonder actors love his plays. My first impression was that Gianfranco was way overacting, but then I loosened up a bit and found what he was doing was very amusing.

When Viola entered, she swaggered like a randy teenaged boy, almost a caricature of Lily's Malvolio. Gabriele watched her carefully. Clearly there were no costumes yet, but Viola was wearing a Robin Hood type of hat with a feather in it, maybe a bow to Peter Pan, who is frequently played by a woman.

He nudged me with his elbow just as I saw Ruth appear at the top of the aisle. "This one come to Ora di Pranzo when Ned bring people."

Lily broke character and waved to Ruth as she sidled into the row of seats where we were sitting. Ruth waved back. "*Lesbica,*" Gabriele whispered in my ear. I guessed he meant Lily and shook my head at him. "Girl from Ned group in Ora di Pranzo, not old woman," he said, making eye contact with me and nodding his head. Viola was talking, and I detected a bit of Irish lilt. She was taller than most women but not as tall as Lily, with bushy red hair that looked completely natural. She also had the very young look that Viola should have as she masquerades virtually the entire play as a young boy, too young to have any growth of facial hair. That causes Olivia to fall in love with her, probably as a means of avoiding the attentions of Orsino, who has been plaguing her with his creepy courtship.

Olivia had just asked her, "What is your parentage?"

Viola answered, "Above my fortunes, yet my state is well: I am a gentleman." Her delivery of the lines fit into my aural memory of Irish speech, especially the way she intoned the word ''my'' twice; it came out as more like ''me'' or ''meh.'' *I bet she pronounces the number after forty-nine as "fufteh." As Irish as Paddy's pig. I'd give odds that Lily will beat that out of her.*

I asked Ruth, who was sitting next to me, if she knew the name of the actress playing Viola. She whipped out a printout of a screen shot that had the list of players. Viola was listed as Georgina Spelvin; Spelvin being a common alias that union actors use when they are performing in a non-union theater or when they are not getting paid, which would be a violation of union rules if they used their registered names. I asked her if she recognized the young woman. She shook her head.

"Does she sound Irish to you?" I asked.

She nodded vigorously. "But Spelvin's not an Irish name, so maybe she's not," she said with a grin. "Maybe she's Jewish."

I said I didn't think Jewish was a national identity.

She rolled her eyes to indicate that I was not really there and said nothing.

Lily called a break, probably because the scene they had been working on was the end of the first act of the play. The first scene of the next act would be up in ten minutes, with two new characters who had not appeared in Act One—Antonio and Sebastian, the latter being Viola's brother whom Viola thinks was drowned in the shipwreck that apparently happened just before the play began. In an ideal world, Viola and Sebastian would look very much alike when Viola was dressed as a boy, although usually the audience has to imagine that part.

Lily strode up the center aisle to where we were sitting, waving with every footstep in spite of what appeared to be a bad ankle.

"Well, *shalom* Malvolio," Ruth blurted out when Lily got to our row.

Lily responded with a stagey smile. She only had a minute but wanted to say hello. Ruth asked her what Viola's name was.

"Lucille McGillicuddy," she said and made a sour face.

"You're kidding. Well, at least it's Irish, even if it's already been used before," Ruth said, alluding to the fact that the name had already been used by a very famous red-haired actress. "If that's her moniker, I don't know why she's calling herself Spelvin on the cast list."

"I'm not kidding, but she probably is. I'd never seen her before. Ned cast her, the same way he cast the rest of us—he sought her out from work she had done in the past and lured her into his den, like the spider and the fly. I have to say she has great timing for Viola and an unusually mobile face with big eyes, so she can make people laugh without even saying anything. Even stranger, she and Sebastian actually look like they could be brother and sister."

I started to ask Lily something, but she chirped, "Toodles," backed out of the row and, limping slightly, headed to the stage, which still looked very much like the choir and altar that it had been earlier in the last century. Other than the figures in the stained glass windows, though, there were no religious symbols or icons, and the part of the stage that had been the altar was just a flat area with a wooden floor; no steps up, like the rest of the stage.

"Help me remember," I said to Ruth, "that I want to find out why Ned had a bad arm and leg."

She tapped something onto her phone and nodded an okay. "Why is that important?"

"I dunno. Maybe it isn't. But we won't know that until we've found out what happened."

Gabriele elbowed me lightly. "Ned tell me he sick when he young, hand go like that." He turned his hand to a sideways scoop shape.

"The thing is," I said to Gabriele, but sitting back so I could address both of them, "I believe Ned grew up in the Los Angeles area, and California has been requiring polio inoculations for decades, so—it's just a guess—I kinda doubt he had polio. When I was a kid, I had friends who had polio, and some of them were like Ned after they had it. But maybe there's another explanation with Ned."

I looked at Gabriele. "Did he have scars on his arm and leg?"

"No," he said, "they smooth, but small, you see bone, not strong."

I texted Mike to ask if the Medical Examiner could tell why Ned had the disability in his arm and leg.

Childhood problem, probably sickness.

In other words, you don't know

Right

Have you talked to his brother. Gabriele knew Ned in the past, but I think only for a short time

Why you interested in brother

Curiosity, looked like a major thing the way he got around. I think you said the candlestick hit him on the left side of his head. Right was crippled side.

Disabled, not crippled

OK

Give him a call

Who

Edgar

Text me his number.

Moments later I had it.

At St Benedict's now, call him later

I looked up and there was a comic scene being read. The two drunks, Feste the jester, Lily as the awkward prude Malvolio and Maria, the conniving lady's maid. Malvolio was reading the riot act to the drunks for being disgraceful in Olivia's house. I stood up and went outside to make the call to Edgar Savage. *Edward and Edgar,* I thought, *odd names for two brothers, easy to get mixed up.*

I got an answering machine or voicemail, hard to tell which one, and left a message, explaining that I was working with Mike di Saronno at the NYPD, and I would appreciate having a bit of his time to fill in some background that might help us find out what happened when Ned died and who was there at the time.

When I got back inside, they had moved to the next scene, and Feste was singing, "Come away, come away, death," in the setting by Roger Quilter and singing it in a high tenor voice that was really quite good while accompanying himself on an acoustic guitar. Lily stood up and raised her hand, and he stopped.

She stepped forward gingerly, favoring her right leg, "Just mark through the song, don't need you losing your voice singing so high."

He finished the song *sotto voce* but playing what sounded like a fairly complicated riff on the guitar as though he did it every day. I asked Ruth what the actor's name was, and she said it was another Spelvin, meaning another assumed name to avoid being in Dutch with Actors Equity.

"*Bellissima*," Gabriele said softly. "What this song about?"

I told him it was a song about a man whose lady did not love him, and he goes off to die from sadness someplace where nobody would find his body. Being Italian, it made perfect sense to him.

I had turned off the ringer on my phone, but it vibrated in my hand and lighted up when Edgar Savage called back. I answered in a light whisper and stepped back down the row to go outside. I noticed Lily looking disapprovingly at me. Very like Malvolio, I thought. Method acting in a Shakespeare comedy, woo hoo!

"Sorry to spring this on you, Mr. Miller, but I just landed at LaGuardia Airport, and I'd like to meet up when you have a chance. I'm not planning to be in town for very long, but I have some things I have to attend to. You know. Ned. Well, I have to arrange a funeral and burial, and I need to have a look at his stuff. We have two sisters, Liz and Mary, and I told them I would put together an inventory of what he, um, left behind. But I know you are trying to help the police figure out who did this, and I'd appreciate the opportunity to shake your hand."

"Call me Hugo. Mr. Miller was my dad," I said mechanically. "As it happens, I'm at St Benedict's watching a rehearsal of *Twelfth Night,* with a cast your brother assembled. Trying to get a better idea of what he was like. I'm with two colleagues, and maybe it would be good if the four of us could meet." I explained about Ruth and Gabriele, and that the three of us had worked with Mike di Saronno of the NYPD on several cases.

"But you're not a cop, right?"

"Right. I'm a civilian criminalist, to be precise. I can help the detectives, but I can't arrest anyone and I don't carry a weapon. Ruth and Gabriele are civilians, no formal connection to the NYPD, but we have been friends for a long time and we work well together. I live in the apartment next door to where Ned was living, and that's why I am helping out."

We agreed that we would meet for drinks in the Oyster Bar at Grand Central. They pour a decent drink and they don't care how long you hang out. Very relaxed atmosphere. Well over one hundred years old too, so there is a patina to it. I told him what I was wearing and that I would have an olive-green baseball cap that has a big WH on the front, for Wave Hill, an old estate that is now a park in Riverdale, the Bronx. In the newspapers, WH means the White House. No danger I would be mistaken for someone from there.

I asked Ruth to see if Lily could set up times for us to talk to Viola and Feste (she said okay). We trooped out and wandered east toward Grand Central in the nearly-sweltering late summer weather. As we left, Lily/Malvolio was reciting what is my favorite of Malvolio's best-known lines. "Some are born great, some achieve greatness, and some have greatness thrust upon 'em." She chewed the scenery in a way that would not fail to get a laugh from all audiences and was waving what appeared to be a table leg in the air. Malvolio is a fool's fool, pitiful in the final analysis, but very funny. Lily knew what she was doing. Maybe the piece of lumber was going to be a sword when there was an audience paying to see the play.

Since I have a sizable bald spot on the top, I have to be careful to always have a baseball cap on. I had a skin cancer on my scalp once, and having it removed was far from a picnic, so I am determined to avoid re-experiencing that and have accumulated a bunch of non-team baseball caps that are generally thrown into the shelf at the top of the hall coat closet. I wear the Wave Hill cap because it is not likely to be the same one that someone else is wearing, which means little risk of an accidental exchange of hats. I don't wear caps that are team caps because they invariably are conversation-starters of a type that I prefer to avoid.

Edgar was easy to spot from the mahogany color of his hair, which matched what I recalled from having seen Ned in the hallway when he was moving in. The only time I ever saw Ned, as a matter of fact. He was taller than average, but not a giant, thirtyish, looked to be in good shape. He smiled naturally as he walked toward us, and I stood up to shake his hand. No disability that I could see; normal walk, normal hands.

He thanked us for the work we were doing to help find whoever did this to his brother. I explained that there were a lot of details that were still blanks. How many people were in the apartment at the time that Ned died or was killed? Was there something programmed happening, like a scene rehearsal?

"Do you mind telling us how Ned came to lose some of the use of his hand and leg?" I asked, making eye contact but trying to look sympathetic.

"D68," he said, tearing up. He wiped his eyes with a napkin.

Ruth looked up, puzzled. "What?"

"D68," he said. "Nobody's ever heard of it, it sometimes seems. It's a bacteria that can get into the intestines, that can cause the same outcomes as polio used to."

"When did this happen?"

"When Ned was a child, about eight. He was thirty-four at his last birthday, so about twenty-six years ago."

Mike said Ned was twenty-seven, probably something to do with his official bio.

"What did the doctors say?"

"Pretty much what I just told you. It's a bacterium, fairly rare to get an infection from it, but if you do, it can really do a lot of damage."

"As I guess it did with Ned."

"My mom told me that Ned had asthma as a child, and I now know that made him more susceptible to D68 than other people would be. It's been on the rise, but almost all the cases in the US are kids, and most recover." He paused, clearly emotional, adding "I'm two years younger than Ned, so I was about six when it happened. I have some memories but not enough to know much. I know about it now because I heard my parents explain it over and over when Ned was growing up. Nate was near-genius-level brainpower, very high IQ, and he adjusted. He even played Little League. You never met anybody more determined to do things than Ned was." Edgar was beginning to tear up. "He was my big brother, and he always tried to take care of me growing up."

The waiter came over to the table and asked if we wanted to order something.

I said I would take a glass of Montepulciano, a red Italian wine. Gabriele wanted a glass of Cannonau, also red, also Italian, but from Sardinia. Ruth asked for a Corona. I looked at Edgar.

"I'll have a double Dewar's on the rocks with a splash," he said. "I don't have to drive."

"Did Ned have a girlfriend?" Ruth asked. Gabriele straightened up for the answer.

"Ned was gay," Edgar said. He said there had sporadically been boyfriends but none of them lasted long.

"Do people call you Edgar, or something else?"

"Anything's okay," he said. "Edgar is fine. Most people call me Edgar. When we were growing up, Ed and Ned sounded too much alike."

"Were you named after someone in the family?" I asked.

"My mom told me I was named after Edgar Allan Poe."

"Very cool," I said. "Quoth the raven, and all that jazz."

"Let me ask my question a different way," Ruth said. "Did Ned have many female friends?"

"Lots," he said.

The waiter brought the drinks. We clinked and took a sip. "To Ned," Gabriele said.

"You knew him?" Edgar asked.

"I knew him," he said, with zero accent. "He was very happy all the time, and he made everybody happy all the time."

"Whoa!" Ruth whispered into her beer, looking into the foam and not looking at anyone at the table. I clenched her hand and told her I already knew that. She leaned over and whispered in my ear. "That's not it. It was the accent disappearing." She looked like her eyes were tearing for a moment.

"We're very close," I said, meaning Gabriele and me, feeling like I was going to swallow my tongue. I put my other arm around Gabriele, who leaned a bit toward me but looked at the ceiling.

"*Era un bell'uomo,*" he said. *He was a handsome man*, meaning Ned.

"He never talked to me about his love life," Edgar said then paused, stood up with his drink and said, "Ned," and downed the whole thing.

"You look like him some," I said. "Although I never officially met him, I did see him when he was moving into his apartment next door to me. I remember thinking 'rock star hair,' which you have too. It's particularly noticeable to someone who's nearly bald, like me."

He looked at me with the beginning of a smile. I took my cap off and bowed my head to show him how sparse the hair was, and how gray. He shook his head and the smile moved closer to being real.

"Do you know any of the people who are working on *Twelfth Night*?" Ruth asked.

"Only by name. Ned's career was mostly in acting. He did some television, mostly on night-time dramas, but he was on a soap opera for a while, did some commercials."

"Movies?"

"A couple, I think, but small parts, and he wanted to make his name on the stage. That's why he was living in New York." He thought for a second. "You know he wasn't getting paid for *Twelfth Night*?"

"We could tell it was a showcase production from the number of stage names that show up on the cast list," I said. "I know this is probably a delicate question, but do you know who stands to gain from his estate?"

He leaned to the left, stroked his hair with his left hand then leaned his left elbow on the arm of his chair. "I guess I do, for one. My sisters to some extent. And the West Side Repertory."

"Is it a substantial estate?"

"Not really, but maybe a couple hundred thousand dollars if you liquidated everything. I haven't been to see his files or checkbook yet, so I'm not really sure. But he had squirreled away more money and stocks than I would have thought he could have done by his age and given that he was not getting paid regularly for long stretches of time. The life of an actor is pretty insecure, he always told me, so he had to be extra careful. He was always smart, though, and he had done well with what he had."

I said he seemed to have been living very modestly—small apartment, not in Manhattan. When I had been in his apartment with the police, the furniture was not expensive looking.

"He liked to come to my restaurant," Gabriele said.

Ruth changed the subject. "Did you know he carried an EpiPen for allergies?"

Edgar stared at her. "A what?"

"A syringe with epinephrine in it, so that if he had an allergy attack, he wouldn't go into shock."

He shook his head. "I don't understand. Allergy?"

I explained that the Medical Examiner determined that Ned was having a severe allergy attack when he died. "He had used a syringe on his thigh to keep the allergy attack from being fatal. It probably would have worked, but he was hit with the candlestick, and that's what killed him."

He closed his eyes and shook his head, like he was trying to shake off water from a rainstorm. Nobody said anything.

"He had asthma," I said. "Isn't that what you told us?"

He nodded.

"Apparently he had some potentially fatal allergy or allergies, and he carried an EpiPen to keep from going into anaphylactic shock if he was exposed to the allergen," Ruth said.

Edgar said he was allergic to mushrooms, but he never ate them.

"How about peanuts?" I asked, knowing that there was a bowl of peanuts on the coffee table.

"Not that I know of." He was looking distressed and confused.

"We need to check to see if there was any mold in the apartment, probably would have been related to the mushrooms," she said. "I mean," she said with a correcting-myself tone, "we should ask Mike di Saronno at the NYPD and see if they found any mold."

"He allergic mushroom and asparagus," Gabriele said, reinstating part of the Italian accent. I wondered if the accent-nonaccent was conscious or if he was unaware that he had been talking differently.

I was running on overload and tried to signal to Gabriele and Ruth that we needed to close this conversation out. I did that by waving to the waiter and making the universal hand sign asking for the check—writing in the air with a pencil that wasn't there.

"Here, let me," Edgar said, pulling out his wallet. I shook my head. He gave in and left after shaking hands around the table.

Chapter Six

The three of us walked up a ramp outside the Oyster Bar and then down some stairs to the subway under Grand Central. We took the 7 train to my stop, which was only about a five-minute ride once the train pulled up.

We walked over to Dominie's Hoek, a good bar with lots of natural air conditioning in the summer and some tables out back with umbrellas and—surprisingly—decent WiFi. I texted Mike to see if he could take some time to answer a few questions. I ordered a dirty vodka straight up with olives. Ruth took the same. Gabriele wanted a sparkling water.

Mike came back shortly via text.

Yeah what

Did CSI find any mold in Ned's apt

Mold?

Yup

They were looking for evidence to tell us who was there

Cool thanks what about mold

Give me a hint why you're asking

Ned allergic mushrooms his brother said, so maybe mold or spores too?

Gonna check and get back

Ruth and Gabriele were luxuriating in the small garden behind the bar, positioning chairs to get maximum shade. I took the sunny chair because I almost always have a baseball cap on and avoid sunburns to my scalp that way.

A waiter brought three drinks, two of which were in martini glasses with olives in them. Clearly those were for Ruth and me. Gabriele sipped at his sparkling water.

"I was surprised at how composed Edgar Savage was," I said, to start the conversation.

"I wasn't," Ruth said. "After Murray died, I couldn't pull myself together, but people said I was bearing up. Believe me, it's disorienting."

I agreed. It had taken me months to adjust after my mother died, and one of my best friends had died suddenly just before she passed. Mom had colon cancer and we knew she didn't have very long, but my friend, Mark, virtually hit the floor dead at fifty-five from an aortic aneurysm; no warning. Heavy smoker.

Mike texted me that there had been some spores that were vacuumed up from the couch with a variety of types of dust mites and schmutz that were normal. They were at the lab to be identified. He raised the priority to high, so he expected results fast.

"Where could mold or spores have come from, to get into Ned's apartment?" Ruth asked. "Don't landlords usually clean an apartment out stem to stern before a new tenant moves in?"

Gabriele spoke up. "Wind can blow in from outside."

"Unless there's a difference from my apartment, there's a screen door if you have the glass door open onto the balcony."

"Spores can be pretty small," Ruth said.

I suggested that we drink up and go over to my apartment. "We can see Ned's balcony easily from my balcony, just next door."

Gabriele wanted to know why looking at his balcony would help. I told him I wanted to see if there was anything on the balcony that could have mold or fungus in it. It had been raining a fair amount, so if there were some old potted plants left there from the previous tenants, for instance, they could have sprouted toadstools. I also told him I would pour him a drink if he was tired of sparkling water. For myself, I was mostly done with my dirty vodka, so I emptied the bit that was remaining into my mouth and down my gullet.

We walked to my apartment, probably the distance of three city blocks in Manhattan, but Queens is not laid out on a grid the way a lot of Manhattan is, so it's harder to estimate. When we walked out onto my balcony, I heard voices and put my index finger over my mouth to signal silence.

There were two women's voices, but I couldn't make out what they were talking about. Ruth was taking smartphone pictures of Ned's balcony—which I noted had several old clay pots on it, but they didn't appear to have any plants in them.

"Is woman from play. *Lesbica*" Gabriele said under his breath as though he were saying it to himself.

Ruth nodded. "The Irish one. Viola. One of the Spelvin sisters."

I put my index finger to my mouth again to indicate that we should be quiet. They both nodded. Still I couldn't make out any words. I motioned them back indoors and quietly rolled the glass door closed.

"I couldn't understand anything they were saying, but it's two women, and like Gabriele was saying, one of them could be Viola from St Benedict's."

Ruth made a sour face. "I think the other voice may be Lily Rasmussen, but I don't know for sure."

"I wonder what would happen if we just knocked on the door."

"It would probably scare the crap out of them. Hard to believe they have any business being there. Can't imagine what they're up to," she said.

I slid the door open and looked out. I could see some motion inside Ned's apartment but not enough to tell what was going on. The sound of voices was still there, but I still couldn't make out anything. Then without warning, Lily Rasmussen stepped onto the balcony next door like a monarch on the balcony at Buckingham Palace, staring into the distance and pointing at what might have been a crowd on the ground below. I stepped quickly back into my apartment, shushing Ruth and Gabriele and pointing to Lily. Then I heard her through the small space left from when I opened the door.

"Go, hang yourselves all! You are idle shallow things. I am not of your element." Then she turned and walked back into the apartment.

"Malvolio," I said, stepping farther inside. "The scene where he makes such a fool of himself in front of Olivia."

Ruth was heading for the entrance hallway.

"You leaving?"

She shushed me and opened the front door a crack. I put the little faux-marble lion doorstop in the opening to keep the door from slamming shut. Sure enough there was the sound of locks unlocking and Ned's door opened. Ruth stepped back into a dark corner of the entrance hall.

There was a knock on the door.

I stepped forward and pulled the door open. It was Lily and the Irish girl. I did my best to look surprised, but I think I just looked like I had been caught in something naughty.

"Lily. The last person I expected to be knocking on my door." Ruth stirred to my left and I asked them if they wanted to come in, opened the door wider, and retrieved the lion doorstop so they wouldn't trip over it.

She said she knocked because she saw the door was ajar then introduced Viola as Siobhan Reilly.

"Oh," Ruth said, joining me at the door. "I thought your name was Spelvin." Siobhan smiled and held her hand out.

Lily and Siobhan stepped in and I showed them to the living room where Gabriele was pouring a glass of red wine.

"What brings you to Long Island City?" I asked them.

"We wanted to have a look at Ned's apartment. The police don't seem to be making any progress in figuring out what happened." She didn't look the least flustered.

"You know the apartment is a crime scene, and you probably have disturbed some evidence just being there?" I said. "I work with the police and will have to tell them about this."

Siobhan cocked her head. "The police?"

"I'm a civilian criminalist, not a police officer. Means I consult with the police and help out with gathering evidence. That's why the three of us were at your rehearsal. We're trying to find some clues to tell us what happened."

"May I?" Lily asked, gesturing to a chair.

Of course, I nodded. "May I offer you something to drink?"

She smiled and mouthed a no-thank-you.

"Why you are coming here?" Gabriele asked.

Siobhan started to say something and then looked at Lily, who answered, "Like I told you, we were hoping to figure out what happened."

"It's a crime scene though," Ruth said.

"There wasn't any police tape there, so we figured it was okay to go in."

"And the door was unlocked?"

"Siobhan has a key," she said, looking at Siobhan.

"Really?" Ruth asked.

"Yes, really," Siobhan answered. "Ned and I were planning to be married."

I looked at Gabriele who was looking at her from the corners of his eyes and squinting.

"We had been told that Ned was gay," Ruth said. "According to his brother, Edgar."

She smiled and said nothing.

"You gay too?" Gabriele asked, still looking out the corners of his eyes.

Siobhan nodded. Lily took a deep breath and let it out loudly.

Ruth looked at Lily. "*Et tu*, Lily?"

Lily shook her head in a vigorous "no" that included her shoulders and would have registered in the last row of the balcony.

"Were you there when Ned died?" I asked Siobhan.

"No," she said. "But I was there earlier that day. I don't have a green card, and I worry that someone will find out when my visa expires. That's why we were getting married."

"Did you pay him anything?"

"No."

"Are you pregnant?"

"No."

"Are you a union actor?"

"I am in the UK but not here."

"So, the cast list says Spelvin to keep prying eyes away from your immigration status while you were performing?" Ruth asked.

"Yes."

"And why did Ned want to marry you?"

"People make wise cracks about him because of his arm and leg, and he said he thought it would cut down on that if he was married."

Gabriele looked at the floor.

"I know you," she said to him. "Don't I?"

He looked up at her and nodded with a vague smile.

"Ora di Pranzo," she said. "Ned told me about you."

"Tell you what?"

"That you were friends. We went to your restaurant for dinner a couple of times with some of the other actors after we did readings of the play." She looked directly at him. "Yes, that's why I recognized you."

"You're Irish?" I asked.

"Armagh. Northern Ireland," she said, "Irish yes, but part of the UK, not part of the Republic of Ireland. That's how I came to work in London a few times. And Equity here has a pact with British Equity, so I would be up for discipline in London if I performed here under my Equity name for less than standard rates."

"What are you going to do about a green card now that Ned's not here anymore?" Ruth asked.

"Nothing yet. My visa's still good."

"I thought you said it was expired."

"I said I was—and I am—worried that my visa will expire and somebody will find out."

"Is your visa good for the run of *Twelfth Night*?"

She nodded.

"Are there a lot of UK citizens with expired visas here? I mean, how likely is it that you'll be found out and deported?"

"Probably not very likely, but if I overstay my visa, I'll play the devil ever coming here again, because the government computers will know what I did, and when I apply for a new visa, it'll get denied."

"Forever?" Ruth asked.

Gabriele answered with a nod. "Many Italians have problem because they work cruise ships and come to US when ship dock and get only three-day visa. Then they stay too long and never can come back."

I didn't say anything, but I was puzzled.

"Look, I'm an actor," Siobhan said. "A British actor. A lot of the work in my trade is in the United States. It would make life very difficult if I were locked out of this country. If my visa is going to expire, I have to exit the United States, go home, or at least go to Canada before the expiration date. I could go to Toronto, but I probably can't get a new US visa if I'm living there. I need to go home to do that."

"But if you marry someone who is a citizen?"

"I could probably get an extension, as long as you understand that they're keen to find out marriages that are just for a green card."

I was still puzzled. She could tell.

"The immigration people have to believe that the marriage is for love, that it's real. They don't want me to marry Ned then divorce him and start getting welfare payments or need healthcare that I can't pay for."

"But how often does that happen?"

"It's not rare. It's especially common with gay people, because both people may stand to gain. Ned was thinking he would get treated better if he was married and probably having sex like a straight guy."

"Really? He looked very handsome to me, although I only saw him briefly."

"He was very handsome," Lily butted in. "And very outgoing, not faggy, but he was open about being gay. If he and Siobhan were married, that might have made him more employable for television or films."

Gabriele chimed in. "We live New York, much liberal city. Other city not so easy for gay like New York."

"You did that, got married, didn't you? Before I met you?" I asked Gabriele.

He nodded and reached in his pocket for his wallet, pulled out his green card and held it up.

"That's how you got it?"

Yes.

"Are you still married?"

No.

"Is she on welfare?"

No.

"Is she still in the United States?"

"Ohio."

"Feel like marrying an Irish girl?" Siobhan put on a flirty look.

Gabriele smiled and shook his head slightly then shrugged his shoulders. "Ora di Pranzo my wife," he said.

"But you and Ned were lovers, right?" she asked. Lily leaned forward.

Gabriele stared at her then looked down. No denial. No affirmation.

Ruth stood up and looked at Lily directly. "Did you find anything in the apartment that we should know about?"

Lily shrugged noncommittally. Siobhan shook her head. "Nothing," she said.

Chapter Seven

Lily and Siobhan left their phone numbers with me and toddled off. Ruth called for an Uber and took the elevator to wait downstairs.

"Do you think Ned would have married that girl to help her get a green card?"

He nodded. "I do same thing, meet *lesbica*, pay her money, marry with judge. One year, I get green card. One more year, we have *divorzio*."

"So, you think Siobhan was going to pay Ned some money?"

He shrugged. "Ned not need money. *Forse* he marry for make people think he straight." He shrugged again. "More job for actor if he straight. Or maybe he want help her."

"Are you thinking about helping her now that Ned's gone?"

He shrugged again. "Not good idea."

"Why not? If you have done it before and it was okay?"

He looked at me squarely. "You want me do that?"

"It has nothing to do with me. Why did you ask me that?"

"*Perchè ti amo.*"

"And I love you. You know that. It's a different kind of love from what you had with Ned, but it's love."

He hugged me and said with a broad smile that made his eyes sparkle that he had to get to Ora di Pranzo or Dante would yell at him.

I called Mike and got his voicemail, told him we had some new information from cast members of *Twelfth Night* about Ned. He called back quickly.

I gave him a condensed version of what had happened. "We were wondering if there was anything on Ned's porch that might have had fungus or mold in it—something that might aggravate his mushroom allergy.

There were some old clay pots that we could see from my balcony, but we couldn't tell if there was anything growing in any of them."

I told him about hearing the voices and then connecting with Lily and Siobhan when they were leaving the apartment.

"Siobhan said she and Ned were planning to get married so that she could get a green card. She was aware that it was an illegal way to try for permanent residence and a work permit, but it seems like something that is relatively common, from what Siobhan and Gabriele said." I didn't mention that Gabriele had gotten his own green card that way, because I was fairly sure that the statute of limitations probably hadn't run out on what he did, and I for sure didn't want him to be deported back to Italy. *I also don't want to marry him so he can keep his green card.*

Mike didn't say anything about Lily and Siobhan being in Ned's apartment, other than asking how they got in. I told him that Siobhan had a key, being as how they were planning to get married anyway.

"I asked them why they were there, and they said they were curious to see if they could see anything that would be a clue to what happened. They said there was no yellow crime scene tape, so they figured it was okay."

"They were right, it was okay," he said. "Did they find anything?"

"They said no, they hadn't found anything. I know they were also rehearsing a scene from *Twelfth Night* while they were there, because I could hear Lily declaiming some of Malvolio's lines."

"Is she any good?"

"Well, I saw her in a Noel Coward play and thought she was hilarious, even though she had a walk-on role. However good or bad she is, she'll still be the best female Malvolio I've ever seen."

Mike observed that there was some gender confusion in a lot of Shakespeare anyway, so casting people cross-sexually ought to be within the rules. He also observed that he'd seen a woman play Richard II once, and although it took a little getting used to, it didn't interfere with the play, which he said was one of his favorites.

"Mine too," I said. "When I was young, I wanted to write a biography of Richard II."

He ignored that one and asked if I wanted to have a prowl around the apartment. I told him I did, and that I would prefer it if Ruth could join me. Two pairs of eyes are better than one; also women see things that men might ignore—and vice versa. He said he would arrange for the concierge to open the apartment for us. I told him I would get in touch with Ruth and see if she could do it this evening.

Ruth said she'd just got out of the Uber, but she could be back pretty quickly.

The apartment was small, but the kitchen was basically the same as mine, and the bathroom was a duplicate of one of mine. Ned had populated it with comfortable-looking furniture, although, as I looked around, I didn't see a bed. There were a variety of artsy items on the tables and some graffiti-derived paintings or prints on the walls. There was an ornate brass samovar that could have used polishing, a lavender-colored glass hookah, a pair of Chinese vases that could have been nineteenth-century, and some small sculptures of animals, several of which were glass. The balcony made it seem more spacious, especially when we opened the sliding glass door and invited in a breeze.

Ruth planted herself on the couch and asked me to stand across the coffee table from her. "Now where did he fall when whoever was here hit him with the candlestick, which I'd guess was the mate for that one," she said, pointing at a single brass candlestick on the pass-through from the kitchen.

I told her I had seen a sketch at Mike's office and I thought Ned had fallen forward, face down, with his head pointing toward the door. I looked at the carpet and could see the ghost of a stain that could have been blood before it was shampooed. I wondered if the property management group would re-carpet the apartment before someone new moved in. My own apartment has wood floors in square parquet pieces that are about four inches on a side; I had to agree to put carpets on eighty percent of the floor as part of my lease.

"Are we sure that he was having a serious allergy attack when this happened?"

"That's what I was told. In fact, they said he had jabbed himself with an EpiPen, so he must have been aware of what was happening. They said if he hadn't been bashed over the head, he would probably have recovered from the allergic reaction to whatever it was."

I walked over to the glass door and looked outside. There were four clay pots, but they looked empty and no green algae on them. No fungus that I could see. I had been hoping for a mushroom or a family of mushrooms in some old wet potting soil or steer manure. *The Attack of the Killer Toadstool.*

My phone vibrated. It was a text from Mike: *aspergillus lungs throat call me.* I showed it to Ruth.

"Do you have any idea what aspergillus means?" I asked her.

No, but she started tapping on her phone. "It's a fungus," she said after a minute. "Not getting a lot of information other than that."

I dialed Mike, who picked up right away. I put the phone on speaker and told him Ruth was with me.

"The M.E. found aspergillus in Ned's lungs and in his throat, and there was considerable swelling and inflammation around the particles he found," Mike said. "So maybe that was what he had that he used the EpiPen on."

He explained that aspergillus is a very common type of mold or fungus that grows in decaying matter or inside animals. Most people breathe in a lot of aspergillus almost every day in the form of spores, and they never get sick from it. But around 10,000 people a year come down with aspergillosis, which can be fatal. People who are most likely to be sickened by aspergillus are people with compromised immune systems or people with asthma.

Asthma. Bingo.

"But how would he have gotten it in his apartment? Airborne?" I was looking around the apartment. No place mold could grow that I could see.

"The M.E. also found evidence that Ned had been using marijuana or hashish."

"I know that's illegal," Ruth said, "but what does it have to do with this mold stuff?"

"Possibly nothing," Mike answered, "but aspergillus is commonly found on the leaves and stems of the *cannabis sativa* plant, which is what most medical marijuana is derived from."

"Is it what we used to smoke when we were in college?" Ruth asked.

He said there are several types of marijuana plants, but the cannabis sativa is grown way more than any other type. The leaves and stems are used for medicines, pain relief, and as we all know, just to get high. Hashish is made from the resin that can be extracted from the main stems of the plant. It can also have aspergillus in it, and it is most often used with a vaporizer these days. Like those electronic cigarettes that use a miniature vaporizer to deliver nicotine without the tar and smoke of a cigarette.

"And did the CSIs find anything like a vaporizer in Ned's apartment?" I asked. "Or a pipe? Or cigarette papers?"

"You're in Ned's apartment now?" he asked.

Yes.

"Look around you."

"You mean that old hookah?" I asked as Ruth was pointing at it.

He said there was no evidence that the hookah had been used any time recently. "But the CSIs found a glass pipe on the coffee table, and it had been used, still had something that looked like weed in it. It's in the evidence locker here. We're sending it to the lab to see if they can find any aspergillus in it."

"Is there any record of Ned having a prescription for medical marijuana?" Ruth asked.

Mike said they were checking, but there was no stash of marijuana in the apartment.

"So maybe the guest brought it?"

"Maybe, just conjecture at this point."

I told him that I would try to get in touch with Siobhan to ask her about Ned using marijuana. What I actually planned to do was to call Gabriele and ask him.

Gabriele answered the phone at Ora di Pranzo. I told him Ruth was with me on the speaker phone and gave him a quick summary of what Mike told us about the mold in Ned's lungs, and that it is commonly found on the leaves and stems of marijuana plants.

"Did Ned use marijuana that you know of?"

He said he didn't know, but it was possible. Lots of people in the entertainment business smoke some weed.

I went over in my mind some of the people we had met at St Benedict's. They were all pretty hip, as far as I could tell. New York has stopped arresting people for marijuana use, even in public, so that distinctive smell is far more common on the streets than it was a couple of years back. And it's completely legal for medical use with a prescription.

"If he was as disabled as you say he was," Ruth offered, "he might very well have needed something for pain management."

"Not disabled," Gabriele said.

"What would you call it?" I asked.

"Not disabled. He do anything anybody do. His hand like fist, but he use it. He even whistle for taxi with fingers from hand."

I called Siobhan at the number she left, and she answered right away. She thanked me for the visit earlier and asked how she could get in touch with Gabriele. I told her that Ora di Pranzo is in the book, and he works there almost all the time.

Yes, she said, Ned did have problems with pain and cramps sometimes, but as far as she knew, he took ibuprofen or aspirin. He liked red wine and also liked to drink scotch ("Wouldn't drink good Irish whiskey like Tullamore DEW, Jameson or Bushmills"). He never had marijuana when she was around, but the smell of it was always there at rehearsals, particularly from Tony Anguilla, also known as Duke Orsino, who was chasing after Olivia, who in turn was falling in love with Viola/Siobhan, who was herself disguised as a boy in *Twelfth Night*.

I didn't recall smelling marijuana at the reading or rehearsal we had been to, and neither could I summon up a memory of Duke Orsino, so I looked up Tony Anguilla on the computer. Sure enough there was an IMDb file that listed several television programs or episodes in his credits, and several of them were shows I had watched, although I couldn't recall the specific episodes. Probably some of them were available on YouTube, I thought. There was a photo that didn't ring any bells for me, but when I clicked on "Images" there were some character shots that looked familiar. Good looking guy in his forties or early fifties, dark hair, probably Italian-looking, at least when the picture was taken. The IMDb file said he was 6'2". Probably wouldn't be using his real name on the program, for union reasons. Another Spelvin.

I logged onto my computer to check emails, something I seldom do on my cellphone because it's too hard to read them on the small screen. Up popped an advertisement from the Hudson Valley Shakespeare Festival urging me to buy tickets for their production of *Twelfth Night*, wouldn't you know.

I've been to the HVSF many times; usually their productions are shockingly first rate, endlessly inventive, and played with a level of energy and intensity that makes them unfailingly memorable. All the plays are presented in a very modern-looking tent on the grounds of an old estate called Boscobel that's open to the public. The tent is three-sided, with the open side facing the Hudson River about one hundred fifty feet below and West Point across the river on the other side. Million-dollar view. I was tempted.

I texted Ruth and asked her to have a look and let me know if she was interested. She asked if she could invite Lily. Of course, why not?

Chapter Eight

The idea must have been a good one, because instead of Ruth and Lily in the rental car, I had Ruth, Lily, Gabriele (surprise), the possibly pot-headed Tony Anguilla (Duke Orsino) and—naturally—our very own Viola, Siobhan Reilly. I expected to hear a babble of whispers throughout the play as my seatmates mouthed and muttered the lines the actors were speaking. I also announced before we left that the car was a no-smoking zone.

We agreed to have an early dinner in Cold Spring, the nearest town to Boscobel. There are several good eateries there, but one is an Italian joint with a lovely garden path to the front door, which happens to be at the back of the building.

We polished off two bottles of a modestly priced *ciliegiolo* from the Maremma, a verdant, former cattle-ranching area that sits between Tuscany and Lazio (where Rome is) on the west coast of the Italian boot. The name is derived from the Italian word for cherry, probably because of something about the taste of the grape it's made from. Gabriele chose it and insisted on paying for the two bottles himself. I know it is one of his favorite wines, and frequently hard to find, even in specialty wine stores.

It was a model summer day in Cold Spring, with a hot sun but low humidity and a breeze. When we finished our late lunch, it was closing in on four o'clock, so I piled everyone back in the car and drove to Boscobel, because I figured we could wander around the grounds at least and marvel at the century-old apple orchard, the spectacular views of West Point, and possibly a jaunt into the forest on a pathway kept free of poison ivy before taking our seats in the tent. We stopped at the ticket office and managed to get six tickets with three in the first row and three immediately behind the three first row seats.

I claimed one of the first-row seats because my legs are long and I didn't fancy being accused of kneeing the person in front of me. Besides, I bought the tickets. Viola, Gabriele and Ruth sat behind. I was between Lily and Tony.

Tony looked like a traditional pick for Orsino, who is the ruler of the place where the story happens, called Illyria, which would mean it'd be part of the modern country of Croatia. Tony is tall, has good features, but looks to be putting on some weight, mostly around his waist, on a small frame for his height. He looks like he was probably rail-thin when he was younger. I'm not good at guessing people's ages, but I'd say late fifties; older than his IMDb profile pic. Carries his shoulders back, chin up, large blue eyes, clean-shaven.

Of course, Orsino is a fool, like most of the characters in *Twelfth Night*, pining after Olivia, who clearly can't stand him, so the actor has to play the part of a foolish aristocrat who can't take ''no'' for an answer, not unlike certain politicians. I began to understand as we walked around at Boscobel how he could make people snicker and snort. He had a slightly clownish way of walking and staring at people. Large features, very mobile face. I thought of the Noel Coward play, "Present Laughter," about an aging but not aged actor—very funny, and oddly enough, the title is taken from dialogue in *Twelfth Night*.

Siobhan attached herself to Gabriele, and Gabriele did not push her away. It made me smile to see the two of them, both young, both probably lonely. The fact that they probably would have no physical attraction to each other didn't seem to matter when I looked at them, and it occurred to me that Gabriele might agree to marry her to help her get her green card. They might even make a very pretty Irish-Italian baby. Stranger things have happened.

Tony reached into the inside breast-pocket of his jacket and pulled out a plastic bag of gummy candies, orange-colored and almost translucent. Pretty. I asked what they were. He said they were medicine. He put the bag in the outside patch pocket of his sport jacket and looked out the front of the tent and made some kind of comment about the view.

"Lucky you, they look like candy."

"They taste good, flavor of tangerines, or I can get them in other flavors. I just like the tangerine ones."

I asked if I could try one.

He shook his head. "It's really medicine. Sorry. Just an easier way to take it." Big smile.

I had a feeling they were cannabis candies, and that he was maybe a little high. I had seen a video on the computer about a company that makes candies like this. New York has been talking about legalizing cannabis for recreational use, but medicinal use was the only way you could buy the candies or brownies or leaves for smoking, at least from a legal dispensary.

But the CSIs found a glass pipe at Ned's apartment, and it had been used recently. That more or less excluded cannabis gummies, unless they were doing both of them. But basically so many people use pot that seeing Tony consume what might be cannabis candy didn't point to anything.

Two young men walked into the tent and sat across from us. They waved at us. I had no idea who they were, but I looked at Lily and she was motioning to them to come over. They were like bookends—same age, similar height, same general coloring and curly hair, scruffy beards, teeth that were the blinding white that you see in toothpaste commercials. They did not look to be related.

Lily leaned over to me. "Feste and Sebastian from our cast."

"Neither one of them looks like Siobhan," I said. Lily gave me a puzzled look. "Well, Sebastian and Viola are brother and sister, right?"

She nodded, "My brother and I don't look anything alike. But Sebastian wears a red wig in this production."

I smiled and swallowed the rest of what I was going to say.

The lights blinked and Lily stood up, walked over to the guys and said something to them, came back and sat down. "We can talk to them at the break," she said.

I asked their names.

"Frick and Frack," she said. "I don't remember. I think the one on the left—that's Feste, Olivia's jester—is Jonathan something. I think people call him Jonny. I don't have any scenes with Sebastian, and I don't know his name. Good looking kid though."

The Hudson Valley cast scrambled into the tent from the twilight with West Point in the background. *It could pass for Illyria,* I thought, *with the river standing in for the Adriatic.*

A man who looked nothing like our Tony—this one short with lots of muscle, shoulder-length hair, in his late twenties—had the first line as Orsino: "If music be the food of love, play on." Several people in the cast produced musical instruments, and they started to play something from what sounded like Monteverdi—very softly, so as not to compromise Orsino's opening lines, which he declaimed as he strolled around looking curiously at the audience, particularly the front row of the audience, which included Tony, Lily and me. I looked around. There were no empty seats. Tony was all ears, listening to the way his lines were paced and emphasized. This Orsino was more like a rich punk than a rich middle-aged fool like Tony's Orsino had been in the rehearsal when we were there. I wondered if Orsino would evolve tonight in Tony's mind.

I am always amazed at how a good actor can make those old lines sing, and if you sit close, you can see the spit flying out of their mouths as they project their lines to the back of the house. Even this short rock-star Orsino knew how to handle the lines so that they sounded natural, even though they were in blank verse. And how to breathe from the diaphragm to make his voice carry.

The short first act flew by. Olivia was watching Malvolio leave and speaking the act-closing couplet almost before it seemed possible that time had even passed: "Fate, show thy force. Ourselves we do not owe. What is decreed must be, and be this so!"

As Olivia walked out of the tent and into the darkling sky, the lights came up in the tent to applause from the sold-out house. The two young men sprang up and walked across the sandy area that the actors used as a stage in the amphitheater-designed seating area.

Jonny and Teddy were their names. I saw Ruth writing and couldn't help smiling; I knew she would look them up in the cast list to get the last names as soon as she could do it without being observed. The young men were clearly very flirty with Siobhan, and Gabriele was gregarious and attentive to them, making me think he knew something that I didn't know.

Jonny and Teddy hustled back to their seats when the chimes sounded. Jonny's character, Sebastian, would make his first appearance at the beginning of the second act, and as the plot thickened, Malvolio would chase down Viola and hand her a ring, saying that Olivia wanted nothing to do with the Duke Orsino, whom he refers to as Viola's "master," keeping in mind that Viola is masquerading as a boy.

"I left no ring with her; what means this lady?" Viola thinks, addressing her thoughts out loud to the audience. And then with a quick black-out, Sir Toby and Sir Andrew, both drunk, were stage-center.

When Olivia's fool, Feste, entered talking jibberish and then sang, "O mistress mine, where are you roaming?" the cast materialized with their instruments and accompanied the jester, using an Elizabethan-sounding setting. Feste had a clear, high tenor voice, most pleasing. I looked at Lily, who was avidly making some notes on her program with a small ball-point pen that was probably designed for keeping score at card games.

The second act is plotty but brief, and as the lights went up again, Jonny and Teddy were back paying court to Siobhan. Teddy was miming playing a guitar; Lily wasn't the only one who liked the instrument-playing cast.

The third act is the crux of the play. It is when Malvolio, the greatest fool of all the fools in the play, commits the unforgiveable sin of making a pass at the lady he serves. Of course he was tricked into it, but he's the butt of every joke and besides, where's the merit involved in fooling a fool? When the lights went up after the third act, there was thunderous applause, and a noticeable rush out the side of the tent toward the line of privies outside. I invited Siobhan and Gabriele to walk with me and get something to drink. Ruth was deep in conversation with Tony, who was looking very superior indeed. Clearly, he either felt the Duke in the cast we were watching was inferior, or perhaps he thought he should pretend that the Duke in the cast was inferior, when in fact he wasn't.

As we walked, Gabriele was holding hands with Siobhan rather ostentatiously. Siobhan declined the offer of a drink and scooted away to one of the privies. I asked Gabriele what he thought about her, thinking he would say something endearing.

"She not care Ned is *morto*. She want me to marry her and get her green card. Then she kill me too."

"Kill? What are you talking about?"

Joseph Allen

He gave me an exasperated look and started to say something, but then suddenly we were at the front of the drink line, and I ordered two glasses of cabernet sauvignon, a deep red from California.

We sipped at our plastic glasses and walked into the darkness that started a few feet away from the tent. The woody, earthy, herbal, slightly rancid smell of marijuana floated toward us and we headed toward it. Sure enough on the other side of a large tree were Jonny and Teddy, each holding a cigarette between the tips of their thumbs and index fingers, drawing long breaths of smoke and holding it in before exhaling.

"Hi, guys," I said brightly.

They looked like deer caught in headlights at first then recognized us and relaxed.

"It may not be legal, strictly speaking," I said, "but nobody cares. Not to worry." We walked to where they were standing and I raised my plastic wine glass. "Cheers."

I asked them what they were thinking about the production we'd been watching. They nodded and said some indistinct things that sounded vaguely complimentary. Not enthusiastic.

Gabriele asked them if Ned had been using marijuana. They looked at me questioningly.

"I work as a civilian criminalist with the NYPD, and I can tell you that there was a glass pipe on the coffee table in Ned's apartment the night he died."

Jonny said that Ned had some pain problems that were probably caused by his weak arm and leg. "I think he had to adjust all the time to try to look as normal as he could, and it gave him a lot of pain. Lots of times you could see it on his face."

"So you think he might have been using marijuana to help him deal with the pain?"

Jonny nodded.

"Any idea where he got it?"

"He had a prescription from his doctor, so he probably got it at one of the dispensaries. There's one on 42nd street over near the UN"

"Have you ever been there? No biggie, just wondered what it's like inside. Are there different types of weed that you can choose from?"

He shrugged. "Haven't been in that one," he said. "I live Upper West, and the one up there is like a natural foods store. Probably a dozen different types of weed."

"So you have a prescription too?"

He nodded. "Asthma."

"Ned had asthma too."

Some chimes sounded from the tent, and we all sauntered back in that direction.

"Why you ask them about that?" Gabriele whispered.

"It's possible that the grass he was smoking, or that he was eating, had some fungus on it that caused him to have a strong reaction that could have killed him."

He looked puzzled.

"It's called aspergillus, often found on the leaves and stems of the plant that gives us marijuana, or at least that's what Mike told me. Ned was allergic to mushrooms, like I am, and mushrooms are also a fungus. The Medical Examiner found aspergillus in Ned's lungs and on his clothing. You know he had jabbed his leg with a needle just before he died, right?"

He nodded. "And tall woman say smell marijuana at church when they work on play."

I nodded, and we took our seats for the fourth act.

"Jon Ostergaard and Theodore Duprè," Ruth said in my ear as we sat down. I felt like I'd won a scratch-off prize in the Lotto, because I knew she would be looking up those names. I smiled broadly at her and mouthed a thank-you.

Before the lights went down, I looked up cannabis companies on my phone, and one popped out at me. It was called "Shaman Inc" and was in Santa Monica. There were also several in British Columbia, which made sense, because cannabis is fully decriminalized in Canada. Several of the companies in BC were publicly traded on the stock market in the United States.

The fourth act is quite short, although it is pithy and plotty. It was over while I was still thinking I wanted to visit one of these cannabis companies to learn more about the commercial cultivation of this popular— and useful—drug. The lights went up and then dimmed quickly for the final act, also short. Before we could shift in our seats, Feste was singing a familiar setting of the final song in his lovely high tenor voice, and the entire cast was accompanying him on instruments, a tambourine, a couple of fiddles, a guitar or two, a clarinet, a saxophone and two recorders. It creates a perfect circle from the first line of the play: "If music be the food of love, play on."

"When that I was and a little tiny boy,
With hey, ho, the wind and the rain,
A foolish thing was but a toy,
For the rain it raineth every day."

The car was full of chatter on the way back to Manhattan, and it was obvious that everyone had enjoyed the evening. It was a little crowded, elbow to elbow, but the mood was light and the air conditioning was on, so the ride, which was just over an hour, went quickly.

Chapter Nine

After dropping off the actors in Manhattan, I drove back to my apartment with Gabriele and Ruth. We had a nightcap of the limoncello that Gabriele had brought before, and I told them I was interested to find out more about how marijuana was being raised for sale in legal dispensaries. If there was aspergillus on the leaves, was there any way to prevent it from causing problems for someone like Ned, or like me? Was it possible to detect if the aspergillus was present?

There were a couple of growers in New Jersey, between New Brunswick and Princeton off Route 27, but I was inclined to want to go to Santa Monica to see the operation of this company called Shaman Inc. It would give me a chance to visit places I hadn't seen in years and maybe even to walk around the campus of UCLA where I went to school.

It's almost never a problem convincing Ruth to go for a jaunt, and we decided to catch a transcon to Los Angeles as soon as we could find seats (meaning business or first-class seats at cheap prices because of Ruth's insider connections with airlines, due to being her late husband's widow). I suggested that we could take Gabriele along with us. She snorted and agreed.

"I promise I will keep him from playing with the buttons on the seats," I told her, remembering his behavior on a trip to London a couple of years earlier when he couldn't stop playing with the seats in business class, where he could lie flat, or sit straight up, or almost anything in between. I thought it was amusing, but Ruth found it downright crazy-making.

I went online and found a hotel in Santa Monica that was close to the pier and within a reasonable hike of the beach as long as you were willing to hike down a long stairway from the top of the bluff that separates Santa Monica from Santa Monica Bay. The next morning, we were riding in an Uber to JFK airport for a 10AM departure on American Airlines. Ruth said she had sent an email to Lily, telling her we would be incognito for a few days; I notified Mike di Saronno of approximately the same thing but noted that we were going to look at a cannabis company to find out if the aspergillus fungus was really endemic on the marijuana plant.

Many years earlier I had been a student at UCLA, in Westwood, just a couple of miles east of Santa Monica on Wilshire Boulevard. A lot had changed in those years—not obviously in the older sections of the university like Royce Hall Quad but in all the residential areas of west Los Angeles, from the parklike VA property that bordered the 405 Freeway on Wilshire all the way to where waves were almost breaking on the doorsteps in Ocean Park and Venice.

High-rises were sprouting up everywhere like golden California poppies after a spring rainstorm. And like those poppies, each one looked like the one next to it—featureless glass towers, sometimes with a setback from the street with maybe a crescent drive or even a drive and a cookie-cutter fountain. When I was a student, there were aging two-story apartment buildings with courtyard swimming pools lining most of the streets. I never lived in Santa Monica, but I did live in Venice, which is part of Los Angeles; not Santa Monica but with the same apartment buildings, just a little more ramshackle in Venice before it became aggressively gentrified. Now almost all the 1950s apartment buildings were gone, replaced along Wilshire Boulevard by high-rise condominium buildings. In Venice, they had morphed into celebrity McMansions as the Hollywood elite moved toward the ocean to escape the heat and smog of Hollywood, downtown LA and Burbank.

The plane flight passed quickly, as transcons tend to do in these days of fast, powerful planes that can carry hundreds of people. It's really not very far from JFK to LAX as the crow flies, unless you have to make a connection in say, Dallas-Fort Worth or Chicago or St Louis. If you fly direct, it takes four to five hours. If you connect, more like eight to nine hours. I find it's a great time to read and snooze, although I occasionally get snagged by a movie. The food is always passable in business class, and the wines are not the kind with screw-tops.

Gabriele is more like a kid in a candy store on an airplane. It's the one time he reminds me of myself when I was younger, when I felt like every plane ride was an adventure, even if it was just going to Denver or Houston or some other place I had been to a bunch of times. I found it nearly impossible to go to sleep on a plane in those days—not because I was anxious or afraid, but because I loved being in a plane whizzing through the sky like somebody in a movie.

These days, plane travel has become humdrum for me, which makes me feel paternal when I watch Gabriele pushing buttons, up-down-up-down.

I always order the veggie lunch, because I don't eat red meat and don't much trust the poultry dishes. Sometimes they have salmon, but it's probably the high-mercury farmed type, so I stick with the pasta. It can be a little gummy, but mostly it's okay. Gabriele, of course, wanted a steak. Ruth waved the lunch away, sipped at a glass of red wine, and drank a whole bottle of water, seemingly in one long gulp. Rule one of airplane travel is to stay hydrated.

I drifted off with my chair leaned back, and before I knew what was happening, Gabriele was lightly shaking me by the shoulder, telling me to sit up because we were landing.

Fortunately, we got through LAX quickly, and since we had checked no bags, we quickly found the Uber car I had ordered when we were allowed to turn on our cellphones as the plane was pulling up to the gate.

Ruth had read up on Shaman Inc, a company whose reputation in the still-exotic cannabis market is for being a technology leader and an easy place to visit with a broad selection of types of marijuana and marijuana-derived or marijuana-enhanced products. So there was a variety of types of marijuana with the types of names one might expect. There was a "Mellow Yellow," for instance. There was a "Maui Wowie," though with a disclaimer that it was not grown in Hawaii.

I pointed to the Maui Wowie and asked one of the employees where the marijuana was grown, if not in Hawaii.

"All our marijuana is grown in California in a highly controlled environment," he said, as though he were reading it off a card. "It's not a good idea to move marijuana across state lines these days, but we're ready to go national when it's permitted." Several US companies had already invested in the newly-public Canadian cannabis companies, and a couple of really big US companies had bought Canadian cannabis companies lock, stock and barrel. There was a gold-rush aspect to it.

I asked why the name referenced Maui, and he said he thought it was from an old song. I said I thought that was true of "Mellow Yellow," but I didn't recall a "Maui Wowie" song. He smiled and shrugged.

Gabriele was hanging back and observing the dispensary as a whole. When he pulled out his smartphone and started to take a picture, an employee covered the back of the phone with his hand and pointed to a prominent sign that said "Photography Not Allowed." I wasn't surprised. Not everyone who wandered in the door would want their pictures taken in a marijuana dispensary.

There were twelve sturdy Parson's tables, each about six or seven feet long, and imbedded in the tables were computer screens with searchable catalog items. On one side of the store there were some shelves with edible products and some small bottles that were about the size of a bottle of nose drops that I might have given to my children when they had a head cold. But they were gaily colored, and as I wandered over to them, I could see that they had labels that indicated what were probably uses. "Sleep" was one, and the label was a sky blue. There was one labeled "relax" in a forest green. I was staring at them, not touching them.

"Essential oils," a voice behind me said. "Like peppermint or lavender oils, but in this case, they are also cannabidiol oils."

I turned to see a young man of about average height with a dark beard, trimmed close but covering the bottom half of his face. He was smiling. "May I help you?" he asked, as though I were in the perfume part of a department store.

Gabriele touched my arm and I looked at him. He was smiling and hooked his arm in mine like a couple out for a walk might hook their arms. The young man smiled again, acknowledged Gabriele with his eyes and said, "Just let me know if I can help."

"I was hoping to see how the plants are grown," I said. "I've been on your website, and it looks like you have some hydroponic technology at work."

He explained that there were different agricultural techniques that were used for different strains of plants and confirmed that hydroponic culture was an important part of the operation. "It's clean, and it's easy to provide a steady stream of nutrients to help the plants grow."

Ruth wandered over and asked the young man if there were any flavor enhancers or if the drops were blended with other herbs to give them a scent.

"Not generally," he said, "but we can special-order drops mixed with herbal extracts." He looked very serious for a moment and said, "but they're not for eating, just for using with a water pipe or a hookah or something like that."

She thanked him and tapped some notes into her tablet then stood close to the product shelves to see the labels.

"May I pick them up?" she asked.

He nodded. "But if you want to buy one, I'll get a fresh one from the back. These have been sitting out for a few days."

"Do I have to have a prescription to buy these products?" I asked, knowing the answer.

"No, you do not. California has legalized cannabis for recreation, so for all practical purposes, it's about like a liquor store. We have to check IDs for age before selling product, but you don't have to be in pain to buy things."

I asked if he was familiar with aspergillus. He nodded.

"I've been told it is frequently found on the leaves and stems of marijuana plants."

He nodded again.

"Would it be on any of your marijuana leaves or in any of your edible products?"

He shook his head. "We work hard to grow plants that are not infected and to clean them scrupulously when they are harvested."

"I had a friend in New York who was infected by aspergillus," I said.

He nodded, "It can happen but usually it only induces some

sneezing or a light cough. I hope your friend is okay."

I smiled and nodded, "Fine."

Ruth asked if there was any way we could visit their growing facilities.

"Are you with the media?" he asked.

She shook her head. "Just curious. When I was in college, I smoked some marijuana, and at that time I had no idea about infections or pollutants. I guess all the pot then was grown out in the country or in forests where it wouldn't be seen by cops."

He smiled and shrugged. "Things are different now. We have products now that do not even get you high." He reached up to the shelf and picked up a clear bottle with a forest green label. "This one, for instance, is for pain. You rub it on the area where you have pain, and it is likely to relieve the pain almost immediately. No high with it. You could use it with children if you have a prescription for a child to use it."

"How about for chemotherapy?"

"There are products here, but not on these shelves, that help chemotherapy patients cope with side effects like nausea or chills." He crossed his arms. "Those are prescription only. They're not dangerous but also not great to combine with some other painkillers."

"But no aspergillus?" I asked again.

"I can't guarantee there is never a possibility, but we work very hard to eradicate it if and when it breaks out." He paused. "And it is usually not capable of making anyone really sick."

"How about grapefruit? Any interaction with grapefruit juice?"

He shook his head. "Not that we know of."

"So, who can we talk to about visiting the place where you grow your plants?" Ruth asked.

The young man took out a business card from his shirt pocket and wrote an email address on the back then handed it to her. "Send them an email, and maybe they'll be able to help you. We're very careful about some trade secrets that we have that help us grow healthy plants, and the company isn't anxious to have anyone taking pictures of our farm."

It was a surprising experience, all told. Very like going into a high-end boutique in some gentrified area of Manhattan. Clean, sleek, polite, well-groomed people with pleasant attitudes. Not a speck of dust anywhere and no pressure to buy anything.

As we left, I said to Ruth and Gabriele, "I don't think there's anything to be gained by hanging out here and trying to visit their farm. They are in the process of opening a store in New York City, in Chelsea, I think. If we have any more questions, we can go there when it opens."

Ruth mused, "I wonder if they have to grow weed in New York to sell it in New York and whether the same lack of that fungus would be true there."

"Wouldn't matter," I said. "It's not open yet, so it couldn't be where the grass in Ned's apartment came from. It sounds like aspergillus is familiar to Shaman, which probably means it's no mystery to other dispensaries either."

That evening we took a blue Santa Monica bus to Westwood Village, one of the few areas in Los Angeles County where there is New York-style pedestrian traffic. "That's because of UCLA being here," I said. "Takes me back, but a lot of these buildings are new since I was here back in the Middle Ages."

We ended up at an Italian place that was entirely new to me though it looked like it had been around for a while. I looked up and down Gayley Avenue when we got there and said it looked like this was where there was a Safeway supermarket when I was in school. "Or maybe a laundromat, not sure."

Being a picky New Yorker and sitting next to a fancy New York restaurateur, I was surprised that the chicken parmigiana that I ordered tasted very much the way I would have expected back home. Gabriele made a slightly sour face when he tasted the *pasta e fagioli* soup—it was made with red kidney beans, not the white Tuscan beans one would expect in Italy or New York. He left it sitting in front of him and the waiter took it away. But he seemed pleased with the salmon he ordered, which was served with fresh pesto sauce on top, reeking of garlic.

He ordered a bottle of Barbaresco, a northern Italian red that in Italy is a weekday wine, Sundays being reserved for Barolo among the well-heeled. It was a little green but pleasant. Ruth had a bottle of Peroni, an Italian beer. I guzzled two large glasses of water in response to the low humidity in the air and then enjoyed the young wine.

    The next morning, we were on a plane back to JFK. Gabriele was less enamored of the buttons on his seat and fell asleep before the plane took off. I am constitutionally unable to stay awake on airplanes and started to read a book I had picked up at a bookstore in Westwood Village. It was a biography of Charles II—interesting, but not interesting enough to keep me awake.

Chapter Ten

Gabriele and I had dinner when we got back to Long Island City, in a very small but fine French restaurant called Tournesol, which is the French word for a sunflower. The menu is mostly from Provence, but the wines are mostly from the west bank of the Rhone. The food is excellent and the prices are reasonable, so it is crowded all the time. The downside is that there is no place to wait for a table to become available, so there is usually a crowd inside and outside the front door. If it weren't so convenient and so affordable, I don't know if I would be willing to put up with the wait.

We were just into the entrees when my cellphone vibrated. It was Ruth.

"Looks like Ned's production of *Twelfth Night* is being cancelled," she said. When I asked why, she said that Siobhan had left the cast and apparently was on her way back to London. "There wasn't ever much funding, but with the cast in turmoil, St Benedict's wanted to rent the space to someone else.

I asked her if she had spoken with Lily, who seemed to be the person she knew best there. Yes, she had, and that was how she had found out what happened. I asked her to see if we could meet up with Lily the next day, which was a Friday, someplace on the West Side. Then I suggested that maybe we could meet at Ora di Pranzo, and that way Gabriele could be with us.

When I told Gabriele, he chuckled and nodded.

"Did you know she was going to leave?" I asked.

He cut a piece of the steak he ordered and nodded.

"She told you?"

No. He was chewing and just shook his head.

"How then?"

He finished chewing. "She kill Ned, not want trouble with police."

I was astonished. He had said something like that before, but I chalked it up to his being angry with Siobhan for trying to get Ned to marry her so she could get a green card.

"I ask her if she kill Ned and she not answer me."

"Why did you ask her that?"

"Because she there when Ned killed."

"How do you know that?"

"I ask her."

"And she said yes?"

"She say she there do practice for play, but when she leave he still alive. She liar." He made a hand sign to ward off the evil eye with his hand vertical and the middle and ring fingers tucked down with the thumb, leaving the index finger and the pinkie upright. It's supposed to represent horns, I think.

I said that she told us she was nearing the expiration of her visa and suggested that she was going back to the UK to stay long enough to get a new visa.

"She kill Ned." He looked straight at me and nodded slightly. "*Si*."

"If she and Ned were there alone, how were they rehearsing for the play? Ned isn't in the cast."

"*Non lo so.*" He didn't know.

"If they were working on a scene, there was probably at least one other actor there as well."

He said maybe the tall woman was there too. They were friends. That would mean Lily. Viola (Siobhan) and Malvolio (Lily) are in several scenes together, but their interactions are not pivotal to the plot. No need to call the two of them for a private rehearsal. Plot-wise the most crucial scene in the play is between Malvolio and Olivia in the middle of the third act. It's also one of the funniest scenes, with the middle-aged and hilariously awkward Malvolio dressed up like a young man with something called crossed garters which would make x's with ribbons up and down his legs—something like a jester might wear—a perfect sign to the groundlings that Malvolio was a fool of the most hilarious type.

I changed the subject and asked him about the steak. He smiled, nodded, and ate another bite enthusiastically. I asked him if I could taste his *ratatouille*, which he agreed to. I stuck my fork in his ratatouille and took a bite. It was perfect, but I love vegetables and olive oil under almost any circumstances. "We'll have a chance to talk to Lily tomorrow, so we can find out more then. Don't say to Lily what you think about Siobhan killing Ned. Okay?"

He nodded and continued to devour his steak.

After dinner I walked with him to the subway station and he disappeared into the maw of the 7 train headed for Manhattan. It was a pleasant evening and as I walked back to my apartment, the skyline of Manhattan sparkled at me. A little breeze blew in off the river. The Chrysler building looked like a postcard with a puffy cloud behind it lighted up by the moon.

I don't ever disbelieve what Gabriele has to say. He is a person of considerable instinct about people. I believe him when he says he doesn't trust Siobhan, but his conclusion that she killed Ned is just him taking his dislike of her to absurdity. Although it was a surprise to me, it is clear that Gabriele had something approaching a love affair with Ned, though Ned apparently did not reciprocate the feelings that Gabriele clearly felt.

If there were two actors there rehearsing in Ned's apartment, they would both have to be involved if there was violence; the place was too small for anyone physically in the apartment not to be aware that Ned was being beaten to death. If someone hit Ned over the head with a heavy brass candlestick, the second actor must have seen it at least, possibly been involved. And what possible motive could there be? Kill the man who was going to get you a green card? Unlikely.

I was wrestling with the evidence that Gabriele could have been thinking about when he decided that Siobhan was involved in Ned's death. It was clear all along that someone was there with him when he used the EpiPen to stop the anaphylactic shock that hit him suddenly—perhaps having to do with the aspergillus spores that were found in his lungs. And it seemed logical that Siobhan would have high-tailed it back to London if her visa were expiring.

When I got home, I poured a dirty vodka and stared out the bedroom window at the Chrysler building while I sipped on it. There was a Mister Softee truck by the pier with an awning stretched out in front. I could see a crowd of people around it. I didn't hear any chimes, probably turned the sound off when he parked.

I logged onto my computer and found the West Side Rep website, still advertising the *Twelfth Night* run to begin in another almost two weeks. I scanned down the cast list and found Olivia. Susan Albright. Didn't ring any bells. I closed my eyes and pictured her, tallish, slimmish, blondish, prettyish. Not gorgeous.

I kept scanning idly down the list and came to the understudies. Well, wouldn't you just know! Georgina Spelvin, *aka* Siobhan Reilly, was Olivia's understudy in addition to being Viola in the first cast. Viola's understudy was the girl who was playing Maria. It would be like a game of musical chairs if Miss Albright was unable to go on as Olivia one evening. But it would also give each actor the right to list another role on their résumés, so maybe there was method in the madness. And if the play wasn't cancelled because Siobhan had decamped to London, Maria would move up to one of the leads, instead of one of the slapstick trio, together with the drunks, Sir Toby and Sir Andrew. Sometimes in these showcase productions, there is an unwritten agreement that the understudies can all count on playing the principal roles they're understudying at least once—and that they will have enough advance notice to invite agents and any casting personnel they can rope in.

Of course none of that was going to happen with Siobhan in London. It was difficult to imagine that the show wouldn't fold. Viola is a mainstay of the plot, and perhaps the only principal role that isn't a fool in some obvious way. Even Viola might get some laughs, though, since in Shakespeare's day all roles were played by males. Viola would be a male playing a girl impersonating a male, with lots of room for broad comedy.

I finished my vodka and poured a little splash into the pile of olives in the glass, swallowed that in a gulp, and took a shower then wandered back to the kitchen and set up the coffee maker for morning. I still didn't feel like sleeping, though, and picked up the biography of Charles II, thinking that would surely do the trick. It was one o'clock on the bedroom clock, which meant it was about 12:45 in the living room—a little self-trickery to help me get out of bed on time. Then I remembered that the sliding glass door to the balcony was open and went to close it so that no bugs would be buzzing around in the dark (there were some small holes in the screen door). The light was on in what had been Ned's apartment.

I leaned out over the railing to see if I could see into Ned's place, but I couldn't. Then the sliding door opened in Ned's apartment. I stepped back into my apartment where the lights were off so I couldn't be seen.

It was Siobhan. *Of course*, I thought, *she has a key*. I wondered how long Ned had prepaid the rent and whether she had a new visa after her visit to London. *Or maybe she had been here all along and hadn't gone to London at all.*

I was tempted to knock on the door but decided that might be a bit hot-headed in the middle of the night. I sent a text message to Mike di Saronno telling him that Siobhan seemed to be in Ned's apartment and went to bed but found that I was tossing and turning with no apparent descent into sleep ahead.

Back to Charles II, who in many ways was a very boring monarch, as British monarchs go (and the truth is many of them were on a continuum between strange and boring). I had read a couple of pages when my phone pinged, indicating a text message. It was Mike, of course.

Thanks we knew, no worries

I have often wondered if Mike ever actually slept, but I had another jigger of cold vodka poured over the much-used olives in the martini glass and found that I could close my eyes without my mind racing through the problems of the world.

And then it was seven o'clock. I woke up with a start, realizing that someone was ringing my doorbell. I got up and staggered to the front door in my t-shirt and boxer briefs.

It was Siobhan, of course. I stared at her like I was sleep-walking, I think, and she said "Hi, Hugo. I'm going to be staying in Ned's apartment for a bit while I try to figure out what to do next with my career and my life."

I motioned for her to come in, which she did. She looked pointedly at my torso, conveying a message without words.

"Sorry," I said. "I was sound asleep when you rang the bell. I guess I'm lucky I had this much on. Sometimes I sleep in less than this when it's hot and muggy."

She smiled and I told her to have a seat in the living room and I would be out to put some coffee on in a couple of minutes. I put on an old white quilted cotton bathrobe and slippers and went back to find Siobhan touring the living room as though it were a gallery.

"Sorry," I said. "I had a bigger place before, more wall space. Now it's all just jammed together. Not the best way to see these paintings, but I can't stretch the walls, unfortunately." I walked into the kitchen and pressed the button on the coffee maker.

Siobhan said she took a little milk in her coffee, no sugar. I handed her a mug with a splash of milk once the machine had stopped brewing; she smiled that it was just right. I drink my coffee black, especially in the mornings. My mother used to love iced coffee with milk in it, but I never picked that up from her. She liked to drink buttermilk, too, and that was also a no-go with me.

I sipped my coffee and fixed my eyes on Siobhan.

She endured the silence for a few seconds, then said, "I know it must seem odd that I'm staying in Ned's apartment."

I shook my head. "Mike di Saronno said it was not a problem."

"When?"

"Last night."

"I didn't even get here until after ten o'clock."

"I figured you'd gone to London to try to get a visa to re-enter and give you some more time here before it expired."

She shook her head. "No need to go all the way to London. Montreal is where I went, actually. Commonwealth, you know. Good enough. I stayed over the weekend and then re-entered, got stamped for ninety days. I've never abused my visas, never been late leaving, so I'm a good girl as far as the Immigration and Customs people are concerned."

"In the meantime, I think West Side Rep cancelled the *Twelfth Night* production."

She nodded. "That's why I went when I did. Now I have to find something else to do, and I needed more time."

"You're not supposed to be working, though. Right?"

"Kinda undecided," she said, without a trace of the Irish lilt I had heard unmistakably in the rehearsal. "Bottom line is I'm not getting paid, so it doesn't matter."

"I figured you needed a job. A paying job."

"I would have, but now that I'm a widow, I have some leeway."

That took a minute to soak in.

"You and Ned had already been married?"

"Few weeks ago."

I asked if she had to wait for probate to clear his assets before she used them.

"Not as his wife, I don't. I can't liquidate his estate and run off with it, but I can write checks and pay bills. Ned added my signature to all his accounts the day we got married."

It was beginning to feel a little creepy. *Why hadn't she told us she and Ned were married when we first met? Why had she asked Gabriele if he wanted to marry her?*

She answered my question without my asking it. "Ned wanted to tell his family first, before we told anyone else."

"But he didn't. I know he didn't because his brother, Edgar, was here and we had lunch together. He was torn up and clearly didn't know he had a sister-in-law."

"I know he didn't tell anyone. Lily was our witness when we were married at City Hall, if you want to verify what I'm telling you. And I have the license. We really did get married."

I asked if being a widow would make it more difficult to get a green card.

"I'm not a lawyer," she said. "But my attorney tells me it shouldn't be a problem."

I suggested to her that she not keep her secret any longer. "It's unkind to his family, at least, and at most, it might make it seem that you are trying to get away with something."

She started to disagree, and I said, "I have no intention of keeping this information confidential. I work with the NYPD and Ned was murdered, according to the cause of death determined by the Medical

Examiner."

"Medical Examiner?"

"Probably what you would call a coroner."

She nodded slowly. "I understand." She stood up and thanked me for inviting her in. "I'll let myself out," she said.

When I heard the door shut, I began to wonder if she had planned in advance that she could get me to notify Ned's family and friends—and the police. Damn.

Chapter Eleven

I called Mike di Saronno and told him about my conversation with Siobhan Savage, *née* Reilly. As I suspected, he already knew of the marriage and already knew Siobhan had moved into Ned's apartment.

"Isn't it suspicious that they married and then he was murdered within days?"

"Depends what you mean by suspicious. If you're asking if we plan to arrest her for his murder, the answer is negative. If you mean that it strains credulity that these two things happened so close together and that she then ran off to Canada to have her visa re-issued at the border, then the answer is a big yes."

"Why wouldn't you arrest her, or at least question her?"

He said the NYPD had every intention of asking her to come in for questioning.

"Can I be there in the observation room?"

He was noncommittal but said he would try to arrange it.

"And Gabriele? He thinks she killed Ned, or at least that's what he said to me."

"Absolutely no evidence that ties her to his death. And no motive for that whatsoever." He said they had questioned Lily Rasmussen about the marriage and their relationship. Lily said they were a normal couple, some small problems to cope with, but smart enough to work through it.

"Ned was gay and Siobhan is too. What kind of marriage could that be?"

He told me not to be naïve and not to make accusations about such things. "There are all kinds of reasons why people get married, and we're perfectly aware at this point that Siobhan needs a green card. Being married to a US citizen is one way to get permanent residency and a work permit." He paused and continued, "It's not my job or the department's job to judge why people get married. Look at the divorce rate if you wonder whether people are careful about who they marry."

"I was certainly careless and nuts to marry my two wives, but at least at the time we got married, I thought I loved them. And I thought they loved me."

"Gonna do it again someday?"

"Not the chance of a snowball in Hell."

"So you're capable of learning something along the way. Almost everyone that gets married is making at least one big mistake in thinking they know what being married is going to be like. They don't. "

He was working up a head of steam.

"Marriage is a massive invasion of privacy, and it's true that divorces are caused because the cap wasn't put on the toothpaste one morning. The one straw that broke the camel's back is a perfect metaphor for a lot of marriages on the rocks."

I didn't reply and he added a post-script. "And if you think gay people can't marry the opposite sex and have as good a chance of being happy as the straight couple that has the hots for each other, then you're stereotyping gay people. That horny straight couple is blind to what they're doing. A couple that is gay on both sides may have thought it through from the outset."

Whew. I wouldn't want to read his diary. I didn't say it out loud, but I must have telegraphed it because his mood changed immediately.

"I'm sorry, Hugo," he said quietly. "I guess I got on my soapbox. I shouldn't have. But you have to think before you say things. You're part of the NYPD now, even though you're a civilian. Just because the man is playing tackle in college football does not tell you his race or his IQ. If you need to know his race or his IQ, you have to find those things out separate from his position as a lineman.

"If two queer people want to get married, you have to wish them well, because clearly they have some issues that straight people don't have. I see stereotyping every day in this job. Every day. And it makes me tired. But I'm really sorry for preaching at you like that."

"Cut it out, Mike," I said with a grin that he couldn't see, of course. "No apologies needed. But I want to tell you that gay couples are something I have thought about a lot. Remember Eddie Hall? That Congressman from Brooklyn who was set to marry a man after his wife walked out on him? The only reason he didn't marry his guy was that his guy got shot on the sidewalk in front of his apartment building.

"And you know? I hang out with Gabriele a lot. You think that topic never came up? Think again. I don't have any answers for the problems that Ned and Siobhan might have had. So you're right that my comment about what kind of marriage they would have was just me talking through my hat. So, I'm sorry for that."

I said it was all beside the point. "If Siobhan is a person of interest in the death of Ned Savage, I think you should talk to Gabriele, who has some very specific ideas about her relationship with Ned."

He agreed and told me he would let me know when she was going to be coming in.

I sent text messages to Ruth and Gabriele asking if we could get together. I told them that I had spoken with Siobhan and learned that she and Ned had, in fact, been married a few weeks prior to Ned's death. There had been no announcement because Ned wanted to tell his family himself, something that he apparently did not do, possibly because he had no warning that his life span would be cut short.

I suggested we meet at my apartment at five o'clock. Gabriele said he needed to be at Ora di Pranzo by seven o'clock, or someone else would have to stand in for him as maître d'. We agreed to meet at Ora di Pranzo at five instead. Gabriele said he hoped we would stay for dinner. He didn't have to ask me twice—the food at his restaurant has always been to die for, so to speak.

The nights were beginning to get cool, although the days continued to be hot and with frequent afternoon pop-up storms that could be drenching at times. I saw no reason to wear Sunday-go-to-meeting clothes and put on the unofficial warm-weather uniform of Manhattan—jeans (always Levis for me) and a black t-shirt. If we'd been in the country, I'd have worn sandals, but being in the city, black athletic shoes and white cotton socks.

Naturally Ruth showed up looking like she just arrived from a photo shoot all in linen that, strangely, had no wrinkles in it, although she must have been sitting in a car to get to SoHo. Gabriele is "old school" when it comes to clothing, and wears a dinner jacket and matching pants with a satin stripe on the side, just like what kids in high school call a tuxedo. And it's true what they say about black. It is the absolute best color on a man, especially when that man is Italian, with hair to match the color of the jacket.

In spite of the maître d' face he put on and in spite of his welcoming people to Ora di Pranzo, he was not quite his normal ebullient self. Ruth broke the ice.

"What's up with you, handsome?"

He shook his head and signaled something to the bartender, who very quickly sent over two dirty vodkas and a glass of red wine, which I guessed would be *nero d'avola*, from Sicily.

He looked at her and then at me and said, "Liar actress kill Ned. *Come ragno.*" *Like a spider*.

Ruth jumped in. "Why do you say that? There's no evidence that she did anything."

"She have *maloik.*" *Evil eye*. He made a horned signal with his right hand to ward it off.

"How can you tell that?"

"I look in her eyes and see *maloik.*" He stuck two fingers into his shirt collar under his ear and pulled a gold chain up that was under his ruffled shirt. Of course it had a *cornetto* on it, a chili pepper in gold, to protect him from the evil eye.

"She's Irish and has blue eyes. Isn't evil eye a dark-eyed thing?"

He looked at her and smiled. Then he shook his head.

"So if she has an evil eye, she killed Ned?"

He nodded.

"But other people must have the evil eye too. Why couldn't one of them have killed him?"

He did his best to deliver a withering look and drank a gulp of his wine. I matched him with my dirty vodka.

I changed the subject. "So, anyway, Siobhan is now Mrs. Savage. I don't know if that means anything about who gets his estate, since they were married such a short time—maybe a week or so. But I think Mike is planning to ask her to answer questions at Midtown North, and I asked him if we could watch in the observation room."

Gabriele drank the dregs of his wine. "She not gonna tell him anything."

My phone vibrated. A text message from Mike. *S Reilly JFK—Heathrow about an hour ago*

I told Gabriele and Ruth. Gabriele responded with an "I told you so" look.

"Well, we know that's not about getting a new visa, since she already did that in Montreal," I offered.

I reached over and put my hand on Gabriele's thigh and patted him. "It's okay to be sad."

"*Son' arrabbia-a-ato.*" *I am a-a-angry.* He signaled to the bartender and our drinks were refilled, which meant Ruth's drink was whisked away although it was still almost full, and a new one replaced it.

"You know," Ruth said. "There's no reason to believe she was even there when Ned died, and bashing in someone's head is not the way women kill people. Women are more likely to use poison or a kitchen implement."

"And men are likely to use weapons," I added. "But that doesn't mean it has to have been a man that killed Ned Savage."

"And it doesn't explain why he was having a life-threatening allergy attack at the same time. If someone wanted him dead, the best thing they could have done was to just sit and watch," Ruth said. "And just to state the obvious, since Siobhan and Ned were married, she had every reason to want him to be healthy, at least until she got her green card."

"Whoever was there, someone had been smoking marijuana, so maybe they were relaxing. And it seems like the aspergillus or whatever fungus was probably on the marijuana leaves," I said. "There was a study that I came across doing research for this case. It was from a year or so ago at the University of California at Davis which has a big program in agriculture and animal husbandry. They found that not only was a large percentage of samples of medical marijuana from across the state of California contaminated with dangerous germs and spores, but that smoking marijuana can send pathogens directly into the lungs and may be significantly dangerous to someone with a compromised immune system, or a serious allergy to something. It started because someone who was on chemotherapy died from a fungal infection that probably came from smoking marijuana to help with the nausea. And it turned out that it's not just aspergillus that's contaminating commercially sold pot but a bunch of fungus types. But as far as I know, aspergillus is the only one that was found in or on Ned by the M.E."

I went to the West Side Rep website and, sure enough, there was a cancellation notice saying that *Twelfth Night* had been cancelled due to the sudden death of a cast member. I showed it to Ruth and Gabriele.

"I figured that notice was up when I read Mike's text about Siobhan being on her way to London.

"I bet Lily is really disappointed," Ruth said. "Playing Malvolio was going to be one of the high points of her career."

All the actors wanted to do the play. They weren't even getting paid.

My phone rang. Edgar Savage. He and his sisters, Liz and Mary, would be landing at LaGuardia from Dallas that evening and wondered if we could get together the next morning. He had gotten my email about Siobhan and Ned. I told him that Siobhan was apparently on her way to London, following the cancellation of *Twelfth Night*. He didn't sound disappointed.

Gabriele and Ruth were okay with the morning meeting, so I suggested we meet at Pershing Square Café, directly opposite the front entrance to Grand Central on 42nd Street. I realized how unlikely it was that we could get a table at one of the most popular breakfast joints in Manhattan, but Gabriele made a quick call to the restaurant and, due to his restaurant magic, secured a hard-to-get reservation for six at 10AM, so the date was fixed.

Ora di Pranzo started to fill up, and it was interesting to watch Gabriele put on his charisma as people lined up for reservations. Clearly the people holding reservations were part of the "one percent," or close to it. *He and Dante really have a gold mine.*

It had cooled off enough that we saw some real couture that evening. And some jewelry. It made me think back decades when I used to go to receptions at the United Nations. Everything was black-tie, of course. And ladies wore jewelry that sparkled. There were a lotta things that were wrong then; the Vietnam War, rampant racial clashes, especially in places like south Boston and south Philly. But going to the opera, especially on a Monday, was like stepping back in time or finding yourself in a movie. I even remember seeing some ladies wearing tiaras, which only married women wore, and even they wore tiaras *only* after sunset, *of course*. And those useless little evening bags that could barely hold a tampon, much less a wallet, but done in petit-point or with gold and jewels and probably worth a king's ransom. I still have a pair of mother-of-pearl opera glasses that belonged to my grandmother. Useless but pretty, like the pair of Chinese vases in my living room; I could put flowers in them, but I don't.

Ora di Pranzo was not an elbow-length-gloves evening out, even in the dead of winter, but when your dinner reservations are wearing real couture—even if it's not Paris—tailored to the wearer, "You're the top, you're the Met Museum," like the song says. Couture is as obvious as a face-lift, and frankly, much more attractive.

Gabriele stayed at the table with us most of the time, so that we could talk without having to backtrack and constantly fill in the gaps.

We decided to follow Siobhan over to London. Ruth volunteered to make the plane reservations if I would get in touch with Rubens at the Palace, a hotel that is a home away from home for us and where the bartenders knew us (which is as important as having a good breakfast—where they also are a winner). It's a bit of a schlep to get to the underground, but you can't have everything. It's across from the back of Buckingham Palace and a short walk to the Gallery, a part of Buckingham Palace open to the public where the Royal collection is shared with visitors on a rotating basis, several hundred at a time.

Ruth was Speedy Gonzalez and had seats for us on American Airlines in business class for the midnight flight the next day, which gave us time to rendezvous with Edgar, Liz and Mary. I like the midnight flight for lots of reasons. First, I can get a bowl of pasta for dinner and a double Dewar's on the rocks and then promptly fall asleep for four or five hours.

Liz and Mary were cut from a different cloth than Ned and Edgar. Where the boys both had mahogany-colored manes of hair and clear white skin, the girls were Dresden dolls, with light-colored hair and blue eyes. It was easy to tell that they were related to Edgar because they had what I assumed was a family resemblance—noses alike, prominent cheekbones, strong chins. The girls were in college, and neither was married.

Gabriele's influence put us in a large curved booth in the back of Pershing Square, and the waiters (two of them) had coffee in front of us almost as soon as we sat down. The breakfast menu is, dare I say it, legendary. I can never resist having crab-cakes with poached eggs and hollandaise sauce and a screwdriver. The Californians had cold cereal with a bowl of fresh fruit cut up into a salad. It looked to be mostly melon. Gabriele had a bowl of strawberries and coffee, and Ruth wanted an "everything" bagel with a *schmear* (translation: a bagel with all kinds of seeds on it and a wipe of cream cheese).

It was a somber gathering, since our only subject in common was the death of Ned Savage.

"Are you sure Ned married that woman?" Liz asked.

"Fairly sure," I said slowly. "I was told that by the NYPD detective who's heading the investigation into Ned's death."

She shook her head and looked at her sister, who started to cry silently.

Edgar said that they would like to go to Ned's apartment to have a look around to see if they could find any photos. He said he had asked the family lawyer to have a look at Ned's will to see if it would hold up with the recent marriage that happened soon after it was signed.

Gabriele listened and said nothing.

"She was in Ned's play that he was directing?" Mary asked.

"Yes, she was in *Twelfth Night,* but it was just in rehearsal and has now been cancelled. She was playing Viola, who is a girl masquerading as a boy. In this production, Ned had set it up so that Malvolio was to be the opposite—a trouser role, what's called a 'travesty,' a woman in a man's role. She's from Northern Ireland and has done a lot of acting in England, I believe," Ruth offered.

"Why did Ned marry her? He was gay, or at least he used to be."

I spoke up quickly, partly to forestall Gabriele from answering. "We may never know the answer to that, since Ned's not here to explain. But

Siobhan is an actor, and actors are a band of brothers. She needed to get a work permit to act in the United States, and the best way to do that is to marry a US citizen." I paused. "But just to be clear, she is gay too, or so we think."

Both girls cocked their heads as though they were being operated by the same puppeteer.

"That's gross," Mary said.

"But would she inherit everything if he died?" Edgar asked.

I explained that I'm not a lawyer, so I couldn't answer his question. "But she's not a person of interest in the investigation, at least as far as I know, and I am working with the NYPD on this case. You should know that New York is not a community property state like California. I think anything he owned before the marriage was and is his solely and not part of the marriage, unless they had a pre-nup, and so far there has been no mention of one. So there would be no financial motive. And frankly, she would have every reason to want him to be healthy and happy, because the immigration service would be likely to investigate the marriage to see if it was just a ploy to get a green card."

We talked about the marijuana, the fungus that had been found in Ned's lung and on the couch, and the EpiPen that was still sticking in his thigh when the police found him.

Neither of the sisters ate more than a bite or two of breakfast. Gabriele devoured his, and I made short work of my crab-cake Benedict. Edgar cut up a banana on his raisin bran and dug into it. He inhaled his coffee and asked for a refill.

I asked if any of them knew of anything in Ned's life that we should be looking into.

They shook their heads.

"He was seeing a psychic or something for a while," Liz said, as Mary rolled her eyes and turned the other way. "I think he paid her a lot of money, but he never talked to us about it. Except he told our brother that he lost some money."

"Was he religious?" Ruth asked.

"He believed in God, if that's what you're asking," Edgar said.

"No, I meant did he go to church or synagogue or someplace like that?"

They all shook their heads thoughtfully. "He went to church sometimes," Edgar said. "He was Episcopalian like the rest of our family, but I think sometimes he went to other churches. Depends on what was nearby, I guess. Why do you ask?"

"Sometimes psychics use a person's religious feelings to get money from them," I said.

"Like what?"

"Oh, maybe they would do some kind of ceremony to contact a spirit to ask questions. Or something like that. Maybe they would bless something to cure a disease. I don't believe in psychics; they're all frauds, but they're clever, and they read people easily and quickly. That's how they can say things that people think are insightful."

Ruth said that the three of us were catching a flight that evening, so we had to be careful of the time. The girls both drank the remainder of the coffee in their cups and pushed their cereal bowls away to indicate they were finished. I pulled out a credit card and Edgar waved it away. "On us," he said.

I told them I'd go with them on the subway and let them into Ned's apartment with the key the NYPD had entrusted to me. "You should know before you go into his apartment that his wife has been living there, even though she's apparently out of town now."

"You don't have to do that," Liz said.

"No problem. I live in the next-door apartment to your brother's place. The only time I saw him was the day he was moving in, but I never spoke to him, unfortunately."

"I know him," Gabriele volunteered. "Good man, what we call *bel uomo.*"

The girls turned to look at him and smiled.

"He bring actors to my *ristorante* in SoHo. Many times. Nice man. Happy. People like him."

Don't go any further. I stood up and reached over to shake Edgar's hand, thanking him for the breakfast then kissed Ruth and Gabriele on both cheeks and left with the Savage band.

We talked a bit on the subway platform about the neighborhood where I lived. All they knew from Ned about his new apartment was that it was not in Manhattan.

"That's all a lot of New Yorkers know about where I live—it's not Manhattan. Which means it might as well be China."

Since it was the middle of the day, the subway was not crowded, but the trains were running frequently, which has been true ever since the 7 trains were extended to the Javits Convention Center. As we walked from my subway stop to my building, I pointed out the Chrysler building in the cityscape of Manhattan across the East River, and told them that the United Nations was directly across from us.

"It may not be Manhattan, but it's a good place to live."

I let them into Ned's apartment and went to my place to pack. I usually pack for a week, even if I'm only going to be gone for a day or so. If I get held over—which happens—every good hotel has some kind of express cleaning service. And I get a week's clothing into a small duffel that fits in the overhead easily. That and my tablet computer, a cellphone, couple of rechargers, a book, and I'm ready to go.

When you take the midnight flight from JFK, you arrive in London just in time for your hotel room to be cleaned and ready for you to check in. It's about a seven-hour flight and a five-hour difference in time, so twelve hours elapse on the clock, which means you land at noon. By the time we clear immigration and get a taxi into town, it's two o'clock and the Rubens checks us in speedily. For me, that means I am in the shower by half-past. Gabriele was in the room next to me, and I could hear his shower before I turned mine on. Ruth was across the hall.

Mike had given me a cellphone number that would get us in touch with Siobhan, who was visiting her parents, maybe to tell them she was married and widowed all at the same time. I sent a text message to that number asking if we could have a drink.

Sure, but I'll skip the drink. I'm pregnant.

Chapter Twelve

I had suggested that Siobhan meet us at the bar in the Rubens at the Palace around four o'clock. She knew where it was and agreed.

She looked normal when she walked into the bar. We had taken a table as far away from the bar and bartender as possible. We wanted to be able to talk without being overheard.

Each of us each ordered a pint of lager, and Siobhan wanted a lemonade with lots of ice. She opened her handbag and took out a plastic bag of champagne-colored sugar-coated candies of some kind. She saw us looking at them and explained that they were candied ginger. "I've been having some nausea, and these help." She popped one in her mouth and took a long draught of the lemonade when it arrived.

The lager was cool but not cold, always a reminder of where you are when in the UK. I told the waiter to put the drink on my room.

Ruth offered a tentative-sounding congratulatory wish.

Siobhan smiled slightly, indicating mixed emotions. "Yes," she said. "It's Ned's." She looked each of us in the eye and said, "We decided to give it a try after we signed the marriage certificate. For me, it's not like I had never been with a man, but Ned had never been with a woman. That part was an extra treat in an unexpected way."

I sneaked a look at Gabriele who was listening and breathing through his mouth.

"We saw Ned's brother and his two sisters yesterday in New York," I said. "They wanted to look at Ned's apartment, the girls had apparently never been in New York before. Both in college."

"And were they upset about Ned and me being married?"

Ruth spoke up. "I think they are upset about everything at the same time, mostly the fact that Ned isn't among the living anymore." She paused. "But they did say that the marriage was a surprise to them because they thought Ned was gay."

"Most people didn't think of Ned as gay," Siobhan said.

Gabriele sat back in his chair like he had been pushed.

"Obviously you knew he was gay," she said to Gabriele.

He nodded and met her gaze without blinking.

"I think I loved him," she said, directly to Gabriele. After two Mississippis, she added, "You did, too, I take it."

He nodded again. But then he glanced at me and said, "I love Ugo more."

I could feel the blood rushing to my cheeks. I smiled at him and noticed a comfortable look on Ruth's face.

"I don't think I've ever loved anyone of either sex that way," she said. "But Ned was very dear to me. He trusted me and he liked my work. Even my parents never appreciated my work. I did Katharine in *The Taming of the Shrew* at Donmar Warehouse and they didn't come to see me. But Ned flew all the way from New York to see me."

"Well, Donmar productions are not exactly unknown, to be fair. If I knew someone who was playing a lead there, I'd be in the front row," I said firmly.

She smiled at me, then looked down at her lemonade. "That he crossed the ocean to be there told me he cared more than anyone else I knew." She patted her stomach. "And now I'm carrying his child." She smiled radiantly, in a way I had not seen before. Then she started to cry. "Pregnant women just cry for no reason," she explained lamely.

"Or with good reason," Ruth said, on the verge of choking.

"So this will be the first Savage Irishman," I said.

"This will be the first American Savage of his generation," she said, with tears dripping down her cheeks.

"I sorry for what I thought about you," Gabriele said, and he started to tear up but wiped his eyes with the back of his sleeve.

She looked at him but didn't ask.

"I know you good person now."

She smiled, started to say something, then decided against it. She blew him a kiss.

I decided to change the subject. "Did you know that Ned got some kind of donation from a famous Turkish writer? Sizeable amount. $50,000. The CSIs found the paperwork in a bunch of files in Ned's apartment, took them to the precinct to copy them."

She nodded. "Omar Ortigan." She pronounced the name without the "g."

"What?"

"That's his name. The writer. Omar Ortigan. It has a "g" in it, but it's silent, or it sounds like a "w" actually."

"How do you know that?"

"Ned and I had some frank conversations before we got married."

"Have you spoken with his brother, Edgar?"

She shook her head.

"Where does he live?"

"Who?"

"The writer."

She shrugged. "No idea, maybe Turkey?" She pulled out her smartphone and tapped on it a few times. "Says on the search engine that he lives in Istanbul. That's not the capital, is it?"

"Ankara is the capital, way southeast of Istanbul as I recall. Usually a plane ride instead of a car drive."

Ruth was waving her smartphone over her head. "He wrote that mystery novel where the narrator is a dog. I read it, but for the life of me I don't remember much, a bunch of years back. Somebody stuck a needle in his own eye. Ugh."

I allowed as how I had visited Istanbul twenty years earlier. "Beautiful city, spectacular blue water and very wooded where there aren't any buildings. You can see immediately why Constantine wanted to live there."

"Why writer give money to Ned?" Gabriele was looking like he might be a dog sniffing something out.

"No idea, sorry," Siobhan said. "Maybe the *Twelfth Night* production?"

I said that I hadn't heard of Ned as a sponsor of the production, but that West Side Rep ought to be able to tell us. "I have zero idea what kind of cash outlay would have kept the production on the boards, but I doubt $50,000 would have been enough."

"Still and all, it's a lot of money," Ruth said. "Worth finding out what it was for."

"Can you do me a favor then?" I asked Ruth. "Send an email to West Side Rep and ask them if Ned was a donor to the production?"

She tapped on her phone for a bit then smiled and gave me a thumbs-up sign.

Siobhan looked at her watch and was clearly anxious to leave. She asked if we could continue the conversation later, because she needed to go to an appointment, "...an audition, actually."

"Break a leg," Ruth said with a smile, as Siobhan shook hands with the three of us and toddled off.

I recalled Edgar saying Ned's estate was larger than he would have expected, given Ned's spotty history of getting paid for his work. I pulled out my cellphone and sent myself a text message to ask Edgar if there was a deposit matching the amount. Then I texted Edgar and told him I was in London and had made contact with Siobhan.

Are the police investigating her? came the reply.

Not that I know of

And you would know, right?

I don't get a daily update, but usually, yes

Can I call you?

I dialed him. When we spoke, I told him briefly about the Turkish writer and what appeared to be a check stub with a letter saying the accompanying check was to further a project that was not described.

"You know, he mentioned Mr. Ortigan to me a couple of times. He was impressed that he was corresponding with someone who had won a Nobel Prize. But I don't remember him saying that the guy gave him $50,000."

"But you have access to his bank statements, right?"

Affirmative.

I got a text message from Ruth, even though she was right there. *No $$ from Ned to West Side Rep. Also no $$ from Turkey*

I nodded vigorously to indicate that I saw the text and texted her back to ask her to find out Ortigan's agent's phone so we could try to get in touch.

Okay

"Sorry. I had to answer a text from Ruth."

"No prob."

"You have Ned's will?"

"No will, or at least if there is, I haven't found it yet."

"You're at his apartment?"

"Yup."

"Liz and Mary there too?"

"Yes."

"Say hi from me, and Ruth too. Must be difficult being there. Sorry."

"Thanks. By the way, nothing here that has to do with his, um, wife except some mail addressed to her with the last name of Reilly."

"She must have taken everything with her."

"She has been using his credit cards, though. The bills have been coming in."

"Spending a lot of money?"

"Not a lot, no, and most of the charges are from before, um, while Ned was alive."

"Do you want to speak with her? Her name is Siobhan."

"Yes."

"I'll ask her to text you at this number. Is that okay?"

"Yes, thanks."

"You have my number if you need me. Just remember I'm five hours later here than you are. Thinking about going to Istanbul to see if Ortigan is there."

We signed off. I sent a text to Siobhan asking her to get in touch with Edgar and gave her his number.

I was tired of the bar in the hotel, and so were Ruth and Gabriele. The three of us went over to a place called The Texas Embassy Cantina just near the bottom of St James's Street, also near the back entrance of the old St James's Palace. It's named for the short time that Texas was a separate nation after it broke off from Mexico (around ten years). In fact, there really was an embassy from the Republic of Texas and it really was in that neighborhood, but not where the Cantina is, although the people who work there wouldn't tell you that. The real Texas embassy was in a building that's now a high-class liquor and wine store called Berry Brothers & Rudd, and there's one of those circular blue historical-site tags on the building. It's on a footpath-alley called Pickering Place that looks like a gap between buildings, but it's paved so it's a footpath.

Anyway, The Texas Embassy Cantina is entirely staffed by Brits, as you'd expect since it's in London. But the menu has entrees with names that sound Texan or Mexican. Ribs, hamburgers, tamales, enchiladas. I've never had them because I don't want to know the Brit concept of Texan dishes or Mexican food. They'd probably have a hard time finding Texas on a map. The enchiladas that the waiters carried by us made me think it's a pseudo-Mexican concoction. Kinda like chop suey—not Chinese at all, just something that someone dreamed up and gave a name that sounded Chinese-ish at the time.

I asked Ruth what she knew about Ortigan. She said she had read a couple of his books and liked them. The one that was narrated by a dog was set in the sixteenth century. The other one was a current-day political novel.

"I was impressed that he could write two books that are so different and still convince me that the characters were real. He obviously did a lot of research and knew what he was writing about, stem to stern, so to speak."

"Does he write in English?"

"Not originally. I don't think so. Must be translations, but whoever the translator is, he or she is good."

"What do we know about him personally? Were you able to get in touch with an agent?"

She said she did have the name of an agent, but she had not been able to get in touch with her. "I think she only deals with the US editions of books that are first published overseas," she said. "She's an independent agent, not with one of the big agencies, but she has a website, so I left messages for her a couple of times."

Ruth's phone made a squeaking noise. "Text message," she said, and tapped on the phone briefly. "No donations to West Side Rep by Ned

Savage or Omar Ortigan."

I was wondering where the money could have gone when Ruth added, "I did some research on Ortigan, by the way. Seems like what we would call a liberal, pushing for equal treatment for minorities and such. On the outs with the Turkish government, which has a religious slant to it. He's also teaching creative writing at a university in Istanbul."

Gabriele was unusually quiet. He was staring around the Cantina and looking at the décor.

"You all right?" I asked him.

He smiled and nodded. "Thinking about Ned wife. Very pretty lady."

"She is pretty. I think she's a bit younger than you are but not a lot."

"She have baby."

I looked at him directly. "Do you think about having a baby?"

He nodded wordlessly.

"I have a son," I said. "And I was a loving father when he was little, but as he got older and I had problems with his mother, I was more distant, I guess, until the divorce, and I don't have a close relationship with any of them now. I think that is one reason why I am so fond of you, to tell you the truth. You're young enough to be my son, and you are friendly like a son would be in my imagination."

Ruth got up with her cellphone to her ear and wandered away, talking to someone.

"Have you slept with girls?"

He nodded.

"Are you thinking about Siobhan that way?"

Affirmative.

Ruth returned with a frustrated look. She had not been able to get a phone number for Omar Ortigan. "The agent seems like she considers herself a gatekeeper."

"Aren't you on some committee with the Public Library?" I asked her.

She nodded. "I hadn't thought about that. Good idea," she said, and marched back out, tapping her phone.

"That would be a big step."

He nodded without smiling.

"You're not a citizen of the United States, right?"

He nodded and smiled. "But I going to school to be citizen."

"You know getting married is a real commitment, right?"

He cocked his head and stared directly into my eyes. "You divorce two times."

"I have made many, many mistakes. Everybody makes mistakes. I'm not trying to influence you, just to support you."

"What is Republic of Texas?" He was staring at the flags and artifacts that covered the walls.

I explained that Texas was part of Spain, then part of France, then it belonged to Mexico after Mexico threw out Spain, and then it became independent, after a war with Mexico. Eventually it joined the United States, then the Confederacy, then back to the United States. But at that time, Texas included a lot more territory than just the State of Texas. It included territories north and west of Texas, including what's now Oklahoma, New Mexico, Colorado, most of Arizona, and even part of Wyoming.

"When it was independent, and before it became part of the United States, it was a country of its own, like France or England or Canada. Because it was run almost entirely by Americans who had left their homes to move to Texas while it was still part of Mexico, the official language was English, and the government was like the states of the United States. And they sent an ambassador to London, just like any other country would."

He looked puzzled.

"It's a gimmick to get American tourists to eat here."

He nodded vigorously and smiled broadly. "Food not good here, I think."

I shrugged and pointed to the margaritas on the menu. "Tequila," I said.

Ruth came back in smiling. "Progress," she said. After she sat down, she told us that she had talked to the agent's assistant who would ask the agent if she could help us get in touch with Omar Ortigan, since our friend, Ned Savage, had died suddenly and Mr. Ortigan had donated a substantial amount of money to one of his projects.

"I think I want get married with Ned wife," Gabriele announced to both of us.

Ruth looked hard at me while I smiled at Gabriele. Then she smiled at Gabriele and scrunched her shoulders up in a gesture of delight. "Have you talked to Siobhan about this?"

He shook his head to indicate no.

Chapter Thirteen

As far as I was concerned, Siobhan was still an unknown quantity. I have a lingering superstition that actors are always acting, so I found it difficult to take anything she said seriously. That was especially true when we found out that she had married Ned a couple of weeks before he was killed. It wasn't that I thought she killed him—not like Gabriele had thought when we first met her—just that I didn't know if what she said was true or improvised for the situation.

I knew I couldn't get an unbiased opinion from Gabriele, although I was inclined to accept his "falling in love" as an earnest evaluation of her. I didn't know then and I don't know now whether Gabriele is gay or whether he is AC/DC, although he had certainly been playing the gay side with me whenever the subject came up.

I asked Ruth what she thought when we got back to the hotel and took up residence in the bar. Gabriele went upstairs for a nap or a shower or whatever.

"Well, I think she's in a bit of a pickle," she said. "She's pregnant, a widow, and probably worried about her immigration status in the US. That's even though as a white British citizen, she's likely to get whatever she needs, especially as the widow of an American citizen. You know, with the white backlash in Washington and what-not."

"Do you think she's telling us the truth?"

"She not spilling her guts, if that's what you mean," she said. "But I think what she does tell us is probably true. She needs us, after all. She's never met Ned's family, and her honeymoon was cut short by Ned being killed. She hasn't told us what they were planning to do, but it's obvious that she thinks she's back at square one when it comes to acting in New

York. She played the lead in *The Taming of the Shrew* at Donmar Warehouse, and now she's going to auditions again."

"Do you think she's noticed that Gabriele is falling in love with her?"

"I don't think she misses anything, if that's what you mean. Just listening to Gabriele, though, and looking at him, I don't think she has been encouraging him. I mean, after all, she's pregnant with Ned's baby. Or at least we assume it's Ned's baby."

"So, what did you think about Gabriele's initial impression that she was involved in killing Ned?"

"Not likely. Maybe not even possible. Have you noticed how slight her build is? Would she have whacked him over the head with a heavy candlestick? Could she have? Is she strong enough? And why on Earth would she do that after they got married?"

I didn't have answers to any questions about Siobhan.

"So, who could have done it?"

"Somebody else, I guess."

Back to the cast list. "How about Lily?"

She snorted. "Think about Lily—who looks like Ichabod Crane in skirts—and then think about her killing the man who cast her as Malvolio, which was apparently something she thought would be a turning point in her career, at her age, whatever that is." She crossed her arms and pursed her mouth, shook her head. "I don't see how it could be a woman unless she was an athlete. Just not something a woman would do. I mean, there are certainly women who kill people, but hitting them with the base of a big candlestick? A heavy one at that?"

"I think what you mean is that it would have been impossible for you to do it. Lily is a good six inches taller than you and probably forty pounds heavier."

"And ten years older, walks with a stoop, and her head shakes when she talks sometimes."

"And an actress."

"You say that like it was an accusation."

"Sorry, I guess it is, in a way. I never know when an actor is on or off stage."

She muttered something in Yiddish, which I think was that I have a hole in my head. I smiled. "I agree with you about Siobhan, and probably about Lily, but both of them have told us lies."

"Lies?"

I pointed out that Siobhan had either lied or withheld the truth when she didn't tell us that she was married to Ned when he was killed. And that Lily—who knew because she was the witness at the wedding—concealed it as well.

"Okay, I'll give that to you. They should've come clean."

"I hear you," I said. "But it was a murder that we were investigating, and they didn't want to get involved. And they're both actors."

After a while, Gabriele strolled back in, stretching and yawning.

"Did you have a good nap?" Ruth asked.

He nodded and waved at the waiter, ordering a ginger ale when he came over.

"We were just talking about Siobhan," Ruth said flatly. "About why she didn't tell us she was married. What do you think?"

"I think she come home to London because she want be with *mamma* when she have baby."

"What about being with Ned's family?"

"Maybe she not feel married. Maybe Ned tell her she get green card."

"She's pregnant," I pointed out. "She says the baby is Ned's. So, he did more than promise her a green card."

"They both gay."

"And you are thinking of asking her to marry you, right?"

He nodded.

"I guess you wouldn't do that if you thought she had anything to do with killing Ned." Ruth was going where I would not have gone.

He looked at her without blinking and said, "She not kill Ned. She not there when bad person kill Ned."

"How do you know that?"

"She tell me. She very sad."

"What do you think about Lily?" I asked him.

"Old lady?"

I nodded.

"She not kill Ned. She like Ned and she like Ned wife."

In my experience, Gabriele frequently makes mistakes when he jumps to conclusions, but he is seldom wrong when he makes decisions about people after he spends time with them. He is inclined to think of women as liars, for whatever reason, and he had to tuck that idea away in order to believe Siobhan. I knew he didn't fall in love with her from his pelvis, so it had to be from his head and heart.

"Why don't you ever use her name? You call her Ned's wife," Ruth wanted to know.

"Her name not Siobhan," he said, pronouncing her name correctly, shi-VAHN. "Siobhan same in Italian like in English. *Irlandese*. Her name Brianna," he said, pronouncing it with the accent on the first "a."

"How did you find that out?"

"She tell me. She show me *passaporto.*"

Of course, a *stage name that shouts that she's Irish.*

Ruth was nodding. "Brianna is easier too." She looked up at the ceiling. "I wonder what Lily's real name is."

I changed the subject. "We're thinking of going to Istanbul to see if we can talk to the Turkish writer that sent Ned $50,000 for a project he was working on."

He looked from me to Ruth and back to me.

"I come if you want me."

"I always want you."

"Then I come. I send email to Brianna and ask her when she come back to New York."

I could tell he was torn. "If you need to stay here, it's okay."

"*Il destino è destino,*" he said. *Fate is fate.* "Brianna come back to New York and we see there what we do." He moved from sitting on the banquette next to Ruth and sat down next to me in a straight chair. He put his arm around my shoulder. "I marry you if you want."

I thought I saw a tear form in Ruth's eye. I smiled at Gabriele, and said, "*Mille grazie.*" And I hugged him the way I would hug my own son if I saw him and he needed hugging.

So we made plans to go to Istanbul. Ruth said she would talk to her guy at American Airlines and see what she could do about a flight on British. I said I would contact the Ciragan Palace Hotel to see if they could accommodate us. Gabriele clenched and unclenched his fists and rubbed his hands together excitedly.

"I go in Asia," he said. "I not been in Asia."

"Istanbul is in Europe," I said. "Sorry to rain on your parade."

"Parade?"

"Ah, it's an old song from a Broadway musical. It means that I'm sorry to disappoint you."

He leaned over and kissed me on the cheek in a way that a relative would, not romantically. "Not disappoint."

I signed the check and we all toddled off upstairs to make preparations, keeping in mind that we had not yet spoken to Omar Ortigan. Fortunately, our rooms were across the hall from each other, so we could compare notes easily enough. And we would meet at seven to go to dinner. There would still be daylight at seven, and I planned for us to go to Le Garrick in Covent Garden.

As it turned out, Ruth had a text message from the agent in New York, saying that Mr. Ortigan would be very pleased to hear any news we might have about Mr. Savage. Obviously, he didn't know what had happened. She said she would call and arrange for us to meet him. I told her that she could tell him we would be staying at the Ciragan Palace—he would know where that is.

Fortunately, I was able to get two rooms in the newer part of the hotel. The main building is a former Ottoman palace, built in the mid-nineteenth century by Sultan Abdulaziz. It is very grand, very gilded, very formal, along the lines of Versailles or Sans Souci, and has been made very comfortable—and scary expensive. The newer building has central air-conditioning and central heat, plenty of hot water, elevators that work all the time, new mattresses and pillows, and a staff that knows your name. Room rates are still high, but in line with good hotels in Europe or New York, not like a Sultan's Palace, so to speak. The rooms look out at the swimming pool and the blue-blue waters of the Bosporus, with fishing boats and huge ships constantly passing by.

Ruth said our flight would leave from Heathrow at one o'clock in the afternoon the next day, which was a Saturday. She had been able to get the front cabin. "But there are only two classes, so it's a small plane," she said. And Mr. Ortigan had responded via email, saying that he would be happy to meet us at the hotel for a drink around five o'clock, if that worked for us. Ruth confirmed.

I wondered what was going on with Siobhan—excuse me, Brianna—whether she was staying with her mommy because she was pregnant but assumed all would come out in the wash. In other words, I just put it out of my mind.

Chapter Fourteen

We were booked by American Airlines on a British Airlines flight, but it turned out that the plane was actually from Turkish Airlines. The last time I had flown on Turkish Airlines was the same route, from London to Istanbul, but it was in 1994, when the world was a different place.

There were no fun buttons for Gabriele to play with on the seat console, but the seats were comfortable and they reclined, with the option of a footrest that could be set at a number of different levels. No matter what you did, it would not be a flat bed though.

When I was on Turkish Airlines in 1994, I was with my second wife, and we were both amused with the smoking arrangements. At that point virtually every plane had a smoking section, but usually it was a Siberia-like section at the back of the cabin. In coach, that gave the smokers an advantage in getting to the restrooms, but it basically created a smoky environment for the rows immediately adjacent to the smoking area.

Not so on Turkish. It was much more straightforward in endorsing cigarette smoking (no cigars allowed; they wouldn't be from Turkey). As you faced the cockpit, the smoking section was the entire left side of the plane, with the right side theoretically non-smoking. It was almost a Marx-Brothers approach to the issue of clean air, but it was clearly an endorsement of the Turkish cigarette and tobacco industry, which supplied a strong, dark tobacco that was used in the smelliest and strongest-tasting cigarettes, like the famous Gauloises that had polluted the air around outdoor cafes for most of the twentieth century.

We were amused, having grown up in a time when smoking was not only common but acceptable. There was no question in our minds that people had a right to smoke, even though our right to clean air was being violated everywhere we went.

The plane we got on at Heathrow was in full compliance with EU rules and regulations. No smoking, no way, no how, anyplace in the plane.

The menu on the plane was a reminder of the excellence of Turkish food. It was a shock to me in 1994. I had traveled to Egypt ten years earlier, and the food there was okay but in no way great or memorable. I was expecting the same in Istanbul. Not.

The Ottoman Empire was in control of Constantinople from 1453 onward until its demise after the First World War. It was a time when rich was rich and almost everyone else was poor, other than a skilled craftsman layer that was a seedling version of a middle class. What does that mean for food? It means that Turkish food had a tradition of excellence at least equivalent to the way we think about French food today. Heck, the Turks invented crispy, *mille-feuille* pastry, that paper-thin layered heavenly pastry that defines baklava, but also Napoleons, *palmiers* and a truckload of fancy dishes, not all of them sweet, like Beef Wellington or maybe even your grandmother's pot pies.

'Nuff said. Neither Ruth nor Gabriele had been to Istanbul. I wondered if they were expecting a dusty, gritty metropolis like Cairo (that was my mental image in 1994 until I got there). But I didn't ask.

"Is like Roma?" Gabriele asked me.

"No. Nothing is like Rome. Nothing in the world that I have ever seen. The Christian parts are Greek and the rest is Turkish. No place, no city is like Istanbul."

The WiFi on the plane was better than I expected. I was able to get onto Google and looked up the hotel, showing Gabriele the gallery of pictures. His eyes opened to double their normal size. I explained that we would not be staying in the old palace but in a new, modern building that was just east of the palace. Much more comfortable.

All three of us have learned over the years not to check bags. We had stuffed our duffel bags into the overhead compartments and since we were in the front cabin, we were quickly off the plane and into the terminal. Immigration took a good deal more time than it had at Heathrow, and Signor Cortese did not just walk in with his EU *passaporto*. But after about forty minutes, we were cleared through immigration and customs and walked outside where a bevy of drivers did verbal battle with each other trying to get us to ride with each one of them.

The Turkish lira is very volatile—up one day and down the next, and I had been told in advance that dollars, pounds or euros would get the job done faster and cheaper than Turkey's own currency. I told one of the drivers in English that we would pay $40 US including tip to get to Ciragan Sarayi. He started to bargain, and I turned to the next one, ignoring the one I had been talking to. The second driver agreed immediately, and I fancied I could hear the first driver gnashing his teeth behind me. We threw our duffels into the trunk and kept our laptops with us. You can buy anything that you might pack in a suitcase in Istanbul. But you can't afford to lose your digital data.

At any rate, traffic was minimal, or so the driver said ("Is not traffic"), and we were at the hotel in less than forty minutes. A dollar a minute. It would have taken half again that much to get from Heathrow into central London.

One of the first things that struck me in Istanbul in 1994 was how European the people looked and dressed. I was anticipating veiled women in long black muumuus with long sleeves and complete head coverings. Instead, the women were reminiscent of Paris. Lots of fashionable frocks and LBDs, lots of four-inch spikes, and lots of bare arms and perfectly coiffed hairdos. That was especially true when we checked into the hotel.

There was a message waiting for us that Omar Ortigan would meet us in the Gazebo Lounge at five o'clock. The concierge assured us that the Gazebo Lounge was the hottest spot in Istanbul, and that the table we would be given would be next to a window looking out at the Bosporus. We checked in at three, so we had time for a quick shower and a quick nap before meeting the Great Man.

I put on a jacket and tie and advised Gabriele to do the same. Of course, he could have gone anyplace in overalls and women would faint like dominoes falling over as he walked by. As it turned out, Ruth met us in jeans, heels, and a Chanel theater jacket with an Hermes scarf worn like an ascot under the jacket.

In the event, Ortigan looked rather younger than his pictures, an almost unlined face, though with a slightly Einsteinian head of hair—curly and graying. He was wearing a blue shirt, no tie, and a beige jacket over jeans. He and Ruth could have walked onto a dance floor together and we would have been left standing in the slightly over-dressed wallflower line.

Except that he was very short, and Ruth was about 5'10" with her platform stilettos.

He told us to call him Omar and spoke English in a British "received" style. The queen's English, so to speak. But his book sales were far higher in the United States than in any other country, and he made it clear that he was comfortable with American argot. We introduced ourselves, and I showed him my NYPD identification.

He was thunderstruck when we told him what had happened to Ned.

"He was going to act in a film based on one of my novels."

"Which one?" Ruth asked quickly.

"Well, at this point, that doesn't matter," he said. "But it was to have been *My Name is Eternity*.

"Oh, that's the one where the bad guy sticks a needle in his eye," she said, showing her teeth clenched together in a fearful or grossed-out expression.

He smiled. "It's a tale of the clash of east and west in the late fifteenth century. And yes, one of the fellows does blind himself purposefully in that way."

Ruth covered her mouth with her freshly manicured hand.

"I should tell you that the way he blinded himself was fairly common as a punishment for criminals, especially high-level criminals."

"High-level criminals?" I asked in an incredulous manner.

"Truthfully, it began under the Byzantines, who had a habit of throwing out their emperors. Since it was unthinkable that an emperor might be disfigured, they frequently cut off the outgoing emperor's nose, but that was fatal more often than they wanted. An emperor is an emperor, and what everyone wanted when they got rid of one was to put them in a monastery someplace where they could be pampered to some extent. Without a nose, the point was moot."

"So, they started sticking needles in their eyes?" I asked.

"No, they started to blind them by holding a red-hot poker in front of their eyes so that the corneas would become opaque. But even that was more disfiguring than they wanted, because each of the incoming emperors knew that he might be susceptible to the same treatment one day. That's when the needles came in. I'm told it doesn't hurt."

Gabriele made a tortured face that did not manage to obliterate his perfect features.

"Of course, I don't know whether it hurt or not, and since it hasn't been done in centuries now, no one could tell me for sure. Dr Guillotin was certain that his means of execution was painless, but nobody ever testified to that after having been decapitated by his machine. Same kind of thing."

"It's very graphic," Ruth said.

"Yes, that's what attracted me to it," Omar said. "That moment of horror, but with no blood."

He paused, and then changed his body position, sat up straighter, and pushed his fizzy drink toward the middle of the table. "So, someone beat him to death? What a terrible shame! So talented and so handsome!"

Since I was the only one with an NYPD identification, I answered. "We're not sure what happened. The medical examiner determined that he was going into anaphylactic shock from an allergic reaction to a fungus that was found in his lungs and in his apartment. He had stuck an EpiPen in his leg." I paused to see if he understood EpiPen, and he seemed to follow. "And the M.E. said that the epinephrine was in his bloodstream when he was killed. He was killed with a single blow to the head. The weapon was the foot of a heavy brass candlestick that was sitting on a side table in his living room."

He shook his head. "Hard to believe someone so young could already be gone."

"Which role would he have been playing?"

"It doesn't matter now, but it was the man who stuck the needle in his eye. Most western readers would see him as a villain. Most Turks would see him as a defeated hero." He looked from one to the next of us. "Our cultures are quite different."

"Are you sympathetic with that character?"

"Ah," he said. "It would be folly for me to comment on that. What I have written, I have written."

Quod scripsi, scripsi I thought. An exact translation. That's what

Pontius Pilate says in the Gospel of John about the plaque that is put above Jesus's head on the cross, proclaiming Jesus of Nazareth to be King of the Jews, frequently turned into an acronym (INRI) by artists and sculptors. The locals objected to that, as one might expect, and Pilate responded with the phrase that Omar had used about the character that Ned would have played in the film of his book. To be fair, all kinds of writers have used that phrase over the centuries. It was not Omar being blasphemous.

"I apologize for this, but I need to ask you about the check you sent to Ned. What was it for?"

"It was a bonus for accepting the role in the film. I wanted him and none but him."

"Had you met?"

"Not exactly. I had seen him play *The Elephant Man* in a small theater in London. Of course he had a slightly deformed arm, hand and leg, which may have added to his transformation from normal to afflicted in the famous opening of that play. But I was overwhelmed. As you Americans would say, I cried like a baby."

"What will you do now for that character?" Ruth asked.

"For now, I shall need to cancel the film. I will most likely revive it, but I admit that I cannot conceive of the role being played by anyone else. I suppose there is probably a Bollywood actor who could step in, but I'm not knowledgeable about Bollywood films."

Gabriele had said nothing but had nursed a glass of *kavaklidere,* a hearty red grape native to Turkey. He raised his glass to Omar and nodded politely then drank to the Nobel laureate's honor.

"Maybe you could do it," Omar said. "Can you say something for me?

"What you want me say?" Gabriele cocked his head to the left and seemed to analyze Omar's face.

"Oh, I like that," Omar said. "Just like that."

"Oh, I like that. Just like that," Gabriele parroted back.

"That's not what I meant, sorry. I was saying I was struck by your face and your composure."

"Composure?" he asked.

"*Compostezza,*" Omar and I both said the word at the same time.

Now it's my turn to be impressed, I thought but did not say. His accent was far better than mine, clipping the vowels and eliminating Americanized diphthong sounds.

"Are you interested?" Omar asked.

Gabriele put down his glass and bowed his head slightly, a sort of noggin genuflection that we all understood as an act of submission.

"I cannot," he said slowly. Then he looked up and directly into Omar's eyes. "I have *ristorante* in Manhattan, and *il mio cugino* never forgive me if I walk away, even if I walk away with famous Nobel man. Is great honor to meet you, *arkadaş.*" That last bit, I later learned, is the Turkish word for "friend." *How the hell did he come up with that?*

Omar handed him a business card.

"Call me if you change your mind," he said. Gabriele stood up and bowed slightly from the waist and remained looking at his shoes as Omar walked away from the table.

I looked at Gabriele the way I would have looked at a child of mine who just played a flawless Beethoven piano sonata.

He laughed, a full-throated laugh. "He not even gay."

"Better cut that out," Ruth said, "or you're going to get laugh lines."

"*Zampe di gallina,*" I said, changing the phrase being translated to "crow's feet."

"I guess we can go home," Ruth said. "I think we got all the news that's fit to print from Omar."

I suggested that since we had come to the edge of Europe for this meeting, that we should take the next day for some compacted sightseeing. I signaled to the waiter, who spoke good English.

"Do you know a good place outside the hotel where we could have dinner?"

The waiter hesitated and looked uncertain.

"The last time I was here, I went to a restaurant called The Cistern, at least in English. Is that still a good place?"

"I am sorry to say this, sir, but that restaurant, called Sarnic, was closed about two years ago. It was a very famous restaurant and very beautiful. Maybe I can ask headwaiter to talk to you?"

I nodded.

In a trice, the headwaiter was there with a white ruffled shirt and black bow tie and a white apron tied around his waist, though obviously with the regulation black pants underneath. He suggested a restaurant called North Terrace, where there is a good view of Hagia Sophia, the great church built by Justinian in 537 AD, later turned into a mosque, and more recently turned into a museum. Several of the original mosaics have been restored in and under the dome that was the largest dome in the world for nearly a millennium. There is also a good view of the Blue Mosque, itself an architectural wonder.

I thanked him and asked if he could arrange for us to have a table at 7:30. He said he could do that. I wrote the room number on the check and signed it, with an amount that looked like drinks cost millions of US dollars. Very scary the first time you do that, but the Turkish lira is indicated by two strokes through a vertical with a squiggle at the bottom, and in a handwritten note, it can look deceptively like a dollar sign. I knew that American Express would not bill me $7 million in US dollars for drinks for four, even at the Ciragan Palace Hotel. I had, by the way, had palpitations about that in 1994 when I was there on vacation.

Dinner was excellent, and we packed a very full day of sightseeing in on Sunday, hitting Justinian's church, a couple of grand mosques and the titanic land walls built by Theodosius in the first half of the fifth century to replace the original walls of Constantine from a hundred years previous. We also went to the Spice Market, a feast for the nose and eyes, and took a short walk in the Grand Bazaar, probably the first indoor shopping mall in the world (begun in 1455), and a more leisurely walk through the Church at Chora, built about ten years after the Norman Conquest of England. We walked across the Galata Bridge. That bridge gave a card game the name of "Bridge" because diplomats who were not allowed to stay in the old city overnight played their form of whist while waiting for traffic to die down at night on the only bridge out of Constantinople. It was the "Bridge" game. And sure enough, there is the Galata Tower on the other side which is where the great bronze chain was stretched to the Old City to block off the Golden Horn when Constantinople was fighting a sea battle.

Then we did a short turn through the magnificent Dolmabahce Palace, built during the 1840s to replace the late medieval Topkapi Palace in the old city, which lacked all of the "modern" amenities. It is a phantasmagoria of enormous handmade carpets, chandeliers bigger than an American sedan from the 1960s, and an amount of gilding that makes Versailles look rustic. Frankly, it's an easy place to overdose on, and we fled back to the hotel after less than an hour in the over-ripe magnificence of the late sultans.

Although I hated to say goodbye to Istanbul after such a short visit, we were back at Ataturk International Airport at 10AM Monday morning and flew directly back to New York. You guessed it, on Turkish Airlines, the only partner of American Airlines to fly that route.

Chapter Fifteen

It had been a whirlwind few days, and I regretted not having spent more time with Siobhan or Brianna or whatever her real name was. There was something yet to find out about what was going on with her.

I sent a text message to Mike di Saronno to see if he wanted to debrief on what we had found out. He did and suggested that I meet him at his office, which was, after all, only a hop-skip-jump from Long Island City. I never walk by my old apartment on 48th Street that I don't wish I was still there. But in fact, it is so ungodly expensive now that only an oil Arab or an expatriate Chinese billionaire could live there without worrying when the next rent increase would come crashing down.

After we said hello, I started with a briefing on Omar Ortigan. "He told us that the $50,000 that we found a stub for in Ned's effects was a bonus to Ned for agreeing to star in a film version of one of his best-selling novels."

"That seems odd, unless they knew each other fairly well."

"Well, according to Mr. Ortigan, they had never met, but Mr. Ortigan had seen Ned in a production of a play called *The Elephant Man*, in the West End of London."

"I've seen that. What was Ned playing?"

"The elephant man—the title role—I forget his name, but it really impressed Mr. Ortigan. He said he had his agent contact Ned and propose a role in the film of one of his books. I think it was called something *Eternity*. Ruth read it a few years back, but I never did, unfortunately. She told me something about one of the characters sticking a needle in his own eye on purpose. Something about a dog too. We didn't talk about what Ned would be doing or where or when, because Mr. Ortigan didn't know Ned had been killed. He seemed wrecked when we told him what happened. But he told us he sent Ned that check to tie it up that Ned would act in the film, or that's what he said. And he's a Nobel Laureate."

"As far as I can tell, none of his books has been made into a movie," Mike said. "I read that book. It was called *My Name Is Eternity*, and there was a character, a painter of Turkish miniatures, who blinded himself with a needle."

"I feel like a bumpkin. Sorry. Anyway, Ortigan seemed thunderstruck by what we told him and didn't have anything useful to tell us other than about the money he sent to Ned."

I told him about our conversation with Siobhan. "By the way, Gabriele had a talk with her offline and says her name is Brianna, not Siobhan."

"Not unusual in the theater. Maybe Siobhan says 'Irish' more dependably than Brianna does."

"Did you know she was pregnant?"

He shook his head. "Ned?"

"She said Ned was the father. I'm strictly an amateur, but I don't see any reason why she would be better off with her husband dead. She was married to him, but her security in being married to a natural-born American citizen would evaporate, I'd guess, with him dead. No motive that I can see."

He didn't reply, although he nodded a bit. "Did she say what she's doing in London?"

I told him that she never explained why she went home, but that I guessed it was because her family was there.

"Didn't you say she was from Armagh? Did she mention her visa?"

"I did. But Armagh is UK, so it's notionally closer to London than it is to Dublin, in spite of the accent. No discussion of visas, that I recall."

He said that his understanding was that UK Equity was pretty tough on American actors working in London.

"I know Equity is very strict about English actors working in New York," I said. "I'm fairly sure that's why she had been planning to use a fake name on the program for *Twelfth Night*. Not that it matters any more, since it's been cancelled."

"I hope you're not planning to put in for your expenses for your long weekend in Europe."

"That was a statement? Not a question? Anyway, of course I'm not planning to ask the NYPD to underwrite our trip to London and Istanbul. Even so, I think we found out some things that will help us figure out what happened to Ned Savage."

"A question about something you said," Mike mused. "You said Gabriele had a conversation with Siobhan and that he told you her real name is Brianna."

"And?"

"Any idea why they had that talk?"

"He's thinking about asking Brianna to marry him."

"Really? Why? He's not a citizen, as far as I know."

"As far as I know too. He carries an Italian passport that gets him to the fast line in Immigration at Heathrow. Although Brexit would end that."

He walked over to his desk and picked up a piece of paper. "According to what our guys tell me, her parents do live near London, so that could be why she is there, especially if she's pregnant."

I shrugged. "Odd that she never mentioned that." I paused and then added, "I had the feeling there was something on her mind that she wasn't talking about."

"Not surprising, given what she's been through. Married, pregnant, widowed, and her Shakespeare gig canceled because her husband was murdered."

I stood up to leave.

"I'd like to talk to Mr. Cortese about Siobhan. And by the way her family name seems to be Dunlaoghaire, however that's pronounced," Mike said, trying to pronounce it with a hard 'g' and then spelling it out. "Not Reilly. But if I was an actor with a last name that nobody could pronounce, I might change it to Reilly too."

"You pronounce it like Dunleary," I said. "It's a town on the sea near Dublin."

"How do you get that from that string of letters? And how do you know?"

"I've been to that little town on a day trip from Dublin when I was meeting a client maybe ten years ago. It's the way the Irish spell a name that's easier to spell in English, but Gaelic isn't English. That's Ireland for you. Most of the cities you've ever heard of in Ireland have English names on maps, but they have Irish names in Ireland. And in my limited experience, Gaelic is like Turkish—looks like random letters stacked up in ways that could never be decoded to something you could say.

"If you want to talk to Gabriele, send him a text. I think he'll pick it up before you can say Jack Robinson." I turned back to Mike, "Where did you find out about her real family name?"

"British Actors' Equity," he said, "her official bio. Although maybe I shouldn't take that literally, especially since it's the name of a town in Ireland, like you said."

Odd, I thought, but I left. Before I walked down to the subway at 50th Street and 8th Avenue, I texted Gabriele: *Mike di S want talk about Brianna*

Mike txt 1 min b4 u

I walked back upstairs and back to the precinct. Mike was still pacing around his office. "Your guys found out about her parents. Can they find out if she was ever married before Ned?"

He nodded, blinking his eyes. "Funny you should ask. She got a marriage license about a year ago to marry a man named Alan Jones. Welsh, I guess, but don't know; it's a Welsh name anyway. No record of a divorce and nothing about when the actual marriage took place."

"She Catholic?"

"That I don't know."

Something else occurred to me. "Was the marriage license for Siobhan Reilly or for Brianna Dunlaoghaire?"

"No idea; good catch. I still need to get in touch with Mr. Cortese."

"I know. You said that before. I texted him and he said he already had a text from you, so I thought you were already in touch. I'm planning to see him in a while. Probably in Manhattan. Since I take the 7 train, I'll probably find a place near Grand Central or the Library. If you want to join us for a drink, let me know and I'll tell you where and when."

I thanked him and headed back to the subway. Less than thirty minutes after that I was walking into my building in Long Island City. I texted Gabriele to call me.

The phone rang as I opened the door to my apartment. It was Gabriele, of course. I told him what Mike told me, about Brianna being married, no record of a divorce.

"*Brianna sposò Ned non validamente?*"

"Not valid? No way to tell with what we know, but I think it's safe to assume it was okay. Maybe there is something we don't know. Maybe the man she married died, like Ned did. Maybe there is a divorce someplace other than England or Northern Ireland. Don't make up your mind before you know the facts. Could be that marriage wasn't valid for some reason. What the forensic team found was a marriage license. He said there was no information as to where or when the marriage was. It could have been cancelled and never happened."

He made a sound that indicated he was puzzled, but it wasn't a real word. More like a grunt with a question mark.

I asked him if he could meet for a drink. He said yes, but he had to check with Dante. He put me on hold and came back a minute or so later. Dante agreed he could take the evening off. They are very close and I'm sure Dante knew how discombobulated Gabriele was about Siobhan.

We agreed to meet at the Croton Reservoir Tavern on 40th Street between 6th and 7th Avenues. It's one of those hidden gems of Manhattan; good bartenders who pour drinks with a heavy hand; tasty, lightly salted feel-good food like an upscale diner, and they don't care how long you sit there. It's got the coolest mural in the front—a big one of the old Croton Reservoir that used to be where the NY Public Library and Bryant Park are now. It was above-ground, and if the mural is accurate, it looked more like a castle than a reservoir like we're used to seeing now. Reservoirs now are really artificial lakes. And it had a huge promenade around the top where the elite went to be seen in the latest fashions.

When Edgar Allan Poe was living in New York, he said the old reservoir was the most fashionable place to be seen in New York City.

Anyway, Gabriele was more agitated than morose about the news of Siobhan's possible earlier marriage.

Mike appeared at the front of the Tavern. I waved while I told

Gabriele he was there. I guess I had forgotten to tell him because he screwed up his face but then smiled when Mike got to the table and sat down. Gabriele and Mike belong to a mutual admiration society; neither one could be cross with the other for more than a minute.

Mike ordered a scotch, which meant he wasn't planning to go back to his office.

Gabriele started talking to Mike in Italian. I'm okay with Italian in short bits or when it's written, but when there is a conversation, I have a hard time. I don't speak Italian as much as I know a lot of words and basically how to translate back and forth between Italian and English. I made a "not this again" face and did a silent palms-up "what's up," and he switched to broken English, even though he knows perfectly well how to speak fluent near-perfect English. American English.

"Hugo tells me that you've been seeing Siobhan Savage."

"Her name Brianna."

"Not on her marriage license. On her marriage license from a few weeks ago it's Siobhan Reilly. I know because I just checked after I talked to Hugo." He sipped on his whisky and waved at the waiter, who came over quickly.

"Anything to nibble on while we have a drink?" he asked.

"I can bring you some bread, sir. Or there's hummus with celery and carrot sticks and some pita bread, if you prefer. But that would be an order from the menu."

He wanted the hummus.

"She tell me her name Brianna."

"Maybe it is. People call me Mike, but my real first name is Peter."

"Why people not call you Peter?"

"I had an uncle Peter, and everybody in the family called me Mike to tell us apart."

"So, you say Brianna not her first name?"

"No. All I said was that her marriage license is in the name of Siobhan Reilly. Now she would be Siobhan Reilly Savage."

"I'm confused," I said, which I was. "You said her last name is the same as the name of a town near Dublin."

"I did, yes."

The waiter put the plate of hummus and veggies on the table with a basket of warm pita bread. Mike dived into it.

"Well, I got it that Brianna could be a middle name or a family name. My dad called me Jose O'Neill for no particular reason. But it's harder to have two last names."

He was chewing. "Unless you're an actor, or unless you change your name."

"So, which is it?"

"On a passport, you can have both names. So, she might be Siobhan Brianna Dunlaoghaire on her passport with a codicil on the opening page that says *This person is known professionally as Siobhan Reilly*. That way she could still be Brianna Dunlaoghaire and be Siobhan Reilly at the same time."

"Why didn't you just say that?"

"Because all I know for sure about her name is that her marriage license to Edward Savage says her name is Siobhan Reilly."

Gabriele was following the conversation like a tennis game, back and forth.

"But baby is Savage," he said. "She Savage too."

Mike nodded.

"I ask her to marry me."

"You did or you going to?" Mike asked.

"I did already."

"And she said?"

"She say no," he said, "but she wrong. She gonna marry me."

"We have a saying here, 'No means no.'"

"For sex, no mean no. For date, no mean no. For kiss, no mean no. For marry, sometime no mean maybe."

I was hearing this for the first time. "I thought you were just thinking about it. I didn't know you had already proposed to her. And I thought you were already married."

"Really?" Mike stopped eating.

Gabriele told him about the lesbian in Iowa who had helped him get his green card and added that the divorce had been finalized two years after the wedding.

Mike said he thought Gabriele had only just met Siobhan a couple of weeks back.

"She have *bambino*, good have *papà*."

"If Ruth was here, she would say 'male chauvinist pig' to you."

He made a sour face and looked down at the table.

"You could be Brianna's friend and still help with the baby. Here in the United States you would probably be called 'Uncle Gabriele' if you did that."

"Want *bambino* be Cortese."

Aha. "But the baby is Savage."

"*Forse adotto bambino.*"

"Siobhan would have to approve if you wanted to adopt her baby," Mike said.

"But I love..." he started to say.

"Love who?"

"Brianna," he said softly, with a puzzled look and a slight shake of his head.

"You mean Ned?" Mike reached over and put his hand on Gabriele's shoulder. Gabriele hunched forward and put the palms of his hands in his eyes with his elbows on the table.

"I want take care of baby. Baby part of Ned."

For a moment I felt jealous, then ashamed of being jealous, then sorry for Gabriele. I wondered how Siobhan/Brianna felt about all this.

Mike straightened up and changed the subject. "Anyway, we need to make some progress on finding out what happened to Ned. I'm planning to ask some of the actors and stage-hands from West Side Rep to come in to answer some questions. Maybe the two of you would like to help out?"

Mike finished his scotch while waving for the check. He had his American Express card in his shirt pocket and had it on the table before I could reach my back pocket.

"I'm paying," he said.

"We're going to have dinner. Let me pay."

Gabriele looked up. "Nobody pay nothing. Everything gonna be free."

Chapter Sixteen

Mike had assigned two young detectives to set up interviews with the cast members of the now-canceled production of *Twelfth Night*. He would handle the interrogations, and he wanted me to react to them. He also wanted Gabriele and Ruth to tell him what they thought, even though, of course, he had no official relationship with them.

Needless to say, both Ruth and Gabriele said they would help as much as they could, and they asked for schedules of when the interviews were to take place.

"Some of them were nearly impossible to get in touch with, because they were using the wrong names and gave bad addresses," Mike said. "Nothing wrong with that. Stuff like that goes on all the time in the theater." He paused and looked at the ceiling. "And nobody knew that somebody in the production was going to be killed. After Ned Savage's death, there were a few rehearsals that were overseen by some of the older people in the cast, particularly Lily Rasmussen and Gianfranco Mirabella."

I looked at the interviews that had been set up. There were only three: Lily, Gianfranco and Tony Anguilla, who had been to the Hudson Valley Shakespeare production with us and who had been scheduled to play Orsino in the production that had now been cancelled.

"As far as I can see, none of them could possibly be a suspect," I said. "What's the purpose in putting them through an interrogation?"

Mike explained that we needed to gather information. Nobody thought that any of the three almost-elderly actors was a candidate for a bludgeoning murder. "The purpose of the interviews is to try to triangulate on what we can find out that probably fell between the cracks before."

It seemed pointless to me, and I'm sure that showed on my face.

But I said nothing. I stared at my hands a lot.

"There's no such thing as a murder that can't be solved," he said, looking up at the ceiling, not at me, not at the two younger detectives, not at Ruth or Gabriele. "Somebody knows something that will help us. They may not even know that what they know is important. It's up to us to find it."

First up was Lily. She was looking as upbeat as she could, wearing a forest green pants suit and flat shoes that made her look almost pretty in spite of her unusual height, odd posture and her voice that varied seemingly unpredictably from bass to counter-tenor. She was wearing a Yankees backpack, which got my attention behind the glass that looked like a mirror in the interrogation room.

Mike started by asking her to describe how Ned was as a director.

"All directors are wrong a good deal of the time, and Ned was no different."

"Meaning?"

"An actor my age knows a lot that a young director may not have thought about. I'm not always right either, but I am sometimes."

"I'm sure that's true," Mike said. "Give me an example of a time when Ned was wrong about something."

"Well, first of all, he was right about casting me as Malvolio. It was a brilliant idea. Not because I'm Laurette Taylor, because I'm not. But Malvolio is different from everybody else in *Twelfth Night,* and Ned knew that. That's why he cast me. Nobody had ever heard of Malvolio as a pants role. But Malvolio is an old lady, isn't he? So, it made sense."

"But he wasn't always right about you and Malvolio?"

"No."

"Give me an example."

"Props."

"Sorry? Can you explain more?"

She explained that props are anything that an actor uses during the play. Could be a belt-buckle that's part of a costume. Could be a sword. Could be a book. Could be a tennis racket. Anything the actor uses to tell the story.

"And you felt you did or did not need the props that Ned made available?"

"For the most part, I don't use props very well. He told me something that I had heard from an old acting teacher who told me when I was still young—back a long time ago—that what I needed to do was to pay attention to my core. I needed to hold my hands and arms within the bounds created by my silhouette. My strength is in my bulk and my voice, which is very distinctive. I can make people laugh."

"So, you didn't want to use props?"

"It wasn't that I didn't want to use any, just none that weren't essential to the plot. Some props are called for in the script, like the letter that Malvolio finds and mistakenly thinks was written by Olivia and intended for him. Of course it's a forgery, but he doesn't know that."

"So, what would you do with the letter?"

"I'd make people laugh. I'd talk to the letter like it was a person. Malvolio is a fool, and the more he acts like a clown, the funnier he is. If I could have got away with it, I would have worn a red clown nose in the fourth act."

"So, where was the disagreement with Ned?"

"The sword."

"What sword? There's no sword in the play that I recall."

She said to keep in mind that it was Shakespeare and men of a certain position in life carried a sword. That means Orsino wore a sword, at least when he was meeting people. Toby wore a sword; he goes by the name Sir Toby Belch, which means he was knighted by somebody, or claims he was. Sir Andrew Aguecheek the same. If you were petty nobility in Shakespeare's time, you wore a sword. Same as if you were a woman with pretensions to be upper-class in the reign of Henry VIII, you wore some kind of headdress that covered your hair and ears and framed your face well."

"Okay, it would be like carrying a cellphone in a play about today."

"That says a lot, doesn't it?" she said with a four-note range of pitches in those few words.

Mike nodded and looked at the mirror.

"If Malvolio had pretensions of being high-class enough to be a realistic lover of Olivia, he had to have a sword."

"But Ned didn't agree?"

"Correct. Ned saw Malvolio as a servant, and servants would never be armed."

"But you thought he should have a sword."

"Not in the first part of the play, but as he sees himself as being more high-class than he is, he would have to find one."

"Find one on stage?"

"No. I didn't want to rewrite the play. He finds the letter. He wouldn't find a sword."

Mike folded his arms and waited.

"He needs to show up with a sword in a scabbard as soon as he thinks Olivia is in love with him."

"Okay."

"Remember that Malvolio is a fool, and for Shakespeare's audiences, fools are supposed to get laughs. There's no such thing as a fool we feel sorry for. Malvolio doesn't see himself as a clown, but he is one. Consider how ridiculous he is supposed to look when he is cross-gartered and dressed like a man a third his age."

"Right. So the sword?"

"It ought to be completely wrong. The total wrong sword and probably totally out of proportion to Malvolio. Think about a silly clown flying a huge kite that pulls him around and makes him look totally stupid, maybe lifts him off the ground, gets lots of laughs."

"But Ned didn't agree?"

She smiled. "He was the director, so it was his decision, and he didn't want it to look slapstick, especially with a woman playing Malvolio, which was already strange for some people."

She made clear that she thought Ned was going to craft a wonderful *Twelfth Night*. Not only that, "He was a dear boy, polite and considerate, and smart as they come. I would have signed up with him for anything he wanted me for."

"Did he conduct any rehearsals at his apartment?"

She cocked her head and looked puzzled. "He was moving from one place to another. His old apartment was on 8th Avenue, not far from St Benedict's. I don't think I was ever in his old apartment. He invited the cast over to his new place in Long Island City, and I went with Siobhan Reilly, who was playing Viola in the first cast and understudying Olivia."

"Were you rehearsing anything there?"

"It was like a housewarming. I took him some towels. It was a small place. We were jammed in there, and there was some drinking. No surprises."

Mike said he believed there had been some rehearsals in the apartment.

"Siobhan ended up going over lines when we went over to his apartment after he was dead. We ran into Hugo that day, and he invited us into his apartment, which is about ten times the size of Ned's place. Hard to believe it was the same building."

"But you never rehearsed in Ned's apartment while he was there?"

"No. Why do you ask?"

"Obviously somebody was there with him at some point, because he was killed."

"And you were thinking maybe it was me?"

"No, Ms Rasmussen. I was trying to find out if Ned was in the habit of coaching actors in his apartment. From my point of view, Malvolio is the star of *Twelfth Night,* so it seemed like he might be coaching you there. That's all. If you were there to rehearse, maybe others were too. At different times. Maybe. Just looking for clues, that's all."

She clutched her backpack as though she were getting ready to leave.

"Did you know that Ned had a severe allergy to fungus and mold?"

She said that she had been told that by Hugo Miller but that she hadn't known it before that.

Lily could tell a lot about an audience, and she loosened up on Mike. She just wanted to help, because she was so fond of Ned, etc., etc., etc.

Mike asked her who else was at the party.

"When your director invites you to something like that, you go. You just go. I think everyone in the cast and crew was there, although not all of them at the same time. That apartment was teeny-tiny."

It was interesting listening to Lily talk about Malvolio, but it didn't seem like we got anything helpful out of the interrogation. Mike tended to agree, but he sent the video of the interrogation for transcribing so we could read through it a few times.

That meant we would have Tony Anguilla up next.

Chapter Seventeen

Tony is tall, Italian-looking with a strong nose, square chin and an overall tanned look. His hair is salt-and-pepper, though still more pepper than salt. He carries himself well, shoulders back, and minimizes the fact that he has a belly by the cut of his clothes.

In most productions of *Twelfth Night,* Orsino, Tony's character in the production that Ned was going to direct, is dreamy-eyed and probably not very well attuned to the people around him. He doesn't, for instance, seem to pick up on the fact that Olivia doesn't want to have anything to do with him. He just keeps on wooing her as though he thinks she will eventually cave to what he wants. He might as well wear a big red clown grin and whiteface with eyebrows painted on looking like birds in flight. But Orsino tends to be cast as a fairly distinguished-looking guy, and sometimes is a "name" actor on the marquee. That's probably because he opens the play with a famous speech as the curtain rises.

Like almost all the characters in *Twelfth Night,* Orsino is a fool, and clearly intended to draw laughs. I always envision him as winking at the audience when he flirts with Olivia and ignores her clearly expressed disgust. That sort of vaudeville comedy would draw laughs.

He was wearing a royal blue sport jacket and a pair of relaxed jeans, not the skinny ones. Mike thanked him for coming to help the police find some clues as to what had happened to Ned Savage.

"We all liked Ned."

"One of the actors told us he was less objectionable than most directors."

"Oh," he said, "so you already spoke with Lily. Lily is notorious for her attitude about directors. But I think it's possible she had a teeny-tiny crush on Ned. Good looking kid, you know."

Gabriele and I were in the viewing room. I was remembering that when we went to Boscobel for their production of *Twelfth Night*, Tony seemed to be eating marijuana gummies, and Siobhan or somebody had said he was a pot-head. When we went to a rehearsal, I thought I recalled the smell of herbal cigarettes or marijuana in the theater.

Mike was asking Tony about how Ned worked as a director.

"He wanted to know from the actors what their ideas were about the characters. If you play *Twelfth Night* straight, it can be a very sour play. I remember being told in college that Malvolio is like Iago, a character that Shakespeare never came to terms with. And lots of audiences feel sorry for him," he said. "If that happens, then the actors are not doing their jobs."

"Meaning?"

"The play is intended to be funny. People in Shakespeare's time would have been gut-laughing through most of the play. The characters are god-damn strange, if you think about it. In a good production of *Twelfth Night,* people giggle as much as they would sob at a production of *Romeo and Juliet*."

"Orsino doesn't seem funny to me. How would you make him funny?"

"I've spent a lot of time in comedy," he said. "I worked up in the Catskills when I was a teenager, and I saw all the great standup guys. I still think the best way to make people laugh is to bend over and drop your pants, or slip on a banana peel and land on your butt. If I could have had a conveyor belt with chocolates on it, I would've been a male Lucy trying to wrap them up. Anything for a laugh."

"How did Ned feel about that?"

He shook his head. "I don't know, to tell the truth. He let me try some things, and when it made the cast laugh, I thought it was working. With comedy, though, you don't know what's working until you play it in front of a real audience, not a bunch of actors who don't care whether your character works or not."

"Did Ned laugh?"

"Yeah, yeah he did."

"So, give me an idea."

"Well, I tried making him kinda swishy at first." He stood and made a limp-wristed waving gesture with his arm in front of him and one hip stuck out as he locked the other knee. "You know, darling?"

"Sure. Did that get a laugh?"

He sat back down. "No."

"And Ned?"

"Ned reminded me that Orsino has hot pants for Olivia, not for one of the guys."

"Ned was gay, right?"

"I guess."

"So, what else did you try?"

"I had a tooter that I used to punctuate my lines."

"A tooter?"

"Makes a farting sound."

I smiled in spite of myself. Gabriele didn't react.

"It worked well in the scene with Feste, Olivia's jester, when he says everyone calls him an ass. I got a big laugh with the tooter there."

"Did you have any scenes with Lily?"

"Not any face-to-face scenes, no."

"Orsino and Malvolio have some similarities as characters, right?"

"Well, they're both pompous, and both are on Olivia's shit-list, even though Malvolio is her butler or steward or whatever you want to call the head of the household staff."

"So, what did you and Ned agree on that would allow Orsino to get some laughs?" Mike asked.

"Well there's a scene when Feste suggests I put my hand in my pocket, which I turned into an exaggerated pocket-pool gag."

"And?"

"Ned was telling me to do slow burns and lick my lips when I went after Olivia," he said. "You know, slobbering almost."

Mike asked Tony if there was anyone in the cast or backstage that didn't get along with Ned.

He shook his head. "Not that I can remember. Ned was good at everything he did, and he cared about what people told him. He told us that he was going to be in a film playing a lead role. Didn't tell us what film, just that he was going to be in a film."

"Have you done films?"

He nodded. "Oh yeah. A bunch. Second bananas, no leads. Some murderers."

"Were you aware that Ned Savage had a severe allergy to mold and fungus?"

He shook his head.

"Or that some fungus that is commonly found on marijuana was found in Ned's lungs in the autopsy?"

He said nothing but looked down and shook his head again.

Mike excused himself and came into the viewing room to see us.

"What do you think?" he asked.

"He's a ham," I said. "But I bet he's funny when he wants to be. My kid always liked farting jokes. His favorite book was about a farting dog. I still think low humor like that is funny."

"Anything he told us helpful?"

We both shrugged at the same time.

The next interview would be Gianfranco Mirabella, who was playing Sir Toby Belch.

Eighteen

Gianfranco Mirabella is a shrimp compared to most actors that play Sir Toby Belch. Sir Toby is sometimes almost like Falstaff—an overstuffed drunk who is hanging on at Olivia's home because his friend, Sir Andrew, is a distant relative of Olivia. He's written as a loud-mouth, and the two things he seems to always have on his mind are alcohol and finding a place to urinate.

Gianfranco is an Italian name, but his real name was Francisco Martinez, part Latin and part Native American from New Mexico, swarthy and dark-eyed, but perhaps looking more like a thug than a knight in shining armor. Ned was turning stereotypes on their heads throughout the production.

Mike started the interview by saying, as he had with the others, that nobody was under suspicion. The point of these interviews was just to compile some potential clues that the NYPD could follow up on, in the ongoing effort to find out how Ned Savage died. He asked Gianfranco what name he was most comfortable with.

"My friends call me Frank," he said. "I thought, or somebody told me anyway, that Ned was hit over the head with something, and that's how he died."

Mike said that Ned was in fact hit on the head in his apartment, but that he may have already been dead or nearly dead when that happened. "But what we wanted to talk to you about is how Ned worked as a director and how he got along with the cast and crew."

Frank looked uncomfortable but didn't fidget. "I hope you're not going to ask me questions about my colleagues," he said.

"Wasn't planning to," Mike said. "We're more interested in your observations about Ned Savage. We're trying to put together a profile of Ned to help us in our investigation."

He shrugged and nodded briefly.

"How did Ned impress you as a director during the time you were working with him on *Twelfth Night*?"

Frank said that he had limited exposure to Ned in terms of his character, Sir Toby Belch, who functions as a scout leader to Sir Andrew Aguecheek. Both of them are drunks, and neither is really a protagonist or antagonist in the story. "Comic relief," he said. "I saw a production recently where they were squirting each other with garden hoses. I suppose that's instead of peeing on each other."

Mike rustled the papers in the folder in front of him.

"But he was interested in my experiences playing Malvolio in some other productions," Frank said.

"Oh, that's interesting. You've been Malvolio in other productions?"

He nodded.

"How did you feel about Malvolio being played by a woman in this production?"

"I thought it was innovative, likely to make the piece funnier. It was in the spirit of the piece, which is already fraught with amusing gender problems. Viola spends almost the whole play as Cesario, a boy played by a girl, who in turn was played by a boy actor, because females were not allowed on stage—so there would have been lots of opportunities for Viola to get laughs—a boy playing a girl dressed as a boy. Now Malvolio is a man played by a woman. Nice balance. And Lily is funny to start with."

Mike asked how Ned had handled rehearsals.

"He posted calls for rehearsal by scenes. That's common, so that somebody who's not going to be needed can do other things instead of just having to sit there and watch."

"Just out of curiosity, how did your Malvolio differ from the Malvolio that Lily was working on?"

"Other than the gender of the actor, I presume you mean?"

Mike smiled and said nothing.

"Well, we're the same in that we are both playing against type. Lily and I had worked together several times, including in a Noel Coward piece that played on Broadway. Lily was up for a Tony in that one. She was a howl, stole the stage from a couple of really well-known famous actresses."

"Playing against type?"

"Well, all actors play against type to some extent, because we're not like the characters we play. We're much more everyday people than our characters on stage."

"For example?"

"Lily has a patent on a certain type of character that might be called an absent-minded lady. She'd be the perfect Mrs. Malaprop in *The Rivals*."

"Mrs. Who?"

"Malaprop, just a very funny character who constantly misuses words, or uses the wrong words in hilarious ways. Malvolio is exactly the opposite, a man who has no tolerance for anyone who is the least bit off the mainstream. So, she'd be playing against the type of person she's more well-known for playing, not to mention that she would be playing a man. She'd be more likely with her reputation to be playing Aunt Eller in *Oklahoma*, for instance."

Mike looked puzzled. Frank stood up and belted out the first line of "The Farmer and the Cowboy Should Be Friends."

"I know who Aunt Eller is. I think it'd be more common for a man to play Aunt Eller than for Lily to play Malvolio."

"Less shocking, you mean. I doubt Aunt Eller has ever been played by a guy. And she's not a funny character. It's not a funny play, although Jud Fry in *Oklahoma* shares with Malvolio that people feel sorry for him. But he doesn't get any laughs. Jud that is."

Mike pulled out his phone and tapped on it, asking me if I had any questions for Frank. Frank sat back down.

I suggested he might ask if Ned had any rehearsals at his apartment.

"Did Ned ever have rehearsals or coaching sessions at his apartment?"

It was Frank's turn to look puzzled.

"Or specifically, were you ever at a rehearsal at Ned's apartment?"

"Ned moved out of his apartment while we were doing readings of the script at St Benedict's."

"Yes, he moved to Long Island City in Queens\ and into an apartment next door to one of our civilian criminalists here at the NYPD."

Frank made a noise that sounded like a grunted version of "Whaddya know?"

"So, you were never there?" Mike asked.

"We were pretty much all there when he moved in. I took a bottle of Johnny Black for a housewarming gift. A lot of the women made things at home and brought them. I think somebody brought a cake and somebody else brought cookies."

"Lily told us she took towels."

"Practical. Everybody can use towels," he said.

I texted to Mike to ask if any of his Malvolio characters used a sword or wore a sword.

"Odd you should ask," Frank said. "Lily and I talked about that too. No, I played Malvolio as an insufferable snob with a Napoleon complex— you know, a short-man complex, like a bulldog grabbing somebody's pants-leg. No swords, but I think the sword would have been a good gag, especially if she waved it around, and it was more than she could handle. Like a kid trying to be King Kong or Darth Vader. You know, tail wagging the dog type of thing."

"When could Malvolio even think about waving a sword around?" Mike asked.

"His big line. 'Some are born great, some achieve greatness, and some have greatness thrust upon them.' It'd be a perfect way to punctuate those three funny lines, especially 'thrust,' for obvious reasons. I've seen other Malvolio actors using that line to do some pelvic thrusting, but not thrusting a sword. Could be a screamer. Gonna remember it."

"Did you know that Ned Savage had a severe allergy to fungus and mold?"

"What?"

"If he was exposed to fungus or mold, he might have had to use an EpiPen to keep from going into anaphylactic shock."

"No, I didn't know that. Poor guy." He obviously wanted the interview to be over.

Mike thanked him for coming in, and for his help.

144

After Frank left, the three of us and the two young detectives gathered in Mike's office.

"That was all real interesting, but I don't think I got any clues out of it about what to do next," I said.

"Have you heard anything else from Ned's brother?" Mike asked me.

"Not a word. I'll tickle him tomorrow and see what I can find out about the will or the wedding."

Gabriele wanted to wander over to Thalia for a drink. I seldom turn that down.

When we sat down at the bar, the bartender sent over a whisky for Gabriele and a dirty vodka for me. We toasted her first and then each other and took a swig.

"Actors not so interesting when they not in film or on stage," he said. He said the three actors who had been interviewed weren't capable of doing anything violent. "Maybe Frank, but he old too."

There was a soccer game on the various televisions around the bar area of Thalia, and clearly some fans were following it because with every kick toward a goal, there was a wave of sound. Gabriele said he had to get to Ora di Pranzo, so I walked him across the avenue to the subway and then texted Ruth.

Did she have time for a talk?

Always my dear. With you always

She suggested I go over to her apartment. It was a nice day, so I walked across from 8th Avenue to Park Avenue (which is really 4th Avenue) and then up from 50th Street to 61st to Ruth's place. Like me, she keeps a bottle of vodka in the freezer all the time. So she poured a dirty vodka for me without my asking.

And one for herself.

"I'm ahead of you," I said. "Gabriele and I had a quick one after we left Mike's office. You didn't miss much in those three interviews. It's interesting to hear actors talk about plays, but after a while it's kinda like having a magician tell you how he pulls coins out of your ears. Do I really want to know that? Probably not."

She said she had heard nothing from Ortigan's agent, and Siobhan was on radio silence. I told her that Mike had asked about Edgar and the sisters.

"I'll send off an email to Edgar to see if I can find out anything, if you'll tickle Siobhan again. I'd guess the agent isn't going to get back to you until she talks to her client."

I told her how put-together Lily looked when she was at Mike's office.

"Just because she plays frazzled old ladies doesn't mean she is one."

"Looks to me like there's a potential clash between Mrs. Savage and Ned's family," I said. "Although I can't imagine what they would clash about. Just looks like they're headed in different directions."

Ruth said it didn't seem like it could be a problem that centered on money, because there was no reason to think Ned had much net worth, even if, as Edgar had said, there was more in his estate that he would have expected.

I texted Edgar, who texted me back within a minute or so.

U have time to talk, I asked.

Sure, just finished lunch

Just got back from Istanbul

U see Omar Ortigan

Yup, nice fellow

Ortigan check in Ned broker acct 50 grand

You find a will yet?

Not yet

In NY no will: everything to the kid(s)

Siobhan pregnant?

Can't tell, but she says yes

She gonna stay London?

Did you ever talk to her?

No. I tried, but she had left for UK

Ok if I call you?

Yup

Then my phone rang, area code 310—Edgar.

"My lawyer says it's not going to help if we try to get her to stop using his accounts. She hasn't charged anything or taken any money out since she left the US, but she could."

"Hey, Edgar, hope you and the girls are doing okay. I know it takes a while to get used to something like this, especially since you may have a niece or nephew in the oven in London."

"Apparently we don't even have a fix on her real name."

"You talked to Mike?"

He had talked to Mike and had retained a lawyer in California. Turns out Ned had always voted in California as an absentee and maintained that his residence was in Edgar's house, although he hadn't actually been there in years.

"But we think that's going to decide where he was a resident."

"Does that make a difference?"

"So far, we don't know. But it seems for sure that anything that Ned owned before the marriage is not part of the estate that could be claimed by the wife. Might have no effect on a child."

"I never met Ned, so I only know what people have told me about him. What do you think he would want?"

There was a pause. "If he had a child, I think we would all want his estate to pass to the child. But we'd have to be sure the child was his."

"And if there is no child? Or if the child is illegitimate?"

"Ned was my brother. I can tell you that legitimacy wouldn't matter if he had a child. We'd want the child to have his name, our name, and to know all about his father—or her father. Ned was a charismatic man, a talented artist and a man of principle." His voice cracked.

"Look, no point trying to solve the woes of the world on the phone. Did you get time to look around Ned's apartment? And did you find any photos or other things you wanted to take home?'

He said that apparently Siobhan had taken a few small things, including a couple of photos of Ned, a group photo of our family, and maybe some other photos of Ned in plays and on a soap opera he worked on for well over a year. According to some industry statistic I found, a supporting actor in a soap probably makes about $400 per episode. That could be as many as two hundred fifty or two hundred sixty episodes per year. At two hundred fifty that would be a gross of $100,000 per year."

"I thought they made a lot more than that, but maybe I was thinking about stars."

"The study I saw said that stars can make $2,000 per episode or even more, so that could be half a million a year, plus they make appearances and frequently get commercials. Some soap actors are pretty rich."

I filled him in on our visit with Omar Ortigan and assured him that Ortigan thought very highly of Ned, "The $50,000 was a down payment for Ned to be a lead actor in a film that's going to be made on one of Ortigan's books. I think the role would be someone that most people would consider the villain."

"I haven't read any of his books," Edgar said. "Have you?"

"I think I did, but I didn't read the book that Ned's film was going to be taken from."

"Is there a name of the book?"

"I think it's *My Name is Eternity*; takes place in the sixteenth century in Constantinople."

"I want to read it, and I bet Liz and Mary will want to read it too."

"I looked at a copy. It's not short, but it's not *War and Peace* either. Maybe five hundred pages."

He wondered if something about the book would remind him of Ned.

"Ortigan never met Ned, I have to tell you. He saw Ned in a play in London a few years back and wanted Ned for this role as soon as he saw him in that play."

"Must have been *The Elephant Man*. He was nominated for several awards for that role," Edgar said. "The name of the man was Joseph Merrick, although in the play he was called John Merrick. I didn't go to London to see him do it, because there was talk at the time that the production would go to New York, and I thought I could see it there. Of course it didn't happen. Somebody else produced *The Elephant Man* in New York, and then nobody wanted to invest in a new production of a play that had just closed on Broadway. I think that's why he got the soap opera role though."

"It was *The Elephant Man*. Ortigan was impressed with the performance, and was particularly impressed that Ned was able to strip virtually all his clothes off for the opening of the play, which was apparently built on a famous drawing of a man by Leonardo da Vinci."

"Mr. Miller, we all appreciate what you are doing for Ned. You didn't even know him, but you're doing everything I can imagine to find out what happened. For whatever it's worth, you're family to us."

Ruth sat through all this, and I had my phone on speaker. She was sipping on her vodka occasionally and probably trying to make sense of my side of the conversation, because Edgar was a little hard to hear. When Edgar and I signed off, I told her the gist of what we had talked about.

"Not that anybody thought anything different, but I don't think Edgar and the girls are going to stand in Siobhan's way if she is pregnant with Ned's baby. If she's not, I guess things might be more adversarial. Edgar was clear that they considered anything that was Ned's before the marriage is not part of the marriage unless there is a child. And since they were only married for a couple of weeks before Ned passed, that would mean virtually everything he owned was his alone.

"As far as Edgar can tell, there is no will, not even an outdated one. I guess if there is a lawyer that might have a copy of it, we don't know who he or she is. Edgar had been pushing him to write a will in case something happened. And apparently Siobhan isn't responding to Edgar's messages."

Loose ends everywhere we looked. And nobody with a motive that meant anything.

I took off for my place because the sky was clouded over and it was obvious we were in for a not-unusual thunderstorm, perfectly timed for the evening rush hour.

Chapter Nineteen

Mike called while I was having my coffee, asked me to meet him at his office. "Got some interesting stuff back from CSIs and lab. Kinda like to bounce some of it off you if you have time."

"Any hints what this is about?"

"Well, it's about Ned Savage, but I'd prefer not to discuss it on the phone, because I'm not recording the conversation."

I told him I'd be there as soon as I could get there. Maybe half-hour if the 7 train pulled into the station when I got there. Or 4forty-five minutes.

In the event, it took about forty minutes, but I was there by 10:30.

There were just the two of us, so we sat in Mike's office; no need to use an interrogation room or to tape what we were talking about.

"Got some data back from the lab about Ned's apartment."

"I'm all ears."

"First, let's talk about aspergillus. The M.E. found aspergillus in Savage's lungs. You knew that I already told you."

I nodded.

"But we found aspergillus mold on the couch, and it turns out there were a few pieces of what we thought was lint that were actually specks of marijuana—maybe spilled when somebody was putting the marijuana in the glass pipe that we found on the coffee table."

"Well, we knew there had been marijuana there. I think there was some evidence in Ned's blood. Right?"

"Yup, not a lot, but enough for us to know he had ingested some of the drug."

"Okay?"

"Originally we thought the marijuana probably carried the

aspergillus into his lungs while he smoked it, or drew on the pipe."

"But?"

"Well, he had either inhaled the marijuana or swallowed it, but the aspergillus in his lungs came from particles of marijuana that was not smoked. Turns out the heat of the pipe would have destroyed the aspergillus, so it would have been unlikely that smoking the grass set off his allergy."

"Okay, I'm not following you. There was aspergillus in his lungs, so it got there how?"

"He probably inhaled some bits of the marijuana that had not been heated in the pipe or in the hookah that was in the room if it was used. We tested the hookah, and it had traces of marijuana in the bowl at the top, but it was older, maybe a lot older, like months. Could have been in the hookah when it was purchased. According to what the movers told us, he was worried about the hookah, wanted it to be wrapped in bubble wrap because he had just bought it and didn't want it to be damaged."

"Such a sixties kind of thing, to have a hookah in your apartment."

"Whatever. At any rate, the aspergillus was aspirated without being smoked. We're assuming that someone brought the marijuana into the apartment—that it wasn't something that Ned had acquired on his own—because he probably would have had an allergy attack whenever he opened it, if the aspergillus was on a lot of the pieces of marijuana. Aspergillus is found on the leaves and stems of the plants in nature, so it could have been on almost every piece of the pot, even very small ones."

"So, if he opened a baggie of marijuana, he could have breathed some of it in. If he could smell it, he could be getting some of it in his lungs. Okay."

"Not wanting to belabor this, it's apparent that Ned ingested marijuana in at least two ways—smoking it and inhaling it through his nose. Maybe snorting, although that seems unlikely. The marijuana is unlikely to have been powdered, and the bits that were in his lungs were not powdered. More likely he stuck his nose in the baggie to smell it and got some in his nose. Maybe it went all the way to the lungs then, or maybe it just stayed in his nose and worked into the lungs later."

"Are you saying that whoever brought the marijuana might not even have been there when Ned had the allergy attack?"

"Maybe, no way to tell that. What I'm saying is that it could have happened immediately, or maybe it could have happened in a delayed way, if the pieces of marijuana that had the fungus didn't immediately make it to his lungs."

"In other words, not every fragment of the grass would have necessarily had the fungus."

"Right, and although he could have had an allergic reaction to exposure in his nose, that might have been sneezing or something short of anaphylactic shock, which is what happened when the fungus got to his lungs."

"If he was sneezing, wouldn't that have expelled the problem?"

"Not always, I guess. That's why sometimes you keep sneezing over and over again as your body tries to get rid of something in the back of your nose or in your throat."

"And where is this taking us?"

"It's possible that there were people who came and went in his apartment. Maybe somebody who smoked some grass and then somebody else who grabbed the candlestick. It's possible that whoever hit him didn't know anyone else had been there. Unfortunately, there were all kinds of fingerprints, which probably date from the day before when he had the whole cast over for a housewarming."

"Are you thinking that he may have been having coaching sessions with the actors?"

"Well, the three we interviewed said they weren't coached at his apartment. And there's nothing that says whoever hit him had to be part of the play he was directing."

"Siobhan wasn't living with him, but there's nothing to say she wasn't there. She was obviously there for the housewarming, but I bet she arrived and left with Lily. She apparently had a key anyway. And it's still possible that there was more than one person there when Ned died."

Mike said he kept thinking about the sword that Lily kept talking about.

"Why?"

"I don't know. It's a weapon."

"But not the weapon that was used to hit Ned. She could have said she wanted to carry a three-foot-long musket. That would have been accurate for Shakespeare's time too."

Mike said nothing and shook his head, looking at his hands on his desk. Then he looked up and said to me, "Right."

I asked tentatively, "Were you thinking that Tony Anguilla was the person who took the pot over to Ned's?"

"Maybe. He could have been, not that it would prove anything. And no reason to make that assumption. No proof. And when I asked him if he knew about Ned's allergies, I thought he was answering truthfully."

"He's an actor. Hard to tell."

"I think about Frank talking about acting against type too."

"There are a bunch of schools of thought on how to learn to be a good actor. I think listening to an actor talk about acting is like listening to a surgeon talk about somebody's internal organs or listening to a snake-handler pray in tongues in the back woods. Gobbledygook. I bet every actor in the world has a different idea of what to do and a different story of how they came to figure it out."

"I knew we weren't going to get anything substantial from the actors. I just thought we might get a better sense of Ned Savage. Or we might hear about something we didn't know."

"I think I did get a better picture of Ned. He was a good listener. That's what all three actors said about him. He was listening to them. In Lily's case, he apparently didn't live long enough to act on the sword thing, but all three of them thought well of him because he was listening to them. I guess that's unusual for a director. There's an old story about an English actress who was playing Gertrude in *Hamlet*. The director interrupted her to give her a note on the speech she was delivering. She looked out over the footlights in the general direction of where the director was sitting in the auditorium, pointed at him and said to the darkness 'Who is that man?' I have always thought that was a funny story."

My cellphone vibrated. It was Ruth. I asked Mike if it was okay for me to take the call. He nodded.

"Guess who just talked to Siobhan?"

"I suppose that would be Ruth Jensen in that case. And how is Mrs.

Savage?"

"She seems pretty upbeat. She's thinking about marrying your Mr. Cortese."

"Careful. I'm in Mike's office and the phone is on speaker."

"Oh, thanks for telling me. Hi, Mike."

"Anyway, did she call you? Or did you call her?"

"She called me. I sent her my cellphone number in an email."

"So, she wants to marry Gabriele."

"She said he wants to marry her."

"She could do a lot worse."

"I told her I was doubtful about how well it would work out, with both of them having careers that were important to them."

"Is she thinking about coming back to New York?"

"She called me from an airplane on her way to JFK from London. Landing in about two hours."

"That's interesting. Mike and I were speculating on what her passport would say her name is."

"I asked her that. She said her passport says Dunleary, Siobhan Brianna. Dunleary spelling the usual American way, not the funny Gaelic way. And she said it does have a place on it where it says her professional name is Siobhan Reilly."

"Neither Mike nor I got it right, so the jackpot goes up for the next drawing."

"Are we going to have a chance to talk to her?"

Ruth said Siobhan was planning to stay in her husband's apartment.

"You mean Ned's apartment?"

"What she said was she would be staying in her husband's apartment. I'm fairly sure she meant she would be next door to the famous Hugo Miller, super-sleuth."

We agreed that Ruth should try to arrange a time later in the day for Siobhan and Ruth to come over for a drink or dinner or both. I knew I wouldn't feel like cooking, so I figured we could go to the fish restaurant near the ferry dock, a short walk from my building. I told her I thought it might be best not to include Gabriele in that plan.

After Ruth signed off, Mike held out his hand to me. I stood up and shook it. "You got these people falling all over you," he said. "Congrats."

Chapter Twenty

My doorbell rang about 5:30. It was Siobhan with a roll-aboard suitcase. "Sorry, just got here. If you don't mind, I'll take a quick shower and then stop over for that ginger ale Ruth mentioned." I held out my hand and we shook.

"See you when I see you then," I said to her.

I texted Ruth *The Eagle has landed. Drinks in about an hour. SYWISY*

That's what I said to her.

Ruth knocked on my door about 6:15. Kiss-kiss.

"No Siobhan?" she asked, peeking into the living room.

"Not yet, but I think sometime soon. How about I whet your whistle in the meantime?"

"You mean you feel like a drink if I'll hold onto one as well and swish it around a bit." She rolled her eyes. She was wearing tight jeans and a bold silk blouse that looked like it had to be Versace, big Roman coins in gold on a yellow background, black accents.

"I don't recall you staring at a drink and not partaking of it—ever," I said, handing her a dirty vodka with several smallish stuffed olives in it. I had one for myself, which I put on the coffee table then retrieved a bowl of salted roasted nuts from the pass-through and put that on the coffee table next to my drink. Ruth was sipping hers already.

"Oh," she said. "I jumped the gun. Cheers." She raised her glass to me. I took a sip of mine, although I had filled it too full and it splashed over the edge of the glass when I picked it up.

The doorbell rang.

Siobhan was wearing a dress and heels. Not cocktail-y. Simple navy empire-line with red piping. Her bronze-colored hair picked up the red in the dress. Not exactly stunning but a lot prettier than I had thought she would be. She wore real heels, not stilts, maybe three inches. I showed her into the living room. Ruth stood up and gestured with her drink, blew an air kiss. Siobhan sat in a Barcelona chair that was at a right angle to the couch, next to a Swedish teak table that had been one of three nesting tables when I bought them, but they were dispersed to different parts of the apartment so they were not a "set" any more.

"What can I get you to drink?"

"Whisky? Just kidding. Sparkling water or whatever doesn't have any alcohol in it."

"Scotch?"

She shook her head negatively. "Preggers, you know."

"Ice?"

She nodded.

"All I have is Canada Dry ginger ale. Not a taste treat."

Yes.

I grabbed a low-ball glass in a pattern reminiscent of every bistro in Paris—smaller than a tumbler, looking more like a normal cocktail glass. I threw a couple of crescent-shaped pieces of ice into the glass, filled it with the amber-colored soda and took it to her on a small silver tray with some pretzels on a paper napkin next to the glass.

"How pretty," she said. She smiled and seemed much more relaxed than she had the last time I had seen her in London.

"Love your dress," Ruth said. Siobhan smiled and mouthed "Thank you" soundlessly. "But I bet you'll be sorry you wore those shoes. Maybe you're not retaining water yet, but if you are, it'll be painful."

"Cheers" I said and raised my glass, as did they. We all took a sip. Siobhan frowned at the ginger ale, clearly wishing it had been scotch. Ruth was sitting between Siobhan and me, and I scooted the bowl of nuts over so that Siobhan could reach them if she wanted to.

I confess that I like vodka. I have been told over and over that it has no taste, but that's not true. The different vodkas are not as distinctive as different scotches or even different bourbons, but they are not the same. My house vodka is Tito because it's made in Texas. The bottle says "handmade."

"I need to ask you a question, Siobhan, if you don't mind."

She smiled and cocked her head slightly, indicating that she agreed.

"What's your name?"

She smiled broadly. "Good question," she answered. "The answer depends on who you are. If you are the immigration officers at the airport, my name is Siobhan Dunleary. If you are hiring an actress, it's Siobhan Reilly."

"Why two names?"

"Well, the original spelling of my last name is more complicated than the simplified version that is on my passport. We had to seek legal help to change the spelling from the Irish version, which even Brits can't pronounce, to the more phonetic version that I use now.

"Before my parents changed the spelling of their name, I adopted Reilly as a stage name because it was easier to pronounce than the Irish version of Dunleary. But Reilly is still Irish, and I didn't want to not have a name that didn't sound Irish. Sorry, that must have been full of double negatives. I wanted a name that sounded Irish."

"Gabriele told me that your name is Brianna."

"It is, in a way. It's my middle name, and it's what my family call me."

"And your family live in London?"

She nodded. "My father is Lord Dunleary. He's the younger son of a viscount. So my mother is Lady Dunleary. They changed the spelling during the IRA years when I was a child, but my birth certificate still had the Gaelic spelling."

"So, your grandfather is a peer?"

"He was a peer and sat in the House of Lords, yes, but he died quite a while back. My uncle, the current viscount, is a stock broker and has no part in the government. Seats for most peers in the House of Lords were abolished in 1999."

"I need to get one more thing out of the way. Sorry."

"All right."

"Mike di Saronno, whom you met—he's a detective in the NYPD—said the police forensic department found a marriage license in what they think was your name to marry a man named Jones a few years back. Is that you, or someone else?"

"Someone else, and this is not the first time I have heard about this. The person who took that license is named, apparently, Siobhan Reilly, which is a name I only use in acting, but both first and last names are common, so there are probably many girls by that name. Otherwise, I am Siobhan Dunleary in everything. The only time I have been married was to Ned. All my taxes and my passport are Siobhan Dunleary."

"Did Ned call you Brianna?"

She nodded.

I smiled. "Thank you for your patience. The police and their records were all confused by the name thing. Now I can straighten it out for Mike. "

She sat forward in the Barcelona chair, which takes an effort, since the chair is designed to make you relax.

"I believe I can trust you both," she said.

Ruth reached over and put her hand on Siobhan's hand. I smiled in a way that I thought would comfort her. Not sure it worked.

"Do you mind if I ask what your parents do?" I asked.

"They live in the country."

"Retired?"

"Not exactly. My father didn't have a job. He has spent a lot of his time putting together his version of the Wars of the Roses. Not finished yet, but when it's published, he thinks it will shake up historians. He has a very Irish outlook."

"Northern Irish, though, right?"

"He thinks of Ireland as one country, north and south."

"So, they're comfortable, as we would say here."

"They live in an old house that has been in the family for ages. The family name is taken from a town in Ireland, but the origins are Norman-English. Ireland was claimed by Henry II and his youngest son, John, was named Lord of Ireland, later became King John, probably one of the most unpopular monarchs in English history, like Richard III or George IV. Anyway, when John became Lord of Ireland, it was a signal for a land grab in what was called the Pale around Dublin. Dunlaoghaire is in the Pale, and somebody in the family who had an estate there five or six hundred years back switched out the name, which was formerly Talbot, for the name of the town. As far as I know, we have no close family in the Republic of Ireland."

"And at some point, they took sides with the English?"

Siobhan nodded. "I think it was about religion, and wanting to be in favor with the English king."

"So, you're C of E?"

"Yes, I am an Anglican in the Church of England."

"So am I," I said. "More or less. I'm Episcopalian. We're part of the Anglican Communion."

She smiled.

"According to his brother, Ned was Episcopalian."

She perked up at the question. "Ned?"

"Your husband?"

"I know who you meant. I was surprised because I don't really know what his religious persuasion was."

"Oh, I figured you probably got married in a church. Doesn't matter. I'm a member of St Mary the Virgin just off Times Square."

"Smoky Mary's?"

"Yes, it gets called that because of the incense."

"Nice church, nice rector. Very inclusive. But no, we didn't marry in the church."

"Do you mind if I ask where you married?"

"A friend of mine who is Unitarian married us. She has a very diverse congregation, very gay-friendly."

"In New York?"

"Yes, Upper West. But we were married in Madison Square. Outdoors."

"Nice," Ruth said. "I like weddings under the sky."

"It was nice, the way we wanted it. Just Janet, the minister who conducted the ceremony, Ned and me, and Lily, who acted as the witness. And some people who were curious about what was going on."

"No friends or family?"

She shook her head. "We wanted to get it done, not to plan some kind of a big wedding. We talked about it, and we both wanted to have a child, or maybe a couple of children."

"Did you exchange rings?"

"He bought me a gold band. I wore it for a couple of days." She reached into her handbag and produced a small plastic baggie. "Here," she said, putting it on her ring finger on the left hand. "This is what he gave me."

I saw that her glass was almost empty. "May I top off your drink a bit?"

She handed it to me, and I walked back into the kitchen to refill it with the dregs of the ginger ale bottle. I put the empty on the counter to remind myself to buy a new one. I heard Ruth ask Siobhan when the baby was due.

"June 21st," she answered. "The summer solstice."

"So, you would have been showing during *Twelfth Night*," I said, walking back in and placing the glass on the little silver tray. I had the bag of pretzels in my other hand and offered them to her. She declined.

"Well, maybe, but we were only planning on a six-week run, so I wouldn't have been obvious. At least I don't think I would have been obvious. I've never been pregnant before."

"Do you know the sex?"

She shook her head. "The test can be dangerous for the baby, and it doesn't make any difference to me whether it's a boy or a girl."

"Have you picked out names?" Ruth asked.

"Edward, if it's a boy. Annette if it's a girl. That would make him Ned or if it's a girl, she would be Nettie."

"So, you plan to name the baby after him. That's sweet."

"You're right to be thinking that we were an odd couple. After all, we're both gay, or we were both gay when we were both alive."

Ruth smiled.

"I never met Ned," I said. "I saw him the day he moved into the apartment, but never said hello or anything. Next thing I knew there was police tape all over."

Siobhan looked down and picked up the napkin that I had put the pretzels on. She blotted at her eyes.

"You were in love, weren't you?" Ruth asked.

"Maybe. If you had asked us in Madison Square about love, we would both have laughed. I realized I loved him after he was dead." She dabbed at her eyes again.

"Was he going to help you with a green card?" I asked.

She nodded. "He wanted me to be able to work in America. He wanted us to be a family."

"Do you think that would have worked?" I asked.

"Sure," she said. "No way to argue with that now."

"My friend, Gabriele, has a soft spot for you."

She smiled, looked at her left hand with the ring on it and made no response. Then she picked up the ginger ale and drained the glass. "That was for Ned," she said as she struggled to her feet.

Ruth and I both stood.

"I'll be next door if you need me. At least for a few days."

"Are you planning to keep the apartment?"

She shook her head. "Not sure. Little Ned or Little Nettie and I will want to live in a house with a yard. Maybe better if we can be close to Nanny and Grandad."

She said she would see herself out, but I followed her to the door to throw the latch when she left.

Chapter Twenty-one

I suggested to Mike that since we had a fairly good idea that Tony Anguilla was using marijuana for a medical condition, it might be a good idea to ask him again if he took any marijuana to Ned's apartment at any point, not just the day Ned died. Maybe a housewarming gift?

"It's legal, isn't it?" Tony responded to a direct question from Mike. As usual, he was nattily dressed when he responded to our request for another Q&A session the next day, with a suede sports jacket that looked expensive and an open-neck, button-down shirt over skinny jeans, looking a bit over-tight.

"There's no way you would get in trouble for giving a friend a small quantity of grass," Mike said.

"Because it's legal, right? You're taping this, right?"

"It's not illegal unless you have a large amount of it on your person, or if it appears that you are trying to sell it. And yes, we are taping this conversation."

"I have a prescription for it."

"I'm not asking you for any reason other than to find out where the tiny bits of marijuana we found on the couch and, during the autopsy, in his lungs came from."

"If it's legal, why does it matter?"

"The bits of marijuana—some of them, not all of them—had almost microscopic amounts on them of a fungus that is common on marijuana and hemp plants. Mr. Savage was very allergic to it, deathly allergic. We'd like to find out what dispensary it came from. And it would be helpful if we could find out how long it had been in his apartment before he inhaled some bits of it."

"So, if I say yes, you're not going to arrest me?"

"Like you said, it's legal, no reason to arrest you."

"Then yes," he said and shook his head like he thought he was doing the wrong thing.

"Do you know where you bought it?"

"Actually, I don't. I usually use a dispensary on 42nd street near 10th Avenue, but I had been in Boston and bought some there then put the two together in a jar in the kitchen where I keep it with a tight lid to make sure it doesn't dry out."

Mike pushed a yellow pad and pencil to Tony who wrote down the name and address of the New York dispensary where he had bought some marijuana. He didn't know the address of the place in Boston but thought he could find out if he called a friend there who had referred him to it.

"Did you take some from the jar to Ned Savage's apartment for the housewarming?"

He nodded. "In a baggie. You know, there are not very many secrets when you're working with actors. We all have things we'd prefer other people didn't know. Anyway, I have a reputation as a pot-head, to use a vulgar term."

"Do you know what type of marijuana you bought at the dispensary on 42nd Street? Like, did it have a name?"

He took the pad and wrote the name down. "I think that's it. Tell them I bought it and if that's not it, they'll know." He paused and looked directly at Mike. "Is this going to stay in this room?"

"No reason for it not to, unless for some reason you are asked to testify at a trial, but you would have plenty of notice before that happened."

"I was hoping it could be kept quiet."

"We're not going to tell anyone who doesn't need to know. Did you and Ned smoke some of it?"

He shook his head. "He wanted to smell it, so he opened the baggie and stuck his nose in. No idea what he did with the rest of it. It wasn't very much, maybe an ounce or two at the most."

"And you didn't take the container to his apartment?"

He said he hadn't taken the container. "I put it in a baggie that was self-sealing, so it would stay fresh. And I put some of the gummies in a separate baggie, because they're colorful. Made it look more like a gift."

"So, you still have the container?"

He nodded. "It has some grass in it now, stuff I bought at the place on 42nd Street."

"We'd like to let our forensic lab test it to see if it has any of the fungus that we are interested in."

Tony agreed and Mike asked a uniform cop to stop by Tony's apartment to pick it up.

"The officer will give you a receipt for the container and its contents. After the lab has a look, you'll probably get everything back, less a very small sample of what we're looking for. That's all we need," Mike said. "Didn't hurt much, did it?" He held his hand out and they shook. Tony left.

"I think maybe we should talk to Siobhan again," Mike said to me. "I wonder if she was there when Ned tried Tony's housewarming gift. Or Lily, or anyone else."

"We know he smoked some of it, right? There were traces of it in his lungs, I think you told me."

He nodded.

"Then why do we need to find someone who was there when he did it?"

"It would be good to know if he had any reaction to it." Mike was rubbing his chin as he spoke.

"My money's on Siobhan knowing more than anybody else. I never saw them together, but it sounds like they had some kind of love at first sight, or whatever." I texted Siobhan to see if she had time to talk to us. She came back quickly, saying she had to stay at home because she was waiting for a callback on an audition she had done. I told her we would meet her at her place and we'd be there in a half-hour.

Turned out the audition she told us about was for an off-off-Broadway production of *Waiting for Godot,* at a well-established repertory-style theater in Tribeca called Aux Puces, which is French for "at the fleas," as in a flea market, which is a *marché aux puces*. Not a bad credit to put on your resume in New York where a lot of well-known young actors would show up from time to time. Best of all, Aux Puces had a deal with Actors

Equity that allowed actors to use their own names on a program or marquee due to a waiver that was part of the theater's alliance with a downtown university which allowed participants to get university credit for their work. So you could have your cake and eat it too. But you still didn't get paid.

We met at her apartment, which is where Ned had lived—and died. We sat around the coffee table, Siobhan in an overstuffed wing chair, Mike and I on the couch. She had made some coffee, "American style," she told us.

It wasn't bad. I drink coffee black, no sugar. Mike loads his up with anything and everything that's available.

Mike told her about our talk with Tony but without naming him and asked if Siobhan had any knowledge about when the pot got smoked.

She had the same questions that Tony had about legality. We told her there were no laws preventing anyone from smoking marijuana or possessing it, as long as the amounts were small and it wasn't done on a public street or in a municipal or state building.

"I knew Ned had some grass. I saw it in a box on the counter over there," she said, pointing to the kitchen area of the one-room apartment. "He told me somebody gave it to him when we were here for the housewarming party. I thought it must have been Tony, because I know he was here—I saw him—and everybody at Westside Rep knew he smoked weed and ate those candies he carried around with him."

She had asked Lily to come over, because the older actress had been present when Ned tried the grass too. When she got to Ned's apartment just after we arrived, Lily was looking frumpier than she had at the precinct interview and was walking with a slight hunch forward, which emphasized her age and gawkiness. She was wearing a flamboyantly flowered silk or rayon dress that looked like a grandmother outfit, with some flesh-toned opaque stockings and low-heeled brown pumps.

"Well, he said he hadn't ever smoked anything before," Lily said. "I figured that was a bunch of bull, because I know he grew up in California, and he had studied acting in school. But it turned out he hadn't smoked anything."

"And how did you know that?" Mike asked.

"Well, I'll tell you. He didn't know how to inhale the smoke. Now when I grew up, everybody seemed to smoke cigarettes, indoors and outdoors, in closed cars while they were driving, in restaurants. Just not in movie theaters. And every kid tried cigarettes. You could buy them when you were sixteen, but I just stole a couple of my mother's Viceroys when I wanted to learn."

Mike asked her to tell us what happened.

She said that he had bought some cigarette papers but that he didn't know how to use them. He had also bought a glass pipe, and he had that antique hookah on top of a shoulder-high bookcase.

"I figured there was no way to get that hookah clean, and it would mean going through a big rigmarole to show him what to do, and anyway, a hookah is usually for hashish resin. So I opted for the pipe, since I wouldn't know how to roll a cigarette if my life depended on it."

She packed some of the marijuana into the bowl of the pipe and used a fireplace lighter that Ned produced to get it going. "I took a drag on it to make sure it was working and then gave it to him." She made a comic face and said, "Boom!"

"Boom?" I asked.

"He started to cough and sneeze at the same time and ran over to the kitchen counter and grabbed a glass, filled it with water, and tried to drink that. But he kept coughing and sneezing. I know how that is because ragweed does that to me sometimes. I wear a cloth mask when I go outside if the pollen count is high."

"Did it seem that he was having trouble breathing?" Mike asked.

Siobhan answered. "No, he was breathing between the coughs, and as he drank the whole glass of water, it started to calm down. Or he started to be able to hold down the coughs. Kept clearing his throat.

"Well, the short version is that he couldn't inhale the smoke without having a coughing fit, so he never managed to try the grass that Tony—it must have been Tony—gave him." She thought for a second, and added, "It's possible he got some of the smoke inhaled in spite of all the coughing and sneezing, I guess. But I doubt he ever tried it again."

"And is there any of it left?"

She shook her head.

"Somebody else smoked it?"

"No idea. I just never saw it again."

"Do you know if he ate any of the candies?"

"I didn't count them, but it didn't look like it. They were in a baggie on the counter, may still be in the cupboard above."

I stood up and walked over to the kitchen area and looked in the cupboards. Sure enough, there was a little baggie with some gummy candies in it. I held it up.

"Do you mind if we take this back to the station?" Mike asked. "I'll give you a receipt for it, and you can get it back at some point."

"I don't need it. Just take it," Siobhan said. "I'm going to clear this place out, I think, so the landlord can rent it to someone else."

"You know that Edgar, Ned's brother, and his two sisters were here in the apartment a few days after Ned passed?"

I told her I thought that they might have taken some of the photos that were in the apartment.

Mike nodded. "They could have taken the pot too, I guess."

"I think it was already gone before I left to go to England," she said then paused and looked up at the ceiling. "In fact, I'm sure it was gone before I left. I remember wondering where it was."

"But going back a bit, you don't ever recall Ned conducting any kind of rehearsals here or in the apartment where he lived on the West Side before he moved in here?"

"I don't think I was in his apartment on 8th Avenue more than a couple of times," she said. "No rehearsals either place, but when there were other actors there, we talked about roles and ideas we had. I said I'd like to play Olivia one day. I think that's why I was Olivia's understudy, which is kinda strange when you think about it, because I was to play Viola. But in showcase productions, they try to give us whatever kind of experience we're looking to have. I might have wanted to invite my agent to see me do Olivia, for instance."

"Who is your agent?" Mike asked.

"Actually, I don't have an agent in the US, although I have one in London. I could probably get an introduction when I need one, I guess. I was just saying that as an example of something that could be anything."

"Maybe somebody in the cast has an agent they like and they could refer you?" I said.

"I'd be happy to refer Siobhan, but my agent only handles characters and mostly mature people, actors who've been around the block a few times," Lily chimed in.

"Actually, Ned was going to introduce me to some agents," Siobhan said. "He never got around to it, and we really only knew each other for a short time, couple of months."

"I thought he was going to help with your green card."

"That he did. When I became Mrs. Savage, I moved close to the top of the list."

"And if you are the widow of an American husband and have his child, you'd be likely to get a green card right away, I'd guess," I said.

"I have an immigration lawyer working on it," she said. "Dad's mum was American too, so that helps."

"But you're sure the marijuana was gone when you left for England?" Mike asked.

She nodded. "I know he was tempted to use it for cooking. He said it smelled like it would be good in spaghetti sauce."

"Good thing Gabriele's not hearing you say that," I said, intending it as a joke.

"Actually, he knew. We were having dinner at his restaurant and Ned said something to him about wanting to make some pot sauce for spaghetti."

"What did he say?"

"I don't remember him saying anything, to tell you the truth."

Mike stood up and thanked Siobhan for letting us ask her these questions. He thanked Lily for her help too. Then he motioned to me and we left, going directly into my apartment next door.

"I don't know if all the coughing they were talking about was a sign of his allergy, but I'm guessing not, because he apparently didn't go into shock," Mike said.

"I'm a serial sneezer too. Once I sneeze, I'm gonna sneeze a bunch more times before it stops. Sneezing is pretty violent sometimes. I almost got punched one time for sneezing in a theater. The guy in front of me turned around and threatened me. I think sneezing comes from something irritating the back of my mouth, like tickling or something. Like a bug was crawling around inside me."

I never could smoke anything. Couldn't get to the place where I could inhale, and without inhaling, it was pointless, I guess. Tasted terrible, too, and I could smell it on my hand. As I remember it, my throat would just close up when I tried to inhale the smoke, made me feel a little like I was going to throw up, but then once I relaxed, everything was okay unless I tried it again. Basically, it was a lesson I learned pretty goddamn fast. No smoke, no gagging. Elementary, my dear Watson.

"But we still don't know who was there when Ned got whacked," he said to nobody in particular.

"I need to call Gabriele and Ruth," I told him.

"And I gotta get back to the station," he said. He stood up and I walked him to the front door.

Chapter Twenty-two

I texted Gabriele to call me. It wasn't two minutes before my phone rang.

"Hi Ri-Ri," I answered the phone when his ID came up on the screen. He hates that baby name, and I know he regrets telling me about it every time I say it. There are times when I can't help myself, and it just comes out.

"Ora di Pranzo, can I help you?"

"Hi Ora di Pranzo. Got a place for me at the end of the bar by the wall?"

"You wanna come here?"

"Or you can come here if you can get away. Mike and I just had a talk with Siobhan and Lily about some things regarding Ned Savage."

He said he'd be here in about an hour, or sooner if he didn't have to wait a long time on the platforms.

There are times when I wish I could be in love with Gabriele. It's not when he's at his most handsome, because, frankly, I'm intimidated by really beautiful people of either sex. When I was a lot younger, I worked for a famous actress; I remember it being said of her that she could stop a Navy battleship in the water with a smile and a wave. I was afraid of her, actively afraid. She was always nice to me. She was married to a football player I was handling some PR for a project of hers. She asked me to do some PR work for an exercise book that she was working on—she was going to release a video. I wondered why, because it seemed to me that she was in the newspaper or on television every day. It didn't last long. She's still a big star.

But when Gabriele shows his soft side, I want to hug him.

In the event, he was at my apartment about ten minutes ahead of when I was expecting him, in spite of the fact that the sky had opened up, replete with lightning and thunder. He had an umbrella, but I think he just walked between the raindrops, because he didn't look like he was wet at all, not even the bottom hem of his pants legs. I had opened a bottle of *nero d'avola* and put two bistro glasses on the coffee table with the bottle on a silver wine tray.

He was looking like he hadn't slept well but had a big smile on his face, even with crow's feet around his eyes. He hugged me and held on for a couple of Mississippis.

"I miss you," I blurted out without thinking. Then I could feel myself start to blush.

"I always miss you," he said. "Because I want to live with you and see you in the morning and when I go to sleep."

"But you still get annoyed when I call you by that baby name."

"No, I never annoyed with you." He picked up one of the bistro glasses and pointed to the bottle of wine with a questioning look on his face.

I nodded.

He poured a glass for me and then one for himself. We clinked and each took a gulp of the dirty, tobacco-y dark red wine from Sicily. One of my favorites, even if it is a "hamburger wine" for most people. I have often thought I would like to have a blind tasting of eight or ten *nero d'avola* bottles against a bottle of some hoity-toity super-Tuscan.

He reached over to me and put his finger on my nose then stepped closer to me with his finger on my nose and kissed me on the mouth.

"I wasn't..." I started to say.

"I know, sometimes I do it," he said. "Like you call me Ri-Ri sometimes."

Tit for tat, only he thinks it annoys me when he kisses me. Ha!

"I wanted to tell you what we learned about Ned when we met with Siobhan and Lily a few hours ago."

He folded his arms and said nothing.

"First of all, we spoke to one of the cast members who said he gave Ned some marijuana and some marijuana candy when he moved into his new apartment."

He nodded and picked up his wine for a sip, but he didn't put it back down.

"You know that the Medical Examiner found traces of marijuana and traces of marijuana smoke in Ned's body. He died so quickly that it was still mostly in his lungs, but there was some in his blood too.

"As we were told, the person who gave him the marijuana was not there when he smoked it, but Siobhan and Lily were. It was after the party he had for the cast of the play, but I don't know exactly when it was. He didn't know how to smoke it. He thought he had to make it into a cigarette."

No reaction.

"He also told Siobhan and Lily that he thought it smelled good enough to put in red sauce for pasta, with basil and oregano."

He made a sour face.

"They told me he said that to you too."

He nodded. "At Ora di Pranzo. I not tell Dante that."

"Anyway, Ned had bought a glass pipe and they tried to show him how to smoke the marijuana, but he couldn't learn to inhale the smoke. They said he started to cough and sneeze a lot when he tried to do it."

"Sneeze?"

"*Starnuto.*"

He nodded.

"Anyway, according to what Siobhan and Lily told us, he never did smoke any of it."

"Why this *importante*?"

"Well, we know he was allergic to the fungus that was probably on the marijuana leaves. He for sure was having a potentially fatal allergic attack from the fungus when he died. When somebody hit him in the head. But we don't know how the marijuana got into his lungs. He didn't have an allergic attack when he tried to smoke it, and Mike said that's not surprising because the heat probably turned the fungus into ash, and he probably didn't react to the ash."

"Maybe eat it?"

"Well, it was in his lungs."

"Why you telling me this, ask me come over here to talk?"

"The point is, Siobhan is going to clean out Ned's apartment and move back to England."

"I ask her to marry me."

"I know that. I wanted you to know that she is going back to England. She also said that her lawyer told her that because she was married to Ned and is pregnant, she'll get the green card she wanted."

He nodded.

"I don't understand. I thought you would be sad."

"I sad because Ned is kill. I sad because I wanted be father for Ned baby."

"Not because you love Siobhan?"

"Brianna," he corrected me.

"Okay, Brianna. I thought you wanted to be married to Brianna."

"I want be father for *bambino*."

"Do you love Brianna?"

"I love you, not Brianna, but cannot be father for your children. They older than me maybe."

He gulped down the rest of the wine and stood up, put both his arms out to me. I stood up and put my arms around his shoulders. "I was very sad that you were going to marry Brianna."

He smiled. "I know. Is good you sad. Make me know how much you love me."

"You know, we could get married. You and me," I said.

"You want that?"

I told him I didn't know. "But I want you to be in my life always, as long as I am alive."

"You want have sex with me?"

I shook my head.

He smiled. "Is okay. I like live in Brooklyn Heights. I like be with you here too. Maybe marry not so good. We should not be married. Not with us, not with other person."

I drank down the rest of my wine. He poured two more glasses. "Is good wine."

He lifted his glass to me and said "*Cin-cin.*"

I echoed him and we drank, but just a swallow. I didn't want to have an alcohol rush from chugging red wine in the afternoon.

"Now we talk about something else," he said. "How 'bout dem Yankees?" he said with a charming Italian lilt to it.

"That's a quote from a play," I said. "It's called *The Boys in the Band*."

"We boys in the band, is why I say that. I love you, Ugo. I be here with you all you life. I wipe you mouth when you old, and I help you walk when you want lean on me."

"I already lean on you, just not for help walking. For other things. I think you should feel free to marry someone if you want to. Maybe not Brianna, because she doesn't want to marry anyone, and I don't want you to be unhappy."

"Very happy now."

Chapter Twenty-three

I called Ruth and ran through the meetings with Tony and then with Siobhan and Lily.

"So, you think he probably inhaled the lethal bit of marijuana straight out of the baggie?"

"I hadn't got far enough to have said it that way, but it makes sense." I thought to myself, *That's what Mike took away from the conversations.*

"He did say he thought the marijuana smelled good enough to put it in spaghetti sauce."

"I don't know where he gets that. Smells kinda stale to me, and kinda bitter or something like that."

"I've put odd things in my cooking sometimes. If anyone had asked me twenty years ago if I would use fennel to start my red sauce, I would have thought they were crazy. I don't associate any smell with marijuana except that kinda pungent herbal smell in the smoke.

"She's going to clean out the apartment next to me and hand it back to the landlord," I told her.

"Good for her. She should go back to her mother if she's going to have a baby with no husband around."

"I don't get the impression that she's very close to her parents, the way she talks about them."

"She tell you scary stories about them?"

"No, she just talks about them like characters in a movie."

"I should get in touch with her and see if I can help her get things in order, maybe call somebody to pick things up and take them to storage if she wants to keep them. And you never know what I might stumble across with her there."

What kept going through my mind after I briefed Ruth was who could have been there when he was sniffing marijuana and then smashed him in the head when he was already dying. Also, I found myself wondering where the $50,000 from Omar Ortigan ended up.

He had told Gabriele about his cooking insight about marijuana in red sauce, and Gabriele rejected it immediately. If he was looking for an Italian who was interested in marijuana, I wondered if he had got back in touch with Tony Anguilla. I didn't know for sure if he was Italian, but he sure looked Italian, and his name is Tony, after all.

You know what FIAT stands for? "Fix It Again Tony." Sorry.

I had a telephone number for Tony, and the area code was 917, which is entirely cellphones, as far as I know. No landlines in area 917.

I sent him a text: *Did Ned ever talk to you about cooking with marijuana*

Cooking?

He thot it wd B gd 4 red sauce

Make red sauce, put MJ in, then make him eat it

Not practical he's dead

Never said gd 4 cooking

OK all I wanted to know

One down. Oh, maybe Mike, but Ned never met Mike. Frank has a made-up Italian name but he's Chicano, or some combination of Hispanic, Native American and European. Dead end. Siobhan may be a lot of things, but Italian she's not. Same for Lily.

Everybody knows that marijuana is good in brownies, so it's not unheard-of to bake with it. Who was it that published a recipe for brownies with cannabis? I think it was Alice B Toklas, Gertrude Stein's partner.

I considered asking Twitter if anyone had cooked spaghetti sauce with marijuana but thought better of it, because once you put something on social media, it never gets deleted. It'll be there as long as there are server farms. So, I did a search on Google instead of putting my name out there on the subject. I never knew Ned Savage, but from what I have learned about him, I have no reason to ignore his idea that marijuana would work in red sauce.

Not surprisingly, given how much marijuana is in the news, there were hundreds of thousands of hits on Google, maybe millions. A lot of them wanted the marijuana to be soaked for a couple of days in olive oil, and that became the basis for the otherwise simple red sauce. A large number included something called Cannabutter, which must have to be made separately, so I excluded those and the ones that asked for brand names of anything. But there were a lot that used chopped marijuana in an otherwise traditional sauce simmered for hours on a low flame. One used the following ingredients:

tomato paste
crushed tomatoes
olive oil or use cannabis-infused oil
onion
other vegetables (carrot, fennel, bell peppers, celery, et al)
chopped marijuana
pepper
garlic
bay leaf
oregano
rosemary
salt
black olives
mushrooms

In my experience, the amounts and proportions are at the discretion of the chef. I always use way more garlic than any recipe calls for. I always use bay leaf too and frequently add rosemary to the oregano. A chef I knew in years gone by told me to put a cheese rind in the sauce while it's simmering, then fish it out before you spoon it onto the pasta. I'm not a big fan of black olives in sauce, and since I'm allergic to mushrooms, they're a no-go for me. I may give this a try if somebody gives me a baggie of marijuana for Christmas (I doubt I will go shopping in a dispensary in Manhattan). And if you want to fly, I guess you power up the amount of marijuana. I wonder if you sprinkle red-hots over the sauce or if you stick with the traditional grated cheese.

But of course that doesn't tell us what happened to the baggie of marijuana that Tony had left with Ned as a housewarming gift.

I knew that Edgar and his sisters had taken most of Ned's personal effects when they were in New York while Ruth, Gabriele and I were in London and Istanbul. I texted him and asked him if they had Ned's cellphone.

Yes, have cellphone, but no sim card
Are there any photos?
Hundreds
Anything that looks like it might be a party at Ned's apt?
I think so, but I'll have to look, and phone needs charged
But you looked through it before and you recall some possible party pics
Not so much me, but Liz
Do you have a charger
Yes
If you plug it in, does the power stay where it is if you turn it on
Try plug it in and see if you can scan through the photos
OK

A few minutes passed, then my phone made a ding sound.

OK, I can scan through them
Tell me if there are party photos
OK

A few more minutes, then another ding.

Yes, photos of party. I see Ned, must be selfies or someone else taking pics
How many pics
Maybe 20 or 25, some blurry
Can you transfer them to your phone and then send them to my email?
I think so, but it'll take a while.
The old phone should be able to access WiFi if you have it in your home
But you'll have to send them from your phone if no sim in Ned's

He signed off and said he'd go to work on trying to send me the photos.

I texted Mike and told him that Edgar, or his sister, found some photos of the party at Ned's apartment on Ned's cellphone.

He texted back: *LMK if he can find photos that he can send us*
Maybe we can see who was there
Might help

My phone rang. It was Edgar.

"Hey, I'm gonna send you several packets of photos, because I don't want to clog up my send or your receive," he said. "There are some with clear faces, but some with mostly backs of heads. Up to you. You've probably met some of these people if they're cast members of *Twelfth Night*."

I told him I was ready to receive and asked him to copy Mike di Saronno on his NYPD email. He agreed and wanted to check that he had the right email for Mike. I said it was the one on the business card Mike had given him.

It took a while for all the photos to arrive at my computer, about two photos to a packet. All told there were twenty-four packets, so probably close to forty or more photos. I saved them and then made them into a photo album with the name "Ned's party."

Once they were all in one place, I scanned through them quickly. I recognized the people I knew well. Some of the rest of the faces looked familiar, maybe people who were at the rehearsal we went to at St Benedict's. Like cellphone photos always are, some images were clearer than others, and some were blurry as some subjects moved while others stayed still.

I forwarded the album to Ruth, because I knew she would recognize more people than I would, or than Mike would, since he had never been to a rehearsal as far as I knew. He had probably only met the three actors he interviewed in the precinct.

When my phone buzzed, Mike's ID appeared on the screen. I picked up.

"Hey, Mike."

"G'morning, Hugo. Just wanted you to know we're running facial rec searches on the photos from Mr. Savage's cellphone."

"I thought that was just used when you were looking for terrorists."

He explained that checking drivers and subway riders against a database of potential terrorists is one application of facial recognition—one that the NYPD is most forthcoming about sometimes because of the public interest in preventing terrorism. "But we can use any database of photos when we're just trying to identify somebody. In this case, we're using the DMV database; people who've had photos made for driving licenses. It's a large base, but of course it's only people with New York licenses, not New Jersey or Connecticut or Pennsylvania. We can get permission to use those if we don't come up with anything here," he said. "A lot of young people in the city don't bother with driving licenses, because they don't need cars."

"How long does it take?"

"It's pretty speedy, considering the size of the database we're programming it to use."

"The DMV data base must be a big one."

"Millions of licenses active in New York State, so it normally takes several hours to scan a face, unless the system finds a perfect match sooner than that. A small percentage of people have more than one license, like a taxi driver, who has a commercial license and a standard license. And in this case, most of the photos we're feeding in have several people in them. The system scans them one face at a time. It will ignore any duplicates, people who are in more than one photo, but I'll guess it'll take the better part of today to give us any information. We'll also run the photos against mugshots from arrests, but that database is much smaller."

There was a ding and a banner appeared at the top of the screen that a text from Ruth was waiting to be viewed. I checked.

Not much help on photos

No worries, talking to Mike about face rec

Later

Well, it was better than nothing. Lucky the cellphone would power up enough to share the photos in the gallery.

I checked on the West Side Rep website to see what was coming up. I wondered if any of the same actors would be working with them even after *Twelfth Night* had been cancelled a couple of weeks before. Surprisingly, there was a notice that there would be another production of

Twelfth Night, this one directed by Lily Rasmussen. It would not be played at St Benedict's, where the next play was a Molière piece about a scam artist named Tartuffe. It would be at a small theater in Greenwich Village that was built inside an old empty gymnasium that was owned by NYU. Appropriately enough, it was called The Gym.

It would be easy to cast, I thought. *Lots of actors have studied it.*

There were no casting details about *Twelfth Night*, but there was a notice that the production was based on concepts of the late Edward Savage, who had made a donation to West Side Rep of $50,000 for a production of *Twelfth Night*, which would be performed at The Gym.

I sent a link to the *Twelfth Night* announcement to Mike, Ruth and Gabriele with a note that the Ortigan check was accounted for now. I wondered why it wasn't mentioned earlier, when Ned was still alive. As an afterthought, I sent the same link to Edgar Savage.

Edgar responded almost immediately, even though it was early in California: *I wonder who did that*

I figured you must know about this

News to me

I thought you were handling his books

Not me. His wife.

Siobhan. She was the one who sent that big check to West Side Rep. I wondered if she was still planning to play Viola. Impulsively I sent the link to Siobhan.

A few minutes later my doorbell rang. It was Siobhan, dressed in shorts and a baggy t-shirt, with a Hawaiian-looking kimono that wasn't fastened in the front.

"May I come in?"

"Of course. Coffee?"

"A glass of tap water, no ice, if you don't mind."

I put a bowl of tangerines on the coffee table, took one out and peeled it. She followed suit.

"You were surprised that the money went to West Side Rep?"

"I was surprised that there was going to be a production of *Twelfth Night* at all. I figured when I read that, it must have been you or Edgar."

"It was me."

"Edgar sent me a text and told me it wasn't him."

She pulled a segment from the tangerine and ate it. "Ned had put the money into an educational trust for the baby. I thought it was better to put it into something that Ned was working on instead."

"That's a lot of money."

She shrugged and ate two more segments of the tangerine.

"Will you be playing Viola in the new production?"

She shook her head decisively.

"You don't need money, do you?"

She shook her head. "I'm not rich, but I have enough to get by, and one day I'll get the country house."

"Most Brits want to live in the country," I said, as though I knew.

"Not this Brit. If they leave the house to me, I'll put it up for sale. Or maybe give it to the National Trust if nobody else wants it. I want to be a cliff-dweller. Worst case I live in a one-story house near some good restaurants and a wine store."

"And you'd be Lady Savage then."

"If people ever call me Lady Anything, you'll know somebody is impersonating me, or I'm being held for ransom someplace."

"Why did you marry Ned?" I should have added an apology for asking, but I didn't.

"The standard reason. I loved him."

"I thought you were both gay."

She looked at me and pursed her lips. "Obviously not gay all the time." She patted her stomach. "And gay doesn't prevent anyone from falling in love, even with the opposite sex."

I thought about Gabriele, who clearly had a fathering gene in his DNA.

"My friend, Gabriele, would have liked to be a stepfather to the baby."

"He'd be a good parent, but I would not be a good wife and it would be a mistake."

"Were you a good wife to Ned?"

She nodded. "But we were only married for a few weeks, less than the run of *Twelfth Night* that we were preparing for."

"You didn't need a green card either, did you?"

She shook her head. "I'd already been notified that I had been accepted as a permanent resident before Ned and I married."

Obviously the truth was doled out on a need-to-know basis.

"So you have a green card?"

"I'm still on a six-month visa at the moment. They told me the green card will come in the mail. That's why I've been staying in the apartment, because that's the address they have."

I broke my tangerine into quarters, and ate it that way, tasting the sweet-sour juice as it squirted into my mouth. I had a glass of *montepulciano d'abruzzi* that balanced it perfectly. Dry vs savory.

I reached out to her. "Nice to meet you, Siobhan."

She smiled demurely.

I told her I had been looking for recipes for spaghetti sauce with marijuana.

She smiled with real amusement. "You and Ned. What is that about?"

"I was talking to Tony Anguilla, who I presume was the source of the grass Ned inhaled. He's Italian, and he found the idea repulsive."

"It didn't sound great to me either," she said. "But I grew up with English food, so anything with a lot of taste is foreign or worse."

"I'm glad we're neighbors," I said.

She stood up and said, smiling, that she would probably be leaving after her green card came in the mail, but she hoped we could stay in touch. She said she'd find her own way out.

I walked to the door with her anyway and threw the latch after she left. I always think it sounds ominous when I do that after someone leaves. They can hear it clearly. Oh well.

Chapter Twenty-four

Mike said the facial rec process yielded a list of the actors and stage hands from the first—now cancelled—production of *Twelfth Night*.

"Not one person who wasn't affiliated with West Side Rep," he said. "That's not true. There were some who appeared to be significant others of actors and others who were at that point with the West Side Rep play. Pictures swapping spit, for instance."

"Do we know if any of them are in the new production at The Gym?"

"Why would that matter?"

"Maybe it wouldn't, but it could make them easier to talk to."

"Have at it then."

I texted Ruth and Gabriele to see if they were available for a short field trip to the Village to see the new theater where West Side Rep would be picking up the pieces of *Twelfth Night*. After a short back-and-forth, we agreed to meet at the Arch in Washington Square at ten the next morning.

I've always been a theater fan, since my parents took me to see my first musical when we were visiting my grandparents in Westchester County. We were living near Galveston where my dad was working for a chemical company, and we drove to where my grandparents lived near Bronxville from Texas. It took several days, and we stayed in what they used to call "tourist homes." They disappeared for a long time, but they're back again with a couple of different names; some are called bed-and-breakfast rooms and some are called room-sharing. Either way, you can find them and reserve them online now. But when I was a kid, you just stopped when there was a house that looked neat and clean with a sign that said Tourist Home.

Anyway, I kept all my program booklets from the time I was little. I never put them in any kind of order, just pitched them in a box next to one of the bookcases. Still do the same now, only my first wife destroyed all the really old ones—out of spite. She put them in the bathtub and turned the water on.

Point being, I knew I had been to The Gym before, and I thought it was to see a production of *Macbeth*, which is another play I have a fondness for. Very showy piece for the actors, and basically a revenge drama, full of blood and guts, screams and torture. I think it was only written about five years or so after *Twelfth Night*, but there was a deep, dark sea of difference between them. *Twelfth Night* was written for a relatively sophisticated Elizabethan audience who could appreciate a silly rom-com. *Macbeth* was written for a rowdier audience after the Scottish king, James VI, was crowned King of England due to his descent from Henry VII. The rough-and-tumble Scots wanted ghoulish special effects and lots of murderous action on stage. Hard to believe they were written by the same playwright. I guess that's one reason why some people think the plays were not all written by the same guy.

I found the program, which was from about 2002. There were no names that were famous then or now and none that were even slightly familiar to me as I read back through the cast. Some of the names seemed like people I had seen someplace, but there were no photos, so it was hard to tell if I actually had seen them or not. No picture of the theater either.

I went online and found a website for The Gym, which, no surprise, looked like a school building from the outside. The gallery of photos showed the interior, which was a theater-in-the-round layout with audience on all sides of the stage so that actors would have to make their entrances and exits using the aisles. I sent the link to Ruth and Gabriele.

The Village was where the beatniks were when there were beatniks. There and in San Francisco, I guess. Now the Village is basically a historical name for an area that is almost entirely owned by NYU. Lots of historic row houses, carriage houses, and the spectacular triumphal arch in Washington Square. Camera heaven, but most of those houses (or maybe all of them) are now student housing, or maybe even classrooms. I used to wander around the streets wondering which house Henry James had in mind when he wrote *Washington Square,* his scary novel of a wealthy woman's vengeance against a suitor who left her in the lurch. That novel was a poster child for the idea that "revenge is best served cold."

But now the Village has neither aristocrats nor beatniks. It almost has no jazz clubs left either, because most of them have closed over the years. Popular music has taken several sharp left turns from the cool days of smooth jazz with Miles Davis and Thelonious Monk or the African "click" songs of Miriam Makeba, who disappeared from the Village after she married the leader of the Black Panthers, Stokely Carmichael, and moved to West Africa to escape American hostility for her husband.

I walked up the street that night and had dinner at a fish place whose primary virtue was quantity. Ever since I was a kid in Galveston, I have had a taste for fried shrimp, and this place had a platter of fried shrimp that even I couldn't finish, with a big lettuce-and-tomato salad with that orange dressing that my mother called French dressing; mostly mayonnaise, I think. I seldom eat out alone unless I eat at the bar in a restaurant with a friendly bartender. That night I sat at a table and played with my cellphone while I gorged myself on large, crispy-fried shrimp that probably had almost no real food value inside the delicious golden batter that hid the animals I was consuming from view. And a spicy red horseradish sauce to dip them in. Heaven.

I woke up early the next morning and turned on the television to a stock-market channel for some reason. I find it interesting that the stock market has enough going on to fill the time all day at a news channel that millions of people watch every day. When I was in the PR business, each time I was in a CEO's or CFO's office, it seemed, people were watching this same channel.

There is something hypnotic about television. It's hard to turn it off once you turn it on. So, I drank my coffee and stared at the screen with its electronic tickertape running across the bottom below the handsome anchors, who never stopped talking or interviewing people I'd never heard of.

Although I had been up at the crack of dawn, when I got to Washington Square, both Ruth and Gabriele were waiting impatiently next to the Arch.

"Sorry guys," I told them. "I don't know what happened. I was up early and all of a sudden it was ten o'clock and I was still on the subway."

"I called West Side Rep," Ruth said. "They told me the cast and crew would be expecting us."

Gabriele looked anxious. I asked him what was wrong. He said nothing was wrong and pasted on a smile.

When we got to The Gym, there was indeed a rehearsal in process. There were some surprises, like Malvolio now being played by Gianfranco Mirabella, where the hallmark of the previous production-in-process was that Lily Rasmussen would be playing Malvolio—and playing him for laughs. Lily, who was designated as the director, was on the cast list as Maria, a second-banana role who tags around with Sir Toby Belch and Sir Andrew Aguecheek, both of whom are continuously drunk throughout the play.

Lily was seated in the middle of the auditorium, and the rehearsal was being videotaped by a videographer with a hand-held camera with sound supplied by three microphones hanging over the stage.

We took seats in the top part of the auditorium, which was no more than about twenty rows back. It's a small theater. The actors paused as we sat down, and Lily turned around to see what was happening. She waved at us then turned around to the stage and told the cast and crew to pick it up from the top. It was the last act of the play, which is short and only has one scene in it. It contains virtually the entire denouement as the confused and disguised characters come clean and most of them realize what fools they've been.

The iffiest moment in the play is when Malvolio is cruelly punished for being a fool and embarrassing his mistress, Olivia, who has certainly been equally the fool, falling in love with a girl dressed up as a boy while the object of her affection falls in love with Orsino, who had been pursuing Olivia. If it's played for laughs, it works. If it's played straight, it puts a sour note in the play. I guess both ways are common, though I'd prefer to leave the theater laughing instead of wondering what would become of poor Malvolio. No matter what you think of him, you wouldn't want to sit next to him on a subway.

For my money, the funniest moment in the play is when it begins to dawn on Olivia that the man she considers her husband, Cesario, is a woman. Viola, who has been masquerading as Cesario, is reunited with her brother, Sebastian, whom she thought had been drowned in a huge thunderstorm at sea just before the play started. It may sound hard to believe, but it is actually a hilarious scene.

The pivotal role of Malvolio was being tossed off easily by Frank, who had, after all, told us he'd played Malvolio a lot of times in the past. And, true to the interview at the precinct, he was wearing a ridiculously large broadsword under his belt with no scabbard and nearly tripped over it every time he took a step, a bit like a child dressed up for Halloween. He loaded Malvolio's last speech with hiccups, tics, and twitches that made me smile but did not obliterate his righteous (and pitiful) accusation of Olivia for wronging him. He left the stage a fool, but a fool with some degree of dignity remaining even after his humiliation and his ridiculous outfit.

So the biggest fool (Malvolio) and the official fool (Feste is Olivia's jester) have the last words in the play.

Lily told Feste to skip the closing song for the rehearsal, but reminded the entire cast that they each have a musical instrument and that they have to accompany Feste's songs.

Lily preached to the choir, "Remember, half the audience already knows that song, and it's our curtain. You like applause? They'll forgive us anything if we give them a good closer. Take a half-hour, we're back on stage at eleven o'clock."

As the stage vacated, one of the doors to the auditorium opened. It was Siobhan, who made a beeline for Lily, but spotted us and waved with a smile. I couldn't make out what they were talking about, but clearly they were having a disagreement—maybe not an out-and-out argument, but not a light breeze in the spring either. Siobhan pointed to Lily and to herself with both hands on her chest, looking defiant.

Both women realized at the same time that they had an audience and turned to us with a smile. They hugged and Siobhan walked back up the aisle to the row we were sitting in and sidled in and sat down next to Ruth, who was closest to the aisle.

In the way of actors, she kiss-kissed Ruth, then waved to Gabriele and me and blew air kisses to us.

"What was all that about?" Ruth asked. We all had the same question on the tips of our tongues.

"I told her she ought to be playing Malvolio, like Ned intended."

"Oh," I said. "I would've guessed you were saying something about yourself."

"I was, more or less. I told her that I had arranged for the gift from Ned's estate to pay for the production, and that one of the main reasons I did that was to see how well Ned's ideas would play on the stage." She paused and took a breath. "She said she couldn't play Malvolio and also direct the play; it was just too much."

Ruth wrinkled her brow a bit and smiled. "And you said?"

"I said I would direct if it would help."

"And she said?"

"She wondered what she was going to do with Frank."

"I told her she didn't have to play all the performances but enough to work the kinks out and show us what Ned was thinking when he cast everyone."

"But he cast you as Viola, my dear, and I didn't see you up there rehearsing."

"Viola has to be able to persuade all and sundry that she is a boy. That would be difficult with a baby bump showing, which mine will be by the time this show opens."

"Baby bump?" Gabriele asked, looking puzzled.

She made a gesture with both hands that indicated a swollen belly.

"This is bump?"

"It's just what they call it in the newspapers when somebody is going to have a baby."

He shook his head and shrugged.

"Why don't you play Olivia then? You were understudying Olivia, as I recall," Ruth asked slyly.

"The cast has a good Olivia, and it's time for me to watch now. The play is what we have from Ned now, not much else."

"Also baby?" Gabriele said.

She smiled and nodded. "I was planning to go back to England for a while. Little Miss or Little Mister will be a dual citizen no matter what, but I'd prefer to be someplace where my own mother can spend time with me when the curtain goes up on the next chapter."

"And I suppose it's free for you in the UK, with the National Health and whatnot."

"The doctoring part is paid for by the National Health but not some of the things that my mum and I have in mind. I intend to have the baby at Seymont Place, not in a hospital."

"And Seymont Place is a what?" I asked.

"It's where my parents live. Bucks."

"Bucks?" Gabriele asked.

"Buckinghamshire, west of London. It's not far from Aylesbury, if you know where that is," she said to all of us.

I tried to summon up a map of southern England in my head. "South of Oxford then?"

She nodded.

"Is it old? The house, I mean." Ruth asked.

"Not in England it's not. In the United States it would probably be landmarked already. It's from around 1780. Not a distinguished house, no famous people except a couple of lady authors in the nineteenth century and a Bloomsbury hanger-on in the twenties."

"I bet you're being modest," Ruth said. "Georgian?"

She nodded. "And there would always be a bedroom for each of you if you wanted to come and visit."

"I thought you said it was a small place."

Siobhan explained that by modern standards it wasn't small. "Houses served a different purpose in the eighteenth century than they do now. You had a staff to clean and cook, and many of them lived in the house with you. And when people came to visit, they stayed for a while—sometimes weeks. Houses couldn't be a cozy three bedrooms and two baths like they are today. But even with all the modern appliances, Mum and Dad still have two maids most of the time, just to keep the dust from settling all over everything. Too much effort for me, but it's home, and it's where I want to have the baby."

"What is there to do at Seymont Place?" I asked, intending to make harmless conversation. I asked it to bring Gabriele into the conversation, although he studiously stared at his smartphone, tapping on it.

"Not much. Clayshooting, riding, hiking in the woods."

"Clayshooting would be what we call skeet shooting?" I guessed. No sign of interest from Gabriele. I nudged him. He shifted to the other side of his chair. *Whatever*, I thought.

"Clay pigeons?" she answered.

I nodded.

"Then yes. And the old blunderbusses there have a kick that will leave a big purple welt on your shoulder if you're new to shooting. Most people bring their own, but to own a gun in the UK, it has to be a long gun, what you would call a rifle or a shotgun, and you must have a license. Handguns are strictly illegal."

"So, how did you resolve things with Lily?" Ruth asked, though she was looking at me as she asked it.

"I think she's going to try to figure out how to move back into playing Malvolio and what to do with Frank, who I would guess will revert to Sir Toby, like Ned had him, but Tony Anguilla isn't in the cast, even though he would be a great Orsino or Sir Toby, who is much more a center of attention and constantly wobbly drunk. Unlike most of the other actors, she'll be able to use her name on the marquee and in the program, because I told her we would pay her Equity scale for the run."

"Eight performances a week?" Ruth asked. "That'll come to a pretty penny."

"Thursday through Sunday with a matinee on Saturday, so five performances a week," she said.

"And who's going to direct?"

"*Moi*," she said. "To tell the truth, if Lily stays the director, she'll alienate everyone in the cast before opening night is even close. A bunch of them have been calling me."

"Have you ever directed something like this?" Ruth asked.

She said she had attended the Royal Academy of Dramatic Arts and had directed several productions, including one of *Into the Woods* in a theater in Islington. Not far from the British Library, she said. "But if you're asking if I have directed a Shakespeare comedy, the answer is no, I have not."

"I wonder if she's going to tuck that huge broadsword under her belt like Frank did," I said.

"Well, at least it won't drag on the ground if Lily's wearing it," Siobhan deadpanned. "Frankly, I love the sword. It's what you call *schtick*, but it works with the character, and it will get laughs, even in Act Five."

Gabriele smiled as Siobhan talked and the tension disappeared from his face and body. I relaxed because he looked like he was relaxing.

Chapter Twenty-five

We were sitting all the way in the back of the auditorium, in the last row, and were trying to decide what to do next. I was in favor of calling Edgar and seeing if he had come up with any ideas. Ruth wanted to watch some more of the rehearsal and see if there was anyone who looked like he or she could have bonked Ned on the noggin and ended his life. Gabriele wanted to eat something. Ruth pulled a couple of packets of saltine crackers out of her handbag and gave them to him. To my surprise, he opened them and ate them. Shades of my mother—always with something in her handbag to keep me busy.

Then Lily appeared on stage with what appeared to be the same broadsword that Frank had been wearing in the earlier rehearsal. She moved like she was doing a rehearsal for a Noh play or a pantomime, posing this way and that way with the sword, and changing positions slowly, like a *tai chi* workout, from one pose to the next. It looked like she had choreographed it.

Ruth waved and Lily saw her. She straightened up and laughed. "Errol Flynn I ain't," she said, "but Errol Flynn would have been a boring Malvolio, so maybe I can outdo him yet." She put the sword on a table that was on the side of the set, where actors who weren't working could watch the proceedings.

"How heavy is it?" Ruth shouted, meaning the sword.

Ruth pointed at the sword with a questioning look.

Ruth nodded.

Lily picked it up and walked up the aisle with it, handed it to Ruth.

"Oh, it's not anything like as heavy as it looks," she said and held it up in the air in a victory stance. Her arm didn't wobble at all.

Joseph Allen

"Surprise, this is the theater. That sword is light because it's a prop. It's not a weapon. If it was a weapon, it would weight thirty or forty pounds, I bet."

"What are you going to do with it?"

"Well, Frank was onto something with this. I thought Malvolio would want to have a sword because it would mean he was a gentleman. But he's not a gentleman, he's a fool, and Frank knew how to slash around with that sword and make him look like a fool pretending to be a gentleman. I have to figure out how to get the same effect with my Ichabod Crane, cross-dressed body. It's all about laughs."

Ruth said it felt like balsa wood with some thin piece of metal or a dull-finish foil to make it look like steel. "It's for knighting," she said and tapped me on the shoulders with it. "I think if I whacked it on anything, it would break—or dent anyway."

"Unlike a candlestick, you mean."

"You were very graceful dancing the sword around on the stage," I said.

"Thanks," she said, weighted with sarcasm, and scowling, "Graceful isn't what's called for. I was just trying to get used to holding it. An actor has to be comfortable with the props. I need to know how long it is, how I have to hold it so it doesn't drag on the ground or stick in my foot. I need to be able to feel with my hands how to keep the broad part of the blade facing the audience so it looks dangerous-but-funny, if you know what I mean. Being an actor isn't just doing what occurs to you on the spur of the moment. Being an actor is like being a dancer, using a prop so that it doesn't appear to be using you."

She had the presence of a middle-school vice-principal about to send me to after-school detention. I could see what Siobhan meant when she said she would alienate everyone.

"I'm sure you can do it. I've never laughed harder than when I saw you in *Waiting in the Wings*," I offered like an olive branch.

Lily exhaled theatrically, retrieved the sword from Ruth, and headed back to the stage, walking like a woman instead of the hips-forward stance she used for Malvolio.

Ruth mouthed a thank-you with a peace-making look on her face, but Lily was looking the other way.

My phone rang; the screen registered Mike di Saronno. After we exchanged how-are-you-fine-and-you, he surprised me.

"Have you been getting any feedback from the folks at West Side Rep?" he asked.

"Feedback as to what?"

"Some of the folks in the cast of *Twelfth Night* feel like they're being stalked, or maybe threatened.'"

"Threatened? For what?"

"Nothing specific, but people are tailing them, they say."

"Kinda the opposite of complaining. They don't talk about it. The new cast is partly the same as the old cast, but some of the actors had other commitments and have been replaced. So, the new kids didn't even know Ned, I think. I guess, now that you mention it, they have been looking a little testy, though."

I showed Ruth and Gabriele the phone with Mike's name on it. They both nodded.

Mike had also taken a call from Edgar Savage, who told Mike he thought Siobhan might have been involved in some way with his brother's death, though he didn't think she had anything directly to do with killing him.

"Siobhan?" I couldn't believe what I was hearing. "I thought they buried the hatchet, so to speak, when we got together at The Oyster Bar."

According to what he told Mike, Edgar said he thought Siobhan was draining the assets that Ned had left when he died. That may have been involved with his discovery that Siobhan Savage gave $50,000 to West Side Rep in Ned's name. That was the same $50,000 that the Turkish writer, Ortigan, had given to Ned as a down payment on a movie role. He also had found that she was married a few years earlier to a man named Jones.

"I told him we knew about that," Mike said, "and the problem was a similarity of names that caused the mistake. Somebody named Siobhan Reilly got a license to marry Jones. Our Siobhan's legal name is Siobhan Brianna Dunleary, even though her stage name is Reilly, and she was not the Siobhan Reilly who got a marriage license with Mr. Jones. It didn't seem to change his mind."

"Well, I couldn't disagree more," I said. "And she has money of her own. Family money. She doesn't need money, not to mention that she expects to inherit the family estate in Buckinghamshire. Her parents have titles."

"I thought she was Irish."

"She was born in Northern Ireland, which is part of the United Kingdom, but she went to acting school in London and has worked there with some big-name theater groups. Her family has English titles with Irish place-names. That money was given to Ned by Omar Ortigan, the Turkish writer we met in Istanbul. Remember? I told you that he told us it was a down payment on a film role that Ortigan wanted Ned to play based on one of his books."

Mike said that some of the actors had reported being followed by people they didn't know.

"Really? That's creepy."

"They think they're being watched by somebody. Some of them are frightened. Some are ready to wring somebody's neck if they find out who's doing it."

I told him I would ask around. "But I don't think you ought to take what Edgar Savage said seriously. Siobhan didn't kill Ned. She's pregnant with Ned's baby, she was his wife, and she seems very calm and happy when she talks about the time that she and Ned had together."

No response from Mike, so I continued, "She's also directing the new production, and has persuaded Lily Rasmussen to play Malvolio instead of trying to direct the play, which was the original plan from West Side Rep. Siobhan thinks the transgender Malvolio is one of Ned's most creative ideas and she wants to see how it will play with an audience."

Mike said Lily Rasmussen had mentioned that she thought she was being shadowed or stalked. Also, Gianfranco Mirabella. And one of the actors that wasn't in the new cast, Tony Anguilla, who Mike gathered was working in a different play now.

"Mirabella was announced to play Malvolio when rehearsals started at The Gym," I said. "That made him one of the leads. But when Siobhan took over directing, she persuaded Lily to play Malvolio like Ned had wanted when he was directing the play. That meant Siobhan either had to fire or demote Mirabella, like sending him back to playing one of the supporting comic roles, maybe Sir Toby or Sir Andrew, which is also what Ned Savage had planned in the first place. Siobhan seems to be putting as many of the players as possible back in the cast that Ned had recruited for his production."

"Except herself," Mike said.

"I asked her about that. She said by the time the production opens, she's likely to be showing, and it would be hard to justify having a pregnant Viola still trying to dress like a boy and still being mistaken by Olivia and Orsino for a male."

Ruth was listening to my end of the conversation, but since she knew it was Mike on the phone, she motioned to me. I asked Mike if I could put him on hold for a few seconds. He agreed.

"Let me talk," she said. "When you go back to the call, put the phone on speaker and tell Mike I'm here."

I did what she asked.

"Mike, you know a lot more about psychology than I do, but I gotta say this," Ruth said. "If I was a cast member when Ned was directing and then he was murdered, I'd be wondering which one of the people in the play did it. If everybody is suspicious of everybody else, there'd be lots of opportunities in Manhattan to think you were being followed."

"Group paranoia," Mike said. "Interesting. I bet actors have good imaginations, and they're obviously competitive, so they'd be good at suspecting things."

"Did any of them have a description of who it was that they thought was on their tail?" I asked.

"The most common description is of a white male with a beard, middle-aged to late middle-aged, stocky," he said. "Not much to go on, probably several million guys in the tri-state area like that."

"But maybe it could mean that the stalking might be organized."

"Organized?"

"What if there is somebody trying to follow the people who were in the cast? Maybe to see if there are any clues that might point to who bonked Ned Savage. Let's say, for instance, that one person in the cast, who knows he or she didn't do it, decided to tail the others to see what they can find out."

"Why would that point to white, middle-aged fat guys with beards?"

"Maybe the cast member has a boyfriend, who's acted as an organizer. Or maybe the cast member has buddies who are helping him. Or her."

Mike thought about it for a couple of moments. "Then there wouldn't be any reason to try to stop them," he said. "I wonder if we should get a sketch artist to try to put together some idea of what some of these guys look like." After a pause, he said, "Hugo, any way you could come up here?"

I said yes and excused myself from The Gym and headed to Midtown West precinct on 54th Street. Thank heaven for subways.

When I got there, Mike picked up his cellphone and tapped on the dial a few times. Shortly, a young woman appeared at his door.

He introduced me. "Madeleine, this is Hugo Miller. Hugo Miller, say hi to Madeleine Skimin, who is a strong right hand of the department." He explained that Madeleine was in charge of Forensic Art, which is the department that sketch artists belong to.

Madeleine explained that most of the sketch artists were part-time civilian criminalists, which is the same designation that I have with the NYPD. Only I am a usually unpaid volunteer, and they are either employees or independent contractors, depending on their availability.

"I worked with a sketch artist here once," I said. "I was amazed at how good he was, but also my friend, Ruth Jensen, worked with a different sketch artist trying to find the same person, and when we looked at the two sketches, I thought Ruth's sketch was more accurate, so it must have to do with how well the witness's memory works and how well he can describe what he remembers."

"All of our forensic artists have a background in anatomy and art," she said, "and they all are good listeners who can respond to a verbal description by using some tools that allow the artist to choose and modify the general shape of the face, ears, hair and eyes, skin color, teeth, etc. Then they can use pencils and erasers to adjust the face they are working on until the witness is satisfied with it." She crossed her arms in front of her. "When we find a good one, we hold onto him or her, because they're very special talents, and they can make all the difference in finding someone that we don't have any video or photos of."

I asked how often the sketches turn out to look like the person who's located or arrested or whatever.

"You'd be surprised," she said. "I'd say at least seven out of ten times they're either right on the money or at least very close."

Mike explained the situation to Madeleine and told her that there were three or four people who might be able to describe whoever it was that was following them. "Of course, there is an even chance that they're imagining being followed, because they're frightened that somebody they know might have bludgeoned Ned Savage."

Madeleine said she would be able to assign two or even three sketch artists to work with people as soon as we wanted to get the witnesses into the precinct station.

As fate would have it, Lily Rasmussen answered her cell phone after a couple of rings and said she could come over to the precinct right away. Madeleine said she would work on getting in touch with Gianfranco Mirabella and Tony Anguilla, as well as three pretty young sisters who went by the un-sisterly stage names of Liesel Blackburn, Annette Hicks, and Melinda Tesserla. All three were understudies, not in the first cast in any role; they were sure they were being tailed, and had been for the better part of a week.

"Who would be responsible?" Mike mused.

"It wouldn't have to be someone in the cast or someone working backstage," I offered. "It could be a relative or friend of any of them. It could be the parent of the three sisters, for instance, if they talked about the murder at home."

Mike reminded me that home for the three girls was in a small town in Texas.

"Whatever. All I meant was it doesn't have to be somebody that had a part in the play or was running the lights or ringing up the curtain or whatever. Those three girls were young, and by the way, I don't think I have seen them on the cast list for the new production down in the Village. But if they're afraid that someone in the old cast might be a killer, it's easy to imagine them finding a guy or a couple of guys to help them figure it out."

Chapter Twenty-six

Lily looked like she was auditioning for a grandmother. Her hair was largely gray, where it had been a nondescript brown in the past, and she didn't seem to be wearing any makeup other than shiny, bright red lipstick. Her dress had shoulder pads that were probably intended to de-emphasize the forward slump of her shoulders; the fabric was populated with childish-looking Marimekko-style blossoms on a solid navy background. She was wearing oversized round glasses that were reminiscent of Holly Golightly's sunglasses in *Breakfast at Tiffany's*.

"Yes, I have been followed by men in suits," she said as she sat down in the interrogation room. There was nobody behind the mirror this time. Mike and I sat across from her. There was a video camera running, but that was because it was almost always running.

"Men, plural?" Mike asked.

She nodded. "But only one at a time. Just not always the same one."

"Two?"

"Or three maybe. I didn't start paying attention to them until I realized that they weren't just neighbors that I see often. They would still be there when I finished lunch and walked out of the deli." She made a disapproving face with her lips puckered and stuck out. "That's when I started paying attention, and that was only a few days ago."

"Are they there all the time?"

She shook her head. "Just when I think it's getting too spooky, they disappear for a while. Then they materialize again after I relax and think it's over with."

Mike asked her if she would work with a forensic sketch artist. She agreed to do it but said that she hadn't gotten a good look at them all, principally the one who was following her when she came out of the deli. "I felt like swinging my purse and whacking him in the head," she said.

"Did they ever speak to you, or approach you?"

No.

"Why did you associate them with Mr. Savage's death?"

"Well, it's not like I have men trailing along after me very often. And when it happens just when the director of the play I'm in gets killed, I don't know, I just thought they were part of the same thing. I thought you or someone from the police told me it was most likely somebody from the cast. Or the crew."

"You know there was no scuffle in Mr. Savage's apartment when he was killed. Whoever was there, came in through the front door. So, we think the person that hit him was somebody he knew."

"You mean somebody from the cast at St Benedict's? Or the crew?"

"Not necessarily from the cast, no. But most likely someone he knew. Could be someone he knew from a previous acting job; here, in London, in California, wherever he'd worked. Could be somebody he knew from where he used to live on 8th Avenue. He probably knew hundreds of people."

"I thought you told me it was probably somebody who was rehearsing at his apartment."

"Sorry, I don't think I said that, and if I gave that impression, I never meant to. I remember asking if there had been any rehearsals at his apartment. Or coaching sessions, I think I said, could have been at his apartment anyway."

She nodded. "Well, he coached us all the time. On the sidewalk, going to the subway, having lunch. He sometimes had a bad case of director-itis. Had an idea about everything."

"Then there was the day when you and Siobhan were there reading lines after Ned was already, umm, gone," I said. "And you ended up coming into my apartment for a coffee."

She nodded again. "I don't recall ever doing a whole scene anyplace but at the church, or in the church basement. Siobhan and I were working on the fourth act that day when we met you in the hallway."

Mike asked Lily if she had time to sit with the sketch artist.

"How long does it take?"

He said usually an hour or so.

She said that would be all right. Mike got up and left the room, saying he would be right back. When he returned, Madeleine was with him. He explained that Madeleine was in charge of the forensic artists, and Madeleine told Lily they had spoken on the phone earlier. She would take Lily to Jake, who was one of the artists.

After Lily was gone, Mike turned to me. "Did you tell her that someone from the cast was the killer?"

"Not that I recall, but I don't have transcripts of all our conversations."

"Do you think it's possible that Ruth or Gabriele said something like that?"

"I don't know who either one of them would have told. I think I've been around when they were talking to the *Twelfth Night* people," I said. "Except maybe when we went up to Boscobel to see a festival production of *Twelfth Night*; a little like a field trip, I guess. There was no way I could hear any and all conversations that night. But why would they? We could ask them. Or you could ask them, I mean."

He nodded. "I think Gabriele—which he pronounced without the final "e"—is sweet on Siobhan Savage."

I shrugged. "Gabriele had a soft spot for Ned, who he knew from Ora di Pranzo. When he found out that Siobhan was pregnant, he wanted to help with the baby."

"So that means he spent time with her when you weren't there?"

"I guess."

"Had you talked to him about the cast being persons of interest?"

"Maybe, but I think all I told him, or Ruth, was that whoever was holding the candlestick wasn't a stranger, because there were no signs of a break-in and Ned wasn't defending himself when he was hit. I remember that originally he though Siobhan might have killed him, but he barely knew her then."

"I thought he knew her from her time with Ned Savage."

"I'm confused," I admitted. "Gabriele apparently was seeing Ned at some time in the past, and it didn't work out. He did say he had met

Siobhan when Ned brought the cast of *Twelfth Night* to Gabriele's restaurant. She was clearly his squeeze, I think, and Gabriele took a dislike to her."

"Okay," he said. "I understand what you said." He said that Tony Anguilla was due to show up to talk about being followed, so he re-set the recording devices, sent the video and sound to his email address, and got rid of the water cups and a paper container of coffee that he had while he was talking to Lily but never drank. Or at least it was full.

When Tony arrived, he brought a lot of energy into the room. He was alternating in two roles with another actor in an Off-Broadway—but professional, he was getting paid—production of *A View from the Bridge*. He and the other actor were taking the roles of Eddie (the villain of the piece) and Alfieri (the man who tells the story, a narrator).

When he told me, I was remembering the play, which I had seen a couple of times and the opera that was made from it—the Met did it several years back. The plot revolves around a girl planning to marry a man who might be gay which would help the guy get a green card. It takes place in Brooklyn, I think, or maybe Queens, and I always thought the bridge in the title was the Brooklyn Bridge or the Queensboro Bridge, but I think it's Alfieri, who is a bridge, kinda, between Italy and the United States.

I congratulated Tony on the roles. "Those are both leading men, right?"

"Yeah, and kinda opposite types too. But they're both Italian. They are guys like guys in my family. It's great to play on both sides of the stage, but nothing's perfect. It's a small theater, not even in midtown, near Union Square. I'm fairly sure it's not eligible for Obies. Or at least I think they're not," he said, referring to the Off-Broadway version of Broadway's Tony Awards. As he spoke, he was primping, smoothing his hair with his hands. It was jet black, a black that you wouldn't normally see on a middle-aged man.

Mike asked him about being followed.

He looked around uneasily and nodded his head. "I'm not a pansy, y'know. I can take care of myself. But there have been these two tough guys that seem like they're keeping an eye on me, and it makes me nervous."

"Why do you think they might be following you?"

"I don't think they're following me. I know they're following me."

"I was asking what reason they might have for following you."

He looked at me then at Mike. "I guess I just thought it had something to do with Ned Savage."

"You guess?" Mike echoed.

Tony said he was a New Yorker, born and bred. He never had anybody following him except maybe years before when he was playing in bigger theaters, and then sometimes people would hang around the stage doors and follow after him. "But that's different," he said. "They all looked like they were from Iowa or something, and they'd never seen an actor before."

"This time you think they're up to no good?" Mike asked.

Tony nodded.

"How could it have anything to do with Ned Savage?"

"That guy got himself killed, ya know. I'm Italian, and I know what people think about Italians and the Mafia or whatever, but it's not like I'm used to having people I know murdered. It kinda stands out when it happens. It's hard not to think about it."

Mike asked if he would see two men together following him or if he saw two guys following him one at a time.

"Nah," he said. "Just one at a time, and they keep their distance."

"Did either one of them ever approach you or say anything to you?"

He shook his head. "No, not even once. As a matter of fact, I don't think they have got closer than half a block."

"So, they just followed you around?"

He nodded. "I guess, but it made me nervous, because nobody wants a shadow following them around."

"Maybe they recognized you from a play or from TV?"

He said he thought about that, but then they kept showing up over and over. "If they were just stage-door johnnies, they'd be gone after a while. And most of those types follow women, not guys."

"But they never threatened you?"

"No." He looked like he might be feeling a little foolish but not anxious or worried.

"And you're still convinced they were following you because of something to do with Ned Savage?"

"Yeah, I think so. I can't come up with any other reason that makes sense."

"Oh, one other thing. Did these guys shadow you just around where you live, or did they follow you to, like rehearsals, or when you were going out to eat?"

He cocked his head and was clearly trying to remember. "Funny you ask that. I think it was just in my neighborhood. If they'd followed me to St Benedict's, for instance, I would have called the cops. But you never can be completely sure what's going on when you see the same people on the street where you live. Maybe they're just neighbors, ya know?"

Mike nodded then took out his cellphone and tapped a few numbers. Madeleine cracked the door a few moments later, and peeked in.

"You must be Tony," she said, walking in and extending her hand for a shake. "I'm Madeleine. We spoke a couple of hours ago, when I called to see if you could come over and give us a hand so we can help find the people who've been tailing you." She said she was head of the Forensic Art program. "What that means is I work with the sketch artists, and we want to see if you can help one of the artists develop a picture of whoever was following you."

He stood up. "There was two of them," he said. "But not at the same time, one at a time, not two at the same time."

"So, Luke will be working on two sketches then." She made a motion that Tony should come with her, and they left.

"Two down," I said. "I wonder if Tony could run into Lily wherever the sketch artists are working."

He said they work in separate areas, not in a bullpen or anything like that. "We try to make it very private." He paused. "So, the answer is no, not unless we want them to see each other, of course."

Mike's cellphone buzzed. It was a text message from Madeleine saying that Gianfranco Mirabella asked if he could come over right away.

"Good," Mike said. "I doubt if the three young sisters with the three last names are going to be able to help us much. The people we have here are likely to be the best of the bunch that we know of right now. One thing

I've learned over the years is that most experienced actors are very observant of what's going on around them, and they have memories like steel traps. They can tell you where the orange vase was on the side table or which edge of the Oriental carpet was frayed. They have to be aware of everything, especially on stage—and even more in comedy than in drama, because making people laugh is all about timing."

After a quick sandbox break and a trip to the coffee dispenser, Gianfranco Mirabella, AKA Frank Martinez was there, every inch the fireplug; short, bulky and defiant was his stock and trade. He looked like he was showing up to have a tooth pulled or to get shots for rabies. Not a shrinking violet, for sure, but an in-your-face bulldog.

"I don't like police stations," he said.

"Why's that?" Mike responded.

"I wasn't one of the good kids when I was in school, I guess. Ended up getting blamed for everything. Cops are cops, whether they're in Manhattan or Albuquerque." I remembered he was from New Mexico.

"We didn't compel you to come over to talk to us, you know. You could have said no."

"I also don't like people following me and my friends."

I tried to change the subject, maybe take some of the stiffness out of the conversation. "I was disappointed that you weren't going to be Malvolio. I liked the way you were playing with the sword."

He smiled big. "It's schtick," he said, "but it can make people laugh. People laugh when somebody looks like a clown on stage, and they like it even more when a clown gets his comeuppance." He frowned for a split second then said, "You know, his name is Malvolio, and that means somebody that has evil thoughts or evil intentions. It's okay to make him look like a clown. Back in the day, people probably threw rotten fruit at the guy playing Malvolio."

"You kinda inhabited that character, turned yourself into Malvolio. I know Lily will be funny, but part of the funny with Lily will be because she is a woman playing a man, just like Viola. Different ages, I guess."

"Ya think?"

"She'll probably try to do the same sort of thing with the sword that you did."

"You know she will. When she saw the crew laughing when I was doing it, she decided right then that she wanted those laughs."

"Actually, Siobhan asked Lily to step in as Malvolio, because that was what Ned Savage had wanted in the first place."

"What does that have to do with it?"

"Well, she's Mrs. Savage, after all. And soon to be the mother of his child."

"I heard," Frank said through his teeth.

"Well, she's pregnant anyway."

"She likes the girls. And he liked the boys. Let's be honest about it. Maybe it's his baby—maybe—but they weren't no *love affair*." He carefully dished up some sarcasm with the last two words.

Mike stepped in. "Can you give us any information about what happened when you were being followed?"

"I'm not sure I was followed. I never said to Lily or the others that I was being trailed."

"But you told Madeleine somebody had been following you."

"She sounds like a cutie," he said with some put-on bravado.

"You go," I said. "She's kinda pretty, by the way. You'll be meeting her in a little bit."

"Did you think somebody was following you around?" Mike didn't drop the subject.

He nodded. "But I wasn't scared or anything."

"We're more interested in what happened than in whether you were scared. What we'd really like is to find out what the guy or guys looked like. Maybe they were the same ones who were following other folks in the cast."

"I know what you're thinking," Frank said, looking Mike in the eyes. "You're thinking somebody in the cast or crew killed Ned Savage. So, you're afraid that if somebody's following them, they might be next."

"Maybe."

"Maybe? What else is it gonna be?"

Mike said that it was entirely possible that it was exactly the opposite.

"Like what?"

"Like somebody in the cast trying to figure out if somebody in the cast was a rotten apple. Maybe they were shadowing you to see if you might be the killer."

Frank took that like a slap in the face. "Whaddya mean?"

"Maybe you bonked Ned and then ran when you saw what happened, for instance."

"You serious?" He puffed up his chest visibly. "Me?"

"I didn't say you did it. I was saying somebody might be trying to figure out who actually did it. And following everybody in the cast to see what they can find out."

Frank just stared at Mike with a scowl. "You wanna talk like that, I'm calling the union to get a lawyer."

Mike asked Frank to sit down and relax. "I'm not accusing you of anything, Mr. Mirabella." He paused for that to sink in. "We're trying to see if it's true that some people from the St Benedict's production of *Twelfth Night* were being tailed. If they were, then we need to offer them some protective services if they think they're in danger."

"My name's Martinez, not Mirabella. Mirabella's my professional name. People just call me Frank."

Mike was sitting, and Frank sank down into a chair on the other side of the table. He was still on red alert though. It was easy to see that. *I wonder what he got in trouble for that made him so anxious about the cops.*

Mike pulled out his cellphone and tapped a few keys on it. Madeleine appeared at the door moments later. Mike introduced Madeleine to Frank.

"Hi, Mr. Mirabella. It's good to meet you. We talked on the phone a little bit ago. Thanks for coming over."

He beamed at her.

She explained that she worked with the sketch artists. "We're trying to get an idea if the people who were being followed, were followed by any of the same guys."

"Do you mind telling us," Mike asked, "what the man looked like who was following you?" He motioned Madeleine to take a seat.

"Kinda like anybody. Medium height, white, maybe Hispanic, but light colored, like me. Street clothes. You know, shirt, pants, I don't know.

Baseball cap. Yankees."

"Did you get a good look at him?"

He nodded.

"See," Mike started, "if these same guys have been bothering a bunch of people, we can charge them with something, get them off the street."

"They didn't really bother me, like I told you." He looked at Madeleine. "They kept their distance, never tried to corner me or take pictures of me."

"But you were aware of being followed," she said.

"Yeah, but when I was in *Waiting in the Wings*, there were always people who followed me away from the theater. I made them laugh, and they just followed me. I would sometimes wave at them, and then they'd wave back and usually turn around and quit."

"Did you try that with these guys?" Mike asked. "Waving at them?"

He shook his head.

Madeleine stood up and gestured to Frank. "Let's go see one of the sketch artists. A woman named Maisie. She's actually a painter, but she's a really talented sketch artist. You'll see."

Frank stood up and followed her out the door.

Chapter Twenty-seven

Mike called after I got home and had my shoes off. The television was tuned to a cable station that ran news most of the time, because there was a hurricane, Hurricane Howard, that was threatening to move up the coast, maybe even as far as New York. I spent a lot of my early childhood near the Gulf of Mexico and have always been frightened by severe weather; tornadoes, hurricanes, even just Hudson Valley thunderstorms sometimes. This particular hurricane was looking like a big one that was going to demolish a lot of the Bahamas and then head north. It could get as far as New York on some of the spaghetti forecasts, and Cape Cod looked like it was going to get inundated almost no matter what.

I had a glass of *montepulciano d'abruzzi* in my hand ready to take a sip when my cellphone buzzed, so I put it down and poured a glass of tap water while I was listening to what he had to say. There were similarities between the three sets of sketches—which were done in interviews with Lily, Tony and Frank by three separate sketch artists who had no communication with each other.

"It's not enough to be conclusive, but it looks like there are only two or three culprits, and they have stalked all three of the people we interviewed," Mike said. "We ran the sketches against facial rec files and came up with about twenty potential matches."

"Did we find any cameras in the three neighborhoods where our witnesses live?"

"Don't know yet. We're checking to see what surveillance or security cameras there are in the three neighborhoods. Usually there are more than you expect, but they're not all pointed in the right direction. But in Manhattan where all three of them live, it's hard to be outside and not be picked up by somebody's security camera. Some are operated by the city, like on traffic lights or in subways or at bus stops, but most of them are owned by landlords or merchants or schools or churches. A lot of restaurants and bars have cameras that are not really operating so that they give the patrons a feeling of security but don't provide any help to us. Most of those are indoors, so we wouldn't want what they had anyway."

I hadn't seen the sketches because they hadn't been finished by the time I left. I asked if they were close enough that they were obviously the same people. Mike said it looked like the same guys, but there were differences too. Like one guy that looked just like another sketch had a scar on his cheek in one sketch and not in the other.

I had put the television on mute, so there was no sound, but I was eyeing the coverage of the hurricane. There was one a few years back named Hugo, but it did so much damage that they retired the name, so I wouldn't be seeing my own name on a television screen again.

"You watching this Hurricane Howard?" I asked him.

"Not really. I dunno. Kinda, I guess. There's more hurricanes every year," he said. "Seems like they're getting worse than they were when I was in school in Brooklyn. You know, stronger, more rain, more damage. Just more of them too. I know a lot of the politicians want climate change to go away because they even prefer dirty air if it might mean more jobs. You know, coal miners and stuff.

"It seems like as soon as the hurricane season is over, it starts up again. But truth is I live on the eighth floor of my building, so I don't have to worry about floods. Where I live it's not a low-lying area that floods anyway. So, unless one of my windows gets whacked by a flying deck chair, they don't have a lot of direct effect on me. I watch the news like everybody, but until we have weather alerts, I try not to let it get under my skin."

"They scare me, always have," I said. "My mom used to hide in the downstairs bathroom if we had tornado warnings when I was a kid."

"Tornados are worth being scared of. Fortunately, we don't see many of them around here."

"I thought there had been one or two in Queens, and maybe one up in Westchester County too."

"Hey listen," he said, "I'm going to email a few of the sketches and face rec results to you. Share them with your team and let me know if any of them look familiar."

After we signed off, I sent an email to Ruth and Gabriele to see if they would have time to look at sketches of people that might have been stalking some of the *Twelfth Night* cast. Both of them were up for it, and I suggested that we rendezvous at my apartment about 7:30. That way we could look at the sketches and compare them to see if anyone looked familiar. Then we could have a drink and see if there was room at some cool restaurant, either near where I live or near Grand Central, which is only one stop away on the subway.

That gave me time to drink my glass of *montepulciano*, which I polished off in about three good gulps, and then take a shower to wash off the police station cooties. I kept checking a weather app to see if there was anything new on Howard, but most weather phenomena take their time to do whatever they're going to do. There was a huge hurricane that hit the Carolinas at one point, barreling in from the Atlantic, and then when it got to land, it almost stopped completely, with the result that it flooded the entire coastline with torrential rains. We had a hurricane-like storm called Superstorm Sandy here in New York—well, all up the east coast, but I experienced it in Queens. It flooded the whole neighborhood where I lived. When I went downstairs the next morning, the waterline in the lobby was about two feet above the floor, although the water had drained out. No more superstorms for me, thanks very much!

Gabriele and Ruth are easy, because they both drink either red wine or vodka, like mini-mes. I put three martini glasses in the freezer when I was toweling off after the shower—the vodka is stored in the freezer because any drink you use vodka in has to be chilled. I do make vodka sauce for spaghetti because it is one of the easiest things to whip up in a few minutes, but keeping it cold doesn't matter when you cook it. Besides, since vodka is the most popular drink in the US, I buy mine in a magnum bottle with a handle on it, and it wouldn't look right on my liquor cabinet. A liquor cabinet is a work of art, adds color and interesting shapes and textures to a room. Odd? Think about it for a minute; it's something I decided when I moved into the apartment. I had the liquor cabinet in the dining room in the last place I lived, but I set it up under a smallish painting from somebody's art-school class—a male torso from the neck to the middle of the abdomen, all in shades of blue. That's when I realized that I liked the liquor sitting on top of the cabinet, which is about elbow-high for me.

Sure enough, they wanted vodka as soon as they walked in the door. The martini glasses frosted right up when I took them out of the freezer, and I threw some stuffed olives in the glasses and poured the vodka over them. I took a bag of tortilla chips out of the pantry and a container of hummus from the fridge and put those on the coffee table. No reason to stand on ceremony.

Long story short, none of us recognized either the sketches or the facial rec photos, which Mike had sent me in an email and I had printed them out. I thought one of the guys in the facial rec photos looked vaguely familiar, but half the people in Manhattan look vaguely familiar to me. We were all surprised at how similar the sketches were, in spite of anomalies like the man with a scar in one picture and no scar in the other picture.

"Maybe it was a Halloween scar," Ruth said. "You know, one of those you can stick on your body and it looks real?"

It was my turn to roll my eyes at her.

"You need to practice that," she said. "In front of a mirror."

We were on to our second vodka after we looked at the pictures. I turned on the TV and flicked the weather station, which was, on cue, doing an update on Howard which had grazed Cape Hatteras in North Carolina and was headed for Virginia and Maryland. The local weatherman was up next and predicted that Howard would run out of steam as it moved north, and all we would get would be a soaking rain or maybe an extra high tide that could erode some of the beaches. Rip currents too.

Ruth, who lives on Park Avenue, and Gabriele, who lives in Brooklyn Heights, were not alarmed. The areas they live in are sufficiently high that flooding was nearly impossible unless we had some kind of giant tsunami. Where I live, I already swam through a flood with Superstorm Sandy, so I was more worried. I said I intended to buy a couple of cases of bottled water.

"And carry them from your car to here?" Ruth asked with the face of a simpleton.

I ignored her but turned off the TV.

"Probably nobody following them, just imagination," Gabriele said, waving his conspicuously empty martini glass in front of him as though there were a bartender who would notice. "But maybe you should show to Brianna."

I marched over to the next apartment and knocked on the door. She answered, with a book in her hand. I asked her if she had a few minutes to look at some sketches of people who might have been following some of the cast members. She put her book down on a table next to the entrance. I could see it was *The Theater and Its Double*, a book by a French author I had to read in college for a Theater Arts elective. It is a bible of sorts for staging plays.

"Artaud?" I asked, naming the author.

She smiled and stepped into the doorway. "I'll follow you," she said.

She declined the offer of vodka or wine, patting her stomach. "Baby on Board," she said.

When we walked into my living room, Gabriele stood up and did his hand-kissing act. She smiled the way you would smile at a friend, not the way you would smile at the balcony.

Ruth handed her the scanned sketches and photos as she sat down in a brown side chair at the end of the coffee table.

She recognized one of the men in the photographs right away. "I don't know who he is, but I saw him more than once at St Benedict's."

I asked if he appeared to be somebody's brother or husband. She didn't know, just that she had seen him hanging around.

"Inside the theater? Or on the sidewalk?" I asked.

She thought for a second. "Probably on the sidewalk," she said, "now that you mention it." She put her right hand on her chin and added, "Any chance he was wearing a clerical collar?"

I told her that none of the three people we had interviewed had mentioned it.

"Doesn't matter," she said. "I couldn't tell you who he is anyway, just I remember seeing him around St Benedict's. Could live right near there, I guess. Even on that block maybe, because it's full of apartments other than where the church is. I don't know."

"Or maybe he could be related to someone in the cast? Maybe a father or brother or uncle?"

She shrugged another "I don't know."

"Just to be clear, you never reported to anyone that you were being followed. Is that because you didn't see anyone following you? Or because you didn't want to report it?"

She clouded up a bit and tightened her mouth before she answered. "If somebody was following me, it would already be on the record because they would have reported that I had kicked him in the crotch or broken his nose." She grinned.

"I guess that's means nobody was following you?" Ruth asked, grinning back. "A woman after my own heart."

"Anything else I can do for you?" Siobhan stood up, intending to leave.

"You seem annoyed," I said apologetically.

"I'm easily annoyed these days. Maybe it's because I'm pregnant," she waved her hand in a dismissive gesture, "or maybe it's because I'm a widow, or because I'm working with the ghost of Ned Savage every day at The Gym. I'm sorry, it is not my intention to offend. I know you're just trying to figure out what happened, and I'm glad you're constantly working on it."

She pecked Gabriele on the cheek, shook Ruth's hand, and threw a big friendly smile at me. "Thanks, neighbor," she said. "I'm planning to be home all day, so don't think you're interrupting if you need something."

I heard her open the door, and then it closed and she walked back into the living room just as I was getting ready to grab the olives and vodka to pour a small dividend into the glasses.

"I know where I saw him. He had a Halal cart at the corner of 8th Avenue, maybe a hundred feet from the church. That help?"

"It could. I don't know. But we'll check it out, see if his cart is still there. It makes sense that he would know some of the actors and crew, I guess."

She exited and I heard the door close again. I poked my head into

217

the entrance hall and she had left, and I picked up the vodka bottle again.

"I'm glad men don't get pregnant," I said, mostly to Ruth. "I would be miserable and nasty to be around if I was deprived of wine and vodka for nine months." I poured a splash of dirty-looking liquid, olive juice to a bartender, from a bottle of olives into each of the martini glasses and then blessed it with an inch or so of vodka in the bottom of the cone-shaped glasses. One good swallow. Salty and terrific.

The Halal carts that Siobhan mentioned are an important part of everyday eating in New York. They are literally kitchens on trailers (not carts) that are parked on the curb and are dragged into place every day behind a car with a bumper hitch. They're licensed and inspected by the city and state but have limited menus, usually a vertical rotisserie of chicken meat, and one of beef-lamb mixture that the Greeks call "gyro." They have tons of white rice and yellow rice colored with turmeric. They serve chicken, the beef-lamb mixture or falafel over rice with some greens and tomatoes—and always pickles—or wrapped in a large pita bread with various kinds of sauces, including a red sauce that is like liquified red pepper. And they fit into anybody's budget. Some of them have hot dogs that are all-beef so they can be halal, which is the Arabic version of kosher. Where else can you have a lunch that's so big you can't finish it for six bucks? Or seven bucks. Plus a buck tip.

The lines at Halal carts—all the operators are Arabic speakers, though not necessarily Arabs—are a constant reminder of the openness of Gotham to immigrants. If we thought Arabs were terrorists, would we be eating their food? No, we would not. The Halal guys I know all call me "brother." Almost all religions have been associated with dark deeds. Christianity has had some bloody bad periods for sure. But the grandma with the rosary and the hook-nosed man kneeling with his forehead touching a prayer rug are salt of the Earth, no matter how you look at it. And Halal-truck falafel sandwiches are like the ambrosia of the gods up on Mount Olympus.

Long story short, I was looking forward to investigating the Halal cart near St Benedict's. Not surprisingly, so were Ruth and Gabriele.

Sure enough, we found the man in the picture at a Halal cart at 8th Avenue and 44th Street. His name was Ahmad, and he was from Lebanon.

It was mid-afternoon when we got there, so there was not a line of people waiting for lunch, and we were able to chat with Ahmad while he made up our orders. He works Monday through Thursday and then again on Saturday because Friday is the day he goes to prayers at his local mosque. He was dressed all in black, so perhaps that's what made Siobhan think he might be a cleric.

I showed him my badge and told him that I am a civilian worker for the NYPD and asked him if he had time to answer a couple of questions about a play that had been rehearsed at the church between 9th and 10th Avenues on his street. He agreed, but a wave of anxiety swept over him visibly.

I explained that a couple of the actors from the play thought they might have seen him following them. No problem, just following them. Was that possible?

He nodded.

"Why?" I asked.

"Because the kids who work in that play say they afraid, because somebody from play get killed, and they afraid because nobody know who is killer."

"Girls? Boys?"

"Both. Maybe five, maybe more. We watch some people and tell young people when they come to buy food. Just young. Maybe same age like my daughter at Hunter College."

I told him nobody was going to give him any hassle. We were just trying to figure out what was going on.

"Do the young people feel safer now?"

He either didn't understand or didn't know how to respond. "Maybe is good now," he said.

He handed us the lunches we ordered and shook his head to tell us we didn't have to pay. I put a twenty and a ten on the counter of the cart. He shook his head vigorously, and I pushed the money closer to him. "You are an honest man and you do honest work. You shouldn't work for free, *habibi*." I was thinking of a Halal guy I visited twice or three times a week when I was working in the office all the time. He didn't know my name, as I recall, but he always called me "brother." *Habibi*, which I think means "friend," is one of about four words I know in Arabic. Like *shukraan* for thank you.

Ruth elbowed me and moved up to the counter, beaming after taking a bite of her chicken *shawarma* sandwich on pita bread with two sauces, tomato and pickles. She said a string of words that meant absolutely nothing to me, and Ahmad brightened up, said something back to her. Then I heard her say thank you in Arabic.

She later told me that she had told him that the food was delicious, and that we respect him and want to be his friend. Then she said *shukraan*, which was the only part I understood.

"I had no idea you could speak Arabic," I said. Gabriele was listening intently.

"I don't," she said. "I learned some things because I grew up close to Atlantic Avenue and all the shopkeepers were Arabs when I was a child. If they say something to me, I usually have no idea what they're saying or talking about. I just memorized some sentences when I was in elementary school, and sometimes they still come in handy. Ahmad was very nervous, and I wanted him to know we were not bad guys."

We decided to walk up to Mike's precinct, since it was only a few blocks. I called Mike and asked him if it was okay for us to come over. He said it was fine.

We reported what we heard from Siobhan and what Ahmad told us. Ruth showed him the photo of Ahmad and where his Halal cart was.

"He passes the sniff test?" Mike asked Ruth directly.

She nodded.

"Food *perfetto*," Gabriele said. "Maybe I ask him come at Ora di Pranzo and make food. Maybe Dante like to have help."

Mike looked a little puzzled.

"Sicilia have many Arabic. In Italia we say Arabic give us lemon and orange. Spanish give us tomato and hot pepper and cactus apple."

Mike smiled and patted Gabriele on the shoulder. "*Buon uomo*," he said. *Good man.*

Chapter Twenty-eight

Gabriele said he had to leave to go to the restaurant, and Ruth said she would keep him company on the subway as far as Bryant Park, which is where he would change trains. I said I thought we were going to have dinner, but Gabriele was intent on getting to Ora di Pranzo. Ruth said she didn't like going home alone in the dark, especially when she was on a subway platform where there might not be a lot of people around.

After they left, I decided to take advantage of Siobhan's semi-invitation and knocked on her door.

She had the Artaud book in her hand when she opened the door.

"I had to read that when I was a sophomore at UCLA. I have to admit it was way over my head at the time, but the professor who was teaching the course on modern theater insisted. There was a chapter called 'The Theater of Cruelty,' that might as well have been written in Chinese. But to tell you the truth, I don't think I was paying much attention, because I didn't want to read some radical essay by an actor who thought he was a philosopher."

She smiled in a way that was intended to tell me that the subject of Artaud was closed. "How about a glass of red?" she offered.

"I thought you were off wine."

"I am, but there is plenty of wine here, in case someone drops by."

"In that case, I'd love a glass."

I told her about meeting Ahmad and his explanation that he had started following some of the cast and crew because several of the younger people told him they were scared. "I didn't ask him who the other one or two guys were, but from what he said, I'd guess they were either friends or family."

She invited me to sit, and I planted myself on an end of the couch where I could put my wine on the coffee table. "Snug, isn't it?"

"You mean small?"

"I was just thinking this would not have been an ideal place to work on scenes."

She looked around, shrugged. "It's not claustrophobic though."

"No, but it's not someplace where you could move around very easily. If you tried, you'd trip over something."

"I suppose that's true. When Lily and I came over here, it was after Ned was gone, and we just ended up reading lines. No swords, no cross-garters. Just the words. When we all went up to Boscobel to see that production up there, they used almost no props, except maybe a garden hose as I remember and some branches to hide behind. Some scripts just work even without props or costumes. *Macbeth* just works that way. So does R and J. I've seen *Romeo and Juliet* performed by schoolchildren, and it's sometimes as good that way as when professionals do it. It's nearly perfect for the stage."

"And what does Artaud tell you?"

"Artaud is a historical artifact. He wanted the theater to be more current, less historical. If we did things his way, there would be no Shakespeare or Molière. Only new plays."

"I always had a feeling that there was a rehearsal going on here when Ned died."

"Why did you think that?"

"I don't know. If the CSIs are right, whoever was here may have been smoking pot, and that's probably part of what set off Ned's allergic reaction. He had stuck himself with an EpiPen before he was hit with the candlestick, so it was the candlestick that killed him. But he barely bled at all, given that he had a blow to the head, which usually means pools of blood. At least that's what I was told, because I wasn't here. So, I think his heart had stopped from the fungus on the marijuana leaves, and when he was hit on the head, the heart stopped again."

"And why does that mean it was a rehearsal?"

"Think about it. Two people are sitting on the couch, smoking some grass and then one of them ends up on the floor over there, having been struck from behind but with no evidence of any kind of struggle at all."

She said she still didn't see what that had to do with rehearsal.

"I just think because Ned was an actor who was probably directing his first Shakespeare play, he probably was living the play, thinking about it all day and all night. So probably whoever was here was part of the production."

"What if whoever was here was just a friend?" She put an earnest look on her face.

"Anything is possible, but in my world, friends don't bash friends over the head with a candlestick." I waited for a minute to let that soak in. "And as far as I know, we don't have any reason to think Ned even had friends outside the theater. You spent a lot of time with him. Did he invite people over who were just friends?"

She shook her head. "Well, you know one of his friends pretty well. That's Mr. Cortese from Ora di Pranzo. But Ned and I were only together for a few weeks, and you're right, there was never a time when he wasn't thinking about the play. All the time, twenty-four hours a day. I found it tiring."

"Is it surprising that you weren't here when it happened?"

"I never thought about it like that. No, it's not surprising. I wasn't living here, you know. I was staying in a bed-sit near to Lincoln Center. The baby was conceived at his place on 8th Avenue in Manhattan, not here."

"But you had a key, right?"

She nodded. "I don't think I ever used the key, to tell the truth, while Ned was alive, except when he first gave it to me and I tried it to make sure it fit the lock." She fished a key ring out of her handbag that was sitting by her on the couch. It had several keys. She held one key up with two fingers.

"Do you mind if I ask about your place near Lincoln Center. Was it about the same size as this apartment?"

"No. My place was much smaller, and there was only one chair. That's why it would be called a 'bed-sit' in England. If there are two people, one of them has to sit on the bed because there is only one chair. And an electric kettle. Now if you ask about Ned's flat on 8th Avenue, it was a good bit bigger than this place. He even had a table for dinner, although there were only four chairs. More like a table for playing cards or chess, I suppose. In this apartment, the table for eating is that coffee table, or your lap, or the counter over there by the kitchen. He wanted to spend less money on rent so he could do other things instead."

"Things like what?"

"Things like directing more plays. He wasn't being paid for *Twelfth Night,* you know. He was financing it himself. And that Turkish writer sent him a check that he intended to use on the production."

"You think he would have given up acting?"

"I think it was a foregone conclusion," she said. "His disability was more crippling than he let on."

She looked down and then up, and then took a deep breath and exhaled. "I want to be clear that I believe we will find in the end that nobody broke in here, or was invited in here, who wanted to kill Ned. Everybody liked Ned. I don't know what happened, but it must have been an accident."

"But you weren't here. So how would you come to that conclusion, that it must have been an accident?"

"No, I was not here. But I know he was planning to see Lily Rasmussen that afternoon. He believed that Malvolio was the core of the play and that his decision to play a gender game would give a talented actress an opportunity to prove that to the audience—and maybe a critic or two."

"So, are you saying that Lily may have been here when whatever happened, happened?"

"I'm not saying anything of the kind. I said that Ned was planning to spend some time with Lily that day. She could have been here, or it could have been cancelled. They could have met someplace else. They could have met and finished what they were working on before someone else arrived. I simply don't know. What I do know in my heart is that nobody wanted to kill Ned Savage."

I looked at her, looking at her hands in her lap. "You loved him."

She nodded. "Yes, I did. I guess I still do. I hope my baby is a boy so I can name him for his father. Ned and his siblings are all named for English monarchs; Edward, Edgar, Elizabeth and Mary."

"Edgar was a monarch of England?"

"He was known as Edgar the Peaceful. He was a about half a century before Edward the Confessor. His son, Ethelred the Unready, is better known."

"You carry these facts around in your head?"

"I went to school in England. These things are part of what England is, who we are."

I nodded. "And you're convinced that Ned's death was an accident?"

"I don't believe there was anyone who would have wanted to get rid of him," she said, looking straight at me. "I suppose it is possible that there could have been a madman, or a burglar, or someone who was running from somebody, but we know there was no break-in, no fighting, nothing amiss. The only possible conclusion I could imagine is that whatever happened, and whoever was involved, it was unintentional."

"Well," I said. "I think it is time for a snack and a cocktail for little old me. And I still have some ginger ale if you'd like to join me. Or I think I have some lemons, could make some fresh lemonade."

She stood up and smiled. "I know what I said complicated things for you, but I really believe that." She patted her stomach, "And so does Baby Savage."

We got up to walk over to my apartment, and as I stood up from the couch, I nearly tripped on the big, free-form coffee table that Siobhan said doubled as a dining table. I visualized sitting on the floor and eating like they do in some Japanese restaurants.

"See?" she said. "Too small for practicing a scene or rehearsing almost anything but a monologue."

I looked back at the furniture in the room. A long couch with the big glass coffee table in front of it, leaving one end of the couch sticking out beyond the coffee table. Either a shelf or a thin table behind the couch, with that hookah on it. To the left an almost overstuffed straight-backed chair that I would guess was French Provincial. To the right an end table and bentwood chair with arms. Very plain. But even with just those few pieces of furniture, almost all the floor space was used up.

"You're right," I said. "I'll have to get in touch with Lily and see if she was here that day."

When we got back to my apartment, I made the lemonade and poured it over some ice cubes in a tall glass. I put some cookies on a plate and put them on my dining table with some blue cotton napkins. I poured a dirty vodka for myself and spread some peanut butter on crackers, and we toasted.

"Gabriele says your real name is Brianna Dunleary."

She smiled. "The name on my passport is Siobhan Reilly Dunleary. With the standardized English spelling of Dunleary."

"Who was Reilly?"

"Family name. My maternal grandmother. Yes, she was Irish, and she lived in the south of Ireland, but at that time it was all part of the UK."

"And Brianna?"

"It's a middle name that I stopped using when I started being Siobhan Reilly, which I believe is easier to remember than Brianna Dunleary. My family call me Brian sometimes," she said, pronouncing the name in Irish, BREE-yun. "Mostly they do it when they want to make me laugh or when I've been acting like a boy instead of a lady. Brianna is Irish, the feminine form of Brian."

I told her I was going to have to report the conversation we had back to Mike. She smiled and nodded. "I'll tell him myself if you want me to."

I told her that I thought she could tell the story better than I could repeat it. I suggested that we talk to Mike together.

"That would be a good next step, to tell the truth." Then I added, "Mike's more likely to take it to heart than you might think. He's skeptical but he's a good detective, studied criminology at John Jay College up near Lincoln Center, in addition to the Academy, and has lots of experience with the NYPD. Me, I'm just somebody who's read a lot of novels. And I raise orchids like Nero Wolfe."

"Nero who?"

"Detective in a series of mystery novels. Like Sherlock Holmes or Lord Peter Wimsey. Doesn't matter. I meant it to be funny."

"Those plants are orchids?" she asked, pointing at my windowsills.

I nodded. "All kinds. For some reason most of them seem to bloom in the winter—which is not what most people would expect—but there are some that bloom at odd times, and some that bloom more than once a year.

And a couple that haven't bloomed in several years but look perfectly healthy." I gave her a pitch on the Orchid Show at the New York Botanical Garden up in the Bronx and told her it was in the dead of winter, too, so maybe orchids are programmed to flower when the days are short. Somebody told me the best way to make them flower is to let them get too dry. Then they flower to make seeds.

She asked if I had any tea, and I saw that she hadn't been drinking the lemonade.

"Of course, English Breakfast, Earl Grey, Darjeeling, or some herbals like lemon tea and chamomile."

"Darjeeling would be lovely. With a little milk if you have it."

I have a small whistling teapot, which I got because I let too many saucepans boil dry because I put them on the burner and forgot they were there. I filled it up and put it on the stove then found an old pottery teapot that didn't have any divots taken out of it. In a surprisingly short amount of time, I was pouring tea into a mug. "I steeped it in the pot, not in the mug," I said and handed her the container of milk, which she poured generously into the mug.

"I wonder if Lily could have been trying out some of those choreographed sword dances she was doing the other day at The Gym." It had been bouncing around in my head. "It looked so much like *tai chi*, that I figured she must have studied it at some point."

"You mean in Ned's apartment?" She shook her head. "Not enough room, and Lily really is gangly and awkward in some ways." She cocked her head and puckered her mouth in thought. "Also, I don't recall seeing a sword in the props at the church."

"When did it show up?"

"The Gym. It was when Frank was cast as Malvolio. He brought a standard-issue sword-fight sword first, and then he found that gigantic broadsword someplace—actually I think he said it was a tag sale somewhere. Anyway, he thought it would get more laughs. He was so delighted with the role that I felt really mean when I put the original casting back in place. I happen to think that Ned's idea of casting Lily in a pants role is a stroke of brilliance." She smiled and shrugged. "But I also just wanted it to be the way Ned wanted it."

"There's no sword in the play, at least not that I recall."

"No, but there are hardly any stage directions of any type. And Lily is right that a gentleman would have been wearing a sword."

"Malvolio is hardly a gentleman, more a fool's fool."

"Right, but as Ned said over and over, Malvolio doesn't see himself as a fool, and he knows that if he is to marry Olivia, he has to be upper-class. So, following that logic, a sword makes sense. Especially a totally inappropriate sword. Remember that everything about Malvolio is exaggerated from the moment he makes his first entrance."

"When you say a regular sword-fighting sword, what would that be?"

"Well, I've never taken fencing lessons, but all the swords used on stage are the type that are called rapiers. They have a narrow, pointed blade, and in reality, they would have been sharpened on the edges like a knife, but never are on stage. The stage versions usually have what's called a basket hilt, which basically conceals the fighter's entire right hand under a solid metal guard, or sometimes a guard with ridges and open spots—more for looks, I think, than any real purpose. The guards were at the time ostensibly to keep the fighter's fingers from being cut off. A little over three feet of blade to a rapier, and they're lightweight."

"And the broadsword?"

"A medieval two-handed sword with very sharp edges used primarily by horsemen in full armor. Used for cutting and slashing, not for running an opponent through. Some of them were very large. That is the type of sword that might have been used to cut off Anne Boleyn's head. She was terrified of the axe, and Henry VIII agreed to have a French swordsman do the deed."

"So, the sword that Lily was playing with would have been a lethal weapon in reality."

"All real swords were lethal weapons. But yes, the broadsword could have cut off your arm or if you were mounted, your horse's head. They were not being used in battle at the time Shakespeare wrote his plays, though. Totally outmoded. So even a proper-sized broadsword would have looked comically antique, not to mention that the gigantic fake sword that Lily was toting around would make the person holding it look like a clown.

It's all about the laughs."

I made a mental note to ask Frank where he got that big sword. My cellphone vibrated. It was a weather warning. High winds and torrential rain coming. I showed it to Siobhan.

"When we had that big storm a few years back, this area was flooded for a short time. I think it was the East River rising, so it may not have been the rain as much as the storm surge." I didn't want to scare her. "Anyway, we lost electricity in this building around nine o'clock at night, and I went to bed because I had already eaten and I couldn't deal with all the lighting being out. I could see in the apartment because the street lights were still on, at least then. And when I woke up the next morning, the electricity was back on. Good property manager. They actually turned the electricity off instead of waiting for it to short out on its own when the transformer was flooded. That would have damaged the whole system. So when the water receded, they were able to turn it back on, no problem. The elevators were no good for a couple of weeks, and the subways were a mess, totally not working on my line because the tunnel was flooded. I took the ferry to Manhattan because I needed to get to my office to see if everything was okay there."

"It's a hurricane isn't it?"

"Not officially, I think. It was a hurricane but I think it's just a big patch of rain and wind now." It occurred to me that she might have been talking about the storm from a few years back. "Unless you were talking about what they now call Superstorm Sandy. But even that wasn't a hurricane, just a really powerful nor'easter that picked up a lot of power from a hurricane that was plowing around in the Gulf of Mexico then ran up the east coast and flooded everything low-lying from Florida to Maine. Washed away most of the sandy beaches too."

I got up and walked into the kitchen and opened the fridge. "I have some chicken and fresh broccoli, if you're game. If this storm is going to hit, I think it would be a good idea to eat sooner than later. If I was feeling flush, I'd probably get to Manhattan and check into a hotel someplace, but even though it makes me nervous to stay here, I don't see laying out a few hundred dollars just to avoid being here."

She frowned. "The building is secure, isn't it?"

"It's not going to get blown over, if that's what you're asking."

"I meant is it going to be dangerous to stay here?"

"Do you still have your place over by Lincoln Center?"

"No, I gave it up when Ned and I married, moved all my things out before the end of last month. I stayed with Lily for a couple of days and then decided to camp out here and wait for my green card in the mail."

"I can't predict the future, but if it's like it was the last time around, everything will be okay. Just that if the electricity goes off, some food might spoil in the freezer or the fridge if it stays off a long time." I opened the freezer again. *Not much there, some frozen vegetables and meatless hamburger patties.* "So, my inclination would be to cook anything that might spoil and have a big dinner."

My cellphone rang. It was the concierge saying that Gabriele was on the way up. It was going on ten o'clock.

"Mr. Cortese is apparently coming up in the elevator."

She looked at her wristwatch just as the doorbell rang.

Of course, he looked like he had just stepped out of a photo shoot, with his black-tie uniform from the restaurant, and although the wind was blowing and his hair had been flying around as he walked, he looked like a photographer had arranged everything just so. They had closed the restaurant early because of the storm warning, because Dante said the area where they were was low enough that it could possibly flood. He was carrying a brown paper bag, and I could see that there were bottles in it, probably wine.

He gallantly kissed Siobhan's hand. She smiled. He took the three bottles of wine out of the bag. All had been opened and had corks stuffed back into them, probably Gabriele's handiwork as he left.

"Ah, a wine tasting!" I said.

He smiled. "Is bottles what was left on tables. We close when city tell us maybe flood happen tonight." He said that they had locked up the wines, which were stored on the third floor of the space, so they would not be likely victims if there was a flood.

"You want to stay here? It could flood here, too, but no problem on the tenth floor, obviously." I looked at Siobhan, nodded, and then back to Gabriele. "I was telling Siobhan that when that big storm came through a few years back, we had some flooding here, and the electricity was out for a few hours, but we were okay."

He gave me a bear hug then lined the bottles up on the pass-through from the kitchen. All three bottles looked more than half full. Two *Pio Cesare* Barolo bottles of different vintages and one bottle of Tignanello, an expensive wine that the Italian wine mob has been successful at naming "super-Tuscan." Most Tuscan wines are Sangiovese grapes—in fact, only a pure Sangiovese can be labeled as a *chianti*. The super-Tuscan wines are blended like Bordeaux wines are blended. The French call them *meritage* wines. But the name "super-Tuscan" has been a touch of genius, and the well-known labels sell like hotcakes, even though you could buy five or more bottles of a fine chianti for the price of one bottle of a super-Tuscan like Tignanello or Sassicaia or Ornellaia.

I explained to Gabriele that we were going to cook anything that might spoil if the electricity went off.

A bolt of lightning lit the sky behind the Chrysler Building, and some raindrops began to pelt the windows. I closed the glass sliding door to the balcony, because it felt as though the wind would start to whip through the living room.

"We hurry cook food," Gabriele said, stripping off his coat and ducking into the kitchen. He opened the fridge and pulled out some chicken parts in a cellophane-covered package, some turkey sausages marked "Italian Hot," and all the vegetables in the crispers. He opened the pantry and pulled out two bottles of sauce marked tomato basil.

"What do you need?" I asked him.

"*Padella di ferro*," he said. *Iron skillet.*

I pulled out a 12-inch cast iron skillet and put it on the stove. He grabbed the large tin of olive oil and covered the bottom of the skillet with it.

"*Aglio*," he said. *Garlic.*

I pulled a plastic container out of the fridge that contained peeled garlic cloves in it. Store-peeled, not home-peeled. He made a slight frown when he saw them, but he pulled out a handful, grabbed a blunt-ended vegetable knife and started chopping. He stopped and pointed at one of the bottles of Barolo. I pulled out three bistro glasses (no stem) and started to pour.

"Not for me," Siobhan said, patting her tummy.

"Righty-o," I said, thinking that sounded British, then fished a bottle of ginger ale out of the fridge and poured that into one of the glasses. The Barolo was excellent, had obviously been breathing for a couple of hours. He sipped his while I gulped at mine then filled it back up.

Gabriele was a picture of concentration as he chopped bell peppers, parsley, and fennel, stripped the leaves from rosemary branches, and tore up all the basil I had into smallish pieces, which he put aside. Siobhan was frozen, standing at the kitchen door, staring at his hands like he was a basilisk or a gorgon.

"Reconsidering something?" I asked in a whisper.

She smiled very slightly and half nodded, just raising her head without ever moving her eyes.

I put a CD into the player, somebody playing the Goldberg Variations on what sounded like a very large harpsichord. The lightning was more frequent, but the rain had paused. I walked over to the balcony doors and looked at the streets. Wet, no flooding. People were walking without umbrellas.

Gabriele found a fileting knife and cut the chicken meat off the bones and into bite-sized pieces that he put into a mixing bowl with some kosher salt, black pepper, garlic powder. Then he poured half a bottle of white wine into the bowl and stirred all of it around with a wooden spoon. He found a plastic bag and put all of the chopped vegetables into it with some olive oil, dried oregano, thyme, more kosher salt and lots of pepper. Then he shook the bag to get everything covered.

"*Ugo, teglia!*" he said loudly. *Roasting pan*, I thought. I fished around in the pots and pans and pulled out an open roaster with no lid and a large Dutch oven with a glass top. He wanted the Dutch oven. I put the big roasting pan back—the only thing it was ever used for was roasting chickens or ducks or a turkey.

A crack of thunder told me to turn off the CD, which was in the midst of a very fast variation. I waited for it to finish then ejected the CD and put it back in the case.

Gabriele was flouring the chicken in a paper bag, the way my grandmother used to do it. I swallowed the rest of my Barolo and made a quick decision to switch to vodka for a bit, so that there would be wine left when we ate. As I pulled the vodka out of the freezer, Gabriele shook his head and motioned for me to put it back. Whatever, I put it back and pulled out a bottle of *nero d'avola*, flashed it at Gabriele, who smiled and nodded. *The vodka would spoil my taste buds.*

The Barolo had been excellent, but truth be told, I prefer the southern Italian wines; cheaper, rougher reds, none of the upper-class pretensions of the Northern Italian wines.

I know that when there is lightning and thunder you should stay away from the windows, but I never can do that. For some reason the lightning fascinates me. The thunder frequently scares me, but with lightning I'm like an insect near a candle flame. That night there was a lot of lightning, and I kept staring, wondering how it is that people get photos of lightning in the sky.

Meanwhile Gabriele was cooking up a storm in the kitchen, just as the storminess was beginning to ease off outdoors, like a pause between acts in a play. Siobhan was watching him the way a child watches an adult. Not exactly trying to learn but fascinated. I heard Gabriele say things to her—things like "hand me that spoon please" but mixed up in English and Italian. I did not hear her respond. Maybe she just handed him the spoon and didn't say anything. I wondered if she spoke Italian.

There was a sudden brilliant, almost blinding, crack of lightning followed by an immediate clap of thunder. I thought I could smell an electrical fire, but I realized it was just something the lightning bolt had done to the air. Then I smelled the chicken cooking on the stove and migrated to the kitchen and away from the sliding glass doors. He had sliced the sausages in half the long way and then cut them into sections and mixed them in with the chicken pieces, the chopped garlic and vegetables, and the two jars of red sauce. I could pick out the smells of garlic, oregano and chicken, and another welter of smells that I couldn't separate.

I suggested to Siobhan that maybe we should set the table, which we did, and the space between the lightning strikes got shorter and shorter, although none of them seemed as close as that one big one that had made it look like daylight for a micro-second.

"The rain is picking up," she said. I had hauled out a tablecloth that was made to look like awning material, with stripes. It made me smile thinking of the high winds and possible flooding outdoors. The table has six chairs, but we laid the places at one end, instead of spreading out.

"You know, maybe you should just ask Lily and Tony and Frank directly if they know anything about what happened when Ned died," Siobhan said, with her eyebrows raised and her brow slightly wrinkled.

I heard her say that and thought to myself *we already did that, didn't we?* I almost said it aloud, but another daylight-like crack of lightning interrupted us, followed a second later by a nearly deafening peal of thunder.

The electricity did not go off. I counted to ten very slowly and the lights were still on. I walked over to the balcony doors and looked at the street. Wet, but not flooded.

Gabriele brought a turkey platter filled with pasta and the chicken-filled red sauce from the kitchen and placed it in the center of the dining table. It looked like any sensible person would have expected, given that the chef co-owned one of the most in-demand restaurants in Manhattan. Perfect, in other words, and with a heavenly smell. He ducked back into the kitchen and came back with a foil-wrapped loaf of bread that reeked of garlic. That's a good reek, by the way.

We had a gourmet dinner that cleared out the spoilables from the fridge and the freezer. Gabriele's wine stood us in good stead; we never had to open one of the bottles of my wine that was lined up like a hedge around the walls of the living room wherever there was wallspace near the floor.

"You were there when Mike interviewed Lily and Tony and Frank," I said to Gabriele while we were eating. "Didn't Mike ask them directly if they were at Ned's apartment when he died?"

He shook his head. "Ask about working at *apartamento*, and they say not happen."

"You're a genius with food," Siobhan said with a broad smile and a fork in her hand.

He indicated with a bob of his head that he appreciated the compliment.

"I have been staying in Ned's apartment," she said. "And it is far too small for a rehearsal of any type. Almost too small for more than three or four people having a drink standing up. There's not too much furniture, just not enough space."

"But we never asked them, I guess," I said quietly. "I should get in touch with Mike. I think he would have transcripts of the interviews we did. I thought I remembered him asking them where they were when Ned was killed."

Gabriele shook his head.

"What would Ruth say if I asked her?"

"Same. Ruth have good memory, remember everything."

"I give up. Like I said, I think Mike has transcripts. But even if we asked them before, no reason we can't ask them again."

Miraculously we had eaten all the chicken and almost all the pasta. There was some sauce left, with a lot of bell pepper and chopped fennel in it. I stood up and picked up my plate and Siobhan's and took them to the kitchen where Gabriele had already washed all the pots and cooking utensils and put them away. He followed me into the kitchen with his plate and the almost-empty platter with a picture of a turkey on the bottom.

I kissed him on both cheeks and then on the mouth. I know Siobhan could see me do it, but I had an overwhelming feeling of gratitude and love for Gabriele. "You know, Gabriele, you are very dear to me." It sounded lame when I said it, but I couldn't think of anything else to say. "Look, you did everything."

"You needed talk to Brianna."

"She told me she almost never uses that name," I said, patting him on the shoulder.

"I no call her that, but she is Brianna for me."

"You love her, don't you?"

He didn't respond, started scraping the plates into the garbage, but shook his head.

"She love me too. But she want have baby alone, and she going *Inghilterra*." The Italian word for England. "And she not like live with man. I like live with man, if man is Ugo. Not like live with man if man is not Ugo."

"Boys!" It was Siobhan, and she was standing next to us, with the wine glasses and the unused spoons. "Where shall I put these?"

Gabriele kissed her lightly on one cheek and put the glasses in the sink. He opened the flatware drawer and motioned to it. She dropped the spoons into the spoon compartment.

"I think this is what they call a Love Triangle," she said. "But maybe a different kind of Love Triangle. A Rainbow Triangle. Two fags and a lesbo. If the baby is a boy, I'm going to name him Edward Hugh Savage. And we'll call him Eddie, not Ned."

"And if the baby is a girl?" I asked.

She shrugged. "Nettie. I wish I were brave enough to call her Boadicea, but that would be like a curse. She'd have to spell her name and explain what it means every time she meets somebody for her whole life. "

I smiled and hugged her, told her to go back to the living room and relax. I keep a Brita filtering pitcher on the counter so that there will be filtered drinking water for people who like that sort of thing. For myself, I drink tap water. But I took down a tumbler and poured it full of filtered water, handed it to her. Then I opened the pantry and took out a candy bar with dark chocolate, tree nuts and sea salt. When I first bought them, I thought It didn't sound like health food. Who knew? Turns out it is actually good for you—and low-cal to boot. She took the candy and the water and went back to the living room. I thought it looked like she might have dropped a slight curtsey, but it could have been that she just tripped on a shoelace or the edge of a rug.

I realized as I was staring out the window that there wasn't any lightning, and I could see through all the windows that there was no rain pelting down. *Either we're in the eye of the storm and heading for the worst or maybe we got lucky and it's moving out to sea.*

Chapter Twenty-nine

Gabriele made it clear that I was not welcome in the kitchen while he was cleaning up. It is a small kitchen, difficult for two people to be there at the same time, but I wanted to help. After all, he had done all the cooking. And "No" is the same in English and Italian. He did a blocking move in the doorway as I tried to edge in.

"Okee dokee, smoky."

"I sleep here tonight. Is storm and rain. And is very bad trains on G line to Brooklyn at night." He closed the cabinets, wiped the counters with paper towels, took off his shirt and walked into my bedroom, grabbed a towel and headed in to take a shower. Just as punctuation to the door closing, there was a clap of thunder—not close, not loud, but thunder. There was rain coming down again—not heavy, not noisy, but rain.

Siobhan was staring out the balcony doors into the night. There is a church steeple almost directly in front of the window, but a few blocks away, and it silhouettes against the pervasive city environment of light very dramatically.

"Saint Mary's," I said. "Catholic."

"I should go home, so that you and Gabriele can get some sleep."

"You're welcome to stay here if you want. At least you won't be alone, and there is a second bedroom, after all. Has its own bathroom too." I thought for a moment, and added, "And it shares a wall with your apartment, so if there's anything going on there, you could hear some noise."

She didn't answer, but I could tell by a relaxing of her shoulders that she was considering the offer. "Sometimes I dream about Ned, and I wake up absolutely certain that I have been talking to him."

"For a girl who likes girls, you certainly were in love with Ned."

She turned to me and smiled. "That's why I'm convinced that there wasn't any foul play about his death. He told me."

I couldn't come up with an answer to that, just made a "huh" noise to indicate I heard what she said.

"That chocolate candy bar was delicious," she said.

I admitted that I am slightly addicted to them as well. "I frequently eat one before I go to bed. I remember reading an article about someone—a woman, but I can't remember who—who always took a spoonful of honey before she went to bed. In her case it was because she wanted to taste sweet if her husband kissed her. In my case, I just like having a good taste in my mouth when I turn off the light."

"Doesn't Gabriele sleep in the other bedroom?"

I shook my head. "No, he sleeps with me. It's a treat for both of us. I spent most of my life sleeping *a deux*; my brother when we were kids, my wives. I don't know about Gabriele, but he seems to fall asleep almost before he takes a breath. It's comforting to sleep with someone, not at all like sleeping alone."

"Do you snore?"

"I suppose I do. Most people do, at least from time to time. My grandmother snored enough to make the walls of the house vibrate, but nobody ever said anything because it wasn't polite to bring it up. The idea was that men snored, but women didn't. I can testify that both of my wives snored at least sporadically. They just poked me if I did, and I learned to turn over in my sleep when poked."

"Does Gabriele poke you?"

"Not that I remember, but I never sleep on my back these days because I have a bit of sleep apnea and wake up feeling like I can't breathe if I fall asleep on my back. I always sleep on my side, with my arm under the pillow."

She turned back to the window and stared in the direction of the steeple.

"What does Ned look like in your dreams?"

"Odd," she said. "He looks odd. Sometimes I can see through him and it makes him laugh when I look through him."

"A ghost."

"Perhaps. I think that must be what Mary saw when the angel appeared to her and told her she would have a baby, 'and shall call his name Emanuel, God with us.'"

"I can't say one way or another, but I sometimes have a sense that the people I love who have died are still there. I don't see ghosts, but I can feel them sometimes, feel them in the room with me."

"Is it scary?"

"No." I changed the subject. "Maybe what you are learning in your dreams is something you already knew but didn't realize you knew."

"I doubt that. Just REM dreams. I did love him, and I think I miss him, even though we were only together for a short time. Maybe it's because we were only together for a short time."

Gabriele emerged from the bedroom wearing one of my t-shirts and a pair of boxer shorts with some kind of silly pattern on them. He looked surprised that Siobhan was still there.

"I asked Siobhan if she wanted to stay here tonight because of the storm. She can sleep in Carl's room."

"Carl?" she asked.

"Old friend, used to be my roommate. He's the reason I have a second bedroom instead of a smaller, one-bedroom apartment. He's married now and lives in Toronto, haven't seen him in years. But I think of the other bedroom as Carl's bedroom. Gabriele has met Carl; he used to be a police detective out on Long Island."

Gabriele nodded.

"Have you ever seen a ghost?" she asked him.

"*Fantasma*," I translated.

"*Sì*," he said. "*Il mio fratello.*" *My brother.*

"When did he die?"

"We was child."

"Was he still a child when you saw him as a ghost?"

He shook his head.

"How did you know it was your brother?"

"I just know."

"Did he tell you something?"

"He tell me Ugo is good man, not be afraid."

"And you believed him?"

I had never heard this before. I opened my mouth to say something and thought better of it.

He nodded. "He right. I know he right when he tell me because he love me."

"What if I tell you that I have seen Ned in my dreams, and he tells me something?"

"What he look like?"

"He looks like Ned, but the light shines through him."

"*Fantasma.*"

She nodded.

"What he tell you?"

"He tells me that nothing bad happened when he died."

"But somebody kill him."

"I know," she said. "But Ned seems to say it was an accident."

"Okay," I said. "It's not Halloween yet, and even though this storm makes it seem like we should be telling ghost stories, it doesn't mean the dead are coming back to tell us things. Dreams are dreams. We dream things that are already in our minds, not things that ghosts bring us."

"Maybe ghosts are things that are already in our brains but that we're not aware of."

"I'm not saying dreams are always wrong, Siobhan. All I'm saying is that we don't need to believe in ghosts to listen carefully to what phantoms tell us in our dreams."

"Fair enough," she said.

"*Non capisco.*" He didn't understand.

"What I'm saying is that your brother told you something that was true, and you knew it was true. Siobhan heard Ned say something in a dream that she believes is true. We should talk to Mike and tell him these things and see what he wants us to do next."

Siobhan said she would head back to her apartment and thanked me for the invitation. Gabriele held his hand out to her. She took it and he pulled her close to him and hugged her then kissed her hand and let go. She waved at me and left.

"Ciao, Brianna," he said to her back. I thought of that Fellini film, *Juliet of the Spirits.* At the end, all of Juliet's made-up friends were sailing away on a ship and waving to her, calling out *"Ciao, Giulietta, Ciao, Giulietta."* She would never see them again.

That night, I had a vivid dream of my grandmother. She didn't tell me anything that I could remember, but I felt better when I woke up in the dark than I had felt when I went to bed. I almost got up to get a fresh glass of water, but instead just turned over and went back to sleep on the off-chance that she might still be there waiting for me. She wasn't.

The storm picked up and the lightning woke me up several times. For some reason thunder never wakes me up but lightning does. Maybe the flash of light goes right through my eyelids. My second wife said nothing could wake me up, not even a train wreck. Not entirely true, because I woke up when the kids were little and would cry at night, but maybe thunder is not unusual enough to wake me up.

Unusually, I woke up before Gabriele and made some coffee. I sent an email to Mike di Saronno about what Siobhan had said to me about Ned's "ghost."

He answered me that it made more sense than the idea that he might have been murdered in cold blood. There had never been a motive established, for instance. But the coroner had declared it a homicide, and that was what we were investigating. He agreed that we should re-visit the scene of Ned's death with the cast members of the original *Twelfth Night,* including Siobhan. There was no evidence that any of them was there when Ned died, but clearly someone had been.

The sky was mostly clear and summery blue. There was a shelf of dark clouds on the southeastern horizon, probably the storm that had passed during the night and was moving out into the Atlantic. The air was dry and the temperature was higher than it had been for several days—autumn weather is as unpredictable as spring weather. In the daylight, I had a hard time relating to Siobhan's dream, but I still was comforted from having seen my grandmother. She looked like I remembered her, an old lady who had been a widow for two decades.

Gabriele tottered out the bedroom door while I was on my second cup of coffee.

He's so young, I thought. He looked boyish with his hair in all different directions and a map of sleep lines on his face and arm. The sight of him took me back to my childhood. I handed him a mug and pointed to the coffeemaker.

He sipped at the coffee and then said to me, "What she said maybe is right. Maybe nobody kill him. Maybe it happen but nobody want to make it happen. It just happen anyway."

I told him Mike had agreed that what Siobhan said made sense from what we knew about Ned, but from what we knew about how Ned died, it was still inescapable that he died at the hand of another person.

He smiled. I knew he was thinking that Siobhan's dream about Ned had the truth buried in it. He took his coffee back into the bedroom to get dressed.

Chapter Thirty

Mike set up several interviews for two days later about the Ned Savage case. He would be talking to Siobhan, Lily, Tony, and Frank as well as the stage manager, Harold Green and two of the St Benedict's cast who were playing Olivia's jester and Maria, neither of whom had been interviewed before. I would be spending my day in the observation booth. Mike also asked Edgar Savage if he wanted to observe these interviews—something the NYPD could arrange because Edgar would have to come to New York. So, Edgar was on a plane from LAX to JFK early the next morning and was checked into a hotel in the theater district by dinnertime.

Mike suggested that the three of us have dinner to go over the situation and to synchronize our watches, so to speak. We met at Chez Josephine, a landmark bistro on 42nd Street that was opened by an adopted son of a famous chanteuse-dancer who spent most of her life in France. In addition to being a unique part of the Hell's Kitchen cultural scene, the food was good and the prices were moderate. I volunteered to pay for the wine and asked if Ruth or Gabriele could join us. Mike agreed. In the end, Gabriele couldn't join us because they were jammed with reservations at his restaurant, and he didn't want to just not show up, or leave it in the hands of one of the waiters. Ruth already had plans, too, so it was boys' night out for Mike, Edgar and me.

Although I never met Ned, I confess I invented a person I thought he might have been by watching Edgar and then remembering what the real Ned looked like when I saw him that one time in the hallway while he was moving in. The brothers had a strong resemblance, but Ned looked like a magazine cover, and Edgar didn't. So, when Edgar walked into Chez Josephine, I imagined him limping toward the table, like I would guess Ned might have if it was him instead of his brother.

"Earth to Hugo," Mike said, snapping his fingers as if to bring me out of a hypnotic state.

"Sorry, I was just trying to remember what Ned looked like the day I saw him. There is a family resemblance. I didn't realize how much you look alike when I first met you, Edgar." We shook hands.

"Stag dinner," Mike said. "We invited a couple of others, but they couldn't make it this time."

"So, I'm easily the guest who traveled the farthest to get here," Edgar smiled. "Hooray for me."

Mike explained that the interviews would include some people that Edgar might know or know of and some who might well be unfamiliar. Edgar said he had refreshed his knowledge of *Twelfth Night* by reading it twice on the plane and by watching a film of the play from 1996 on a streaming service. ("Veddy British" he said).

"Have you had any further thoughts about anyone who might have a grudge against Ned?" Mike asked him.

Edgar shook his head slowly, with his eyes looking down at the table. "Honestly, I know Ned was human and so he probably wasn't loved by everyone he ever met, but I have never heard anyone speak ill of him."

"How about actors he worked with?"

"He must have had some disagreements with people he worked with. I don't remember much, but I remember once he didn't like the blocking in a scene because the director seemed to purposefully upstage him—made him speak to the back of the stage. But mostly he considered all the people he worked with to be his friends."

"Anybody ever take a poke at him?"

"Not that I ever knew anything about. He was kinda fragile-looking when he was relaxed. You know, because of the arm and the way he held his hand, the way he dragged his right foot. Nobody would hit him if they were in their right mind. People were drawn to him. He was like a magnet for all kinds of people. If we went to a party, he would know everybody who was there by the time we left. He got very gregarious when he had a couple of drinks, but I never saw him tipsy or slurring his words. No idea what he would have been like if he was plastered, but I doubt he ever was.

Plastered, I mean."

"Hugo and I are at a disadvantage because neither of us ever met him, so we have to put together our pictures of him based on what other people tell us."

We ordered a round of drinks and a plate of goat-cheese "Chinese" raviolis. I always stick with dirty vodka. Mike had a very pale dry sherry, and Edgar wanted a Manhattan.

"You know they're going to make your Manhattan with rye whisky, right?"

"I've only ever had Manhattans made with bourbon or sour mash."

"That's why I said that. Most people from out of town aren't expecting the rye whisky—most of it is made in small distilleries upstate. Not the least bit rough on the palate, most of them very smooth, but they don't have that sweetish taste that bourbon has."

"I'll be brave," he said with a slight smile.

We clinked our glasses and toasted Ned.

"Do these look Chinese?" Mike asked, pointing at the raviolis.

"Dim sum," Edgar said.

"I guess, but they're not shaped like dim sum; they're shaped like raviolis. I'm Italian, you know, and my grandma made raviolis all day before any holiday or anybody's saint's day. For me, since I'm Michael, that was September 29, my saint's day, also called Michaelmas. Actually, it's for all the archangels, so Hugo's buddy Gabriele would have the same day. Anyway, they look Italian to me. Who cares if Marco Polo brought them back from China? He was Venetian anyway. The only thing Italian about Venice is the map. They speak a different language."

The waiter brought over a platter of oysters with several sauces to dip them in. Looked like there were a couple of dozen, all different kinds.

"On the house," he said. "Welcome to Mr. Miller."

I thanked him.

"Look," Edgar said, "I'm still uncomfortable seeing Ned's wife is going to be interrogated. Does she have to be one of the people you're interviewing?"

"These are not people who might be suspects," Mike said. "It's possible that however Ned died, one of these people could have been in the room, but that's not why we want to talk to them. One of the things we want to find out is what happened the day before Ned was killed. He apparently had most of the cast of the play over for drinks, and some of them apparently brought housewarming gifts. We want to know whether they remember anything that might help us. Could be that's when the marijuana specks landed on the couch, for instance."

A man with shoulder-length hair and red silk pajamas strode over to our table. It was the owner, Josephine's adopted son, Jean-Claude. He kiss-kissed all three of us and welcomed us to Chez Josephine. He and I had known each other for years. An investment banker who died in about 1999 introduced us, and we stayed friends, although we don't socialize outside the restaurant. Then he could see we were talking about something serious and excused himself, hoping we would enjoy the oysters.

"I want to tell you that several of the people we've interviewed, including Siobhan, Ned's wife, refuse to believe he died at the hand of someone else. They're all convinced it was some kind of unfortunate accident."

"And you think?" Edgar asked.

"We don't know what to think. But, however you look at it, it's hard to imagine someone smashing him over the head with a heavy candlestick by mistake."

"Didn't you tell me he had an EpiPen stuck in his leg when the police got there?"

Mike nodded. "He apparently had an allergic reaction that we think was caused by a fungus that is frequently found on cannabis plants. We tested the couch and found some of the particles of leaves there that had the fungus on them. It's called aspergillus. For most people, it's harmless, but obviously not for Ned."

Edgar didn't say anything, just sipped on his Manhattan.

"But the allergy didn't kill him. The candlestick killed him," Mike said softly.

"So, the smoke from the marijuana might have caused the allergy attack?" Edgar asked.

"Not the smoke," Mike said. "The medical examiner said the fungus could not survive the heat and probably would not have caused any problem by smoking, which was what they were doing. We found some un-burnt particles on the couch and there were some in his throat and lungs. They were using a glass pipe, so they probably were handling the marijuana, putting it into the pipe, and it would have been possible to inhale a couple of small bits from the air without even knowing it, like a particle of pollen outdoors in the spring or fall."

"I saw him have that kind of attack one time when I was in high school. They called paramedics and took him off to the hospital. He was okay, but they gave him a shot of something that he said hurt like hell, and that's apparently what saved his life."

"Probably epinephrine; that's what's in an EpiPen," Mike said. "Most people who have an injection like that are unconscious, but I guess he wasn't the time you saw him have an attack. The result from an EpiPen injection is almost automatic, and probably the dose isn't nearly as big as what he might have had in the ER a decade or so back."

"So maybe the two things are unrelated? That never occurred to me," Edgar said.

"Almost certainly unrelated," Mike said. "And nothing to say that they even happened at the same time. The fungus particles on the couch could have been inhaled way after they were deposited there. Whoever had the candlestick probably had no idea what was going on when Ned started to pass out and stuck the EpiPen in his thigh."

"But he bashed him anyway, instead of trying to help."

Mike shrugged an I-don't-know.

"I'm just a bystander," I volunteered, "but almost all the people we've talked to seemed to think it was some kind of weird accident. No ideas how or why it happened, but nobody can believe anyone would want to kill Ned. He was a very popular guy. Everybody liked him, or at least that's the way it seems."

I ordered spaghetti with marinara sauce. I'm not Italian, but I think I must have been in a previous life. Edgar ordered the specialty of the house; a gigantic salad with a whole steamed lobster on top. Mike had the fish of the day, mahi-mahi with lemon-caper sauce. The food was good, but the treat at Chez Josephine is the place itself; the bizarre posters and portraits of Josephine Baker that crowd the walls. I plead guilty that I regularly have the fried chicken that is like the centerpiece of southern cooking (Josephine was from St Louis, but her mother was from Arkansas). That night, though, the pasta with red sauce sounded great to me. I asked the waiter to bring a dish of basil leaves with the entree.

"Tell me why you said that Siobhan was involved in Ned's death," Mike said, looking at Edgar.

"I know I said that, and for some reason I was thinking it, but for the life of me I don't remember why I thought that," he said. "I think I may have had a dream about Ned, and maybe his wife was in it too. I was confused. Try to forget I said that."

Without saying it out loud, we all changed the subject, and Mike was asking Edgar if he was planning to see a show while he was in town. We talked about several of the shows that people said were good. I hadn't seen any of them—wouldn't you think I could have found tickets to at least one? Of course what people in California heard about most was *Hamilton*, but the tickets were always scarce as hen's teeth, and more expensive than diamonds.

As we left, the sky was black and there were bolts of lightning to the south. The smell of rain was in the air. It had the look of another nor'easter.

Chapter Thirty-one

I remember when I was a child being told that only "fools and foreigners" tried to predict the weather. Meteorologists would disagree, but it does turn out that even with satellites watching 24-7, we still get taken completely off-guard by the weather at times. And that's not just when a hurricane strengthens at the last minute before it makes landfall.

In New York City—and the entire Northeastern part of the United States—there is a phenomenon of storms that brew up in the Gulf of Mexico or the warmer part of the Atlantic just above the Caribbean and then sail up the east coast, causing havoc every inch of the way. Basically, that was the story with Superstorm Sandy which actually was a product of two weather fronts joining forces before they started north.

Well, this one was not a superstorm like Sandy, but it was a dilly. We could watch its progress as it swept up the coast toward us. The weather services and the television stations were running video of flooded towns, huge storm surges washing over seawalls, and cars being tossed around in rivers that were overrunning streets. It was eerily like the plot of *The Rise and Fall of the City of Mahagonny* by Bertolt Brecht, considered these days to be an opera of sorts with music by Kurt Weill, who also wrote *The Threepenny Opera*.

As it happened, the actual damage the storm that night did in New York City was less than we were braced for; lots of trees down, lots of limbs of trees down, lots of power outages, lots of clogged drains that were blocked with fallen leaves and whatever had been swept to the grated drains and piled up, and in some places, water backing up onto the streets. The subways were okay, but the commuter railways were awash in floodwaters and two to five inches of rain, depending on where you happened to be.

Mother Nature's pyrotechnic department really outdid itself though. Cracks of lightning went on for what seemed like hours, and everyone kept counting to see how far away the lightning was. I think the concept is that if you count and multiply the number you get to by one thousand before the thunderclap hits, that would be about the number of feet away that the lightning was. So, if you could get to six or seven, that lightning was more than a mile away. If you could get to ten or more, it was either not there yet or moving away. If you could only get to one and a half, that lightning was right on top of you. When it's on top of you like that, you stay away from the windows, and you don't even think about using the plumbing, because the metal pipes can carry the electricity to toilets, tubs, faucets and even appliances like garbage disposals or washing machines.

There were a lot of one and a half counts that night, and for many people, restful sleep was beyond impossible. For me not so much, because as my mother used to say, I could sleep through an air raid, which I fortunately have never had to prove. I confess to leaning on a martini glass full of vodka to put me in the mood to fall asleep with the lightning creating strobe effects on the glass of the buildings outside my bedroom windows. That meant a moment of quandary about two o'clock when I woke up needing to urinate. But I determined that it was okay to lift the lid on the toilet because it was plastic, and I did what I needed to do without being afraid of being electrocuted. Then I went back to sleep.

I remember dreaming about Ned Savage, but I don't remember much of what I dreamed. I think in my dream he may have showed up alive, so that the murder victim must have been someone else. I don't think I could see him, but I knew he was there, maybe like Banquo's ghost. I woke up with a start, and there was heavy rain beating on the window, with not nearly as much lightning as there had been earlier. I looked at the digital display on the clock next to my bed. It was 4:37. I went back to sleep and pulled the quilt up so that it reached my hairline in the back and tucked under my chin in the front.

When I woke up, the digital clock said it was just after seven o'clock, and since the daylight matched that, I was happy and guessed that we had not lost electricity. Sure enough, none of the electronic clocks, like the one on the stove, were blinking and needing to be re-set. I verified that by opening the freezer and seeing that the ice-maker was full of pieces of ice. If the electricity had been off, the ice would have partially defrosted and become welded together when it refroze.

It was still raining, and there were still flashes of lightning, but since the sun was somewhere up there behind the clouds, it was less like a nightclub strobe. Still, the thunder was loud when it hit.

My doorbell rang. I grabbed a bathrobe and scurried out to see who it was—no doubt someone at the wrong apartment.

It was Tony. He was shaking out an umbrella that had clearly not kept him dry, because his pants were clinging to his legs and his shirt was soaked. He was shivering. I ushered him in and gave him some orange juice, promising to put the coffee on presto.

"It was my fault," he blurted out.

"What was your fault?"

"Ned. I took that pot over there, and I guess he went into a coma or something."

"When?"

"When he had the apartment party."

"No, I mean when did he go into a coma?"

"I don't know. I wasn't there."

"You just said you were there, didn't you?"

"What I did was take the pot over there, and I guess they smoked it later and Ned was allergic or whatever. I didn't know." He was still shivering. I walked him into the bathroom off my bedroom and handed him the heavy terrycloth robe I was wearing. I told him to take a hot shower and pointed at the towel on the rack.

"Don't worry about it. It's not your fault. The pot didn't kill him," I said to him as I closed the door.

When I heard the shower start, I called Mike, who answered, and I gave him a short version of what had happened. I put on a long-sleeved t-shirt and some jeans while we talked. When I heard the shower turn off, I told Mike I had to go, because Tony would be out of the bathroom shortly. Mike said he would be over in half-hour or so, depending on the subway.

Tony appeared in my robe, carrying his wet clothes. I told him to put them in the dryer in the hallway. While he was doing that, I explained to him that Ned's death was caused by a head wound that was obviously inflicted by the candlestick that was found on the floor with blood all over it.

As we stood in the hallway, there was a knock on the door. It was Lily, who shrieked, standing at the door, "It was my fault." Clearly the electric storm had caused a wave of guilt to wash over New York.

The door to Ned's apartment opened and there was Siobhan. "What do you mean, it was your fault?"

"I knew Tony had brought that grass to the party, and I didn't say anything to you or anyone, but especially to you, because you were his wife."

"How does that make it your fault?" Tony asked, stepping behind me and peering over my shoulder.

"What are you doing here?" Lily said more softly.

"I came over to tell Hugo that I took the pot to the party, and I thought it was my fault that Ned died."

Lily pushed her way into my apartment and did a head-to-toe visual exam of Tony in the bathrobe with no clothes on underneath.

"What are you doing here again?" she asked Tony without looking at me.

Siobhan was standing in the doorway, looking surprised at what was going on. There was a huge flash of lightning and an almost immediate thunderclap that sounded like it was in the room with us. The lights went out.

"Of course," I said to no one in particular, looking around the apartment to see if anything electric was still operating. Nope.

"Might as well come in, and I'll see if I can find something to drink. May end up being tap water." I looked Lily up and down and congratulated her on having walked between the raindrops. "Tony was soaked when he got here. How did you stay dry?"

"I took a cab."

Siobhan looked like someone at a tennis match, looking from one of them to the other and back. Fortunately, there were enough places to sit in the living room, and there was enough ambient light from the windows that it didn't seem like dusk. There was a clatter of hail on the balcony.

"If it was anybody's fault, it was mine," Siobhan said. "If I had just stayed with Ned, I would have been there when whoever was there was getting ready to hit him with the candlestick."

Mike walked in the door that I had left ajar. He was slightly out of breath from having come up the stairs. "Elevators are out, but you probably already knew that," he said. "Hugo tells me that you thought Ned's death was your fault, Tony. Unburden yourself if that's what you think. The pot had nothing to do with Ned's demise. He died from being hit with a blunt instrument."

"I already told him that," I said. "I don't know about the rest of you guys, but I am going to have a screwdriver. It's five o'clock someplace in the world." I keep fresh orange juice in the fridge as a condiment for vodka in the hours before noon. "Rats, no screwdriver, everything is in the fridge and freezer."

Siobhan, Lily and Tony all seconded the motion. Lily was tapping on her smartphone but looked up and smiled. Mike wandered into the kitchen and found a tumbler in the cabinet, filled it with tap-water and took it back to the living room. I had a magnum bottle of a cheap Italian red wine that I have with dinner a lot of evenings. I took down four wine glasses and handed them to the guests first. As I gestured to the wine and was about to say "cheers," Edgar arrived.

"Did you leave the door open?" I asked Mike. He shrugged and nodded. I walked out and closed it.

"Wine?" I asked Edgar. "Electricity is out, can't open the fridge, so it's either wine or water."

"They told me downstairs that the electricity was out, and I came up the stairs," Edgar said.

"I forgot to tell you that I called Ned's brother, Edgar Savage, and told him that he might want to come over here," Mike said to everyone.

"Edgar, you have arrived just in time to hear that all three of these actors decided during the storm that they were probably at fault for Ned's death. Of course they weren't at fault, but they all felt like they were guilty of something.

"That happens when there is no clear resolution of a case. Suspicions grow, and that includes feelings of self-guilt," Mike said. "I bet even Edgar has wondered if there was any way he could have prevented it from happening, and he was on the west coast the whole time."

Edgar looked at his lap and nodded.

The lights flickered several times and there was an audible clunking sound as the electricity turned back on. Siobhan walked over to the balcony sliding doors and pointed. "The electricity is back in the whole neighborhood, or at least the traffic lights are on, and I see some neon too."

There were several flashes of lightning, but the electricity didn't go off. The thunder began to sound more distant, and I could feel tension dropping off me.

"Well, here's to Con Ed," I raised a glass of wine to the utility company. The others with wine said "Con Ed" and took a sip. I pulled out my phone and sent a quick note to Gabriele and Ruth to let them in on what was happening.

The concierge called to let me know there was a man coming up, but he hadn't understood the name, sounded like "miracle something." Why not? It must be Frank.

I told the room that someone was coming up. Lily put her hand up and said, "Probably Frank. I texted him about what was going on here."

Frank rang the doorbell just as there was a flash of lightning that seemed close, followed maybe five seconds later by a fairly loud clap of thunder.

I opened the door and said, "I suppose you're here to say it was your fault that Ned Savage died." He looked surprised but didn't say anything, just squinted at me like I had a bright light behind me. Lily appeared behind me and took Frank by the hand, leading him into the living room.

Mike smiled and said to Frank that all the seats were already taken, and suggested that Frank might want to sit at the dining table, since it was all one room anyway.

"What did you mean when you opened the door?" he asked me across the room.

"Nothing, really nothing. Several people who are here seemed to think they were at least partly responsible for Ned's death, so I asked you if you were responsible, because it would be like following suit."

"Well, you guessed right. I am responsible, but I had no intention of hitting him, and certainly no intention of hurting him in any way."

Mike straightened up and said, "Are you saying that it was you that hit him with the candlestick?"

He nodded and explained that he and Ned had been talking about Malvolio. "I think Lily is a born comedienne, and she is perfect for Malvolio, much better than I would have been. But I agreed with her that if Malvolio was trying to raise himself above his station, he would be wearing a sword."

"Where are you going with this?"

"Well, it was just Ned and me, and I told him that it would be uproarious if Malvolio learned how to do a musketeer-like obeisance with the sword. But Ned didn't understand what I meant, so I picked up the candlestick and waved it in the air, basically drawing figure-eights with it."

"And then you hit him with it?"

"Well," he said, looking panicky, "sorta, yes, but that was when Ned looked like he was having an epileptic fit or something, and then he looked like he was passing out. He turned pale and stuck something in his leg. He staggered at me and then fell on the floor and I tripped on his leg. It happened so fast, I don't know how to describe it. I know it sounds impossible."

"So you tripped, fell and hit Ned when you fell?" I asked.

Frank looked stricken and like he was going to say something but couldn't decide on the words. He started to sob. "I should have told you right away, but I was scared."

The doorbell rang. I said, "Hold that thought," and went to the door. It was a daily double; both Ruth and Gabriele at the same time.

I whispered to them, "You're not going to believe this, just be quiet and watch," I told them as they walked into the living room that they might want to take chairs from the table so they could sit down.

Mike picked up the conversation.

"So, if I understand what you said, you're saying that you tripped and fell and the candlestick in your hand hit Ned Savage by accident."

He nodded. "But it wasn't in my hand. I let go of it and it hit Ned when I let go. I was wearing gloves because I had intended to find a stick or something and show Ned what I was recommending. Gloves made me feel more like I was holding a sword. But the candlestick slipped away as I started to fall, and it hit him."

Siobhan and Lily both had I-told-you-so teary smiles. They nodded in unison. Gabriele looked puzzled, and Ruth was clearly trying to figure out what had gone on before they arrived.

Frank looked downcast and leaned forward with his head in his hands, looking down at the floor.

"Frank," Lily said in a collegial tone, "Frank, I learned how to do that three-musketeers thing, but it doesn't work with the big broadsword." She looked at the ceiling then said, "Maybe my broadsword is a little too much anyway. This play shouldn't be like a burlesque show, after all, with comics dropping their pants."

Frank stood up and walked over to Siobhan, clearly to say he was sorry, but no words came out. Siobhan stood up and hugged him.

"It must have been horrible for you," she said to him. "Ned was probably semi-conscious at most, and maybe completely unconscious. He's in heaven now, so don't worry about him," she said sweetly and calmly, with a valiant attempt at a smile. "You can't help tripping and falling when a guy throws himself at your legs."

Frank burst into gagging sobs, turned to the room and said to everyone, "I'm so sorry, everybody. It just happened. He fell, he tripped me, I fell, and the candlestick hit him. I was so scared, I just ran. I knew he was dead. He wasn't bleeding much, but I knew he was dead."

Mike stepped forward. "He wasn't dead, although he probably was within a couple of minutes. We will have to talk to the D.A. about whether to charge you with leaving the scene, but I suspect the decision will be negative. And the gloves are why there were no prints."

"I killed a man. A good man. That's a horrible thing to carry around. I can tell you that I thought I would be struck by lightning so many times that I almost got used to it. The mark of Cain."

"Okay, bring the curtain down," Tony said. "No more bows. No more ham fat." He walked over and hugged Frank, towering over him. "You okay, Shortie?"

Frank kept on sobbing but smiled while tears were dripping down his cheeks.

I grabbed Ruth and Gabriele and steered them into my bedroom, where I explained what had happened; how Siobhan, Lily and Tony had all said they were responsible for what happened, and that if things happened the way Frank said, it really was an accident.

Edgar put a cap on it. He was streaming tears but not sobbing. "I knew no one would have done this to Ned on purpose. And anybody who was Ned's friend is my friend." He hugged Frank. I poured wine in all the glasses except Siobhan's. We drank to Ned. Then Lily proposed a toast to "all fools." We drank again.

Chapter Thirty-two

An hour after the rest had left, Gabriele and Ruth were still at my apartment. For some reason I had turned on the television to an all-news cable station, and we were all staring at it. There was some coverage of the storm; downed trees and tree branches blocking streets, and there was some roadway ponding. Subways were running, surface transportation not so much. Major delays on the bridges and tunnels. It was getting dark outside.

"So, what do you think about all that?" I asked.

"All what?" It was Ruth making a puzzled face.

"That Frank tripped over Ned Savage and accidentally clubbed him with the candlestick that he was waving around like Malvolio waving a sword."

"Is make sense," Gabriele said slowly. "Why you ask that?"

"We had been hearing for quite a while that the people who knew Ned didn't think he was murdered, but that it was some kind of accident," I said. "I never could imagine how the guy could get whacked over the head by accident. Do you think what Frank said was possible?"

The doorbell rang. It was Siobhan.

"I didn't want to sit in that apartment by myself, so here I am," she said.

"So, I'm gonna ask you," I said. "Do you think what Frank said made sense? Could it have happened that way?"

She looked up in thought and then walked over to the glass doors to the balcony. She turned. "Yes, I think Frank was telling us what happened, not just something he made up, if that's what you're asking me."

"That he tripped over Ned while Ned was falling down with the EpiPen in his thigh and hit Ned with the candlestick by accident?"

258

She nodded. "I think I told you I couldn't imagine anyone wanting to kill Ned."

"But there's a difference between thinking he wasn't murdered and believing what Frank said."

She thought for a minute and said, "I have worked with Frank, and I can tell you for sure he wasn't acting today. He was telling the truth."

Ruth cocked her head and Siobhan said, "Frank telegraphs a lot when he's acting. You wouldn't notice it from the audience, but to the other actors it stands out like a sore thumb. None of that today."

"Telegraphs?"

"He has little signals—I'm sure he's entirely unaware of them—that can tell you where he's getting ready to go with his act. Maybe that doesn't make sense, sorry. For Frank, little things like putting his teeth on his bottom lip, or touching his upper teeth with his tongue. He looks at the ceiling briefly when he's starting a line. Things like that. Very obvious when you work with someone day after day. I probably have some too, but of course I'm not acting in the new production."

"Why would you think he would use the same telegraph signals if he was making something up as opposed to saying what is written in a script?"

Gabriele leaned in to hear the answer with Ruth. I realized that they had become good friends over the years. I tended to think of them as my friends, not as friends of each other.

"Telegraphing isn't part of the work of acting. It's just something that people do. Just like Gabriele and Ruth both telegraphed that they were interested in my answer by leaning toward me and turning their heads so that the dominant ear was at the front."

They both sat back. Ruth crossed her arms and Gabriele stood up and walked into the kitchen.

"I wonder if Frank would have run away if he hadn't been waving the candlestick around when Ned started to pass out," Siobhan said.

"You mean if Ned was still alive?" Ruth asked. "None of this would have happened without the candlestick hitting Ned. We'd probably already have finished the run at St Benedict's, and since you're not showing much, you probably would have been Viola all the way through. If Ned was still alive."

"I hadn't thought about it that way. Or, actually, that's not what I meant."

Gabriele was leaning against the wall of the living room, drinking a glass of water. "Frank not bad man." He drank a big gulp of water. "Not liar." He finished the water and put the glass on the pass-through, picking up a wine glass. He grabbed the magnum of red wine, which was the kind with a screw-off top, and filled the glass.

"In Italia, we no drink wine that cost big money," he said. He proposed a toast to Frank. "Frank feel very bad for what happen. I hope he understand what is accident."

We all took a sip of the *montepulciano d'abruzzo,* which is an Italian version of what's sometimes called "hamburger wine" in the United States—cheap and easily drinkable.

My phone vibrated in my hip pocket. It was a text from Mike. *ADA decided not to charge Frank. Chance of winning remote.*

I told my guests that Frank was off the hook. There wasn't a dry eye in the room as we took another sip of the wine to Ned.

Chapter Thirty-three

By the time *Twelfth Night* opened at The Gym, Siobhan's pregnancy was obvious. She watched the opening night (which came after two weeks of previews), from an aisle seat in row K and was wearing a green silk caftan with gold thread woven in such a way that it created a repeating pattern that gave the impression of vertical stripes. She sat with her in-laws: Liz, Mary and Edgar Savage.

The audience loved the production from the moment the lights went down. The sets were minimal because the production was in the round. The stage was covered with dirt and sawdust that could have summoned up an impression of a single-ring circus. It was flooded with dry-ice smoke as the lights went down and a projection on the ceiling gave an impression of a storm at sea and a ship sinking.

The costumes were a movie-ish imitation of about a century of Tudor fashion. Orsino wore the club-toed shoes that Henry VIII favored and a white shirt embroidered in black silk, a style that was called blackwork. His shoulders were well-padded and his flat, beret-like cap had been part of a fashionable look during the time of Henry VIII.

Olivia wore gowns made to stand out with farthingales, with neck ruffs and wrist ruffs, but made with fairly plain pastel materials that would have passed muster at the court of Elizabeth I, where it was nearly a capital offense to wear anything that even approached the fanciness of the queen's elaborate gowns. Sir Toby and Sir Andrew were very showy drunks, and Maria was dressed like a somewhat upscale streetwalker with a lot of cleavage showing. Olivia's jester had the wild hair of a modern rock star and was dressed in traditional motley with a large, three-pointed hat that had bells on the three peaks.

Given the stripped-down stage, the costumes were so sumptuous and colorful that they created a feeling of a story being told in a dream (or so more than one reviewer wrote the next day).

Lily's Malvolio was an immediate hit. She did retain the sword starting after Malvolio finds the counterfeit letter that proves to be his undoing, but it was a period-inaccurate fencing rapier with a slightly rusty look. She had more tics and jerks than any less-experienced comic actor could have gotten away with, and her pomposity started the audience laughing the minute she stepped onto the stage. She later said that she knew that Ned Savage was watching the performance, and she played to him instead of to the audience.

The applause and cheers at the end of the play, after Olivia's jester sang, "When that I was and a little tiny boy," seemed like they would go on all night until Lily stepped forward and signaled for the audience to be seated, which they did.

"This production was designed by a brilliant man named Ned Savage," she said. "He's not here tonight, but everyone on this stage knows that he was looking down on us from heaven. We are all dedicating our performances for the run of this play to Ned Savage, and it is my very great pleasure to introduce the director who took over from Ned when he died." She pointed at Siobhan and motioned to her to come down to the stage. Tony handed her down the two steps to the stage from the aisle, and Lily continued, "It was Ned's concept, but what you have seen tonight is due to the brilliant work of this soon-to-be mother, Siobhan Reilly, who in real life is Ned Savage's widow." She applauded, and the entire audience sprang to their feet, clapping loudly and cheering.

Siobhan said nothing, bowed her head, looked up and threw kisses to the cast then turned to the audience and threw a kiss to Edgar and his sisters.

There were offers to take the production to Broadway, but it wasn't possible, so the three weeks of the announced schedule was the full span of the production's life.

The next day, Siobhan told us that she was going to leave for England after the play closed and wouldn't be back until the baby was born and she felt safe flying back to New York. She had worked out with the building management that she would keep the apartment with the intention of spending some time there when she returned to New York with the baby. She explained that she would continue to work in the theater, so she would most likely move to Manhattan. She felt like Ned's baby should be brought up in America.

Edgar, Liz and Mary decided to spend a few days in New York. I invited them to dinner, and texted Ruth and Gabriele, asking them to join us. Gabriele texted back immediately saying that Ora di Pranzo would be at our service. How much better than that does it get? But I said I would accept only if Gabriele could join us for dinner. He agreed, and I invited Mike to join us. On an impulse, I also texted Siobhan and asked her to join us as well.

To tell the truth, I was not satisfied with the way things were turning out. After all the dust settled, it just didn't seem like we knew everything that went on. I didn't think Frank was very convincing when he said he just panicked and ran off. Maybe I would have, too, but I hope not. If someone was bleeding out on the floor, literally beneath my feet, I hope that I would at least call 911 and give them an anonymous tip, even if I ran away like a scared rabbit right after that. And possibly because Frank didn't have a key as I recalled, Ned was found by an employee of the building who noticed that his door was slightly ajar.

Gabriele had set up a table for us in a back corner of the restaurant and had moved all the tables that would have been nearby away to create a band of empty floor to give us some privacy. We were seated as we arrived, not waiting for the whole party to assemble. Mike was there at the table when I got there, and of course Gabriele was there. Ruth appeared on time, and the Savages were not late. Siobhan was a few minutes late and was wearing a maternity dress, the first time I had seen her do that.

Dante had outdone himself in the kitchen. The menu was pre-set and dominated by seafood, vegetables and pasta, typical of southern Italy. Gabriele had selected some wine, a white and a red, that would complement the food, and we had several toasts, most of them to the cast of *Twelfth Night* or to Siobhan for directing it, or to Ned for having fathered the production.

Neither Mike nor I wanted to open the conversation about what

Frank had told us until it was time for dessert, although everyone there already knew that it was Frank who was there when Ned died. As the dinner went on, however, and the courses were served one after another, the subject of Ned's death became more and more the 800-pound gorilla in the room. Siobhan in particular began to look anxious, fearing, I thought, that we would have to go back over what happened that day yet another time.

After the fish course while we were waiting for the meats to be served, I tapped Siobhan on the shoulder and asked her if she was okay. She smiled, but was obviously uncomfortable as she said she was fine. Then she turned away and took a piece of Italian bread and dipped it in the garbanzo dip that was by each place setting. Liz Savage said something to her, and Siobhan stood up, turned to me, and trotted off to the ladies' room.

"I knew he was dead." When she came back from the restroom, she didn't sit down, stayed standing, making eye contact with each person at the table one by one. "He was just there on the floor, and there was some blood around his head. He was face down, and there was that candlestick right next to him."

We all reacted the same way—shocked, staring, silent.

"I let myself in. I had the key that he gave me. I didn't move in with him because nobody knew we were married, but I didn't want to be alone, so I went over to surprise him." She looked from person to person. "And when I went in, he was dead on the floor, that gun-metal color, like there wasn't any blood left in him."

She sat down at her place then and looked at her hands on the table. "I thought it must have been some kind of accident. I sat down on the floor next to him and stared at him, hoping he would twitch or move, but I knew he wouldn't. I don't know how long I sat there. I told him I loved him and that I would name the baby after him. Somebody told me one time that when somebody dies suddenly, their soul lingers around the body for a while, so I was hoping he could hear what I was saying."

She started to sob and put her face in her hands. Liz, who was sitting next to her, scooted her chair over toward Siobhan and put her arm over Siobhan's back, patting her lightly like a sister would do. Siobhan leaned into Liz, and Liz put both arms around her. Then Gabriele was there, kneeling next to Siobhan and holding her right hand.

"When was it that you went to Ned's apartment?" Mike asked.

She looked up, shrugged, and said she thought it was around four o'clock.

"And why didn't you call 911?"

"He was dead. It was obvious. No point calling anyone. I didn't know how to get in touch with his family. I couldn't face talking to the other people in the cast. I think I was in shock. I probably left the door unlocked when I left. That was probably me." She smiled at Gabriele, her face wet with tears, and stroked his cheek lightly.

"You shouldn't leave the scene of a crime, you know," Mike said.

"He was dead. He had been dead for a while. I didn't touch him because I knew he would be cold. And I thought it had been an accident."

"Did you feel for a pulse?"

"No. He was dead," she said, staring at Mike. "There was no way he might still be alive. He was gray, almost blue." She wiped her nose with her hand then grabbed at a napkin to wipe her hand and face. "I'm so sorry I didn't call someone. It just didn't occur to me. He was dead, and we had been married less than a month. I knew I was carrying his child. I don't think I knew what was going on, and I just left."

"Where did you go?"

"I don't remember. I walked along the river. I was frightened."

"Frightened because you were afraid someone would hurt you?"

"No. Frightened because he was dead, I guess, and I didn't know what to do."

"Did you talk to anyone while you were out walking? Did you get a drink of water or a lemonade? There are usually food trucks out there. Did you get anything to drink or eat?"

"I walked for a while and then went into an Asian restaurant and sat at the bar. It was a big place and decorated like a dinner restaurant, although it was only afternoon when I was there. I had a Virgin Mary. I would have liked a real drink, but I'm not supposed to drink alcohol while I'm pregnant. It was very spicy, odd I remember that. It must have had some kind of pepper sauce in it. I don't usually tolerate spicy food, but I drank that one down, even though it was stinging my mouth."

"Were you in shock?"

She looked at Mike quizzically. "I don't know. Maybe, I suppose. I felt like I was in a bubble. But do you go into shock just because you saw something like your husband dead on the floor? I didn't hit my head or anything. Nobody punched me. I felt stunned, like I couldn't talk, like I was going to throw up while I was in the apartment. I just had to get out of there."

"When we saw you, you seemed normal," Ruth said.

Siobhan smiled a little. "That was a couple of days later. I was in a trance that day, like I was in a balloon that separated me from the rest of the world. That had passed. And remember, I'm an actor."

Epilogue

The production was overall a triumph in the press and at the box office and became a major New York calling-card for Siobhan as an actor and director. She delivered a touching curtain speech on closing night, remembering her husband and dedicating the production to his memory. She was in her fifth month, and Ruth said it looked like she was hiding a basketball under her loose-fitting, floor-length caftan.

Edward Reilly Savage was baptized in the Anglican Communion at St James-in-the-Fields on Piccadilly, a Christopher Wren church that had also hosted the baptism of the poet, William Blake, nearly two hundred fifty years earlier. The godparents were Edgar Savage and Fiona Durbanville, a cousin of Siobhan Reilly Savage on her mother's side. When Eddie was six months old, his mother moved the two of them back to New York City and found a small apartment in Hell's Kitchen on the west side of Manhattan.

I had a party for Siobhan at a favorite restaurant where the owners were friends of mine when mother and child moved into the new place. Virtually the entire cast showed up, and Ned's siblings flew in from Los Angeles. Gabriele escorted Siobhan into the restaurant and to her table, to a "standing O" from all. At the end of the evening, Toby Finch, who had played the role of Olivia's fool in the production, accompanied himself on a guitar as he sang the curtain song from *Twelfth Night*.

"When that I was and a little tiny boy,
With hey, ho, the wind and the rain,
A foolish thing was but a toy,
For the rain it raineth every day.

"But when I came to man's estate,
With hey, ho, the wind and the rain,
'Gainst knaves and thieves men shut their gate,
For the rain it raineth every day.
"But when I came, alas! to wive,
With hey, ho, the wind and the rain,
By swaggering could I never thrive,
For the rain it raineth every day.
"But when I came unto my beds,
With hey, ho, the wind and the rain,
With toss-pots still had drunken heads,
For the rain it raineth every day."

The whole cast sang along for the final stanza.

"A great while ago the world begun,
With hey, ho, the wind and the rain,
But that's all one, our play is done,
And we'll strive to please you every day."

About the Author

Joe Allen's first success in "trade" books (books for retail buyers) was *Sandcastles: The Splendors of Enchantment* (1981). His first mystery novel, *Rocky Point Road*, was published in 2015, followed by *The Monteverdi Manuscript: A Hugo Miller Mystery* in 2016. *The Hanging Man*, published December 1, 2018, is a second Hugo Miller Mystery, set largely in Manhattan. With characters including a murderous "gypsy" dwarf, a papal legate with an overactive Twitter account, a woman promoting canonization for a nineteenth century New Yorker, a long-dead gangster who may have left buried gold in the basement of a condemned building, the wife of a murdered man on the lam with her infant son, and a tribe of possibly mutant males who live in tunnels underground on the west side of NYC.

His other forthcoming novel about a sprawling New York family from the Eisenhower years to 2015, *Where All Past Years Are,* published September 1, 2018, is set largely on the west shore of Lake Champlain in New York near the Canadian border. *A More Perfect Union*, published early in 2019, is the third Hugo Miller mystery, following the fortunes of Eddie Hall, an African-American lawyer and politician whose intended same-sex marriage is cancelled by the murder of his intended on a sidewalk in SoHo. He is currently working on a fifth Hugo Miller mystery and a mystery, *Boom!* that starts with a deadly explosion at a fireworks factory in Arizona.

Joe is also the author of five nonfiction books, including *Effective Business Communications: A Practical Guide.* His *Systems in Actions: A Social and Managerial Approach* was used as a text in advanced problem-solving in several MBA programs, including the UCLA Anderson School of Management. He contributed chapters to two Aspatore (Thomson

Reuters) books on investor relations.

Most of Joe's business career was with Bozell & Jacobs and then at Allen & Caron Inc., a consulting and investor relations firm he founded in 1981 in Irvine, California. Under his leadership, the company worked with clients in the UK, Ireland, France, Belgium, Sweden, Denmark, Italy, Greece, Germany, Poland, Switzerland, South Africa, Singapore, Australia, New Zealand, Brazil and Argentina, among other countries.

Joe served on the boards of several small companies, was vice chairman of the United Way in Orange County, California, has written on a variety of topics for numerous leading magazines and newspapers, and has published interviews with financial luminaries on SeekingAlpha.com.

Joe studied Classical Languages and English Literature at UCLA in the 1960s, prior to becoming an editor of scholarly journals at Sage Publications, and was then a marketing manager at Benziger Bruce & Glencoe, a college publishing subsidiary of Macmillan. He was married for forty-seven years. Now widowed, he has two children and two granddaughters.

Also by the Author
at
Rogue Phoenix Press

Rocky Point Road

When his ex-wife drowns in a hot tub in California, Denis Rosa sets out to bury her and sell the house. He confronts her philandering history and her fixation on young Chicano boys and is the victim of a vicious attempted murder without ever knowing why. The house on the cliffside on Rocky Point Road holds a ghost, a hidden treasure of some kind, and decades of memories for the Rosa family. When Detective Sue Mason is assigned to the case, her son and his soon-to-be husband and two dogs move into the house with Denis to protect him from further attacks. Is it drug-related? The wife was alcoholic and smoked grass, but nothing hard. Denis confronts his ghosts as he finds himself attracted to Sue. The key to the plot is found when Denis slides off the edge of the cliff.

Chapter One

The apartment was cluttered with art.

Denis Rosa's unfocussed appreciation of different styles ended up in a kind of warehouse approach to everything. There was a rubbing he'd bought in Cambodia, and a pair of late Ching dynasty vases, probably not worth a lot. An early Chinese brazier or incense burner, coppery green on a Noguchi glass-top coffee table with his grandfather's crystal pipe ashtray that took two hands to pick up. Then an old Syrian inlaid wooden chair with bits of shiny mother-of-pearl diamond shapes here and there, a ragtag assortment of flat-weave kilim rugs, a Barcelona chair, a walnut harpsichord. His grandmother's heavy sterling candlesticks with Christmas red candles, an African table carved from a single ebony tree trunk, and a mismatched assortment of African sculptures bought here and there, one a red-faced West African piece with monkey fur for hair. A dark, moody painting of Chief Joseph in television pixel patterns, a ghostly painting of shadowy figures on a bridge, an abstract oil of student riots in 1968 at the Gare du Nord, a couple of big academic nudes, a late impressionist picture of two people on the Staten Island ferry with the Brooklyn Bridge, a gaggle of Victorian tourist watercolors of Italian stereotypes (a cleric, a street musician, a woman with a big hat), two Persian miniatures of animals, a pair of impressive storytelling copperplate etchings from the 1960s, and five non-objective mystery pieces in bright colors by a well-known Irish artist. That was plus two dozen or so family photos scattered around the room and seven or eight pieces of high-fired ceramic bas relief.

What a fucking mess. Why did I accumulate all this stuff?

His wife had died and he was walking in circles with his back to the walls, looking from the walls toward the rooms, trying to make sense of something that didn't make sense no matter how you looked at it. *I could just start hitting things, pick up that African ebony head shaped like a scythe and just hit the canvasses until they are all ripped and shredded.* But like the temptation to throw her wedding ring in the river, the impulse subsided. Till death us do part. Death was here, and they were parted.

Why do you make a home after all? So it will be a place where you are comfortable, where you feel safe, where you can store all your pieces of string into a huge ball if you want. Then you pull away one of the foundation stones and what happens? Ashes, ashes, we all fall down.

He walked out the front door of the building. *It's odd how lucid I feel while I am nearly unhinged in the way I am thinking. Almost like I had taken some kind of designer drug that would make me high, but let me drive a car.*

It was chilly outside and the sidewalks were wet. He scuffed through the puddles in the pedestrian mall that used to be Broadway, stopping to watch the lights dance across the buildings. A man on stilts with a tall red hat was handing out flyers for a comedy club, or maybe a nude club, and that man with white underwear and a cowboy hat was strumming a guitar for a group of people who were busily snapping smartphone pictures of him and probably giving him money. How does he stay warm enough to play the guitar? How does his guitar stay in tune when it is so damp?

He turned onto 46th Street and headed for St. Mary the Virgin, hoping the door would not be locked. It was Sunday afternoon, so there was an even chance he could get in and smell the ghost of stale incense that constantly floated in the air. The door was, in fact, open when he pulled on it. There was to be evensong. Could he wait for that? He looked at his watch, which he had buckled on upside down, so he had to twist his wrist around and cock his head to read the clockface: four thirty. He scooted into a pew on the side. There was a scattering of people: a couple of ladies, a man who seemed to be dressed as a Gray Friar with a rope around his waist, and a man with a young child walking the Stations of the Cross.

He stared at the beam that crossed above the old communion rail that formed a rood screen about thirty feet off the floor. It had a life-size crucifix, and six pendant, red glass altar lights in gold or brass fixtures at regular intervals across the span, swaying slightly from the motion of the earth, or the vibrations of the subways. The church couldn't get a permit for a crypt even though it was well over 150 years old because, basically, the idea of burying dead bodies under the theater district was too gross for the city to consider. And you can't dig very far in midtown without hitting something that makes the city run anyway.

Someone started to play the organ, stopped, and started over. *If you play the organ you have to practice on an organ. Makes sense. Hard to have a full organ in your apartment, so you have to practice in a church. Well, evensong, after all, is only an hour or so away. Maybe that's it.* The organist stopped again, and there was silence for half a minute. Then he started to play Bach's Toccata and Fugue in F Major.

Tony Perkins was speeding along a cliff edge in his little sports car yelling goodbye, John Sebastian, and singing along with the organ music on his radio. *Odd the things that music makes you remember.* "It's raining," Melina Mercouri had said shakily, staring out the window with half a pound of mascara on her magnificent burning eyes. Her husband would kill her, of course; that was the fate of Phaedra. But Tony Perkins had to drive his car off a cliff into the water with a randomly chosen Bach organ piece playing as he flew through the air toward the rocks.

His eyes filled with tears, remembering that time long ago when he could take Phaedra seriously. Hell, his wife had died out in California and he had so far felt no discernible emotion other than anger and a certain level of disorientation, even though he'd been alone when he got the call and could have cried. *But crying is a communal thing.* He'd cried fountains in the past; it wasn't that he was so macho that he couldn't cry.

"Yeah," he said, "I'm OK, I'll be OK. I'll get a flight right away, I'll, um, I'll call you later."

Sitting in the church listening to the organist practice made the knot in his stomach loosen up a bit, although he still felt on the edge of nausea. The slightly bitter sweetness in the air was restorative. In most churches you smelled candle wax, but in this church you smelled frankincense. They call it Smoky Mary's because they use so much incense it makes your eyes water if you sit in the front of the church. He knew to sit in the back on the side, and even so his throat sometimes coated with phlegm when the deacon came down the center aisle to read the gospel, and flung the censor back and forth, creating a cloud of gray-blue vaporized resin for the congregation to suck into their lungs.

He couldn't just sit there and wait.

He took out his smartphone and looked up an airline flight service, walked out the front of the church and booked a flight to LA Monday morning, getting in about noon. "Yes, first class, upgrade with my miles. I'm not made out of money."

Bond 45 was dismantling the afternoon brunch. He waved at the maître d', walked over to the long bar, and ordered a vodka straight up, a little dirty, with olives. A drink would help. He asked the bartender for some roasted vegetables, too, cauliflower, string beans, and eggplant.

You'd think something would be different when someone dies. Something would happen, people would not watch ballgames or something. But I'm looking around and Times Square is normal, even though Elissa drowned in the back yard hot tub on a sunny late afternoon at the south end of Santa Monica Bay.

The vodka had little bits of ice floating in it from having been shaken vigorously in a theatrical, over-the-head show that the bartender did. *Show-off. Well, it's Times Square.* It was deliciously cold and there were three big olives. The salty olive juice took the edge off the alcohol and he took a big loud slurp from the martini glass while it was sitting on the bar. He put his phone down on the bar and waved at the bartender, pointed at the restrooms, and mouthed *Be right back.*

Well, something was different. He had never felt like masturbating in a public restroom before. Just as he didn't destroy the paintings, though, he just peed, rinsed his hands, and went back to the bar.

The apartment was chilly because he had left the windows open. The vodka had cleared his head, and that businesslike avatar of his took over when something dislocating happened. He packed a few things, but didn't need to take much other than a suit because he had plenty of clothes in the house in Palos Verdes Estates (PVE).

He had to inject himself with a blood-thinner after a deep vein thrombosis years before, and if he waited until after he got on the plane because he did not have a membership in the right airline club, he did it in the head after he got seated in 4D on the aisle. He had never learned, after all those years, to just jab himself with the needle, had to push it into the fleshy part of his thigh and then push the plunger down. It seldom hurt, and frequently was almost sensationless, but there was a sense of dread when he pulled out an orange-wrapped syringe and wiped his thigh with an alcohol swab with his jeans around his calves. He threw the used syringe back in his cosmetics bag after the protective plastic sheath snapped up to protect anyone from getting stuck with the needle. And for some reason after he finished the shot, he felt more relaxed, as though he could fall asleep before the plane took off. There was still the minute coal-like bit of blood clot in a vein just below his left knee, and he had to be careful. He pulled on the doctor-prescribed, tight rubberized support stockings before he put on his jeans. *They're so tight I can't wear them.* But he always managed to forget about them and today was no different. He only had to wear them in the air, and it seemed like a penance.

The flight attendant gave him a screwdriver with an extra little bottle of vodka that he dumped into the drink. He reclined his chair a bit and stared out the window at the sky that was blue and glaring at the same time, left his eyes unable to focus momentarily when he looked back into the cabin. How could she drown? She was afraid of water because she was a bad swimmer, but you don't need to swim in a hot tub. Did she fall? Did she have a heart attack?

Theirs was not a standard-issue marriage, although they'd had children who had dutifully reproduced and given them grandchildren, so on Christmas Day they seemed Norman Rockwell-ish. They'd both been unhappily married before, but the scars from the previous experiences were deeper than they had thought, and they were not able to achieve that easy trust and companionship that some enviable couples had. They didn't distrust each other, and they usually got along well. They shared some interests, notably baseball and classical music.

Things danced around in his head. A strong practical streak in him thought about what to do with the house, a house that meant even more clutter to deal with over and above the apartment that had driven him to the brink of despair the day before. He wanted "Simple Gifts" to be played. He would have her cremated as they had talked about, and he would scatter her ashes at sea. He saw himself dropping a lei of plumeria flowers onto the blackish-blue choppy water of the Catalina Sound.

They loved each other, but they found after the children were grown that they couldn't get along without bickering, and he had moved to New York and opened a new office of the consulting business he had founded. He learned to cook because he did not want to eat at restaurants all the time, and she had taken up with a string of short-term boyfriends, some of whom tried to take up residence in the house with her, but she apparently drew the line at that. Backwards, right? He was supposed to be tomcatting and she was supposed to be cooking, but it didn't work out that way.

He wondered if one of the guys had been with her when she died. His business partner had not said anything other than that Elissa had been found by the gardener in the hot tub with the Jacuzzi function still running. She had apparently been there for a day or so. Ignoble to be all wrinkled and partially parboiled. The coroner had taken her, of course. He had not talked to the rest of the family; not a word. *In centuries past, the women in the family would have cleaned her up and packed herbs around her in a plank-made coffin, strong-smelling herbs: -basil and verbena and rosemary and mint.*

Other Books by the Author
at
Rogue Phoenix Press

The Monteverdi Manuscript

The action revolves around the death of a famous musician, who hits the pavement outside Carnegie Hall from the window of his apartment seven stories up. He has recorded keyboard versions of a lost opera by Claudio Monteverdi, the man who "invented" opera. Set in New York, London and Venice, action includes a kidnapping, drug use, prostitution, LGBT characters, one character who comes back from the dead, and three classic New York detective characters led by Hugo Miller.

Where All Past Years Are

Starting on Thanksgiving Day 1954, the Chadwick family encounters wars, financial crashes, 9-11, and the Great Recession. As a family with a WASP history they discover the wider world that is America, marry across religious, racial and ethnic lines, live, love, laugh and celebrate Thanksgiving and Independence Day at the Old Home on the shore of Lake Champlain near the Canadian border in New York.

The love of husbands and wives, the closeness of relatives who are an increasingly rainbow-like group, the touching beauty of the Old Home on the Lake as some family members move back to the property into new cottages—all are major themes. Children running a three-legged race watch the young man, Gray Chadwick, drop to his knees to beg his pregnant girlfriend, Melissa, to marry him. Births, deaths, burials, 4th of July fireworks, boating and bass fishing, and the strengthening power of love lead to a final surprising and unexpected reunion of two branches of the family for the first time in over three hundred years.

A More Perfect Union

Former ADA Eddie Hill, divorced African-American father of two, plans to marry Jimmy van Gelsen, wealthy gay man who, like Eddie, has been unlucky in love. Eddie is injured in a car accident on the NY Thruway, and Jimmy is shot in the forehead, killing him instantly. Was it Eddie's gun? If so, with Eddie in the hospital upstate, who pulled the trigger? Hugo, Ruth and Gabriele sort through a thicket of clues—a stolen Bentley, a shabby vacation home on Antigua, a multimillion-dollar co-op in Greenwich Village with fabulous art. Major political demonstrations with thugs and tiki torches, reminiscent of the Charlottesville riots with protesters battling in the streets—one at a prayer vigil, one a "Million Woman March" down 5th Avenue, another outside the Copley Plaza in Boston. Eddie runs for Congress from a mixed-race district in Brooklyn. Jimmy's will left a fortune to Eddie, who doesn't want any of it. Is it a right vs left murder? A gay-bashing murder? A robbery gone wrong? The answers are close to home.

The Hanging Man

When wealthy investment banker Luigi's body is found hanging from the crossbars of the George Washington Bridge, it is immediately thought to be a Mafia hit. Is it? Not according to a Catholic bishop with a diplomatic errand from the Vatican and an out-of-control Twitter account. As the truth unfolds, the reader meets a mad dwarf who eats insects and small rodents, a long-dead candidate for canonization, a deceased gangster who owned The Cotton Club in Harlem, and a tribe of mis-shapen males whose lives have been spent in tunnels under Hell's Kitchen.

Explosions, whispers coming from walls, mysterious billionaires from Grand Cayman, Luigi's terrified young wife with a suckling baby at her breast, treasure-hunters looking for buried gold in the basement—provide a frightening backdrop to a mystery that literally goes deeper and deeper into Manhattan as the story develops.

Hugo Miller, Ruth the Sleuth, handsome Gabriele Cortese and stalwart NYPD detective Mike di Saronno pool their considerable resources to solve a series of crimes that may hark back as far as seventy-five or one hundred years.

www.ingramcontent.com/pod-product-compliance
Lightning Source LLC
Chambersburg PA
CBHW071451170626
46811CB00007B/2540